Dear Reader,

For as long as I have been reading and writing, I have always loved a bit of a thrill in my stories. Maybe that's why I had so much fun going all out with the drama, suspense, and twists in *The Perfect Ruin*. This novel is a gripping tale about betrayal and revenge. It's also about the importance of mental health and therapy for minorities. As a Black female author, I am so honored to be bringing representation and voice to the thriller genre.

The Perfect Ruin is about a young woman named Ivy Hill whose childhood was torn apart due to a tragic accident. In the years since, as she's battled mental health issues and outside abuses, she's been desperate to know the name of the person responsible for ruining her life. When she finally discovers it was a popular socialite named Lola Maxwell, Ivy becomes obsessed. She begins to watch Lola's every move, first on social media, and then in person, slowly creeping her way into Lola's world and eventually becoming her best friend. She's determined to sink deep into Lola's domain, certain that nothing can stop her plan to ruin the life of the woman who unapologetically ruined hers. What Ivy doesn't realize is someone out there is watching her every move too…

Women of color are often expected to always be strong. We're told our emotional responses to traumatic situations are overreactions or invalid. We feel we have to suffer through pain in silence and bottle it in. I want to change that narrative. I wrote *The Perfect Ruin* in part to spotlight the importance of mental health for women of color. As you read this story you will see clearly that Ivy and Lola are not perfect. You'll also notice there are many moments when they are crying for help but are too afraid to seek it, either because of their pride or simply because they think it's something that will pass. Ivy is a woman whose unhealed trauma has festered into hatred and obsession.

I hope that by witnessing the destructive thoughts and actions of a woman who hasn't gotten the help she needs, more people will understand how serious this issue is. Women in general are often so strong, and I hope this book helps readers realize there is no shame or weakness in getting the help they need and deserve.

I am beyond thrilled to have the opportunity to share *The Perfect Ruin* with you as a Target Diverse Book Club Pick! Fun fact: My dream has always been to see one of my books on a Target shelf, and here we are today. I am over the moon with excitement! If you decide to give this book a chance by taking it home with you, I want to thank you so, so much for your support. I do hope you enjoy it.

And if you'd like to share your Target Diverse Book Club Pick with the social media world, please tag #ThePerfectRuin or #ShanoraWilliams so I can join in on the fun with you!

Sending all my love,

Shanora Williams

The Perfect Ruin

Shanora Williams

www.kensingtonbooks.com

DAFINA BOOKS are published by

Kensington Publishing Corp.
119 West 40th Street
New York, NY 10018

All Kensington titles, imprints, and distributed lines are available at special quantity discounts for bulk purchases for sales promotion, premiums, fund-raising, and educational or institutional use.

Special book excerpts or customized printings can also be created to fit specific needs. For details, write or phone the office of the Kensington Sales Manager: Kensington Publishing Corp., 119 West 40th Street, New York, NY 10018. Attn. Sales Department. Phone: 1-800-221-2647.

The Dafina logo is a trademark of Kensington Publishing Corp.

ISBN-13: 978-1-4967-3920-9
ISBN-10: 1-4967-3920-5
First Trade Paperback Printing: August 2021

ISBN-13: 978-1-4967-3113-5 (e-book)
ISBN-10: 1-4967-3113-1 (e-book)
First Electronic Edition: August 2021

10 9 8 7 6 5 4 3 2 1

Printed in the United States of America

Dedicated to my boys.
I love you all dearly.

PROLOGUE

You are just a woman. A woman with hate in her heart and darkness in her soul.

You hate yourself, so you take it out on everyone else. You are scorned. Broken. Pathetic.

You will suffer at my hands.

I will ruin you . . . and you won't even see me coming.

CHAPTER ONE

Ivy stared at the fish tank across from her, scratching at her cuticle, simmering with irritation. She'd studied all the fish in the bubbling water so many times she'd lost count, but there was a new one in the tank today.

The new fish was blood-orange with white spots. Its body was flat, its left fin ugly and stubby, just like the right fin as it rotated in the tank. The fish appeared lost—like it had no clue what the hell it was doing in the glass box. It had been snatched from the comfort of its own home. Trapped in a tank.

Ivy knew the feeling of being trapped—except she hadn't been trapped in tanks. She'd been trapped in box-sized rooms or, worse, forced to share a box-sized room with another person around her age whom she'd never gotten along with. How it must have sucked to share a single tank with eight other fish, glugging the same water and fighting over pellets of food.

A door opened to the left and a woman with cornrows down to her shoulders, narrow, rectangular glasses on the bridge of her nose, and bright pink lipstick walked out. The woman was always dressed like a hippie. Loose blouses and pants, and god-awful sandals that Ivy used to call Bible sandals. The woman loved wearing colorful scarves around her neck, even when it was almost one hundred degrees outside. Today she was wearing a yellow and green one.

"Welcome, Ivy," Dr. Harold said from the door, bringing her hands together joyously. Ivy stood up with her purse and sighed. It was the same old thing with her therapist, Dr. Marriott Harold. Big smiles and gratefulness.

Her name was Marriott to rhyme with Harriet, as Marriott had mentioned once. Marriott's mother liked the name Harriet . . . so why didn't she just name Marriot, *Harriet*? It never made sense to Ivy. It made her confused and she hated confusion.

Marriott was single and didn't have much of a life outside of being a therapist. No family and not many friends. She had three cats—Whitney, Stevie, and Mikey. All three of them were named after her favorite musical artists, Whitney Houston, Stevie Wonder, and Michael Jackson. Ivy found her life boring and irrelevant.

Nonetheless, she met Dr. Harold every single Wednesday to perform a therapy session. Dr. Harold insisted Ivy call her Marriott, stating that "Dr. Harold" was too formal and that they were friends who could trust each other. Ivy often wondered if Marriott meant it—that she trusted her. No one ever trusted Ivy. She was a rebel, a liar, a thief, and a con artist. She could steal from babies and not feel any remorse.

"How are you today? I trust you have been resting." Marriott watched as Ivy walked past her.

Ivy walked into Marriott's office, placed her purse on the usual chair in the corner, and then flopped down on a cushioned brown chaise. It was her favorite spot to get through her fifty-five-minute sessions, but it was starting to get worn. Marriott would have to replace it soon.

The older Ivy became, the less often she'd have to come to this cuckoo's nest. She could have been done sooner, but when she had turned twenty-one, Marriott had the choice of keeping Ivy in therapy or considering it safe for her to move on and start a new life. Marriott told the judge Ivy needed more time to cope. Ivy had despised the damn therapist ever since. So why did she continue her visits? Why not just stop showing up? A part of her had to like the sessions, right?

Apparently, the whole world thought Ivy was suffering from post-traumatic stress disorder, depression, and a host of other issues. She'd heard Marriott tell the judge that she was having some obsessive behavior with a boy and with certain events from her past, which was sparking other mental disorders within her.

Ivy considered it all bullshit. She was fine, just dealing with shit like the rest of the world. Was it *not normal* to have to deal with shit?

"How can I rest?" Ivy grumbled, staring up at the ceiling. "It's close to the anniversary. I haven't slept all week."

"Yes, I remember the anniversary is coming up." Marriott fidgeted by the door. Ivy side-eyed her. She was acting weird. Smiling, but not as wide and bold as usual. "Have you been taking your antidepressants?" Marriott asked, sinking down in her usual brown recliner across the room. Finally. She was sitting. Relaxing. Ivy's body relaxed too.

Ivy avoided the therapist's eyes as she recalled dumping all the antidepressants down the kitchen sink and then turning on the trash disposal. "To hell with those," Ivy had muttered as she watched the pills disappear. She didn't like how they made her feel. Her head was often foggy while on them, and she became too sleepy, was losing too much weight. She was fine without them.

"Yes, I've taken them." She held back a grin, glancing at Marriott's degree tacked to the wall, just above her desk, which was stacked with papers, folders, and a cold cup of coffee sitting close to the edge.

Ivy always stared at the degree and couldn't believe a

woman like *Marriott* had one. She shouldn't be a therapist for adults. Marriott was too cheerful and bright and colorful. It made Ivy sick. She'd suit kids much better.

"Good." Marriott sighed. She was avoiding Ivy's eyes. Still acting strange. "So, since we're close to the anniversary, can you tell me how you're feeling right now?"

"Oh, you want to know how I feel? Annoyed—actually, no. Pissed off." Ivy gritted her teeth. "I'm going to the police station tomorrow. I'm old enough now—almost twenty-six. I deserve some answers about what really happened. I'm telling you, something is not right about what happened and no one is questioning it but me."

Marriott gave Ivy a sympathetic nod and her eyes saddened. She stared at Ivy for a moment, her hands stacked on her lap, tapping her finger slowly.

She then stood up and walked to her desk in front of the floor-to-ceiling window. Ivy watched as Marriott collected a folded sheet of paper and brought it back with her to the recliner.

"Ivy, I have something to share with you. I don't want to, because I'm not so sure I would consider it a great thing for you to know, but I need to," Marriott murmured, and she had her serious voice on, which meant Marriott wasn't fucking around. This voice was rare, and Ivy took notice.

"What is it?" asked Ivy.

Marriott drew in a breath. Her heart was beating harder. Her hands began to tremble. "I have the name of the person you've been looking for. I was instructed to give it to you."

The room grew absolutely still—so quiet Ivy could hear the construction happening on Palm Green Avenue, which was three blocks away.

"What are you talking about?" Ivy sat up in the chaise, her brows dipping with confusion.

"The person you claim has ruined your life—I have their name."

"What? *How*?"

"I have it written on *this* sheet of paper," Marriott said, raising the paper in the air, "but I want you to realize if you read this name, it may not make you feel better. I only have this name because someone came to me and told me it was what the person wanted. Perhaps their conscience has caught up to them and now they want to own up to their demons. I don't believe you deserve to live in the dark, but I also don't think you are ready to know this name. Unfortunately, as your therapist and confidante, I don't want to keep information like this from you. Do you understand what I'm saying?"

"How did you get it?" Ivy demanded, ignoring all Marriott's therapist mumbo jumbo talk. "Are you sure it wasn't a cop?"

Ivy remembered all the times she went to the police station and demanded answers. She remembered slamming her fists on the desk after the detective in charge of her case, Detective Jack Shaw, told her he couldn't relay those facts, because the person wanted to remain anonymous and because it was considered an accident, they had the right to keep the name private.

Apparently, this person was powerful, and the cops in her city were crooks. They could easily be bought, she figured. Or maybe they weren't telling her because, just like Marriott, they knew it would only lead to conflict. Ivy had no lawyer to back her up, nor did she have money for one, so she always walked out of the police station furious and in tears. All she wanted was an answer—a *name*.

"No. It was not a cop—at least, not that I'm aware of."

As if Marriot had read Ivy's mind, she went on with, "I spoke with Detective Shaw the day after receiving this name, just to confirm the information was correct. There is a reason he never told you the person's name; it's because he knew you didn't need to know this so young—not when you had so much going on mentally. I didn't know the name before now, and I had no desire to know it. You were assigned to me for therapy and counseling, I wanted to help you, and that was all that mattered to me. During all our sessions, I'm glad you didn't know who the person was. In cases like this, the unknown is best, and you've progressed so much without knowing it."

Marriott focused on the sheet of paper in her hand again before shifting her eyes to Ivy and saying, "You have a choice today, Ivy. You can read the name on this paper and let it consume you, or you have the option to *not* read this name, accept what happened all those years ago, and let it go. Realize that all things happen for a reason and that it is okay to forgive and move on with your life." Marriott was quiet for a beat. "I'm hoping you will take the stepping stones I have given you and create a wonderful future for yourself, knowing this name or not." Marriott placed the paper on the coffee table between her and Ivy and slid it forward, but Ivy didn't hesitate a second.

She'd wanted to know who the person was ever since she was fourteen. No need for modesty at this point. She deserved to know—she'd worked hard to know.

Marriott sighed and sat back in her chair, watching Ivy unfold the paper. Her fingers were still trembling.

The person had a name now. *Lola Maxwell.* She hated Lola with a passion, despite the fact that she didn't know who she was, where she lived, or even what she looked like.

Ivy wanted to find Lola and confront her—tell her that she was a selfish bitch who'd destroyed everything good in her life, and then she'd move on and build a future. Lola deserved that much—for someone to scream in her face and make her own up to what she did instead of being a coward.

Ivy shot out of her chair with the paper clutched in her hand. "I need to go," she said in a hurried voice. She walked to the chair and picked up her bag.

"You still have forty-five minutes left, Ivy." Marriott

stood with her. "Don't you want to complete your session for today? Talk about this?"

"No, I don't," Ivy muttered on her way to the door.

"Does knowing the name upset you?"

"Of course, it upsets me, *Marriott*! Why wouldn't it?" Ivy snapped. "But look, I'm glad you didn't keep this information from me. Now I can let it all sink in."

Ivy turned for the door, but Marriott caught her by the wrist before she could flee. Ivy noticed her fingers were cold and shaking. Her eyes shifted up to Marriott's, whose were now filled with something Ivy couldn't quite put her finger on. Worry? Guilt?

"I hope to still see you next Wednesday," Marriott said with a forced smile. There was no warmth in her smile like usual. It was lukewarm at best.

"Yeah, you will." And she would. Ivy wanted to find this Lola person, yes, but she also knew she'd need to keep up appearances for a while—prove to Marriott that she could handle the responsibility of knowing the name of the person who'd ruined her life.

Lola Maxwell.

Lola Maxwell.

Lola Maxwell.

The name was running in circles in her mind, taking over every single one of her thoughts.

"Okay, then." Marriott pushed one of her braids behind her back. "I'll see you on Wednesday. Call or email me if you need anything, and remember, if there's ever anything you want to talk about, I'm always here. You can write to me if it's too much to say and I'll read it to get an understanding." She gently squeezed Ivy's hand. "I'm here for you, Ivy."

"Okay." Ivy forced her own smile, pulled her hand out of Marriott's, and left the office without looking back.

★ ★ ★

As soon as Ivy stepped into her apartment, she went for her laptop, booted it up, and did an Internet search for Lola Maxwell.

What did Marriott think? That she was just going to forget about the name as soon as she got home? Of course not! She needed to know who this woman was, and she knew there was only one place she could find her immediately—a place you could find anyone if you looked hard enough. On the Internet.

And, good Lord, this Lola woman was *everywhere*. She was on every major social media outlet there was. For an evil bitch, she sure made it easy to find her.

Ivy clicked Facebook first, but she didn't have an account set up. She'd never felt the need to have any social media accounts. She saw the way it consumed her peers when she was in college, and even in the real world as she worked, and she hated it.

Her friend Alexa used to just sit and scroll through her phone, looking at other people, wishing she had their lives. It was strange to Ivy, to be so consumed with someone else's life instead of your own.

She recalled one time when a guy almost walked in front of a car on campus because he was so focused on the screen of his phone.

Ivy never understood how humans could be so simple-minded. How did they not realize there were dangers everywhere? One wrong move could kill you. Ivy liked to be in the present moment, not worried about what a fellow classmate ate for dinner, or that someone had just gotten engaged. She knew to really pry on Lola, though, setting up an account was vital. She'd make this an exception.

She quickly created a Facebook account with a fake last name and used a random photo of a white rose she'd found on Google Images as her profile photo. After it was all set up, she searched for Lola again and sent her a friend request. Her page was private, but her profile and cover photos were visible to the public.

Ivy studied Lola's profile picture.

She was beautiful. Silky, honey-blond hair that paired well with her tawny skin, perfect white teeth, and a thin frame with curves in all the right places. She had gold hoops in her ears and was wearing all white in the photo—crisp and clean, and yet Ivy knew that pretty bitch had blood on her hands.

Ivy clicked through more of Lola's profile photos, and there were images of her in her kitchen, and her office, and even in her pool. Every image seemed like one out of a magazine. So, this woman was pretty *and* rich? That pissed Ivy off even more.

To her surprise, Ivy got a notification that her friend request had been accepted. She grinned and refreshed the page to look through Lola's profile.

Ivy scrolled down until she caught a photo of Lola arm in arm with a man. He was a very handsome man, with perfect teeth too, and a faded, wavy haircut. This woman was married! Happily married too, from the looks of it. How was it that she got to be pretty, happy, *and* in love, while Ivy suffered for years because of her?

Ivy didn't trust being in relationships. She was in one before and it didn't end well, and now she blamed Lola for it. The relationship only ended badly because Ivy's ex couldn't accept the fact that she needed to see a therapist every week. He didn't want to have a "crazy girlfriend," so she made it easy for him and dumped his ass. He called her names, told her she was no good. Used and abused her.

Ivy gritted her teeth as she pressed down harder on her mouse pad, clicking through Lola's photos.

How could Lola just *live* like she'd done nothing wrong in her life? Lola had a big, fancy home with a handsome husband and wore expensive clothes and jewelry. She didn't deserve *any* of what she had.

Ivy continued scrolling, but couldn't help noticing that even though Lola smiled brightly in every photo, there was something about her eyes. Her eyes told Ivy everything she needed to know. She'd gone through something tragic. Lola was definitely responsible for destroying her life.

Ivy saw an Instagram post on Lola's page. She clicked it, and it took her to the photo. It was a blue-and-white graphic for a charity named Ladies with Passion. It was for volunteer jobs for a charity Lola had founded in 2008. A year after the incident. Yeah, that wasn't a coincidence at all. Put up a charity to cover up the guilt.

Lola had just posted the graphic two days before. Everyone was welcome to apply for the charity if they wanted to work as a volunteer, but background checks were required and spaces were limited, which meant they would be picky about who became one. There was a link to apply in her biography on Instagram.

Ivy stared at the link for a fleeting moment, tapping the pad of her finger on the edge of her laptop. The last thing she wanted was for the perfect Mrs. Maxwell to run a background check on her; then again, she could always use her mother's maiden name on the application and have Alexa's boyfriend make her a fake ID.

She clicked the link to apply, filled it out diligently, and sent it off. With all Lola had going on, she figured the woman wouldn't even know who she was or give her first name a second thought, if she was aware of it.

It seemed she'd already forgotten about the incident, with her handsome husband, fancy home, and amazing life. For all Ivy knew, she didn't even exist to the rich bitch.

But who'd given her therapist the name? Why would Lola jeopardize all she had just to feed her name to Ivy now? Did she know Ivy? Know what she looked like? How did she even find Marriott?

Lola would know who Ivy was . . . right? She would be waiting for Ivy to come to her someday, confront her about the past. All of it could backfire or even be a trap. Ivy had to be careful, plan her approach wisely.

Ivy sighed as she looked at the confirmation email that let her know her application had been received, then she took a look around her cramped, one-bedroom apartment. The leaky faucet was dripping. The brown stain on her floor was getting darker instead of lighter, no matter how much she scrubbed at it. The AC never worked properly and caused her to break out in a sweat every hot night.

Fury blinded Ivy.

It wasn't fair that Lola got to live in luxury and style while Ivy struggled day in, day out just to pay her bills. Ivy worked retail and faked smiles all day. She never quite had enough money to buy a new outfit for herself, or new shoes, because all her money went to her rent or recurring bills. Her life would have been so different if it weren't for Lola Maxwell.

After shutting the lid of the laptop, Ivy poured herself a glass of the red wine she got from a coworker, sat on her dingy brown couch with her iPhone, and scrolled through Lola's Instagram account, absorbing everything she could about the woman who'd ruined everything good in her life.

CHAPTER TWO

Ivy couldn't believe it.

Her application for the Ladies with Passion charity had been rejected, the email typed in big, bold, red letters.

THANK YOU FOR APPLYING TO BE A LADIES WITH PASSION VOLUNTEER. AT THIS TIME, WE ARE CONSIDERING OTHER OPTIONS, BUT PLEASE FEEL FREE TO APPLY AGAIN NEXT YEAR.

WITH LOVE AND GRACE,

LOLA AND TEAM

What a bitch. And here she'd worked so hard on the application to make it sound believable. Lola opened volunteer applications every year, though, so it was fine. She could wait. She needed time to plan anyway, and perhaps Lola would forget about Ivy completely after another year.

As badly as she wanted to see this woman face-to-face as soon as possible, it had to be at the right time and the right moment.

Ladies with Passion was an organization for pregnant teen girls and women who needed financial support for prenatal and postnatal care. It was thoughtful, but a load of shit. She should have put all that energy into owning up to what she'd done instead.

It was obvious to Ivy that the charity was created so Lola could avoid the truth . . . which still left the question: Who gave Marriott Lola's name? Was Lola waiting for Ivy to show up and planning on paying her off to keep her quiet while clearing her conscience? Because, hell, she would have loved that. Perhaps she should have emailed her and gotten it over with, or even met her for lunch somewhere to discuss money . . . but that was too easy for her. Money alone wasn't going to cut it. Ivy needed more.

Opening her laptop with a weak cup of coffee beside it, Ivy typed in the name of Lola's charity organization in the Search bar. She then went to the website and absorbed as much knowledge as she could about it. Just because her application wasn't approved didn't mean she couldn't show up for the events.

She clicked through the photos of all the pregnant women who'd been helped or given large checks, and then clicked through the volunteer images, all of them in their sky-blue shirts with "Ladies with Passion" in swirly pink font. Lola was in several photos, smiling like an angel . . . which she was not.

Ivy abandoned the website and picked up her phone, going to Instagram and finding Lola again. She'd done this many times since discovering Lola had an account.

Her Instagram account was where she posted the most. She wouldn't follow her just in case Lola noticed her name. Not yet at least. She only needed to see Lola, and because Lola's profile was public, it made things a lot easier.

She scrolled until she found an image of Lola slathered in sweat, with a pair of pink boxing gloves on her hands. She was flexing her toned arms, her honey hair hanging down in a low ponytail, wisps clinging to her wet face.

"Kickboxing? Seriously?" Ivy muttered, then rolled her eyes. Lola had tagged her location with the photo. Best Rounds Kickboxing was the place, and the address was even attached. How foolish could Lola be? Ivy wondered. She made her life so . . . *accessible.*

Did she really think the world cared about her latest workout or charity sponsor? Then again, according to the twenty-to-fifty-thousand likes and hundreds of comments, many people did care what Lola was up to.

Ivy chewed the flesh on the inside of her cheek, tapping on the next photo. It was an image of Lola and her husband. Ivy lingered on that photo—on the husband.

He wore a black tuxedo, and Lola was in a platinum dress, her hair pulled up into a tight bun. Her skin was glowing and flawless. They were attending a fundraising dance.

Ivy's eyes shifted back over to Lola's husband. She tapped the photo, and a username popped up where he was tagged. That took her to a profile for a man named Corey Maxwell.

So that was his name. Corey Maxwell. Corey was divine, really, and that said a lot coming from Ivy, seeing that she didn't care much for men in general after her ex. She never felt normal with that fucker, and she hadn't trusted many people afterward, especially men.

There was something about Corey Maxwell that drew Ivy in, though. He had deep brown eyes and a beautiful, boyish smile. He even had dimples that sank into his brown skin when he revealed his teeth. She could tell, despite only seeing him in photos, that he was tall—she guessed six feet or taller.

Corey Maxwell had broad shoulders and his face was cleanshaven in most photos, but when he rocked a five-o' clock shadow, it made him appear more rugged and handsome. He was eye candy for sure, and something about him made her want to talk to him. Touch him. Hear his voice for the first time.

She scrolled through his profile pictures until she found an image of him in front of a building with his hands in the air, as if he were proud.

Maxwell's Aesthetics. It was a #throwbackthursday photo, to when he first opened his company in 2003.

Ivy quickly left the Instagram app and went to Google to search for the company.

So, Corey Maxwell was a plastic surgeon? He was the best in South Beach, Florida, according to several articles. He even performed surgery on celebrities. Now *that* was interesting. No wonder Mrs. Maxwell was so well off.

Ivy was filled with so much knowledge now about the infamous Lola. With a smile on her face, she walked to the kitchen with her phone, going back and forth between Lola's profile and Corey's.

Her phone rang. She rolled her eyes and ignored the call.

She prepared a hot turkey sandwich with potato chips and then sat down on her patio to eat it all, letting the seed of an idea plant itself in her mind.

She didn't have a great view from her studio apartment, and it always smelled like fast food, thanks to the McDonald's across the street. Music was blasting in the apartment downstairs from Streeter, the punk weed dealer who loved having parties every weekend and playing loud hip-hop music all day long, but she didn't mind the noise today, or the smell of the greasy burgers.

Normally, she'd go downstairs and bang on Streeter's door and demand that he cut the music off, but not today. Streeter could have his stupid music because she had something much better to deal with.

A plan.

Ivy munched on a potato chip. Scrolled through her phone.

There was one thing Ivy knew for certain: Lola Maxwell would not live a picture-perfect life for much longer. Ivy would tear it down bit by bit, but she'd have to be patient, make sure it worked in her favor.

She wanted to ruin this woman's life, just as she'd ruined hers . . . but first she had to sit, think, and devise a plan. Despite the delay it would cause, she was very much looking forward to witnessing Lola Maxwell's ruin from a front-row seat.

PART ONE

BEFORE THE RUIN

CHAPTER THREE

IVY

Hey, Marriott.

You told me to write to you when I needed someone to talk to, even if I decided never to share what I had to say.

Get the words out, you'd always tell me. *Express the way you feel on paper if you don't want to talk about it out loud. Thoughts come out way clearer when they're written on paper, Ivy.*

Well, I'm taking your advice for once. I'm writing it out. After all, I have nothing but time on my hands.

As you know, I don't have any friends—at least not many I can confide in. There was Alexa. Remember her? But I can't trust her with my secrets.

She did more judging than accepting, and there was something off about her. She started asking too many questions and was always popping up when I didn't even invite her over. So, that leaves me with you.

After all I've been through, you will probably never acknowledge these words, but it feels good to know I'm telling this story to you. Someone needs to know my side of things.

When you told me the name of the person who'd ruined my life, I think something inside me snapped. I lost all sense of self-control and became *obsessed*—way too obsessed for my own good. Maybe you were right about my obsessive behavior before.

If you're blaming yourself right now for anything, stop. You shouldn't blame yourself for what happened. Really, you shouldn't. None of this was your fault. You tried to do the right thing with me, but I just didn't want to listen. Now look at me.

Still, I suppose I needed to know who the person was. I wouldn't have lived in peace if I never knew, and you know that.

I quickly learned things about Lola Maxwell. I knew things about her husband too. I'd come up with plan after plan, making sure each one had a plan Z. I was finally ready to take the risk—ready to face this woman and see if she'd recognize me as the girl whose life she ruined.

But before I did that, I had to do some legwork. Pay some expenses. Get in good and make my mark. It was cool. It needed to be done to create the outcome I'd originally wanted.

That's why I started with her handsome husband, Mr. Corey Maxwell. Or Dr. Corey Maxwell, I should say.

I want you to read this slowly. No, really. Digest it all, and then when it's done, you can form your own opinions of me. I want you to understand my every angle because at the end of the day, you know my mind better than anyone else does. You studied it for over a decade, inhaled my habits, and continuously diagnosed me with disorders I never even knew I had.

You know me, Marriott. But for now, just read this. Pay attention to the details. And *don't you dare* judge me until you've read every single last one of my words.

I'll start from the beginning.

CHAPTER FOUR

Fourteen Months Before the Ruin

The day was May 22, 2019. That was the day when my plans were truly going to kick in. I had just turned twenty-seven and was ready to conquer the world.

It was hot as hell in downtown Miami, the air thick with humidity and the wind blowing with gusts from the salty ocean.

I collected my bag from the passenger seat—a purple handbag I found on the clearance rack at Target. After applying another coat of lip gloss while looking in my visor mirror, I fingered through my hair to loosen my soft, natural curls and then climbed out of my two-door Honda Civic.

I dressed as flashily as my budget would allow. I'd found a black dress that hugged my waist on the clearance rack at my job at Banana Republic and a pair of open-toed heels from Target. The dress was strapless, and because I had a follow-up appointment, I didn't need a bra.

I walked up to the door of Maxwell Aesthetics and swung it open. A woman with twists in her hair greeted me behind the counter. "Good morning. How can I help you?"

"I have a follow-up appointment with Dr. Maxwell at ten."

"And what is your name?" the woman asked, already typing on the keyboard in front of her.

"Ivy Elliot." My last name wasn't Elliot, but you know that. That's my mother's maiden name.

The woman typed my name on the keyboard and then nodded. "Okay. I've got you signed in, Miss. Elliot. Dr. Maxwell will be with you shortly. Would you like a cool beverage while you wait?"

"No, thank you. I appreciate the offer, though." I took a seat in the waiting area. It had a man's touch. Upholstered black leather sofas, glass tables with sharp silver corners, and square mirrors on the white walls.

As I waited, I bunched my breasts together and looked down, focusing on my cleavage. I had to get used to that. Dr. Maxwell had done a wonderful job with my breast implants, but it had cost me a pretty damn penny.

I'd saved up all last year to get them specifically from Dr. Maxwell, and also dug into the money I had been saving when I was receiving my government assistance checks to kick-start the fund myself.

You would say this was a waste of money, but . . . well, I considered it necessary for everything I had in store. A little over the top? Yes. But I needed it for many reasons.

My surgery was six weeks before. My breasts were now two sizes bigger and I even had to go up a shirt size. The healing process was a bitch and I had to take off work the first week, but I didn't mind it. I was tired of being an A-cup anyway.

I'm pretty sure I've told you about how annoyed I was with my tiny breasts a time or two. You always told me to love my body. Well, Marriott, no one loved a boy's body, and now that I knew who Lola was, I found myself regretting the sleeve of tattoos on my left arm that I'd gotten while in college. Ink drawings on my skin of geometric shapes, leaves, roses, and crescent moons. My sleeve took me a year to complete. I was proud of it at one point because it was made of some of my favorite things. Now? Not so much. Rich people—the type in Lola's world—didn't have sleeves of tattoos, but perhaps mine would make me stand out more.

"Ivy Elliot." A deep voice carried through the waiting area, and I picked up my head, spotting the ever-so-handsome Corey Maxwell standing near his office door.

I smiled and stood as elegantly as possible. My chin was raised and my eyes were locked right on his. He smiled at me as I approached.

"It's a pleasure to see you again, Ivy." His smile was warm. Infectious. Dimples creased his cheeks. I loved a man with dimples. Did you know dimples are a genetic defect? And yet people with them are much, much cuter than those without. To me, at least.

"Thank you for fitting me into your schedule," I said, entering his office. "I know how busy you are."

"It does get busy around here, but you are my client." He glanced at my chest. "I trust you are enjoying your new luxuries?"

I did the laugh I had practiced in the mirror—the flirtatious giggle that would make him feel good and stroke his ego. I'd once read about flirtatious laughter in a magazine. Men loved when pretty women laughed at their jokes, no matter how corny the jokes were.

"My luxuries. That's funny." I guess I should have considered them luxuries. These new breasts of mine cost me close to twenty grand.

I took the seat across from him, purposely pressing in the insides of my upper arms to make my chest appear fuller. "They are great, though. All of my friends are in awe. I recommended they come to you if they want a great boob job because you, sir, are amazing." Who was I kidding? I didn't have any friends.

Corey chuckled as he typed away on his keyboard. "That's

good to hear. Have you had any pain while you've healed, other than the usual soreness?"

"Not much."

"Any back issues?"

"Nope."

"What about sensitivity of your nipples and areolae? Everything still feel about the same?"

Why don't you find out for yourself? I wanted to ask, but instead I nodded my head with an innocent smile. Look, Marriott, I said don't judge me yet. "I still feel it all. Very much."

I didn't ignore the way he avoided my eyes after my statement, but he was still smiling, revealing those dimples, so that was good. He loved when women flirted with him.

"Okay, this is all good. You can follow me to the examination room and I'll give you a quick check." I followed him through the white door behind his desk. The examination room had walls painted robin's-egg blue, but the floors and chairs and counters were so white and sterile they were almost blinding.

I climbed on the table and lowered my straps immediately. Corey pretended not to notice my ministriptease as he slid his fingers into latex gloves. I lay back with a smirk, and he finally faced me.

"All right. I'm just going to feel around a bit. Make sure your sensitivity is okay."

"Sure." I smiled up at him.

Look, I know what you're thinking. What kind of woman purposely gets breast implants from the husband of the woman who ruined her life?

Me. I'm that kind of woman. Come on, you can't be surprised by this. I can be petty when I want to be.

After discovering that Lola Maxwell lived a little less than four hours away from me, I decided I'd move to her. Other than what I had saved for my implants, I'd used the rest of my savings to get an apartment in Miami, and got a retail job at a

store close by. Granted, I didn't stay in the best part of the city, but it would do. It was cheap and temporary.

The first step of my plan was to meet Corey, get him to remember my face and recognize me, so that way the rest would carry out. The only way I could truly do that was if I came into his place of business with something he could be passionate about. He loved his job, and I had breasts, so it seemed reasonable enough.

I was saving money for this part of my plan, but it still cost a lot to get in the door with Dr. Maxwell. I had to take out a loan for the surgery, and even after I did, his waiting list was a mile long. Fortunately, someone canceled an appointment and I was given their spot.

I'd also moved up to a manager's position at Banana Republic within six months of starting and got paid a few dollars more, which helped with stacking my money and paying off the loan on time. The money didn't matter right now, though. I was getting closer to Corey and the plan was in motion. The finances would be taken care of later.

"Everything feels fine," he murmured to me. He hovered above, kneading the sides of my breasts. He rolled one of my nipples between his forefinger and middle finger, and I purposely let out a gentle moan.

"You okay?" he asked.

"Yeah. That was just *very* sensitive," I purred.

He smiled and then moved away. "Well, it's good you can still feel everything. I'm glad to see you have healed nicely and are happy."

I did another giggle, coquettishly sliding my dress back up to conceal my breasts. I had to be a little modest here. I didn't need him thinking I was some desperate woman who was after him, even though I was, but I still wanted him to know I was an open door.

"Do you have any questions for me?" he asked, snatching off his gloves and tossing them in the trash.

"No—none at all."

"Well, then, I suppose this is where I thank you for following up with me. I would like to see you in three months as well, just to make sure everything is still okay, but from the looks of it, you may not even need the three-month check. Anyway, if any problems arise, please feel free to call or email me and I'll be happy to discuss any issues you may have."

I climbed off the table. "I will, Dr. Maxwell. Thank you again for everything."

"Of course. Have a good afternoon, Ivy." *Ivy*. My name sounded so sweet as it spilled from his magenta lips.

I left the exam room, sliding the strap of my handbag on top of my shoulder with a smile. The girl behind the desk gave me a farewell after I booked my three-month follow-up and then I left.

When I was inside my car, the air conditioning blowing on my face, I logged onto Instagram and searched for Lola. It was that time of year again. She was taking applications for volunteers for her charity. I would do it right this time.

I drove to my apartment, logged onto my computer, and found the website to apply.

This time, my sob story was even better than the last, albeit a complete lie—but it was a lie I knew Lola would be able to relate to. If she didn't approve my application this time, I was going to have to rework my plan.

Regardless, I was going to get to know this woman personally, and everything she stood for, no matter what it took to make that happen.

CHAPTER FIVE

I couldn't believe I was doing this.

For starters, I hated anything that revolved around boxing. What did people find so entertaining about it anyway? Men and women punching each other in the face until they had fat, swollen lips and purple rings around their eyes? Blood all over the floor of the mat? Spitting blood into buckets?

But *kickboxing*? Kickboxing was a fucking joke—just a way for a person to feel strong because they could punch and kick a defenseless bag.

I had a new, expensive-as-hell membership card on my keychain and it was a bright and early Tuesday morning. Kickboxing it was.

Lola posted often that she loved Tuesdays and Thursdays because that was when she could visit Best Rounds Kickboxing. She went on about how the coach of her class always kicked her butt with a good workout and kept her in tip-top shape.

She was so full of shit.

She had a personal trainer and a nutritionist to keep her in shape as well, I was sure. Kickboxing was just another way she could flash her money and pretend to have a busy schedule.

I didn't exactly consider myself out of shape. In fact, I worked out four times a week in my apartment. Sit-ups and crunches to keep my abs tight. Squats and lunges to keep my ass perky. Some light lifting with dumbbells to keep my arms slim and toned.

Before knowing who Lola was, I hadn't worked out. I was soft around the middle, but I wasn't fat, per se—more so what people would call "skinny fat." You always told me I was healthy and slim, Marriott. I know you were just being nice. Doesn't matter. I needed to work on myself for once, and I'm pleased to tell you that I found a reason to do it.

When I found Lola, my desire to get fit came at me full speed. I needed to get in shape so I could fit in with women like her. She hung out with slender women who had snatched waists and great asses that I was sure they all paid high-dollar amounts for. They wore expensive jewelry and packed on their makeup heavily.

Makeup wasn't a go-to thing for me either, but I learned how to wing my eyeliner and use concealer to cover the dark circles under my eyes from all my sleepless nights, so that was a start, and it was better than nothing.

Xavier had liked me natural—no makeup. I have to give it up to him, Marriott. He wasn't all that great a man, but he did help me gain a smidge of confidence in myself when he made remarks like that.

A natural beauty, he'd call me. *You don't need all that makeup like some of these other bitches do, L'il I. You're good the way you are.*

Yeah, he seemed nice, like you said when I first told you about him, but being with him was like having constant whiplash. One minute I was the sexiest woman alive and the next I was a dirty, ugly, basic bitch. To this day, I can say that I don't miss being with him.

Grabbing my gym bag from the passenger seat, I let out a ragged breath and made my way across the parking lot to the kickboxing studio. When I had first walked into the studio to sign up, I'd hated the smell of it. Leather and sweat masked with some kind of perfume-y fragrance.

The walls were black, as well as the large mats on the floor. The punching bags were royal purple, and definitely vomit-inducing on their own. Nothing in this place matched. It was like it was all just thrown together, and I was curious what attracted Lola to it. Perhaps it was a recommendation. Or maybe she knew the owner and got perks. You never knew with that woman, there was always a catch.

"Hello, Ivy!" Chanel, the lead fitness instructor, greeted me as I walked in. She wore a pair of yoga pants with the Best Rounds Kickboxing logo on the thigh and a tank top that revealed her toned, russet arms. "I'm so glad you could join me on this lovely Tuesday! Go on and put your stuff in a locker in the back and meet me back on the mat. We'll be getting started soon."

"Thanks, Chanel." I forced a smile at her, then turned away with an eye roll. She was too damn chipper for me, but I couldn't be too hard on her. She'd squeezed me in and had given me a membership even though spots were limited.

This place normally reserved spaces for upper-class people, which I was not, but with a perfect woe-is-me story about how I used to be the fat girl in high school who needed to empower herself, Chanel slid me in.

I wasn't fat in high school. I never had been in my life, but lying came with the territory. Hell, some nights I didn't even get to eat as a teen. You'd feed me. Pick up a burger and a shake for me so I could eat during my therapy sessions.

I walked to the back where the tan lockers were, but came to a rapid halt when I saw a person already standing back there. Damn. I thought I'd beaten her here. I didn't see her car outside. She drove a blue Tesla every single day, but I suppose she'd switched things up and gotten a new car to ride around in now.

Lola Maxwell was bent over with a bare foot on the bench in front of her, tugging on the leg of her yoga pants to adjust them. I hated that she was here so soon. I figured surely she'd prance into the studio late with some excuse about being so swamped and busy, like all rich people do, and I could study her as she trotted around in all her artificial glory.

She picked up her head, as if realizing she wasn't alone, and a smile spread across her glossed lips. The photos she'd posted on Facebook and Instagram hadn't done her justice. If anything, she was even more stunning up close.

I hadn't been this close to her before. I'd always watched her from a distance, seated in my car across the parking lot or coasting by her office, but to see her standing right there almost left me stuck in place. There was a sudden urge to say something to her—the rage building up inside me and clawing at my throat.

Do you know what you did to me?

Do you realize what you've done?

Do you know who I am?

You ruined my life, you know that much!

I hate you!

But that would have been too easy, and I hadn't spent a year plotting just to let it all go to shit with five little sentences. No. I needed more out of this.

I envied her skin and how it glowed with warm undertones, and how her teeth were so stark white they could probably blind you in the sunlight.

"Oh, hello," Lola said to me, still smiling. "You're new here, aren't you? I haven't seen you around before."

It hit me in that moment, Marriott. This woman I despised so much didn't know me at all. I'd been bracing myself for the day I would collide with her world, waiting for the moment she'd see me and automatically recognize me, guilt clouding her eyes and sweat beading on her forehead.

But she'd never seen me—I mean, she couldn't have. She'd sent someone to tell me her name, get it off her conscience, but she'd obviously never seen me before, otherwise she wouldn't have been smiling in my face.

Granted, I had changed my look. Shorter hair. More makeup. Nose piercing was gone, but the changes weren't all that dramatic.

This was good. I had one up on her.

I blinked quickly and pulled myself out of my stupor. "Hi. Yes, I'm new. Signed up last week, and I'm so nervous." I walked to a locker that was past hers and opened it. Through the corner of my eye, I watched her drop her bare foot and stand straight.

"Oh, don't be nervous. You made a great choice by signing up. Chanel is *amazing*. The first couple of classes are pretty brutal, but once your body knows what to expect, it gets better. Not easier, but better." She laughed, and it was a harmonious laugh that could make any person feel warm and happy. But not me. Fuck her and her laugh.

"That's good to know." I stretched my lips to smile at her when really I wanted to pounce on top of her and slap her for being such a fake bitch.

"See you on the mat." Lola turned around with her blue gloves in hand, and I watched her walk away. Hell, even her walk was elegant. Everything about her screamed elegance and I couldn't stand it.

When I heard her talking to Chanel, both of them squealing with laughter, I walked close to where she had been standing and checked each locker until I came across the one she'd dumped her belongings into.

She didn't have much with her. Just her cell phone, her car keys, and a pair of black Adidas slides. I picked up her phone, but of course it needed a passcode or her face to get into it. Her screen saver was an image of her and Corey standing in front of a crystal-blue ocean, smiling like they had no worries in the world. I wanted to slam the phone to the ground and crack it, but I resisted the urge.

I heard someone coming and put down the phone, shutting the locker rapidly and then grabbing my gloves and making my way to the mat. A Caucasian woman with dark hair smiled at me on her way back and I gave her a tight-lipped smile in return.

When I walked out, Chanel instructed me to place my gloves on top of whichever bag I wanted to kickbox with for the day. I chose a bag that was two away from Lola's blue gloves.

Class started, and Lola wasn't kidding. The class was *brutal*. All the burpees and push-ups and sit-ups were likely going to kill me and were making me lightheaded. By the time we could take a water break, my face was hot, and I was drenched with sweat in places I didn't even know I could sweat.

Turns out, that was only the warm-up. We started our next round, which was the kickboxing one, but it was much easier to punch the hell out of a bag and pretend it was Lola than do full-body workouts on the floor.

I glanced over every so often at Lola, who was punching her bag with stealth and grace. I tried mimicking the way she punched, but I wasn't good at it. Chanel watched me a lot because I was new, which irritated me because I hated being watched. She taught me how to roundhouse kick, not even realizing how badly I wanted to roundhouse her ass.

Then the partner drills began. We could pick partners, and to my surprise, Lola looked at me with a smile and said, "Come on, new girl. Let's do this." I put on a sweet, bashful smile on my way to her.

Oh, Lola Maxwell wants to partner with me? What a dream this is! Not.

I knew any girl in South Beach would have thought the world of this, but I wasn't any girl. Still, it was good she

wanted to partner with me. Perhaps it meant she saw something in me . . . or maybe she did know exactly who I was and
was pretending not to.

I had to be careful.

Partner drills started, and Chanel instructed us on what to
do before we got into it.

"So, do you live around here?" Lola asked, lightly punching my glove with hers for our first drill. We were exchanging
light punches on each other's gloves.

"I do, yes. I live about fifteen minutes away."

"Oh really? What part of the city, if you don't mind me
asking?"

"Close to Liberty City," I panted, punching her glove when
it was my turn. Liberty City was bad news and she'd know it.
Anyone who lived around that area clearly didn't have much
money. I wanted her to know that about me from the start. I
was poor. I needed assistance in any way, shape, or form.

"Oh, that's cool," she chimed in. Really, Marriott? Please
tell me how it was cool to live near Liberty City? Oh, I'll tell
you how—it fucking wasn't. "I live close to the beach."

I resisted the urge to roll my eyes. She really had the nerve
to be modest. I'm sure what she really wanted to say was that
she lived *on* the beach, in a mansion with six bedrooms.

I said, "I really love your hair! I've always wanted to dye
my hair that honey color but never thought highlights like
that would look good on me."

"Oh, thank you! Yeah, I've had this custom color for a
while now. I've been thinking about switching it up lately,
though. Maybe to something darker." She winked.

Chanel told us our time was up and Lola dropped her
arms, placing her hands on her waist to momentarily catch her
breath. "I think your hair is lovely the way it is, though. Natural suits you."

I provided a smile—the same smile I'd practiced in the
mirror—and then we both sat to stretch with Chanel.

"So . . . um . . . don't you run the Ladies with Passion project?" I asked in a quiet voice.

Lola's hazel eyes lit up. "I do! How'd you know?"

"Well, I'm just a little obsessed with that charity, is all." I laughed, and waved it off like my obsession meant nothing. Little did she know how deep my obsession ran.

"You are? That is so amazing to hear!" Lola reached for her foot to stretch her thigh and back.

"I especially love how you bring all those new mothers together after their babies are born and have parties for them. It's such a good thing you do. Makes women feel like they're safe in this world with a newborn, you know?"

"Oh yes, that is my main goal with the charity." She gave a serious nod. "No one should have to carry a baby without support, let alone worry about finances or necessities while raising their baby."

"You wanna know something funny? I applied to be a volunteer for the charity this year," I said, giving her a sheepish grin. "But I probably won't be approved."

"Are you serious? You're interested in volunteering?" Lola sat up, back straight, looking me in the eye.

"Yeah." I waved it off dismissively. "I applied last spring too, but I didn't get the opportunity. I totally understand why, though. There are people who are way more qualified out there than I am."

"What is your name?" Lola asked, and my heart beat a little faster.

"Ivy Elliot."

She didn't show me any sign of disapproval or recognition of the name. If she knew it, she had a mean poker face because she revealed nothing. I let out a slow, steady breath when she tilted her head and sighed. It was a good thing I'd used my mother's maiden name.

"Well, Ivy, how about after class I take you to my office close to the bay and we can go over your application?"

"Oh—no, Mrs. Maxwell, you don't have to do that. It wouldn't be fair to the other people who I'm sure are much more qualified."

"That's nonsense. I love to hire *passionate* people who are willing to help! Plus, you have a mean right hook." She winked at me. I blushed, as if I was so flattered to receive a compliment from *the* Lola Maxwell.

Chanel wrapped up the class and clapped for us, but I kept my attention on Lola. "If you have the time now, you can follow me to my office. I was going to make a quick stop there anyway before heading home."

Home. Home. Her home. I needed to get into her home. Not yet, but soon.

"Are you sure?" I asked.

"I'm positive. I'd love to chat more."

"Okay, then. I don't mind following you there."

I went with Lola to the lockers and we collected our things. Chanel commended me on my good work on the way out the door, but I brushed her off, not leaving her much room to talk.

The plan was in motion now. There was no room to keep playing the friendly new girl.

I watched Lola get into what I'm sure was a brand-new, pearl-white Escalade as I climbed into my Civic.

This was happening, and I was ready.

CHAPTER SIX

I followed Lola across town, but I didn't need to follow her to know exactly where her office was located.

She did all her work with a small staff in an office close to the bay. I'd driven past it so many times I'd lost count. Most times I'd never see Lola there, which led me to believe she mostly worked at home.

Because I was a fresh face, she wasn't going to take me to her house, which was understandable, but her office was good enough for now. One step closer, I figured, and at least now I wasn't sitting in the car watching from across the street. I was going to be *inside* the office.

Be patient, Ivy, I told myself. *You'll get there.*

I pulled up to the familiar white-brick building that had over a dozen wide, rectangular windows, all of them squeaky clean. Two palm trees delivered shade around the front of the building. From where I was parked, I could see right through the windows. There were desks in each corner, and walls separating the offices that appeared to be made completely of frosty glass.

Lola stepped out of her SUV and waved at me as I met up to her. "I believe Noah and Olivia are here today, which is a

good thing. They may be able to get your application pro-
cessed today," she said when I met her at the door.

I followed her into the office, feeling a sense of accomplishment as we walked across sparkling, porcelain floors.

"Olivia, Noah! Good morning!" Lola greeted from the
door, meeting them and giving them kisses on the cheek.
"Forgive me, you guys! I am so sweaty! I just left kickboxing
class."

"Oh, stop it," the one I assumed was Noah said. "Even
when you sweat, you sweat diamonds, girl!" I avoided an eye
roll as they all hugged and squealed like baby pigs. She needed
people like this in her life. People eager to compliment her.

Lola turned to me. "This is Ivy Elliot, and believe it or
not, she was in class with me today and brought up the Ladies
with Passion project!"

"Did she now?" Noah exclaimed with way too much enthusiasm. He was extra and flamboyant, with his blue, skinny
pants, white loafers, and floral button-down shirt. And what
was up with his hair? He had the thickest dreads I'd ever seen,
but I guess that was the hip thing now—having a hairstyle that
made you look homeless.

"Yes, and she told me she applied to be a volunteer. Isn't
this a small world?" said Lola gleefully.

"It sure is." Olivia gave me a bold smile. She was a petite
woman with a short, pixie cut and bronze skin. She wore a
white linen dress and hideous jeweled sandals.

"I told her I would sit down with her so we could look
over her application today," Lola went on.

"Oh, for sure. I actually just wrapped up on getting some
volunteers for the gala. Competition was fierce this year,
honey!" Noah stepped toward me and offered a hand. I shook
it firmly. "It's so nice to meet you, Ivy. And you are so damn
gorgeous, by the way."

Smile, Ivy. Just smile. "Thank you."

"Ivy, would you like some cucumber water or some coffee?" Lola asked as she walked to a wide, white door with her name on it. Of course her name was on a gold plate on the door.

"Cucumber water sounds good," I said. Might as well enjoy the luxuries. She told Noah to fetch the water and then instructed me to follow her.

She walked into her office, which was immaculate. Not that I expected anything less. Her office may as well have been made all of windows. It revealed turquoise waters, white sand, and sailboats not too far off in the distance. Her glass desk was free of papers. The only thing atop it was a Mac desktop and keyboard.

There was a teal love seat against the only painted wall, which was a very light blue, and a coffee table with white lilies on top of it. Everything was clean, crisp, and perfect. Just like our dear Lola.

"Please, have a seat." Lola sat in the cushioned chair behind her desk and I pulled back the clear chair across from her. This chair had to be made of glass. I was almost too afraid to sit my sweaty ass in it.

"So, tell me about yourself, Ivy," Lola said, booting up her laptop and clicking away on her keyboard to log in.

"What would you like to know?" I asked, pretending to be nervous, fidgeting in my chair. Truth be told, I was prepared for this.

"Are you originally from Florida?"

"I am, yes."

"Oh really? Were you born here in Miami?" she asked, looking me in the eye.

I wasn't about to tell her I was from St. Petersburg, and not the lovely part of that city either. She'd catch on. Figure out my past. "I'm from Tampa."

"Oh, Tampa is amazing. My husband and I go there a lot to visit his mother."

"Really? I bet that's nice."

"It's funny, because you remind me of someone. Are you related to anyone I know?"

"Not that I'm aware of," I answered quickly.

She narrowed her eyes. Studied my face, every detail of it. Then she shrugged, and I held back a sigh. "So, what makes you so interested in volunteering for Ladies with Passion? Other than helping the future moms, of course."

"Well, um . . . I sort of have a personal story, but I didn't want to say much about it during kickboxing to throw off the mood or anything. It's on my application, but I don't go into a lot of detail on there."

"Oh?" Lola sat up higher in her chair, giving me her undivided attention. "Are you okay with sharing your story? Everything in this interview remains confidential, I assure you, but if you aren't comfortable telling me, you absolutely don't have to."

"No, no. It's okay." I drew in a breath, ready to play the inspired good-girl-with-a-tragic-past. My true story is already a bit of a tragedy—you know all about it—but this new one I'd made up would butter Lola up for sure. "Well, when I was eighteen, I suffered a miscarriage."

"Oh my goodness." Lola swallowed hard, then closed her eyes for a brief moment. For a second I thought I'd come on too strong with my little fib, and that I should have eased into it, but she opened her hazel eyes again and pressed her lips together. "I am so sorry to hear that."

"It's okay. I feel like I've healed from it now, you know?"

"Honey, trust me. We never heal," she murmured.

We? One step closer.

"That's true." I worked hard to swallow, and tears crept to my eyes, right on cue. I swiped at my eyes. "I'm so sorry," I whispered. "It's just when I think about it I, um . . . I get a little choked up."

"No, no. Please." Lola pushed out of her chair and I hung my head in shame. She walked around her desk and took the chair beside mine, placing a hand on my upper back. "It's okay. You don't have to tell me right now, sweetie."

"No, I want to," I whispered, and my voice cracked. Damn, I deserved an Oscar for this shit, Marriott! I almost had to fight a smile. I'd practiced this sob story in the mirror too many times to count, making sure all my facial expressions were clear and worthy of tugging on the heartstrings.

"I'm just . . . well, it still haunts me sometimes. I was seven weeks along. I was only eighteen years old, but I wanted the baby. I know I was young, but I had a job and I knew I could take care of it if I wanted to. I was so prepared to live life as a new mom, but then I woke up with these really bad cramps one night, and when I turned on the light, blood was all over my bed. I—I didn't make it to the hospital in time."

"Oh, sweetie, I am so sorry." Lola rubbed my back as I dropped my face into my palms. I had her right in the palm of my hand.

"If I'd had insurance or money to set an appointment, then I could have gotten the proper care, but as a young girl, I couldn't afford to go to prenatal appointments or anything. I was just saving up for the birth and afterward. I should have gotten the care I needed."

Lola was quiet for a moment, but she still rubbed my back in soothing circles. She stared off in the distance for a long time—so long that I thought she was ignoring me.

After several seconds, she said, "I went through something similar."

I picked up my head and purposely separated my lips to gasp. "You did?" Of course I already knew that. She'd posted about it on Facebook several times, stating that her miscarriage was part of the reason she'd started a charity for pregnant women who couldn't afford proper care—especially if they were high risk. Apparently, she had met a woman who'd suffered a miscarriage around the same time she did while she was in the hospital. The woman couldn't afford the medical bill when all was said and done, so Lola paid the bill for her, and that inspired her to start up Ladies with Passion a year later.

"I did," Lola went on. "I was thirty-four at the time, seven weeks along. I remember being so happy that I was pregnant, but then watching it all vanish into a pool of red. It was just . . . I can't explain it, but I understand your grief. I am so sorry you went through that, Ivy."

I nodded, and Lola sighed, blinking away her tears and standing up. She walked to a bookcase against the wall and took down a box of tissues. After offering one to me, she snatched one for herself and dabbed at the corners of her eyes.

Noah walked into the room, and I was so thankful he interrupted our tearfest. It was getting harder and harder to fake the waterworks. He handed the water to me with a sympathetic sweep of his eyes and I thanked him graciously.

"You know what? I've heard enough. I want you as a volunteer," Lola said with utmost certainty. "I know how hard it is to endure what you've gone through, and to know that someone who is passionate about this project is around to encourage these moms is exactly what I need."

"A-are you sure?" I asked, lowering the tissue as she walked around her desk.

"Positive, sweetie. I found your application and I'm going to forward it to Noah so he'll have you on file as an approved member. Just lend me your ID so I can get it photocopied and you'll be good to go."

"Oh my goodness! I can't thank you enough! This is a dream come true, it really is!" I thought maybe I was laying my excitement on too thick, but Lola only smiled a sweet, caring smile.

"I'm lucky to have met you. It's very rare to find the passionate eggs, but I can tell you're one of them. We will be having a seminar next Saturday to discuss Passion Camp, which is coming up very soon. Do you think you'll be able to join us to learn the ropes for camp?"

"Of course. I don't work too often on Saturdays, so that's perfect." I fingered through my wallet, handing her my fake ID. Ivy Elliot from Tampa was what she'd see on it.

"Wonderful." Lola accepted the ID, typed something else, and then pushed back in her chair to stand. I stood with her. "I just forwarded your application." She walked to me and held me by the upper arms. "I am so happy to have you on board for the Ladies with Passion Project, Ivy. You are so strong. I know you'll make a great team member."

My eyes filled with tears. Don't ask me how I was doing it. I read something once that said you have to think of something that makes you really sad to conjure tears, but for me, I would have considered these tears of joy.

I had a foot in the door. I was going to be a volunteer, and our dear Lola just took me in with wide-open arms because of a made-up sob story and a few crocodile tears.

Truth is, Marriott, I didn't have a miscarriage when I was eighteen. I had an abortion. I did want to keep the baby, though, so it was like a loss, wasn't it?

Look, I told you not to judge me. I couldn't afford to have a baby, and the guy who'd knocked me up was a complete asshole and wouldn't have been a good father.

Xavier was bad news and you know it. I was barely making ends meet at eighteen, so if anything, I was sparing that baby from a life of struggle, hopelessness, and anger. I didn't want the baby to end up like me—alone and mad at the world. I had to build up my life first. I was too young for a baby.

For a while I didn't know how I'd build my life and make it greater, but then you gave me a name, Marriott. I found the face that went with that name and my whole perspective on life changed.

This rich woman in front of me owed me her *life*, and the only way I was going to be able to provide for myself was if I took what she had. I wanted a child one day, but I had to make sure the child could be protected and taken care of financially first.

I walked out the door of Lola's office after Noah scanned my ID, still carrying on with my hopeless-girl charade as I walked past Olivia, but when I got inside my car, I did a small jig, glad I had won Lola over.

There was more work to be done, though. Lots more. This was just the beginning. The next step was going to be the trickiest, but if I could get her to believe my made-up story, I could get her to believe almost anything.

I know how fucked up it is to lie about something as serious as a miscarriage, but it was the only way, Marriott. How else was I going to connect to the charity *and* to Lola?

She felt automatic sympathy for me because she could relate to what I'd gone through, and I was going to use that to my fullest advantage.

CHAPTER SEVEN

I couldn't wait for Saturday to arrive.

Most times work went by in a flash, but it was slow the week after officially meeting Lola, not to mention the customers who did come in were starting to get under my skin. A few more months and I would be able to quit this damn job.

Still, Saturday rolled around eventually, and I wore a black maxidress with stud earrings to keep it subtle. I wanted to give off the appearance that I was well-off enough to look presentable, but that I could still use a hand if Lola ever wanted to generously offer a shopping spree and take care of the costs.

I dreamed of all the new clothes I could get with her at my side. I bet she didn't have a shopping limit. I could shop 'til I dropped and still go back for more with her.

Lola liked to give. She was charming and kind, and between her and her husband, they made so much money that handing over fifty thousand dollars was probably like handing over a single dollar bill for them.

I got an email from Lola the same night she'd sent my application to Noah. She sent me the address of the location where the seminar for Passion Camp would be held. It was my desire to be prompt—show her that I was fully invested in becoming a volunteer.

I arrived at the place, which happened to be a Baptist church. There were already dozens of cars parked in the lot. I collected my purse and scurried right inside. I was greeted with smiles and hugs at the door and tried hard not to stiffen as they all wrapped their giving arms around me.

I had to get used to this. Hugs weren't my thing, but I was Ivy Elliot, a nice young woman who loved to help and was so unassertive that it was almost embarrassing.

I signed in with one of the women at the tables and then walked into the room that was set up for our event. There were tables covered in white tablecloths, with sky-blue balloons and blue place settings. Many women stood around, mingling and sipping coffee or wine.

I stood near a table to the far left, hoping to avoid conversation. Unfortunately, avoiding conversation was not in the plans.

A plump woman walked up to me with a moonlike face. Her smile was wide and her eyes were thin, like almonds. "You must be Ivy!" The woman was loud. I hated that her voice was drawing attention my way. The less attention I received, the better this plan of mine would work out.

"I am," I said, patting her back as she reeled me in for a hug. I was seriously never going to get used to the hugs.

"I'm so glad you could make it! I'm Vonyetta, Lola's organizer and assistant. You are going to love it as a volunteer, especially for Passion Camp! We have so many mothers coming to enjoy camp this year, it's nice to have your helping hands."

"Thank you so much."

"I'm so glad God sent you our way. Lola has been talking about all the new volunteers she's interviewed! She told me you have a beautiful story. If you ever wish to share it with any of us, just know we are here to listen with open arms, sweetie."

"Thank you!" Like hell I was sharing anything with these bitches. It was like pulling teeth for you, wasn't it? Why would I share a thing with them?

Vonyetta gave me a friendly pat on the shoulder, and as she did, someone walked in, catching her attention.

"Oh, Meera! Look at you! Glowing with that bump, girl!" Vonyetta rushed toward the pregnant woman who'd walked through the door in a red sundress, and I turned away, glad she was gone.

I sat in a chair, gritting my teeth as the women in the room cackled like old hens and exclaimed over how blessed they all were.

Yes, yes, they were blessed. I got it already, but was it necessary to keep saying it? I'm not very religious, as you know, Marriott. After losing everything that mattered, how could I be? All hope was lost when I was fourteen.

Fortunately, Lola sauntered into the room and stole the show. Everyone greeted her with smiley faces and gave her so many compliments on her clothes.

I watched her stroll by, dressed in linen white pants and a baby-blue blouse. Her hair was half up, half down, and her face was free of all makeup except mascara. She was flawless, and I envied the hell out of her.

Still, when she looked my way, I smiled, and she gave me an urgent wave, like she was so happy to see I'd made it.

She was starting to like me, Marriott. I could feel it. The start of something great . . .

Well, for me anyway.

The camp training was a snoozefest. I can't even count how many times I was about to doze off as Vonyetta went on about how the pregnant moms were nervous, but so thankful for the opportunity to kick their feet up and enjoy camp this summer.

I suppose if I were pregnant and got a chance to get into Passion Camp, I'd be grateful too. Passion Camp was a week-long event where pregnant women would be pampered with pedicures, manicures, facials, boat rides, three hot meals a day, and prenatal massages.

Rumor had it that it was hard to get accepted into Passion Camp. You had to truly need the escape and the help of a charity, and they also ran background checks on the women. Any hard convictions and they wouldn't take you. Basically, you needed to be as poor as dirt and pure as snow to get treated like a princess for a week at Passion Camp.

When the volunteer seminar was over, we had a lunch catered by Lola. I slinked my way past a few volunteers to get to the front of the line and get my food first, making sure I could secure a seat close to Lola.

Because Vonyetta was her assistant, she had a seat beside her. Some other woman named Keke, who I was sure was going to cause me problems just from her nasty looks alone, took the chair to Lola's right.

I didn't care for this Keke woman. She was late to the seminar and had this weird, territorial claim on Lola. She was obnoxious, and I had no clue how the classy Lola Maxwell dealt with someone like her.

I sat next to Vonyetta, unfortunately. I had a rotisserie chicken club sandwich on my plate, with apple slices and a glass of champagne offered from the food line.

"I love bringing on new volunteers." Lola sighed as she sat down with her glass of champagne. I noticed she wasn't eating, though she insisted everyone take as much as they wanted. The serving area was filled with food—sandwiches, fruit, desserts, sangria, and champagne.

"It's a blessing for sure," Vonyetta said, and I swore I

would stab her with my fork if she said the word "blessing" one more time.

Something crashed in the corner and a burst of gasps set the room off. We all looked over to see a woman standing in front of shattered glass. She'd dropped her wineglass. I'd been watching that woman. Her name was Alyssa. She'd been drinking during the whole meeting.

"Oh, Lyssa! You okay?" Vonyetta asked, pushing out of her chair and helping her step around the glass.

"Yeah, I'm okay, girl. Just feeling a little lightheaded. You know I work third shift," Alyssa said, forcing a laugh.

"Yep, that's right. You know you could have skipped the meeting today and I could have filled you in. You need to rest, honey. It's a blessing you got that new job, but you work too hard."

Have mercy.

I sipped my champagne to fight the urge to scream. As I did, I felt eyes on me. Lola was looking right at me with a warm smile.

"How are you feeling? Excited or overwhelmed?" she asked.

"A little bit of both," I said with nervous laughter, sitting up higher in my chair.

Lola slid over to Vonyetta's chair, but I didn't miss the scowl Keke gave me before biting into a grape.

"No need to be overwhelmed at all," said Lola. "We have a great staff, and they'll walk you through everything. I know it seems like a lot to take in right now, but I promise you, the volunteers have just as much fun at the camp as the expectant mothers."

"That's good to know."

I looked up to see Vonyetta sweeping up the glass.

"Do you have any relatives around here?" Keke asked, leaning forward.

I shook my head. "No, I don't."

"Really? But aren't you from Florida?"

I stared Keke in the eye. "Yes, Tampa, actually."

"And no family there?"

"Keke," Lola hissed. "Why are you so worried about her family?"

"I'm just wondering." Keke sipped her sangria with flared nostrils. There was something about her. I could see that Keke wanted to be just like Lola, except she didn't have the grace of gentleness. She was just a hostile, jealous bitch who hated being second best, but kept Lola close to make herself look good. It was sad I could read all that about her, and I didn't even know her last name.

When lunch was over, it was time for everyone to part ways. I took my time finishing another glass of champagne and watching Lola give everyone sweet farewells. Keke had long gone, thank goodness.

I walked toward the exit, slipping past Lola and a woman she was speaking with. "Oh—Ivy!" I peered over my shoulder before reaching the door, and Lola was holding up a manicured finger for me. "Just a minute! I need to chat with you really quickly."

I waited for her to finish with the woman, and by the time she did the room was mostly clear of bodies. "Is everything okay?" I asked.

"Oh, everything is great. I just wanted to apologize for Keke's little interrogation. She can get a little ahead of herself. She sometimes forgets that not everyone is so open and willing to share their lives with the world."

I huffed a laugh. "Oh, it's okay."

Lola studied my face for a fleeting moment before saying, "I am curious about you, though. Noah and I looked at your application, and you mentioned being adopted?" Her voice was quieter, even though not many people were around.

I knew this was coming and I played my card, nodding and swallowing. "Yes, I was. I was adopted into this huge family, didn't really like it there, but I survived." I gave a shrug.

"Oh. Do you still keep in touch with them?"

"Sometimes. Not often. I gave them a lot of trouble. I'm trying to be a better person and they know that, but sometimes it's hard for them to forgive the adopted girl."

"Oh Ivy." She placed a hand on my shoulder. "I bet you have had it rough."

Yeah, because of you, bitch! I wanted to shout. Instead, I nodded, and to my surprise my eyes did sting, but not with tears of sadness. Tears of anger.

"Well, listen—Corey will be in Vegas with a few friends and I'll be free tomorrow after my morning yoga. What do you say you come to my place for brunch?"

"Brunch at your place? Really?"

"Yes. Call me crazy, but I see something in you and I'd like to get to know you a little better." She paused and laughed a little. "This might sound silly, but you feel so familiar to me. It's hard for me to form connections like this, but I like you, and I see myself in you. Of course if you're busy, I completely understand."

"No—no. Not at all." That was a lie. I did have a shift in the afternoon, but it wasn't until four. I could make a brunch with Lola Maxwell work.

Wasn't this all strange? She was being too nice to me, a new girl who was just a stranger to her a week before. It felt like she was up to something, that she could see right through me at times like this, but then, when I really looked at her, it was as if she knew nothing at all.

Did she know? Did I need to continue pretending to be Ivy Elliot?

"Perfect. I got your number from the application," Lola told me. "I'll text you my address as soon as I get home."

"Great." I followed her out of the church and into the

Florida sun, then watched her climb into the navy-blue Tesla. She waved as she drove away. I stood by my car, watching her go.

Sure enough, Lola sent me a text with the address. I had just gotten out of the shower after a quick workout when my phone buzzed on the bed. I was quick to pick it up and read it.

Brunch was at twelve.

I would bring a bottle of cheap champagne, just to show her how excited I was to be invited. Truth is, I *was* excited. This would get me one step closer to Lola.

It was game time.

CHAPTER EIGHT

The next morning I woke up early so I could take my time getting dressed and practice my humble mannerisms.

I found an ivory dress in the closet that I'd bought when I first moved there. I'd decided I would create a new wardrobe. Long gone were the days when I wore crop top shirts, shorts with fishnet stockings, and leather boots. I'd even gotten rid of my septum piercing. Face jewelry seemed to be frowned upon in Lola's elite world, and I needed to fit in as best I could.

After getting dressed, sliding into a pair of sandals, and then pinning pearl earrings in my ears, I grabbed my phone and wallet and left my apartment. I locked up and went downstairs, spotting my neighbor Julius sitting on the stoop. He had a cigarette pinched between his lips.

"You look like an escort," he said as I walked past him.

"And you look like a bum," I said back.

"You're a real bitch, Ivy. You know that?"

I rolled my eyes and climbed into my car.

Funny story about Julius—we slept together once. It wasn't intentional. I'd had a little too much to drink one night and he had a lot of friends over next door who were really loud. I was stewing about Lola over some accomplishment she'd posted, and because I was already ticked off, I went over, banged on his door, and told him to shut off the noise.

Because he had friends over, Julius was embarrassed. We got in each other's faces and he walked out of his apartment, bumping me back with his chest toward my apartment. The next thing I knew, we were making out on my bed. Angrily. Aggressively. It was weird, but good.

I have no idea why I slept with a guy like him. Julius had a tongue piercing, which I admit he made good use of, corn-rows, and had arms that were covered in ink. He wasn't my type, but I suppose I was desperate and needed some. He was okay in bed. Good enough to go to again if I needed it. I could tell he always wanted more whenever I passed by, always focusing on my ass or my new breasts, but I couldn't stoop to Julius's level anymore. I had to go for men like Corey.

I drove away from my run-down apartment complex and through town, following the directions of my phone's GPS. I couldn't believe I had her address. I knew where she lived by now—I'd followed her once—but the place was under twenty-four-hour security and you either had to be an owner of one of the homes or on someone's visitors list to get inside, though lately I'd noticed security had been kind of slack due to all the rented-out Airbnbs in the area.

I was tempted to rent one once, just to have access to the neighborhood, but the costs were too extreme and I didn't have thousands of dollars to spend per night.

I drove for twenty minutes, riding along MacArthur Causeway, before the GPS told me I had arrived on Star Is-land, right off Biscayne Bay. I knew anyone who lived in Star, Palm, or Hibiscus Island, or anywhere near Biscayne Bay, had deep pockets. It didn't surprise me to know Lola lived there when I first followed her.

I checked in with security at the gate, pleased that Lola

had me listed on her visitors' sheet. This was a big step for me in my own eyes. As a visitor, I could come and go in the neighborhood without her knowledge, and without raising any red flags.

I made a right turn, riding through the neighborhood made of immaculate mansions I couldn't even imagine owning. There were droves of palm trees and thick, monogrammed iron gates and neatly paved roads.

How was it that people could become so rich? These millionaires made it seem so effortless, and yet I had no clue where to even start.

When I was near Lola's estate, I made another turn, and the black asphalt smoothly transitioned to cobblestone. The driveway was lined with palm trees and fresh flower beds in between. I drove until a wrought-iron gate appeared with a gold letter M in the middle of it. M for Maxwell.

There was a silver speaker box at the gate with a camera, and I rolled my window down to press the white button.

"Ivy! Come on in!" Lola's voice was shrill through the intercom. The silver box buzzed and the gates rolled apart, separating the gold M. I drove through the gates and up more cobblestone. There were more shady palm trees lining the driveway.

The palm trees soon cleared and the ocean came into view. I collected a breath when I noticed the luxurious mansion built right on a hill, surrounded by turquoise waters from behind.

"Wow." It was the only word I could muster. I'd always imagined what her home would look like. I saw many photos of the front of her mansion when she'd pose with a new car or just take a photo for her Instagram, but seeing it on social media was nothing like seeing it in person.

The home was stunning—not that I expected anything less. Just like her office, the mansion was practically made of glass. Windows embellished the entire front side of the home, intricately designed in sharp-edged rectangles and squares. The grass was bright and green, the leaves of the palm trees swaying with the wind. A terra-cotta roof covered the large abode, giving it color and life.

I parked and climbed out of the car with the cheap bottle of champagne I'd picked up the night before from a corner store and made my way to the front door. I rang the doorbell and the door opened in a matter of seconds.

A woman who appeared to be in her midthirties, her coily, black hair pulled up into a bun, answered the door. She was dressed in khaki pants, flat black shoes, and a blue shirt with the letter M monogrammed on the heart of it. Her face was clear of makeup, her brows bushy and untamed. The woman really needed them arched and plucked.

"Hey there. You must be Ivy," the woman said, letting me inside as she took a step back. "I'm Georgia, Mrs. Maxwell's household manager and personal assistant. Can I take that from you?" She lowered her gaze to the bottle of champagne in my hand and I nodded, handing it to her. "Wonderful. Right this way." Georgia walked across polished marble floors, the bottle of champagne resting in her palm, and I followed her, but I couldn't help taking in my surroundings.

Lola's home was stunning in every way, shape, and form, from the crown molding in the ceilings and well-picked chandeliers to the tan paint on the walls. We passed a sitting area consisting of a matching love seat and single chair made of white leather. I could tell this room was hardly ever used, but a furry gray throw was placed on the top of the love seat, positioned in a way that made the room appear used and cozy.

Georgia continued walking, into a kitchen made predominantly of white marble, from the counters to the backsplash. The counters were a light gray and spotless, and sunlight from the floor-to-ceiling glass double doors bounced off them, the light almost blinding.

Georgia slid open the doors, and as she did, I spotted Lola

standing in front of a wide, blue pool, her hip cocked, a cell phone to her ear. She wore a red sleeveless dress that hugged her curves, with gold earrings and gold bangles connected by red rubies. On her feet were red stilettos with gold straps. Why did she always look so great, Marriott? Please explain.

At the sound of the doors opening, she turned around and smiled at me. "Yes, I'll discuss it in depth tomorrow. I'm just about to have brunch. Talk to you soon." Lola ended the call and then walked to me, opening her arms. "Ivy!" She sang my name. She gave me a squeeze and I returned one, patting her back for emphasis. "I am so glad you're here."

"I wouldn't have missed it." Not for the world.

"Would you like something to drink?" Lola offered. "Georgia had our chef whip up these *delicious* raspberry mimosas. So good. Would you like to try one?"

"Sure, I'll take one."

Lola gave Georgia a nod, and she walked off right away, making her way back into the kitchen. When she was gone, Lola walked to a seating area on the deck. It was shaded with a turquoise umbrella, and there were air ducts above, blowing out cool air. An air-conditioned patio? This woman really *was* rich.

"You have a lovely home, Lola. I can't believe you get to wake up here every day."

Lola laughed, but waved it off. Even so, I could tell she was flattered. "Corey chose this place. I just made the most of it. He wanted to be able to park his boat close to the house. No better place than on the bay, I suppose."

I took a look to the right, where the ocean was past the pools—yes, she had two—and saw a small, white yacht at the end of the pier. Corey had a yacht. That was nice. It would come in handy.

Georgia returned with two red drinks in champagne flutes, two fuzzy raspberries floating at the tops of each glass. Lola moved to the end of her chair after accepting her drink, then tipped her glass toward me. "I want to propose a toast."

"Okay," I said with a smile. "What for?"

"For having you join Ladies with Passion and devoting yourself to the cause. I am so grateful for you."

"Oh, please. I'm so thankful you let me join. Seriously, I'm honored." We tapped glasses and then sipped. "This is really good."

Lola gave me a wink. "My chef is one of the best in Florida."

Of course he was.

Two men wearing white gloves came to where we were seated and placed food down on the short, wooden table in front of us. There was all sorts of food and my belly grumbled at the sight of it. Fortunately, Lola couldn't hear it. I hadn't eaten that morning. I was saving my appetite for this brunch.

"Will you need anything else, Mrs. Maxwell?" Georgia asked, popping up after the men walked away.

"We're okay for now, G."

Georgia nodded and left. When she disappeared around a corner, I took a hard sweep of Lola's home again, absorbing everything I could see from where I was seated.

Palm trees towered over the pedicured green grass and just past Corey's yacht, I could clearly make out the Miami skyline in the distance. It seemed only a skip, hop, and a jump away.

I turned my head left, and a wooden shed was across the pedicured lawn, nestled beneath the shade of the palms.

"I'm going to dig right in. I'm starving," Lola said, picking up a slice of cinnamon toast. I dug in as well, picking up a plate grabbing a small bunch of red grapes, a slice of watermelon, and a croissant stuffed with warm strawberry purée and cream cheese.

"All right, Ivy. So, I'm going to be honest with you here

and cut straight to the chase. I didn't just invite you here because you volunteer for me now."

I froze a moment, wanting to avoid her eyes. Had she done her research? Found out more about me? I knew it! She knew exactly who I was.

"No?" I kept my face casual but slightly confused.

"No." She dusted the crumbs from her hands and then reached for a folder beneath her seat. She handed it to me, and I quickly set down my plate to open it. I glanced up at her and she nodded her head. "Go on. Read it." She was smiling; what was happening?

I kept my hands steady as I opened the folder and read over the sheet of paper inside. My jaw instantly went slack as I did. My heart, which was beating like a drum in my chest a minute ago, settled a bit. She had no idea.

"Wait . . . are you serious?" I asked.

Lola's features drooped a bit. "I can understand if you don't want to do it. With volunteering already, I realize this is a lot for you to take on so soon, and I know you work full-time, so I don't want you to feel—"

"No—I think this is great! I'm just really surprised you actually want *me* to model the Ladies with Passion shirts this year."

"Of course I do! Have you looked in the mirror? You are a beautiful young lady! Noah is the one who brought it to my attention, actually—you being the perfect fit to model the shirts. He said you have a unique appeal and I agree. I'd love for you to be the face of the shirts this year."

"I mean, this is an honor, Lola! Really! But I'm so new to all this. Are you sure you don't want someone else to do it? Someone who has been around longer than I have, like your friend Keke, maybe? She's really pretty and would make a great fit." I was pushing it, I knew, but I had to play my role. I'd done my research on Keke.

"Well, Keke used to model the shirts," Lola said, and I knew that, "but she doesn't seem as interested anymore, and her schedule never coincides with Bailey's. She's a busy momma. I brought up the idea to her, about someone new modeling the shirts and tank tops this year when we met for dinner a few nights ago, just to feel her out. She didn't seem to mind me asking around. Although I call the shots, I'd still hate for any of the ladies on my team to feel offended."

Well, she'd read Keke completely wrong then. Now I knew why she kept giving me dirty looks during the seminar yesterday. Lola must have told her she was considering giving me the model slot and she felt replaced, but of course she wasn't going to flat-out tell Lola not to ask me.

"Well, if Keke's okay with it and you really want this, I'll be happy to do it." I wanted to laugh. *Fuck Keke*.

"Great! And as you probably know, all proceeds for every shirt sold goes to the charity. We also want to present them in a slideshow for our gala this fall, to raise a few bucks for them, so you would be the face for that too. I hope that's okay."

"Gotta admit, that makes me nervous." I giggled. "But featuring the shirts during your gala seems like a good idea. I'm down."

"Yay! So, the only thing is, I'll need you to come next weekend for the shoot. I know it's short notice, but you'd be surprised how hard it is to find a model who will do this voluntarily. Many of them see my name involved and see dollar signs, and it's so sad. But you won't have to worry about makeup or anything—I'll have it all covered, and I'll even have a lunch planned for you afterward."

"I should be able to do next weekend. I'll just see if I can switch my shift." There was no way in hell I was missing this photo shoot.

Full-blown relief struck me then. I'd thought surely she was going to confess to her crimes when she said she needed to be honest and flat-out tell me she knew who I was, but this was much better, honestly. She didn't know who I was. I could keep up with my plan, play my part.

Lola sighed and laughed. "Oh, this is wonderful. I was a little nervous to ask. You just joined the Ladies with Passion, and not only that but you seem so reserved—like this wouldn't be your kind of thing."

"Well, I've never modeled before and I am kind of camera shy, but this is for the charity, so I really don't mind." I gave her a wide smile, putting down the folder and picking up my raspberry mimosa.

"So good to hear. Well, just so you know, the photo shoot always happens here, on our deck. I hire a photographer who does a wonderful job of capturing the images I need. I invited you today so you could get a feel of my place, get acquainted with the atmosphere here," she stated, gesturing to the area around us.

Well, that wasn't an issue. I felt right at home walking into her mansion. I'd dreamed of the day I'd be able to walk in and breathe it all in. Get a taste of what she experienced, a feel for how she lived her life, even if it was all for just a moment. I put on a grateful smile. "This place is lovely. There's no reason not to love it."

"Corey will be so glad I found someone. Now I can stop talking his head off about searching for a model every night over dinner."

I sat up a little higher in my chair at the mention of Corey. "Well, you totally could have modeled the shirts yourself. You're gorgeous, Lola."

She laughed. "Oh girl, you sound just like my husband. He constantly says that to me. I like to keep things fresh, though. Younger faces work better for LWP, considering most of the moms are women who are under thirty."

"That makes sense." I sipped my drink. "And Corey is your husband, right?"

"Yep, he is," she answered, but not as excitedly as she had about the charity topic.

"Does he help out a lot with the charity?" I asked, still trying to keep it light.

"He does what he can. He's always busy, so I don't expect him to do much for it, but as far as hiring the right catering teams and getting donations from the men who feel they're too good to donate to women's charities, he's good for that." She chuckled.

I tried not to roll my eyes.

"Oh, that's cool." I paused for a moment. "You know, I follow you on Instagram," I said, smiling coyly. "That's how I know Corey is your husband . . . ."

"You do?" Lola laughed. "That's so great! I love Instagram! I'll have to find you on there and give you a follow. It's my favorite app."

Yeah, it was her favorite because she was a conceited bitch.

"I always see pictures of you with him. You guys always look so happy together."

"Well, we try to be, you know? After everything we've been through, we try to live with smiles on our faces." Her whole statement seemed practiced, like she'd said it many times before.

"You mean with the miscarriage?" I asked, treading carefully. I kept my voice gentle, my face compassionate. She'd brought up the miscarriage before, and because I'd told my sob story, I hoped she wouldn't take too much offense at my question.

Lola nodded, then sipped her drink. She was quiet for a moment, looking at the ocean, scratching a manicured nail over her thumb cuticle. "Things change after having one, but it made our marriage stronger. Impenetrable."

Nothing is impenetrable. There's always a way to break through something, especially a marriage, right? A warm breeze brushed by me as I finished off my mimosa and then picked up a strawberry. "How long have you guys been married, if you don't mind me asking?"

"Just short of seventeen years." She smiled at the reminder.

"Wow, that's such a long time. Definitely goals."

"Things moved fast with us at first. We'd only been together two years, but I loved him so much—still love him so much. We woke up one morning and decided we wanted to be together for the rest of our lives. Didn't want to live without each other for a second."

Oh, kill me now. I refrained from sucking my teeth and instead said, "That must be so nice—knowing you've met your soul mate." I wanted to swallow those words. *He was my soul mate.*

"Truly. So, are you dating anyone?" Lola asked, then sipped her drink, her hazel eyes on me.

"No. I try to focus on working and building a future for myself for now. I just came here to start over."

"You must have had a rough childhood," she murmured sympathetically. "Same as I did."

"I did," I replied, holding back on a clipped tone.

"What exactly are you trying to start over with, if you don't mind?"

I sat back and crossed my legs. "Well, I told you about my miscarriage at eighteen, and I also mentioned my shitty ex-boyfriend."

Lola nodded.

"I suppose I just look at Miami as a fresh start. I know it's not a long way from where I was raised, but it feels good to be somewhere else, around other people."

"I bet it does." Lola sighed. "Well, I'm so glad you moved here. I can already tell you and I are going to get along just great."

Oh yeah. We were going to be the best of friends. Right

now, I had to be gentle about how our friendship blossomed, though. I wanted her to know I was an asset, not a burden, or someone who was coming for her pockets . . . or her husband.

I knew I'd gain more of her trust with time, so for now any little favors she needed from me, I'd do.

Model for the charity? No problem, Lola!

I'd do anything to take her down.

After we talked a little more over brunch, Lola gave me a tour of her home. She showed me four guest bedrooms, all of which were designed beautifully, but none of them could top the master bedroom.

Lola and Corey's bedroom had an ocean and pool view, and their walk-in closet was the size of my apartment. The bathroom was like something out of a magazine. A freestanding tub facing the ocean, heated marble floors, frameless shower doors, and a wide, silver rain-forest showerhead.

Her office was upstairs, across from her favorite guest room. A MacBook on a glass desk, and two glass doors at the end of the room, revealing turquoise waters and a white deck.

Envy coursed through me as she sauntered into a room she'd called her "thinking room" and pointed up at a crystal chandelier. This room was her motivation room, where she came to pace and think. It was fucking ridiculous, Marriott. She'd mentioned having the chandelier custom-made and that it had cost her several thousand dollars.

"I come in here sometimes to look at this chandelier because I remember it was one of the first things I splurged on for this place," Lola said, staring up at it. I had to admit, it was a gorgeous chandelier. Wide, with gold throngs and dangling teardrop crystals.

Simple.

Eloquent.

Definitely a Lola Maxwell chandelier.

"I didn't care for the pool or the kitchen," Lola went on.

"This chandelier represents all my hard work. I look at it and I remember that even when things are tough, or if I'm having a bad day, I must persevere. I work hard for what I want and what I have, and I don't quit."

I wanted to break the damn thing with a metal baseball bat. She didn't deserve the chandelier or any of what she had. She lived her life like she had no secrets and told no lies. It annoyed me that she was one of the most well-paid and respected women of color in Florida. Knowing she got to attend extravagant dinners and be invited to private parties with celebrities ticked me off.

My life was a living hell and had been for *years* because of her, and yet she had it all—a gorgeous home, a gorgeous husband, a gorgeous car, a gorgeous fucking *thinking room* with a gorgeous fucking chandelier.

It wasn't fair, but only children pouted about what was fair and what wasn't. I was grown, and I would make things right again. Make it fair.

I continued a smile and pretended to be in awe of the chandelier that inspired Lola's lavish life.

When it was time for me to go, Lola handed me a bottle of white wine from her wine fridge—it was her favorite and I *needed* to try it right away—and gave me a kiss on the cheek, reminding me to be at her place next Saturday for the photo shoot.

I strolled past her blue Tesla and a black Chrysler 300 with bold silver rims that I could only assume belonged to Corey.

Lola gave me a final wave as I started my car and even watched me leave her driveway from the front door. As I drove through the gates, though, making sure my windows were rolled up, I screamed as loudly as I could, until my lungs felt like they were about to pop.

When I was far enough from her house that she couldn't see me, but still in the privacy of the cobblestone driveway, I rested my head on the steering wheel while gripping it.

Playing nice with her was killing me slowly, but I knew in the end all this would be worth it. I just had to keep following through. I had to keep Lola close, no matter how badly I wanted to wrap my hands around her throat and strangle her.

"Gain her trust, then ruin her," I said, putting the car in Drive and rolling out of the driveway. "Gain her trust, then ruin her."

I repeated the mantra off Star Island and the whole way home.

CHAPTER NINE

When I woke up the morning after brunch with Lola, the first thing I did was grab my phone and open the Instagram app. I could see why people became addicted to watching other people's lives now, Marriott. You can't help it, really. It's human nature to see what other humans are up to.

It was a surprise to see Lola had found me and followed me back, despite the fact that I had no photos on my account. Only thing I had was a profile image. It was all so pointless to me, but I suppose to keep up appearances and to let Lola know I was the average millennial, I had to start posting *something* soon.

I sat up and stared at the half-empty bottle of white wine on my nightstand that Lola had sent me off with after brunch. I had looked it up while on my break at work. The bottle was worth three hundred dollars. I almost had the urge to dump it down the drain with a chuckle, just to know I'd wasted her money, but after spending all that time with her at her mansion, seeing how she got to live her life, and then dealing with rude-ass customers at work afterward, I decided to drink it when I got home instead.

My head was throbbing as I clicked through Lola's stories.

I never did well with wine. I climbed out of bed and walked to my bathroom, taking down a bottle of painkillers. I popped two of them in my hand, then walked back to my nightstand to grab the wine bottle. The pill was in my mouth and I chugged down a good bit of wine before swallowing it all. I know, I know. A bad thing to do—a dangerous cocktail—but it was fine. I lived.

I lay in bed again, picking up my phone and visiting Corey's profile this time.

He was in Vegas with his boys, as Lola had mentioned. He'd posted several photos, and even had an image of him with one of his guys and a woman who looked like a stripper between them.

I wondered what Lola thought, seeing that image; then again, I bet she wasn't even bothered. She seemed like the kind of woman who trusted her husband more than anyone in the world.

Men are pigs, but I had hoped Corey didn't have any piglike traits. He seemed like the perfect gentleman. Strong. Kind. Funny when necessary. I was sure he had his flaws, as all people did, and the only way I was going to find out what they were was through Lola.

It was a shame I spent the better half of my day off stalking the couple on my phone. Corey had added videos to his Instagram stories of him walking in Vegas, taking shots of liquor with his buddies. I wished I could be with him.

There was an image of him on his profile. A new one. He'd taken a selfie on the balcony of his suite. The city of Las Vegas was behind him. He smiled wide, and his teeth were so white, and he had that stubble on his chin that proved he hadn't shaved in about two weeks.

He was so sexy. So dreamy.

I envied how he could just run off and have a good time in a different state with no repercussions. Meanwhile, I killed myself for every dollar, pulling extra shifts just so I could pay my rent and afford my new membership at Best Rounds Kick-boxing.

The things I did to get close to Corey and Lola truly astounded me, Marriott, but it would be worth it. It had to be. And of course I'd cancel the membership later . . . once I had my foot completely in the door.

Then a thought hit me.

I went back to Lola's profile to find an image of her with Keke. I'd seen one before but never paid much attention to it because I had no idea who Keke was or how important she was to Lola until the meeting for camp.

In the photo with Keke, they were at a charity event, and both were wearing soaking-wet T-shirts and covered in bubbles. Lola had organized a slip-and-slide bubble race at a park for people of all ages to join them and raise money.

I had to give it up to Lola; she did have some very good ideas for raising money . . . or maybe it was her team who had the ideas and she just threw money at it. Either way, good for her on that front.

I tapped the photo, and Keke's username popped up. I scoffed at it. KeeQueen. She was a joke. Still, I went to her profile, as I'd done once before, read her arrogant biography about being owner of a flower shop and being a queen and a boss, and then scrolled through her pictures.

There was a photo of her with a child that caught my attention most. I clicked it and read the caption.

Not sure what I would do without this little angel
in my life.

Keke had a kid. A girl. She looked about three or four. That explained why she was a part of Ladies with Passion, I supposed.

I combed my way through more of Keke's photos and could tell her life was a hot heap of shit. She wanted to seem like some high-class, entrepreneurial woman, and yet she was a single mother who owned a flower shop and drove a Camry. It was pathetic, and I could tell even from a mile away that Keke loved sniffing on Lola, probably hoping to get rich off her somehow.

I wouldn't have given a damn about someone like Keke to begin with, but there was something to be said when it came to her. I couldn't have another person standing in my way when it came to Lola treating someone like a charity case. From what I could tell, Lola donated generously to Keke's flower shop and, in return, Keke was a sponsor for the charity, though I was sure Lola didn't need it. But it served as loyalty.

She constantly buttered Lola up to get close to her. Served her compliments. Went on lunch and hair dates.

I wasn't having it.

If anyone was going to be close to Lola and get to waste her millions of dollars, it was going to be me, someone who deserved it.

I needed to work harder to get in really good with Lola. I was sure she'd known Keke for years, but all it would take was one little mistake for Lola to kick her out of her life for good.

I was going to make that happen.

CHAPTER TEN

For the rest of the week I worked, and during any of the free time I had, I kept up-to-date on Lola's social media posts. What? It wasn't like I could text her every day to check in. I didn't want to turn her off.

She'd posted on Facebook one day about having lunch with Corey and how much she'd missed him while he was in Vegas. In the image with her post, they were sitting in a fancy booth of some restaurant, their fingers entwined on the tabletop.

Corey was looking at her lovingly, clearly about to nuzzle the tip of his nose in the crook of her neck, and I scoffed at that. He was so infatuated with her that it made me sick. I bet Corey had no idea what kind of secrets his wife held—the kind of shit she did to people. He probably thought his wife was some perfect human being just like the rest of the world did. He was dead wrong.

The day after that, Keke had shared a photo of Lola holding her daughter. Of course Keke had come around again, playing her single mother card. She had a toddler she could use to make her look like she'd always need a helping hand. I rolled my eyes when I read the caption.

My bestie Lola got my baby some new summer dresses!
#bestfriendsforlife #LolaistherealMVP #thatsmybestfriend

I sat on the bench outside my job beneath a palm tree, stewing over the photo. Her daughter was cute and all, but that bitch Keke was really starting to annoy me. I mean, "bestie"? Come on, now.

When Saturday arrived, I was filled with glee. It was my time to shine and get all Lola's attention. I took a long, hot shower that same morning, and made sure my face was as bare as possible, but I didn't forget the mint lip gloss.

After cutting a Gala apple and eating a buttery slice of toast with strawberry jam, I walked to the door of my studio apartment, preparing to leave but taking a look around first.

I hated this place. I didn't have much, which was probably why it annoyed me so much. Just a love seat, a small, flat-screen TV that I never watched, and my lumpy queen-size mattress on the floor, against the wall. When I first moved in, it smelled like mothballs. Candles did the trick, but the mothball scent would still show up here and there. The only good things about it were the double patio doors. They gave me lots of natural light, which you always told me was healthy to have.

No matter. None of this was going to last long anyway.

I slammed the door behind me and locked it, trotting down the steps to get to my car. Julius was sitting on the stoop as I walked by, but we ignored each other. I was glad he didn't talk to me. I wanted to be in the best mood possible when I arrived at Lola's, and talking to Julius always aggravated me.

I didn't need my GPS to find my way to Lola's house this time. I'd visited every other day of the week since she'd sent me the address. Most times it was after work. I didn't go up her driveway or do anything that would cause suspicion of course, but I did drive past her private driveway, just to see if I could capture anything, or maybe spot her or Corey walking around the neighborhood. I gathered the idea they weren't joggers.

But with security at the main gates, I had to be cautious. Visiting every day would have caused one of the men to get curious.

I drove with a small smile pulling at the corners of my lips. When I arrived at her house, I pressed the buzzer on the gate and was invited right in.

There was a black SUV parked in the driveway as I pulled up, along with Lola's Tesla and the same black Chrysler I'd seen last week. I also spotted Lola's pearly white SUV parked close to the house, and I was itching to drag my key across the shiny paint. *Not today.*

Climbing out of the car, I walked up to the wide, brown door and gave the bell a ring. Georgia answered again with a subtle smile on her lips. Her eyes were not welcoming at all, though. It was clear she hated her job . . . or she hated me. Either way, I didn't care. I wasn't there for her.

Georgia escorted me to the deck, where there were cameras, laptops, photography umbrellas, and backdrops already set up. Several men were piecing equipment together.

I put down my bag just as Georgia walked up to me with a tray in hand and drinks on top of it. "Would you like a blood-orange sangria, Miss Elliot?" she asked.

"Sure." I took one from the tray but didn't miss the once-over she gave me as she stepped back.

"Mrs. Maxwell is still getting ready, but she should be down any minute now."

"Okay. No problem." I took a seat on one of the cushioned pool chairs beneath the turquoise umbrella, sipping my drink and watching the men work.

A woman with box braids that reached her lower back, wearing pink shorts and a gray crop top, walked outside, and I sat up a little higher in my chair, studying her as she made her way to the group of men who were piecing together another backdrop.

I knew who she was on sight. Xena Whitley, the photographer for today—and not just *any* photographer. Lola used Xena for almost every photo shoot she had. She was her personal photographer and had even done the headshots for Lola on her charity website. Xena was also a well-known Instagram photographer, and everyone in South Beach wanted to do shoots with her.

Xena turned to me and her brown eyes grew wide. "Oh, heyyyy!" She dragged out the word. "You must be Ivy!"

I smiled, putting down my wineglass on the table in front of me. "I am. And you must be Xena."

"I'm your girl!" she sang, and I held back an eye roll. "Well, don't just sit there! Give me a hug! We've gotta get acquainted because we're doing this photo shoot together!"

I stood, begrudgingly of course, and wrapped my arms around her as she squeezed me tight.

"So, Lola told me you're helping her as a volunteer for the charity. I swear, she's so good, isn't she? Her heart has to be made of gold. You know she's the reason I can even do my job? If she hadn't hired me when I first started doing shoots, no one would know who the hell I am right now. She took a chance on me and my life hasn't been the same since—in a good way. I am so lucky to have that woman in my life."

So, this was a thing with Lola, I realized. She loved to save people, or more like let people know she had a hand in others' success. This was good news. If she wanted to save sad souls, I could lay my sob story on thicker and she could *save* me too. And by save me, I meant give me all her money.

"Lola is so, so good." I wanted to throw up after saying the words.

"She is a great person, and the fact that she chose you to model says a lot. That means she sees something in you." She gave me a wink, her faux lashes batting at me. "Anyway, I'm gonna get you in the chair with the makeup artist. The look will be subtle today—nothing too extravagant. Honestly, though, you don't even need it. You're gorgeous—but makeup for this shoot with this sun will give the charity images a fresher look!"

Xena led me to a chair in the sunroom inside, where I could still see the pool and the ocean. The floors were made of hardwood in this room, and there were cushioned lavender chairs in two of the corners. A vase of peonies was on top of a wooden table beside one of the chairs, and skylight windows were in the vaulted ceiling, giving the room a breath of fresh air.

A woman with wavy black hair and tan skin pranced around the corner with makeup brushes and introduced herself as Gena. Gena got straight to work on my makeup. As she did, I became antsy as more time passed, wondering where the hell Lola was.

I hoped she wasn't leaving me to do this shoot by myself. That would have been rude as hell, and it would have completely thrown off my plans for the day.

Gena was halfway done with my makeup when Lola finally strolled into the sunroom. She wore a flowy blue dress, her honey-blond hair hanging down and touching her shoulders. Her baby hairs were sleek on her forehead and at her temples, and her lips were plump and glossed. All that beauty. Such a waste on a selfish soul.

"Oh, Ivy! Look at you!" Lola rubbed my shoulder with a wide smile. "Sorry it took me so long to come down. I had a few phone calls to make, but I'm so happy to see you here! You ready for today?"

"That's okay. I'm excited to be here, but also really nervous."

"No, no. Don't be nervous. This is a private shoot where you can be yourself. You're going to do great, plus, Xena always knows how to get people to let loose and have fun." She gave my shoulder a squeeze and then looked at Xena, who was sitting in one of the chairs and fiddling with the lens of one of her cameras.

Lola excused herself from me to go to Xena, and they murmured about the shoot and other things I didn't care to listen to. Lola left the room and I watched her go, only to return moments later with a stack of shirts.

"Ivy, we're going to get started soon," she told me. "I'll let you get dressed in my favorite guest room."

"Okay, great."

Gena finished off my face with setting spray and I climbed out of the chair, following Lola down the hallway.

"Did you have a sangria to warm you up a bit?" Lola asked as I met up to her. "I swear, a good drink always has me feeling good."

"I did. Georgia gave me one. Though I'm sure I could use another."

"Well, there's more if you'd like. I'll have Georgia bring another glass to you after you're dressed."

Lola sauntered past the den and one of the stunningly decorated seating areas until she reached a molded white door. She opened it, revealing one of the rooms she'd shown me the first time I visited.

There was a queen-size bed swathed in a white duvet and fluffed blue and white pillows at the headboard. The walls were painted a very light blue—by now, it was safe to say this was Lola's favorite color—and the floors were made of a light oak. The floors were so polished I could see the blur of my reflection.

Lola placed the shirts on a velvet, royal-blue chair in the corner and then stepped in front of a door beside it. She slid the door open, revealing a walk-in closet. I followed her into it, and for a guest-room closet, it was packed with clothes and was about half the size of my apartment.

"Okay, so as far as bottoms, pick your poison, but I would suggest shorts because this is to raise money over the summer. You told me your size via email, so I ordered several styles of shorts, skirts, and jeans and they're all on this rack here." She gestured to the front rack. "Experiment the bottoms with the shirts and see which look best for you. There's a full-length mirror in the bathroom over there."

I nodded. "Wow. This is all so much, Lola. I could have just brought some bottoms if you needed me to."

"Don't mention it, sweetie." She smiled with her perfect white teeth as she walked up to me, then placed her hands on my shoulders. "You'll do great. Think about the charity and how wonderful it'll be to bring so much goodness to these women."

"Yes. I want to give my all to the charity." I couldn't give a shit less about it, if I was being honest.

"Great." She gave my shoulders a squeeze, and I wanted to break every single one of her skinny fingers. "I'll have Georgia bring you another sangria, but there's a minifridge by the bed with heavier drinks if you need one." Another one of her winks. "After the shoot, I'm taking you out for lunch."

Lola pulled away and left, but not without a confident smile over her shoulder. When the door clicked shut, I took a look around the room and sighed.

Fuck that photo shoot, Marriott! Taking pictures could wait. I needed to get acquainted with this guest room. I mean, it was stunning! I'd have much rather lived in it than my apartment in Liberty City.

I made way to the minifridge and opened it, spotting minibottles of wine, champagne, vodka, and water. I grabbed a bottle of pineapple CÎROC, twisted off the cap, and chugged the majority, then let out a wet gasp. This would definitely get me to loosen up.

I walked to the closet, taking down a pair of jean shorts that were shredded at the hem. I picked up a blue T-shirt from the stack of charity shirts, knowing Lola would favor it, and got dressed. As I looked at my reflection in the floor-to-ceiling mirror, there was a knock on the door.

I answered, and Georgia had another sangria in hand. "Enjoy," she said in a prim-and-proper voice, offering it to me.

"Thank you so much." Georgia started to turn, but I called after her. "What is it like to work here?"

She put on a courteous smile and said, "I love my job, Miss Elliot. I love this home and I'll do whatever I need to do to protect it."

She turned away quickly, but I couldn't help noticing the look in her eyes before she walked off. A flash of annoyance or disappointment? I had no clue.

I poured the liquid of the sangria down the bathroom sink, dumped the fruit in the waste bin and, when I felt good enough, walked out of the guest room and back to the deck. Lola was sitting in a chair beneath the umbrella, sipping a sangria.

"Look at you! You chose wisely!"

I knew she'd say that. "Thank you."

Lola stood and went to Xena. "Let's get started. I want to take Ivy out for lunch early so I can make it back in time for dinner with Corey."

"Yep, got it."

Dinner with Corey? I had to find a reason to stay longer—

just to see Corey. I was sure between now and lunch I'd be able to come up with something.

The photo shoot started, and it was awkward as hell at first. I'm not a model, Marriott. I had no clue what to do with my hands, but Xena told me to tug on the shirt or twirl with it, which I thought was kind of stupid, but it worked.

I'm far from model material, and the only way I got through it was by thinking about Corey. What would it have been like to kiss him for the first time? Hold his hand? Feel his breath mix with mine?

Would he dare leave his wife for me?

Would he dare risk it?

He would for me because I would love him. Please him. Take care of him.

Xena egged me on, clearly loving my sudden spark of confidence. I found Lola's eyes every so often, and she was giving me a proud smirk with her hands clasped together. I had to give her reason to think she'd chosen wisely.

Someone ambled into the kitchen and stopped, and when I realized who it was, my confidence burst like a balloon.

I held back a gasp as the person stared at me from the wide island counter, brows dipped in confusion. The sleeves of his gray dress shirt were rolled up, revealing strong forearms, and his head was cocked to the left.

Corey. My Corey.

"Corey, honey, what are you doing home so early?" Lola asked, moving to him in her heels when she noticed him too. She seemed annoyed by his presence.

Corey finally looked away from me to focus on his wife. "My last client was an hour ago," he said.

Xena stopped shooting and told me I could take five minutes while she went through the set of photos. I stood where I was, picking up my new glass of sangria from the table nearby as a distraction.

"Speaking of clients—baby, I didn't know Ivy worked with you," Corey boomed.

Shit.

"She's your client?" Lola asked, laughing as she turned a fraction to look between us. "I didn't know that."

"Yeah, she got lucky and was squeezed in for an appointment a couple of months ago."

"Wow, Ivy. I had no clue! What did you have done?" Lola was looking right at me. "No, wait. Let me guess. Girls your age are usually going for . . . lipo? No—fillers?"

"No, I . . . um . . . I had my breasts done," I murmured. "Breast augmentation."

"Oh." Lola's eyes dropped to my chest on cue. She gave me a strange look—a look when I couldn't tell if she was annoyed by that fact or still just curious.

"That's interesting." She gave me a once-over with her eyes and then faced Corey again, patting his broad chest. "Okay, well, we're just wrapping up on the shoot. Think you can keep yourself occupied until dinner?"

"Yeah. Didn't mean to interrupt. I'll catch a drink with Clyde." He kissed her cheek. Splayed a hand on her upper back. "See you at dinner."

Corey pulled away and Lola watched him go. She then turned to me, putting on a forced smile. The light in her eyes had faded, or maybe I'd just imagined it. Either way, she didn't look very pleased at the moment.

Though I was glad I was making progress with my plan, it was awkward with Lola after the encounter with Corey. She did her head nods and passed her smiles, but they weren't as genuine as before.

The shoot was over and Xena had gotten some great shots of the shirts, which Lola had praised her for, and when it was time for Xena and her team to pack up, I went back to the guest room with a smile riding my lips.

I needed Lola to trust me, and now was the perfect opportunity to dig a little deeper. I probably should have told her I had my breasts done beforehand to spare the awkwardness, but I liked the direction things had taken, and I was looking forward to watching it play out.

After I changed back into the casual jeans and blush blouse I'd worn to come over, I slipped into my sandals and walked out of the guest room.

Lola was standing in the sunroom, where I'd gotten my makeup done, with her cell phone in hand, scrolling through it.

As much as I loved watching her wallow a bit, while probably asking herself a million negative questions about her husband, I decided it was best to keep playing my part. Right now I was supposed to feel guilty. Embarrassed. Ashamed.

I needed to show it.

I lightly cleared my throat and said, "I think I'm going to head home. I forgot I have to be at work early tomorrow to do inventory."

"Are you sure you can't stick around? I still want to take you out for lunch," Lola offered, facing me.

That surprised me. I thought of all people she'd shoo me off once she suspected foul play or mistrust. I still had to play my cards right. "Aw, Lola, that's so nice of you, but you really don't have to. The snacks you had today were great."

"I insist, Ivy. Please." She took a step forward and looked me in the eye. So maybe she wasn't upset, or maybe she was taking me out so she could collect her thoughts and go about this the right way.

With a sigh, I agreed and followed her out of the mansion.

She walked to her Tesla and I climbed into the passenger seat, loving the feel of the luxurious, warm leather against my backside. The engine came to life and she drove through the gates.

"Ever been to Hatteras?" she asked me without taking her eyes off the road.

"No, I haven't, but I've heard it's very nice." And way too expensive for my budget.

"Well, I'm glad I get to take you there first. It's a beautiful place, with tables that have ocean views. You'll love it."

Okay. Why wasn't she talking about the boob job thing and her husband? Why wasn't she pissed? I looked at her through the corner of my eye every few seconds, waiting for her to tick, but she was calm. Her eyes were on the road, and she tapped her finger on the steering wheel as a song by Rihanna played.

When she pulled up to Hatteras, she handed her keys to a valet and I followed her inside. At a place like this you needed to make a reservation weeks in advance, but one look at Lola Maxwell and they had a table prepared on the air-conditioned deck overlooking the bay in less than two minutes.

"This view is amazing," I said, hoping to keep up with her complacent mood.

"Isn't it?" She picked up the drink menu. "Get whatever you want. After all your hard work today, you deserve it. I'll order a good wine for us." She gave me a sugary-sweet smile.

I smashed my lips together and looked over the menu. Everything was priced way too high for my budget.

When a waiter came to the table, Lola ordered an expensive bottle of chilled white wine. The server poured us glasses when he returned with the bottle and I sipped it, despite still feeling buzzed from the bottle of CÎROC and sangrias I'd had at her mansion.

Lola had had several drinks herself, and I took a mental

note of that. The woman loved to drink, almost like it was a slight addiction, and I would use that to my advantage one day.

We placed our orders, and as soon as the waiter was gone, Lola sighed and said, "Okay, Ivy. Look."

Oh, shit. Here it comes.

"About what you got done from Corey—I'm not bothered by it at all. In fact, I've sent my friends to Corey for things they've wanted done many times before. I'm sensing some tension from you and I don't want you to think I'm upset by that at all."

Wow. That was shocking. "Really? Oh, thank goodness." Relief, relief, relief. I have to say, I was a little worried there, Marriott. Not too much, but a little. "I really thought you were upset with me about it. I—I know I should have told you beforehand, but it slipped my mind so many times, and I always get so shy around you."

"No." She laughed. "Why would I be upset about that? There's nothing wrong with getting something like that done!"

"Well, mainly because I know he's your husband, and having a woman you just met get a boob job from your spouse seems kind of . . . odd."

"It was a little weird when he first started doing it," she said, swirling her wine in her glass with her upper back pressed to the chair. "But I finally came to the realization that it's his job, and it makes him great money. He doesn't look at it the way I think he does, and that gives me peace of mind."

Yeah, I bet it did. She was so full of shit, Marriott.

If my man was doing breast implants every week and then getting as many looks and feels as he wanted after the woman healed, it would annoy me. I'd wonder if he wanted to wrap his lips around their taut nipples during the checkups. Maybe that's just me, though. I suppose rich people think differently.

"I went to Dr. Maxwell because I found him on Google," I confessed. "He was so highly recommended, and he had stunning reviews. I wanted to be in good hands for the job. It wasn't until I followed you on Instagram that I put two and two together. I didn't even realize he was your husband."

"That I can understand. There are many cosmetic surgeons in Miami who are so expensive but are complete trash."

I laughed on cue.

"If you don't mind me asking, though, what made you get them done?" She gestured to my chest with her glass in hand. "Was it just a spur-of-the-moment thing?"

I sat up in my chair and sank my teeth into my bottom lip. This was the moment I'd been waiting for. I knew one day Corey would pop up and mention I was a client, and that Lola would be curious about it.

I had wanted her to ask this question, to feed her more of my story, get her to connect with me more. Granted, she wasn't supposed to ask *today*, but things would move quicker this way. It was fine, Marriott. I had this all under control.

"Um . . . well, it's kind of personal and kind of messed up. I probably shouldn't get into it right now."

"Oh—no, you don't have to tell me, then. Don't even worry." Her voice was filled with compassion, and I knew I had her interest when she sat forward to look me in the eye.

"It's just . . . when I think about it, I get really upset. Going to get them done was a big step for me, and a challenge, but talking about it is . . . it's kind of hard sometimes."

"Right. Of course." This woman had no idea what to say, but the curiosity was burning deep in those hazel eyes of hers.

I sipped my wine slowly, letting the crisp taste burst on my tongue. "It's just . . . well, do you remember when I told you about my ex?"

"And how he was a piece of shit? Yes, I do." She put down her glass, her arms folded on the tabletop, fully alert.

"Well, he used to have this . . . *fetish*. He would um . . . put these metal clamps on my nipples and tug them really hard. I hated it, but I did it for him because I had nowhere else to stay, and he always threatened to kick me out if I didn't do what he wanted. Anyway, he tugged too hard one time, and one of my nipples actually ripped."

"Oh sweet Jesus." Lola closed her eyes briefly, like she could imagine the pain.

"It took a while for it to heal, but when it did, there was this ugly scar on my nipple and across my areola. When I got out of the relationship with him and decided I deserved better, the scar always reminded me of him, and I hated it. I hated my body and I hated myself. One day I got sick of feeling that way. I knew I could change the way they looked and get rid of the scar . . . so I looked up plastic surgeons. And that's how I found Maxwell Aesthetics. I figured go big or go home, you know? So, I had the nipple slightly reconstructed and got implants as well, I guess to make a statement." I shrugged.

"Wow, Ivy. I am so sorry you went through something like that." She reached across the table and placed a caring hand on top of mine.

"It's okay." I sighed. "It's the past and I'm learning to heal and move on from such a toxic, abusive relationship."

"And I'm so glad you've moved on. Is that why you came to Miami? To get away from all that?"

"Partly. I didn't want to live in Tampa anymore, that's for sure. Everything there reminded me of him. I also saw Miami as a new opportunity for me. Start over. Rebuild."

She nodded with understanding. "Well, you did the right thing. You're a beautiful young lady and you deserve way better than what that asshole did to you."

I nodded appreciatively. Telling her this would lead her to believe that I trusted her to keep my secret, and in return, she could trust me to keep any secrets she told me in the future.

It was only a matter of time before she started pouring them on the table to me, like she did all these fancy bottles of wine.

Not only that, but this piece of my sob story would make her want to keep me close. Lola loved sad women. Crazy but true. She loved women she could build up and make stronger.

She liked to treat women like me, Xena, and Keke as projects. A smile from one of us made her proud. Why do you think she created Ladies with Passion? She knew those mothers couldn't afford shit, so she made their pregnant dreams come true by paying for their insurance or hospital bills, or by buying their diapers and formula when they couldn't afford it.

Our food arrived shortly after that, and we ate while Lola talked about how great she thought the photos would turn out. While we ate, I couldn't help glancing at my steak knife.

My mind wandered.

I always wondered how she'd react if I cut her. Just one little slice, preferably on her face. I could imagine her shocked expression, her jaw slack and her eyes round like saucers, once she realized her face was going to be scarred for the rest of her life. Not that she couldn't afford to pay for a new face.

But nah. The face wouldn't do it. It had to be her heart. Break that and not even all the money in the world would mend it.

After lunch Lola took me back to her mansion with brighter spirits, and I knew I'd won her back over. Before, she wanted to pretend the thing with Corey didn't bother her, but I knew it did deep down. Now that she knew the reason, her confidence in her husband and me had been restored.

She gave me a hug as I got out of the Tesla. "Lunch was great today, Ivy. I can't remember the last time I actually got to relax, eat, and drink, you know?"

"I should be thanking you. Lunch was amazing."

She stepped sideways, like she wanted to let me go about my way, but didn't all the same. "Okay, this might sound crazy, and maybe it's a little too forward," she chuckled, holding up a hand, "but what do you think about rooming with me at Passion Camp?"

I blinked quickly, pretending to be speechless for a moment. All a part of the act of course.

I'd heard from the other ladies during the volunteer meeting that Lola had her own cabin for Passion Camp. Vonyetta was so upset she wouldn't be able to stay there this year—something about her back—which meant a bed was open. All the women were trying to figure out ways to get into Lola's exclusive cabin.

"Wait, are you serious?" I squawked.

"I'm so serious! Passion Camp is always such an amazing time. We go on trail walks, have movie nights and spa days. My cabin has six beds, and usually Vonyetta stays with me, but she's been having back problems and decided she'd drive home to sleep in her bed at nights. There'll be an extra bed and I'd hate for the spot to go to waste. I'd love to have you there."

"Wow—I mean, Lola! I don't even know what to say to this! I would love to!"

"Yay! That's so good to hear! You'll have an amazing time with the other girls too. It'll be a good way to meet new people and make new friends. We all love it."

"Who all rooms with you?" I asked.

"Well, there's Faith, Arabel, and Keke. Also Xena, but she'll be all over the place taking pictures. Faith and Arabel are really good friends of mine and have husbands who sponsor the charity. And you already know Keke."

Ugh. Fucking Keke. Of course that pathetic bitch would be sleeping in the CEO's cabin. Wouldn't be like her to miss it, would it?

"That sounds so fun! It'll be like a sleepover!"

"Exactly! And we have the works, girl. There'll be movies, snacks, wine, face masks, sugar scrubs—everything. I love Passion Camp. It really creates an escape for women, you know? We all get to get away from our daily lives and breathe a little bit."

Yeah, I doubted that. With so many high-class women and pregnant women in one place, it meant increased amounts of estrogen, and women were catty, jealous creatures. They'd smile to your face and talk shit right behind your back, and the truth is, women just can't help it, Marriott. It's been imprinted in our DNA to be jealous or envious. Some women can control their emotions, but others—like me—can't.

If I could control it, I wouldn't have been standing right in front of Lola, pretending I wanted to be her very best friend, when really, I wanted to punch her in her damn veneers.

"Well, I'd love to room with you all. I just hope the other ladies won't mind. Do you think they'll feel like I don't belong?" I asked with a hopeless smile.

"Nah-uh. Don't you worry about that. You're part of the LWP family now. I wish someone would make you feel like you don't belong. And between you and me, I could have asked Olivia, but she snores way too loud."

I huffed a laugh. "Right. I guess I'm just nervous. I'm so new to all this."

"If you want, you can meet me here the day we leave and we can drive to the church together."

"Sure, that would be nice."

"Wonderful. Well, enjoy the rest of your day, Ivy. And again, I loved lunch. We'll have to do it again soon."

Oh, we would. Trust and believe.

We hugged again, and Lola walked to her front door, unlocking it and stepping inside. I went to my car and climbed inside, starting it up and cranking the AC.

As I pulled out of Lola's driveway, though, I noticed someone standing in front of one of the windows in the middle of the house on the upper level through my rearview mirror.

It was Georgia, and she was looking right at me. If I weren't mistaken, her eyes were narrowed.

I didn't like that woman, Marriott. I felt like she could see right through me, but she wasn't about to throw off my plans. It was a good thing Lola didn't seem like the type to listen to the help . . . then again, I knew she had Lola's ear in a sense, seeing as Georgia was loyal to her.

Didn't matter. I was going to keep my distance just enough to make sure her household manager could keep whatever suspicions she had of me low and out of the way.

CHAPTER ELEVEN

Lola probably assumed we hadn't seen each other in two weeks. The reality was, I saw her every single day.

I saw her in her office, during lunch meetings, and even when she drove home from lunch dates with her friends. I once spotted her at a Japanese restaurant with Corey, watching as they sipped expensive wine and shared a bowl of edamame, and I even saw her walking the beach with him in a flowy purple sundress one Sunday evening.

With my work schedule, it was tough to catch her, but I always managed to find a way. I was staked out across the street from her office during my lunch breaks most of the time, peering through the windows, munching on sandwiches or chips.

She was at her office more often now, probably because the date for Passion Camp was getting closer and she needed to know all the plans. Noah and Olivia were the duo keeping her charity afloat. She could fool everyone else by having them think she was the queen of ideas, but not me. Without Noah and Olivia, her charity would have been a lost cause.

The Passion Gala was happening in September, which was

three months from now, and I knew they were planning for that as well.

I was hoping she'd invite me soon. It would have been lovely to have Lola buy me an expensive designer dress and heels specifically for that night. Hell, she'd probably invite me to get my hair and nails done too, just so she didn't have to get ready for the event alone. I was very much looking forward to that. I just needed to stick with the program.

Even if she didn't invite me, though, I would find a way in, either as a waitress or a part of the staff. The annual Passion Gala was special to her, and I had to work hard to get invited, I knew. She didn't fully trust me just yet, but by the time Passion Camp was over, she would. She'd have to.

To prepare for camp, I went to Walmart the weekend before and bought new shorts, tank tops, and hiking shoes. I collected bug spray, tampons, and other essentials as well. Camp was in three days and I had to be prepared. My first mission was going to be to remove Keke from "bestie" status. The only question was how I could do that without too much backlash against me.

I needed to get closer to Keke to truly get her out of my way. I had to learn more about her so I could use it against her, but Keke wasn't the type to trust easily, and something told me it had something to do with the father of her child. He'd left her to raise a baby alone and, apparently, she grew a backbone afterward and *didn't take any shit from anyone*, per her arrogant Instagram posts.

My second mission would be to have a moment alone with Lola to bond. Both of us out in the open, sharing stories and confiding in each other with no one else around. That wasn't going to happen unless I conquered mission one, though, and that was to get Keke the hell out of my way.

There was no way in hell Keke was going to lose her place to me. She'd have her head so far up Lola's ass during camp that it would take a miracle to wrench her out.

★ ★ ★

The day camp began, I left my apartment in a flash. I didn't want to be in that run-down place any more than I needed to be.

When I left, Julius was sitting on the stoop, his loose hair pulled up in a half ponytail. I hated when he did that to his hair. It made him look too feminine, and I liked masculine men. Sometimes I was sure he wore his hair that way just to get a reaction from me, seeing as I'd mentioned how much I'd hated it once before.

I stepped around him. "Did you get my text?" I asked.

"Yep," he said, taking a drag from his joint.

"And you got it done?"

"Yep." His tone was nonchalant. "And for the record, I'm not your fucking errand boy. You don't know what I had going on. Next time give me a few days' notice before you come to my door demanding shit from me."

"Oh, shut up, Julius. You got something out of it, didn't you?" Just as I asked that, his eyes drifted down to my bare legs; then he stood up with the joint and looked me in the eye.

"It was straight," he mumbled, then he turned his back on me and went up the stairs to his apartment.

I rolled my eyes and walked to my car. Julius was extra. Yes, I'd had sex with him in exchange for a favor, and no, I didn't feel good about it, Marriott. It is what it is.

I arrived at Lola's house twenty minutes early so we could ride to Passion Camp together. I took my bag out of the trunk as soon as I pulled up and walked to the door. Georgia answered.

"Hello again, Miss Elliot."

"Hi, Georgia." I gave my head a bob and walked past her when she stepped back. I didn't have time for her and her weird looks today.

"Mrs. Maxwell is in her office. She told me to send you up when you arrived," Georgia said after shutting the door behind me. "You can leave your bags here. I'll have them placed in the SUV."

"Thanks." I walked down the corridor, where the furniture looked crisp and dusted, the wall tables polished, and went up the stairs with the flair of confidence. I knew every room—had studied this place so much, it was engraved in my brain. This was my time to shine and really get cozy with Lola before camp started.

I found the double doors to Lola's office, remembering them from when she gave me the official tour of her home, but before I could knock, I heard voices.

Brows dipping, I knocked, and Lola sang for me to come in. I pushed one of the double doors open and Lola was standing beside her desk, laughing.

And seated in Lola's desk chair was Keke.

Fucking Keke! I swear, Marriott!

I gritted my teeth before giving a tight-lipped smile.

"Oh, hi, Ivy!" Lola rushed my way, wrapping her arms around my shoulders to hug me. "I've been looking forward to seeing your gorgeous face. You remember Keke?" She gestured back at the so-called bestie.

"Of course she remembers me!" Keke stood from the chair with all her arrogance in tow. She had on a sundress and wedged heels. For a first, Lola wasn't wearing a dress. She had on a white tank tucked into army-green shorts and a pair of Nikes.

"I do." My smile was forced. I had to remember I'd only met Keke once, but after watching her Instagram like a hawk, I felt like I'd seen her every damn day and knew her like the back of my hand. "I didn't realize we were supposed to dress up." I threw shade. All the shade.

"Oh, um, we aren't," Lola said, then glanced at Keke's shoes, as if embarrassed for her. "But that's Keke for you! She loves to dress for any occasion. I told her she was crazy wearing those heels on day one! There'll be a lot of walking and moving around."

"I have backup flats." Keke laughed, but I didn't miss the way she cut her eyes at me.

"Well, don't worry. We're going to have fun, especially because we'll all be riding together to the church." Lola looked at me. "You guys can get to know each other before the swarm."

Ugh.

"You know, I'm so thankful," Keke said with a voice full of bogus compassion. "I can't think of any other way to spend this week. I'll miss Bailey, though."

"Who is Bailey?" I asked, pretending I had no clue.

"My daughter. She's four." Keke picked up her phone and unlocked it, then walked to me to show me a photo of her daughter. She didn't need to show me her daughter for me to see what she looked like. I knew exactly how she looked.

It always annoyed me that people just posted pictures of their babies online. Were they not aware of predators? Stalkers? Pedophiles? Someone could have been fondling their dick to the thought of her daughter's *chubby little cheeks*, as Keke liked to call them.

"Isn't she so gorgeous?" Keke's voice sliced through my thoughts.

"She is! So adorable!" Her daughter was gorgeous, but giving Keke any sort of compliment grated on my nerves.

"Look at you two, hitting it off already," Lola said, grinning from ear to ear. "I love it."

I don't.

Lola flipped her wrist to check the time on her rose-gold Cartier wristwatch. "Okay, we have forty-five minutes to get to the church. I don't want to get stuck in the Miami traffic, so let's have some of the coffee and bagels downstairs in the dining room and then get a roll on, ladies."

Keke walked past me, sashaying her hips as she left the office. Lola walked beside me, giving my shoulder a squeeze before we could walk out. "I hope you don't mind Keke riding along with us," Lola murmured when Keke was out of earshot. "Her car was giving her trouble, so I picked her up this morning."

"No—I don't mind at all. She seems like good company."

"Okay, good. I don't want you to feel like I didn't want us riding alone or anything."

"No, I get it. You have to look out for your friends. I would have hated if she missed camp." That couldn't have been any further from the truth. Did I always lie this effortlessly with you, Marriott?

Here's the truth: Keke's car was giving her trouble because I had Julius pull a few wires under her hood last night. What kind of person leaves her car unlocked in *Miami*? She was such a dumb, oblivious bitch.

I knew where she lived because I'd followed her home from her flower shop one day. She always closed at five thirty, and I made sure the time aligned with my schedule before the trip so I could follow her.

I assumed Keke would get so caught up with getting her car started the morning of camp that she'd miss the bus to get there, but no, she called Lola, who swooped in and rescued her. Not that I didn't expect Keke to show at camp, but her having a setback would have paved a golden runway for me with Lola.

Our bags were already in the SUV when we walked out of Lola's house, so we climbed in the car, and of course Keke took the passenger seat.

She was now talking about how she had to renew her gym membership soon. I wanted to slap a hand over her mouth. She talked too damn much! All it would take was a tight grip around the back of her neck and a quick shove forward for me to slam her face into the dashboard and shut her up.

But I had to be nice, even if I really wanted to strap duct tape over her mouth.

Lola drove to the church, all while Keke chatted her head off. Lola could hardly get a word in edgewise, and I had no idea how it didn't drive her crazy, considering she liked talking about herself just as much.

When we made it there, I lurched out of the car and out to the humid Florida air, escaping Keke's chatter about how expensive day care was for her daughter. She was the one who decided to have a damn kid. She needed to shut the hell up about it already and deal with the burdens of it.

We carried our bags to one of the charter buses, where two men were working to store the bags. I handed mine to one of the men and then met up with Lola. Two more women had gathered around her, and I knew on sight—and from stalking Lola's social media—that they were Arabel and Faith.

Arabel had shoulder-length, relaxed hair with blond highlights. She was just like Keke, in a dress and heels, only her heels were a bit shorter than Keke's and seemed a little more comfortable. The diamond on her ring finger screamed *I'm married to a millionaire.*

Faith was an average-looking woman, nothing spectacular about her. She was on the chubby side, with too much makeup and long, black hair that I knew wasn't hers.

I remembered these women from a photo on Lola's Instagram. They'd met at a book club and bonded over some romance novel they really loved.

"Arabel, Faith, I want you to meet Ivy. She's the young lady I told you would be rooming with us at camp."

Arabel took my hand and shook it. "So nice to meet you, Ivy! I saw the shoot you did for the charity shirts—love them, girl! Lola gave me a little sneak peek!"

I smiled. "Thank you." I didn't get a damn sneak peek. I glanced at Lola, who simply smiled, like the comment Arabel had just made meant nothing.

"I loved them too," Faith said, giving me a lukewarm smile. I could tell she didn't like that I was staying in the cabin with them.

Despite Faith's halfhearted compliment, she and Arabel were two women I felt I could actually deal with. Even though they were looking at me like I was some stray, adorable cat, at least they weren't completely snobby and codependent upon Lola, like Keke. These women seemed more concerned about themselves—in fact, they probably didn't give a damn about this charity but were around for show and to support her cause.

"Say cheese!" A camera shuttered as we all turned, and Xena was there, her black camera in front of her face. She'd changed her hair, and had fresh black-and-pink-ombré braids now.

"Xena!" Lola waved a playful hand at her. "I told you to hold it until we get to camp, girl! That's where all the fun will be!"

"Don't even worry! I have so much space on my memory card for the week. We'll have so many good pictures this year! Oh, hey, girl!" Xena rushed my way, hugging me with one arm, her camera in the other.

What do you think her reaction would have been if I'd accidentally knocked that expensive camera out of her hand? Bet she wouldn't run to hug me anymore, and I would be cool with that. "I'm so happy to see you!" Xena went on.

I told myself to be nice. Be the chill girl who went with the flow. "So happy to see you too!" I said back, with as much enthusiasm as possible. I swear, I wasn't going to be able to take much more of this. I am not a people person, Marriott.

When it was time to board the buses, I released a sigh of relief. I made sure to stick close to Lola, but as we walked up the steps of one of the buses, Keke lightly bumped against me and stood in front of me, thinking I wouldn't notice, but I did.

That was strike two now.

Strike one was her talking too damn much in the car.

Lola took a seat in the very back by the window. Keke excused herself as she brushed past a few volunteers in purple shirts to get to the back and took the seat right next to Lola.

I took the seat on the opposite side, by the window. I still needed to appear independent—like I didn't want to be in Lola's way, but still garner enough attention from her so she could check in with me here and there.

Faith took the seat next to me, and Arabel sat in the aisle in front of Keke.

"I swear, that girl isn't gonna let Lola breathe all week," Faith mumbled, rolling her eyes.

I glanced at her, but her focus was on Keke, who was already talking Lola's head off and moving her hands animatedly.

I laughed. "Lola's probably used to being around her."

"No, honey. Trust me, she isn't. No one can get used to someone so self-absorbed. Plus, we can all tell she uses Lola, but Lola is too damn nice to see through her crazy mess. Lola loves to pick up strays, honey. Oh—no offense to you or anything. I've heard good things about you."

I straightened my back. I guessed I'd read Faith wrong. Just like me, she could smell a bad fish from a mile away, and she considered me a stray to Lola. In her eyes, I was a moocher. I wasn't really a part of Lola's world.

Bitch, please. She would see.

She gave me a kind smile, and I relaxed—only a little.

"You seem like a nice girl who could be spending her summer doing something else. How'd you get into volunteering for the charity?" she asked me.

"Oh well, I've always been interested in Ladies with Passion. I actually told Lola my story, and told her how I found the charity inspiring for young mothers and wished I would have found this foundation a few years ago."

"Aw, that's sweet. It's always good to know we have charities like this, right? Makes women feel good. You know they have a story night every year at camp. Lola sets up sparkling juice and we light a fire, and those who are interested tell their story for others to hear. It's inspiring. If you tell yours, I'll be looking forward to hearing it."

Yeah, yeah, yeah.

She turned when Arabel asked her for something, and I took it upon myself to stick my earphones in my ears and look out of the window. I wasn't in the mood to make friends with any of Lola's entourage.

My only focus was Mrs. Maxwell, but with these women in the way, it was proving to be difficult. They were lucky I didn't mind a good challenge.

CHAPTER TWELVE

We arrived at camp, where the cabins were made of thick, brown logs and a mixture of palm and live oak trees surrounded each one. After everyone was off the bus, we were directed to the main hall, where we picked up name badges in the cafeteria and were offered water bottles.

Noah, Olivia, Vonyetta, and two other women were sitting at a table in the hall when we arrived, greeting people and ready to sign them in. Volunteers signed up at one table and picked up their blue volunteer shirts, while the pregnant guests took up another.

After I collected my name badge, I took a sweep of the main hall. For it to belong to a camp, it was pretty damn fancy. Seafoam-green walls, sparkling, waxed floors, and picture windows that revealed the outdoor scenery.

Of course Lola dearest wasn't going to settle for some average place to camp. There still had to be some luxury involved. "Glamping" is what people call it, you know? Never knew it was a thing until Lola mentioned it during the volunteer meeting. I could only imagine how the cabins looked inside.

I looked at the front table, and Lola was chatting with Noah and Vonyetta. I realized then that it was going to be tricky getting Lola alone this week. How naïve of me. The only times I was going to catch her was in her cabin, or between activities.

We were all escorted to an outdoor stadium, where the seats were made of smooth logs. To my surprise, they were handing out blue pillows to the guests so they wouldn't have to sit on the hard wood. Everything had a touch of Lola to it, from the blue name badges to the pillows.

I grabbed a pillow myself and went to the front row, and as we all settled in, Lola and Vonyetta stood up front and welcomed everyone with wide smiles, chipper voices, and microphones in hand.

I felt someone looking at me and glanced over my shoulder. Keke was looking my way. She put on the fakest smile for me, batted her fake-as-hell eyelashes, and turned away. I rolled my eyes, focusing on Vonyetta, who was talking about camp safety.

I guess I could say the first day wasn't so bad. Lola was so busy with the camp rangers, and Noah and Olivia had my hands deep in the volunteer stuff, which I actually found enjoyable.

They had me helping the expectant moms design onesies for their babies. I was certain the onesies would never be put on the babies because of all the hot glue we had to use and the way the permanent markers leaked through the fabric, but it was entertaining for the time being. It would make a good keepsake for the moms.

I overheard Keke being sent to help get the paints ready for belly painting in the room next door. I saw her walk around a corner thirty minutes after the first round of activities had started. She'd changed into clothes and shoes that were more comfortable, and I laughed. Why she'd even worn a dress and heels astounded me. It wasn't like she was going to find a man among this sea of pregnant women.

When dinner rolled around, I found Lola sitting at the back of the cafeteria. She waved at me, and I was glad she'd spotted me. The seat beside her was wide open, and praise the heavens, Keke was nowhere in sight.

"I'm so happy to see you." Lola breathed out as I approached.

"Everything okay?" I asked, laughing a little. She seemed anxious.

"Oh yeah. First days are just really overwhelming. Some of the women get feisty about where to sleep, shower—all that." She took a sweep of the cafeteria with her bold, hazel eyes before focusing on me and asking, "So, how are you liking camp so far?"

"Oh—it's amazing. I love it." I bit into my bread roll. I had to give it to her. The food looked and smelled good. It wasn't basic camp food. We had gourmet meals. Tonight's dinner was almond-crusted salmon or buttered cod, with roasted vegetables and yellow rice.

"I can see why so many people fight for a spot to attend," I said after chewing a bit. "Helping with the onesies was fun, and I could tell the ladies enjoyed it a lot."

"Oh, yeah. Onesie decorating is a good one. Tomorrow you'll be helping with the second round of belly painting, right?"

"I am. I'm looking forward to it." I took a bite of salmon. "Do you plan on doing any of the activities?"

"Well, I've been helping here and there, but I've mostly been floating around to make sure everything is running smoothly." She shrugged. "I've found that when I stay out of the way, though, the moms are more excited. Vonyetta mentioned something about staying out of the way last year, so I decided I'd take a few steps back. Truth be told, I wasn't going to stay here this year."

"What do you mean, you weren't going to stay here? Why wouldn't you, when you organized all this?"

"Well, Vonyetta told me she overheard some ladies last year saying they felt like they were being watched too closely by me—like they were nervous because I was around."

"Like you intimidate them?"

"Something like that." She picked up her water to sip it as she looked around the cafeteria. I bet she wished it was something stronger. Maybe that was why she was on edge—she had no alcohol in her.

"Well, I wouldn't be too upset about that." I needed to make her feel better, butter her up. That was what a good, trustworthy friend would do. "A lot of people know your status. They know you're one of the most well-paid women in Florida. Maybe they feel like they have to be perfect around you and that makes them nervous—sends their hormones on a rampage."

"You think so?" she asked, swinging her gaze to me. "Do you think I'm intimidating, Ivy?"

I put on a sheepish smile. In all honesty, hell no I didn't find her intimidating. If anything, her presence probably annoyed the hell out of people, the way she walked around like gravity defied her and politely gave orders. The way she pretended she didn't love to be in charge, and that she didn't take any of her success for granted. Such bullshit. All of it.

"Well," I started, "when I first met you, I was a little nervous—but only because I'd heard so much about you and couldn't believe I was actually meeting you for the first time."

"Really?" Her mouth did a thing. Not a smile, but not a frown either. She was clearly flattered. "See, I wish I could understand that. I don't want the women to look at me as an

idol or anything. I want them to think of me as a friend—
someone who doesn't mind taking care of another sister."
First of all, I never said I looked at her as an idol. See how she
loved to put ideas into her own head?

"I say take it with a grain of salt. You're practically a goddess among mortals here. You can't be too hard on yourself,
but I really do admire your humbleness." After saying that, I
wished the fish in my mouth would get lodged in my throat,
or at least that there were bones in them to choke me.

"Well, thank you, Ivy. You're so sweet." She rubbed my
shoulder. She always did that, like I was her little pet.

Something dropped down on the table and we both looked
up to find Keke standing on the other side of the table with
her tray of food. "I swear, I thought I'd never make it to dinner!" Keke griped. "Ugh. What are you two over here talking
about?" She plopped down in the chair and picked up her
bottle of water to crack it open and sit.

"Keke, why weren't you on time for dinner?" Lola asked,
completely ignoring her last question.

"Girl, I had to help one of the pregnant ladies because she
accidentally peed on herself! I swear, Lola, some of them pretend they are so handicapped. I mean, when I was pregnant, I
still knew how to walk and make it to the bathroom. Yeah, I
had a few mishaps when Bailey hit the third trimester and was
all on my bladder, but I wasn't full-blown peeing on myself."

"Keke, you have to remember some of them have been
through some really hard times. Lots of it is traumatic." The
way Lola coddled Keke made me sick. She treated her like her
long-lost sister. Now that I thought about it, it didn't shock
me that Keke was around my age. I guess taking on Keke and
Bailey gave Lola purpose too. She couldn't have a child on her
own, so younger women made up for that somehow—like
raising a sister or a daughter. It was weird as hell, but it worked
in my favor, I suppose.

Lola yawned. "I'm really tired. I had an early start this morning and it's catching up to me."

"You should go to the cabin and rest. You've been running around all day," Keke said, eating her bread.

I looked at Lola's plate, which only had vegetables on it, and noticed she'd barely touched her food. Then I looked up at her, but she was already focused on me. "You won't mind if I run off, will you?"

"Not at all, no."

She gave me a grateful smile and then gave my shoulder a pat. I was ready to burn off her hand by this point.

"Okay. I'll see you two in the cabin later—that is, if I'm not already sleeping." Lola stood and walked away from the table to Noah to say something to him, and then sauntered out of the cafeteria.

"I hope she's okay," I said but avoided Keke's eyes. I knew she'd heard me, but she said nothing in response to my remark. We finished our meals in silence, listening to the chatter of the expectant mothers and some of the volunteers.

A fork clinked against porcelain. "All right. I just have to say it. You know what I find interesting?" Keke said, looking me over.

I carefully yet curiously slid my gaze up to hers. "Interesting about what?"

"About *you*."

"What about me?" I asked with a nervous laugh. A sweet, innocent smile.

"I tried to find you on Facebook, but I couldn't, so I searched Google for your name and a few Facebook accounts came up, but none of them were of you. I saw an Instagram account for you, but you don't even have any pictures." Keke narrowed her eyes and stared right into mine. "There's something off about you and I don't like or trust it."

Well, if she was playing that card . . . "Funny, I was thinking the same thing about you when we first met." I couldn't let her think she intimidated me, Marriott. Fuck that.

Her nostrils flared at the edges, but she tried to keep a cool head. "You don't have to like me, honey," she shot back. "I love myself enough."

Did she really just go there? This was a joke, right?

I rolled my eyes and picked up my grape juice. She really went there, Marriott. I simply couldn't.

"I just can't help but find it interesting that you met Lola in her kickboxing class and became a volunteer all in the same day. Then she wants you to model for her shirts—*you*, a new volunteer, when there have been *dozens* of girls who have been *dying* for that position—and now you're here at the camp, sharing her VIP cabin?" She scoffed and shook her head, her silver hoops catching the light in the ceiling. "Something doesn't add up with you. Girls like you, who just pop up out of nowhere in Lola's life, are always after something."

I bet she'd know. "Maybe Lola just likes me as a person," I responded, avoiding the urge to pick up my empty tray and slam it across her head. "I have nothing to hide, Keke. I just don't believe in posting my life all over social media the way others do."

Keke scoffed, pursed her lips as she looked me up and down, and then locked on my face again. "Lola needs to stop wearing her heart on her sleeve. People like you are leeches. You worm your way in, try to get close, and think you'll have a foot in the door with her for life. Well, here's a piece of advice for you," she said, leaning over the table. "The same way Lola took you in with open arms, she'll drop you just as fast if you do something to hurt or betray her."

I matched Keke's stare, refusing to back down. I could speak nice, but there was no way in hell I was going to let this bitch think she could intimidate me.

I'm certain there was something a bit more vicious about

my stare because she leaned back and clenched her jaw before picking up her tray and taking it to the nearest trash can.

She left the cafeteria, but not without looking back at me.

This was strike three. I'd had enough of her.

I watched her leave and then made a mental note to take her out. Immediately.

I was done playing games—letting her think she had the upper hand. Keke was a flaw in my perfect plan, and it was time to get her out of my way.

CHAPTER THIRTEEN

I've always had a problem with my temper, Marriott. I remember my mother giving me spankings for throwing tantrums over things I couldn't have or couldn't do.

I remember being thirteen and purposely breaking Mama's favorite lemonade pitcher because she wouldn't let me go to a sleepover. Granted, my grades weren't so good, and it served as a form of punishment that I couldn't attend said sleepover, but all I remember was thinking how unfair she was and getting pissed about it.

If only I'd known that a year later, she would be gone forever. I never would have broken her favorite pitcher and hid the glass pieces. I never would have been such a pain in the ass.

I wish I could say I had outgrown the tantrum phase at this point in my life, but that would be a complete lie. If anything, my tantrums manifested into something much, much worse. How does the saying go, when you bottle up too many emotions? Yeah, it's that sort of thing for me.

I was desperate to get closer to Lola. No one was going to stop me, spread rumors about me, or get into Lola's ear on my watch. Keke was going to keep telling Lola that she didn't like me—that she found me weird and off. I couldn't have that, Marriott.

I guess Keke's blabbermouth was good for one thing, though. Last night, Keke told the whole cabin she couldn't wait to wake up early and go for a run so she could keep her body in shape. Faith and Arabel forced smiles at her, and Lola was so out of the mix that she didn't respond to her.

There was something on Lola's mind. Was what Vonyetta told her about being intimidating to the pregnant women really bothering her that much?

Too bad I didn't get the chance to ask. Keke must have noticed the same thing about Lola because she climbed out of her bed to sit beside Lola and ask her what was wrong. I overheard Lola mentioning she was tired, and then she told her she was going for a shower. When Lola walked out, Keke glared my way before going back to her bed.

Who would have known Keke was into jogging? She always seemed like the shake-your-ass-and-dance-to-workout type. A little twerk here and some jumping jacks there.

Keke woke up at five fifteen in the morning, got dressed, and left the cabin at five thirty. I know because I watched her as she did so the morning after she mentioned going for the jog.

Five thirty was right before the sun slipped over the horizon—before the palm trees would begin to sway, and while the soil in the earth was still cool.

I stepped out of the cabin, barefoot and in a matching set of pajamas, watching Keke run toward the first trail in view. I peered up at the sky, which was a mass of lavender and blue, the orange swirls from the sun slowly filling in, and then I focused on the trail Keke had taken again.

There were many shadows and trees on that trail.

I looked around. The camp was quiet. No one was awake at this hour.

This.

This would be the way I got rid of Keke. While everyone was sleeping. On a shadowy trail, where no one could see. It would be quick. Easy.

But it wouldn't be right now.

No, the next morning seemed much more promising.

An alarm went off at 5:15 a.m.

Keke groaned as she sat up, then she sighed and rolled out of the bed, going for her suitcase. From where I was, I watched her take her workout clothes to the bathroom. She flipped a switch, and part of the room illuminated with light.

Faith, Arabel, Xena, and Lola were all sleeping, practically dead to the world. Arabel was a light snorer but, according to Lola, nothing in comparison to Olivia.

Keke got dressed quickly and trotted out of the bathroom. She stuffed her feet into black Nike running shoes, grabbed her phone and headphones, and headed out the door, clicking it shut quietly behind her.

As soon as she was gone, I twisted the doorknob in front of me and stepped out of the only closet in the cabin, dressed in yoga pants, a black T-shirt, and tennis shoes. I adjusted my black baseball cap and hurried for the door, making sure to keep my steps light. The door creaked as I shut it and I mentally cursed it for being so loud. But no one woke up. The coast was still clear.

I jogged toward the trail. I couldn't let her get too far ahead of me.

I'd thought about how I'd handle this situation all day yesterday. In between painting protruding bellies, prepping snacks, and helping Lola make mocktails for the dine in movie, all I could think about was getting Keke out of my way.

Keke had rolled her eyes at me so much the day before that I'd lost count. And anytime she saw me alone with Lola,

she'd interrupt, only to talk about herself or something someone did that reminded her of Bailey.

She was too much for Lola, and I wished Lola would
fucking say something about it already. A friend with no
boundaries is unhealthy . . . but perhaps I should digress, so as
not to seem like the world's biggest hypocrite, right?

The path of the trail was a simple one, and I could see why
Keke jogged on it. It was a straight shot to the lake. Not only
that, but there was a cliff where, not far beyond it, you could
watch the sun rise above a shimmering ocean.

Below the cliff, though—like, right below it—were jagged
rocks. The rocks weren't too far down. In fact, if you took a
few steps to the right, you could climb on the rocks. You'd
have to sit close to the edge of the cliff to witness the sunset
from the top of the cliff.

That particular cliff was amazing—a beholder of beauty
and destruction, something I could relate to all too well. Get
too close to the edge and you'll see the ugly, scary rocks at the
bottom. But stand back just enough, keep your distance, and
you'll only see the beauty of it.

I kept my steps light, spotting Keke's white T-shirt ahead.
She was running with her headphones plugged into her ears.
She couldn't hear me. I was sure of it because I could hear her
music from where I was, about twenty steps behind her.

She did a light jog, nothing too intense. I could keep up.

Fifteen steps.

I lowered my baseball cap.

Keke's panting grew louder.

I grew closer.

Ten steps.

She rapped one of the lines from the song she was listening
to out loud. J. Cole lyrics. I liked J. Cole . . . but I didn't like
Keke.

Six steps.

Could she feel my presence?

Two steps.

Feel someone breathing down her back?

The cliff was ahead of her, but to be wise, she'd make a right turn, follow the path to the lake. Keke wasn't the type to watch sunrises or sunsets, let alone interrupt her life to witness basic, everyday nature.

But maybe I'd make her look this one time.

One.

Before she could prepare to make the right turn, my palms were pressed to her back to shove her forward with all my might. She made an audible gasp and whipped her head to the left to look over her shoulder to try to see me.

The push wasn't hard enough. She caught herself and began to turn to see her culprit, but I couldn't let her see me. She would recover, tell Lola it was me. Ruin all my plans.

I grunted and shoved her harder on the back, and she screamed, tripping forward and falling.

Falling.

Falling.

It only took a split second for her to fall and land, but in those moments leading up to the big fall, I couldn't help but watch her. Her back was to me, arms flailing, trying to stop her impending doom.

She'd never know I did it. It could have been anyone at the camp, but when she recovered, I was sure she'd pin it on me. The new girl. Her biggest threat with Lola.

But what proof would she have? She'd only accuse me, right? She could scream about it until her face was blue, or maybe Lola would assume Keke had fallen for attention. It would be like Keke to do something drastic for all to think and talk about her.

I rushed to the edge of the cliff right before Keke hit the rocks.

A loud thwack as the back of her head hit the sharp edge of a boulder. Blood instantly pooled around her head, dripping down the curves and edges of gray and silver stone.

Oh shit.

A breath left my body.

Shit, Marriott. I think I pushed her a little too hard.

She was only supposed to fall, hit her head, break a limb or two, and be rushed off to the hospital. But from this angle, she didn't appear to be breathing. There was too much blood.

Oh my God.

She looked . . . she looked *dead*.

CHAPTER FOURTEEN

*R*un.

My thoughts screamed at me. I couldn't stay here much longer. Someone would come by eventually. One of the park rangers, maybe. They'd see Keke's body. Sound the alarm. I couldn't be spotted here when that happened.

Run.

I ran away as quickly as I could, finishing on the trail that led to the lake. No way was I going back to the cabins. I'd act as if I got breakfast early—a quick pudding at the Night Mommy cart by the cafeteria for the pregnant women with insomnia.

I made it to the Night Mommy cart and opened the top lid, panting wildly. I'd run fast—faster than I ever had before.

There was a broad selection of healthy refrigerated treats and snacks inside the cart, and on the side were containers of veggie chips and bags of dried fruit, which I was certain Lola had picked out. She loved incorporating veganism into everyone else's lives.

I picked out a chia seed pudding and grabbed a spoon from one of the cabinets on the cart, but before I turned away, I noticed a camera in the corner above me.

My heart froze for a moment, then beat to life again like a drum.

A camera? I only saw one camera, and it was in the cafeteria. But there was one here. Were they all over the camp? On the trails? The cliff?

They could have been hooked to the trees. After all, this was an upscale camp. They had great resources. Who was there to stop them from making sure they had an eye on every single thing happening at their camp?

I put my back to the camera casually. "Shit," I cursed under my breath.

I walked away, keeping cool. Those cameras couldn't work . . . but if they did, then they'd put the times together. They'd investigate and they'd know I had come off the same trail Keke was found on.

My plan would be over way before it even began.

I'd worked too hard. I couldn't let that happen.

CHAPTER FIFTEEN

There were three rangers in the main station. It appeared they'd just woken up, dumping creamer and sugar into their coffees with sleepy faces.

As I peered through the window, I made out a room for security in the back. Was it occupied? Was someone watching?

There was no way I'd be able to get in there with three men on duty. I walked away grudgingly and made my way toward the lake. I sat on a bench for a little over thirty minutes, watching the windows of each cabin across the lake light up. The volunteers and soon-to-be moms were waking up now. Some were already out and walking about.

I stood up and took a different trail to get back to my cabin, but I didn't go straight in. I waited, until I saw Arabel, Faith, and Xena leave.

When they were gone, I made my way inside, trying to keep my nerves from frying. Lola was already fully dressed as she stood in front of her bed, pushing a diamond stud through her earlobe.

She wore brown hiking boots, black shorts, and one of the Ladies with Passion shirts I had modeled for the photo shoot.

"Oh, hey, Ivy. You're up early," Lola said when she spotted me coming in. "You hangin' in there?"

I smiled at her, trudging to my bed. "Kinda. I couldn't really sleep last night. Woke up around four this morning and went to the Night Mommy cart. Grabbed a snack and sat by the lake." I winced regretfully. "I know there are cameras here, so if you see me on one of the security screens sneaking a couple of snacks, I hope you can forgive me."

Lola laughed. "First of all, that cart is for *everyone* at camp. We refill them if needed, so there's enough to go around. Secondly, the cameras here are turned off during the week of Ladies with Passion, other than in the cafeteria and front entrance."

Oh my goodness, Marriott! Never had I felt so religious! The cameras didn't work. They didn't work! This was more than enough reason to break out in gospel.

"There was an incident about two years ago," Lola continued. "One of the rangers—who was terminated—took footage from our week at camp and uploaded it online. It was a video of one of the moms going into premature labor. She was screaming at everyone. Hysterical. It was a mess. To keep me in his good graces, the owner of the camp made an agreement that cameras would be off for the week of Ladies with Passion so that it could never happen again. Not only that, but when the mom in labor saw it, she filed a lawsuit against the charity so . . . that didn't end well. I value the moms-to-be and like for them to have as much privacy as they can, so when we're at camp, cameras are off. I don't have time for another lawsuit."

"I can't believe that asshole did that." I wanted to squeal. This was great news, and I know it's horrible to say, but thank goodness for the mom who drew the lawsuit. If it weren't for her, the cameras would still be on. No one would ever know I was on that trail.

"Speaking of, I actually might stop the Night Mommy cart next year," Lola said, cutting into my thoughts. "Not many moms flock to it anyway."

"Maybe they all just so happen to sleep really well between the hours of midnight and five a.m.," I offered.

Lola huffed a laugh as she bent over to tie her boot "I wish that were the case. No, a lot them tell me they can hardly sleep with so much kicking at the ribs, their constant urge to use the bathroom, and so on."

"Valid point."

Lola sighed. Shrugged. "Probably best to save that money, fund it into something else . . ."

Silence rained down on us. "May I make a suggestion?" I asked, filling the void.

"Of course. Anything. What are your thoughts?"

"Well, if I were pregnant and waking up at least four times a night, I think I'd go for doughnuts and cookies and something sweet over veggie chips and dried fruit." My smile was sugary sweet. "Not that anything is wrong with those choices, and I do think you should still keep them as an option, but those aren't exactly midnight snacks I'd keep around, you know?"

Lola appeared stunned—taken off guard, almost. What? Did I hurt her precious pride? "You know what, Ivy?"

Ah, shit.

"That makes perfect sense. It's a lot of work being pregnant."

Oh.

"Yeah, there is so much the body goes through, and comfort food can work miracles. Maybe I'll start incorporating those sorts of snacks we women love to indulge in, but also keep the healthy snacks as an option too. Some chocolate and popcorn here and there." She stepped closer to me and held my upper arms with a toothy smile. "You are so smart. Always on your toes. I'm so glad you came to camp this week. It's nice having a younger mind to bounce ideas off of."

"It's my pleasure, Lola." It was anything but.

"Would you like to take a walk with me before going to breakfast?" Lola inquired as she picked up a blue folder. "There are a few other changes I've been thinking about making and I'd love to get your thoughts on them too."

That was a lie. She had no one else to ask to take a walk with her, and if Keke were here—which she would have been if I hadn't pushed her—she would have asked us both to join her.

But there was only me. No one else. The way it should have been from the start.

"Sure," I said. "I'd love that."

But, of course, the walk couldn't even begin for us. As soon as we walked out the door, we saw women rushing toward the trail. The trail Keke took. The trail I *followed* her on.

"What in the world is going on?" Lola took a step forward, watching the pregnant women move quicker than they usually did. "Shouldn't everyone be heading to breakfast?" She took off after them.

I followed behind her, making sure to keep close.

"Ladies, what's going on?" Lola asked, catching up to two of the pregnant women walking together.

"We heard one of the volunteers was involved in an accident," one of the women said, winded. "By the cliff, where you can see the ocean."

"Jesus," Lola whispered. She excused herself from the pregnant women and jogged ahead. I jogged with her until a crowd came into view. Lola pushed her way through the crowd. I stayed close behind her. When she was finally in the front, she came to a halt and looked down.

"Oh my God! *Keke!*" she screamed. It was a bloodcurdling scream. One that made my ears ring. A scream I would never forget. She rushed to the side of the cliff and started to climb down the rocks, but one of the rangers told her to stay back.

"I am the organizer of this entire event! She is my friend! What the hell happened to her? Is she okay?" Lola demanded.

"Ma'am. I need you to stay back while we take care of this."

Lola did as she was told, pressing her knuckles to her lips and staring down at Keke's body. I came up to her side, looking down with her.

Keke was still there, yes, and there were also more rangers down there. Two were picking up her body and putting her on a stretcher. I frowned as they moved her. Why would they do that if she were dead? Wouldn't this be considered a crime scene? The body can't be touched unless . . .

"Lola!" I looked past Lola and Vonyetta was rushing toward us. "I was looking all over for you!"

"Vonny! What happened to Keke?" Lola screeched, climbing back on the trail and to steady ground.

"I'm not sure, honey! I got here about twenty minutes ago and the rangers were talking to one another on their walkies in the main hall. I heard them say someone was below the cliff and I followed them here, saw this." Vonyetta closed her eyes and pressed a hand to her chest, as if her heart was physically breaking.

"Keke takes this trail every morning when she's here at camp. W-what would change?" Lola asked Vonyetta, desperate for answers.

"Don't panic, sweetie. I spoke to one of the rangers. They've already called for an ambulance, but right now they're taking her to the nursing hall to patch her up. The ranger who found her said she was still breathing!" Vonyetta's plump face broke out in a smile. "By the grace of God, she's still breathing, honey!"

Wait . . . *WHAT?* She wasn't dead? How was that even

possible? I mean, don't get me wrong, I was relieved about it. Death would have resulted in an investigation, and I didn't need that right now.

Lola bubbled out a hysterical laugh. "Vonny, are you sure? She's breathing?"

"By the grace of God." Vonyetta pulled Lola in for a tight hug.

I couldn't help but stare at them both. This was good news . . . right? Why was I suddenly nervous about all this?

Keke was still alive. Still breathing.

She was going to wake up eventually. What if she remembered everything? What if the damage wasn't as bad as I thought? What if she did see my face after all? The sleeve of tattoos on my left arm? Caught the smell of my shampoo?

Fuck.

This wasn't good, Marriott.

CHAPTER SIXTEEN

Only . . . Keke never woke up.

No. In fact, the ambulance arrived and took her away. She was still unconscious.

Lola freaked out. She insisted that she catch a ride to the hospital with Keke to look after her, make sure she was okay, so she hopped in the ambulance and left with it.

Even while unconscious, Keke was still in my way.

"Welp," Faith said, watching the ambulance become smaller in the distance. "What the hell are we supposed to do now?"

Faith, Vonyetta, Arabel, Xena, and I were standing near the gates of the camp. We'd watched them load Keke into the ambulance on a stretcher, witnessed Lola have a meltdown and tried to soothe her, and now the entertainment was gone.

"Camp will continue," Vonyetta confirmed in a strong voice. "I have the schedule for today, and I'm sure it's what Lola would want. Let's occupy the expectant mothers, keep them distracted from what happened on that cliff."

"That sounds really good," Xena said, then blew a breath. "Lola should really consider having liquor around for us. I could use a few hard drinks after all this."

"I still can't believe she fell," Arabel murmured as we turned and walked toward the cafeteria.

"I can't believe she was still breathing," Faith added. "That cliff is dangerous."

"Y'all know Keke is strong. She'll stumble or fall, but she won't ever quit on herself." Vonyetta's voice was proud. "The Lord was watching over her. She will survive this. I feel it in my spirit."

I rolled my eyes, trailing behind them.

"Ivy, you've been really quiet all morning," Xena said, slowing her pace to walk next to me. "You good?"

"Oh yeah. I'm good," I assured her. "I mean, that was really scary. I'm just worried about her, you know?"

Bull. Shit.

"Yeah. I am too. I mean, the girl is extra as hell and all, but the last thing I'd wish is for her to get hurt like that." Xena slowed her pace as the other women kept walking. "You wanna know what I think, though?" she asked me in a quieter voice.

"What?"

"I don't think this was an accident."

My heart shot up to my throat. I locked on Xena.

"Keke pissed somebody off. Got under their skin. With her attitude, somebody probably got mad and pushed her off that damn cliff."

I worked harder to swallow. "Who would do something like that?"

"I don't know. Keke thinks she's number one to Lola. Hard to say, when Lola has so many friends around. Could be any one of us."

"No way. It had to be an accident. She fell."

Xena stopped walking and focused on my face. "Lola said Keke has never gone close to the cliff—that she used to jog with her in the mornings last year and *always* stayed on the path to get to the lake. She didn't fall on her own. Someone wanted her down there."

I stared right back her. What did she know? There was no way she saw anything. If she did, I was going to have to get rid of her too. I couldn't have any loose ends when it came to my plan and I had no problem getting rid of a childish photographer to keep my name clear.

"But who knows?" Xena chuckled. "My boyfriend always tells me I watch and read too many conspiracy theories, and don't get me started on *Law and Order*. All that shit is probably getting to my head."

"Ha. Yeah." I tried to relax. It was hard to do.

"Anyway, I heard they've got cinnamon rolls today from Benny's Bakery. Have you ever had them? Girl, they're so good. We gotta grab some before they're all gone."

Xena took me by the hand and rushed past the other ladies to get to the cafeteria. She didn't assume I was a suspect of her conspiracy theory, otherwise she wouldn't have been ready to shove cinnamon rolls in my face.

That was good. The last thing I wanted was to bring Xena into it, Marriott. Enough blood was shed for the day. Xena wasn't really in my way. In fact, I kind of liked her. All she cared about was her camera. As long as it stayed that way, she'd be safe.

Matter of fact, all of Lola's friends would be safe if they minded their own business.

I was curious when Lola would return to camp, or if she even would.

What happened that day was embarrassing, to say the least. Rumors were already spreading, journalists popping up at the front gates firing questions at Vonyetta, who insisted they leave during their private event.

With so much heat, I figured Lola would cower and never

return—let her staff handle it all—but around nine the same night she was back.

I was the only person in the cabin, on my cell phone, scrolling through Corey's Instagram. I had to keep tabs on him as well. He was just as much a piece in this little chess game of mine as Lola was.

When she walked in, Georgia trailed in behind her with the straps of a plastic bag in hand.

I climbed off the bed. "Lola?" I gasped.

Lola sat on her bed and pulled the comforter over her legs and thighs without a word. Georgia came up to her and handed her the bag, and Lola immediately tore into it, taking out a pint of ice cream. I knew the brand. It was a vegan ice cream. She sponsored the company and the ice cream on her Instagram often.

"Is there anything else you'll need, Mrs. Maxwell?" Georgia asked.

"No. I'm okay, G. You can take the truck back to the mansion."

"Okay." Georgia stepped back and looked at me. Pursing her lips, she turned away and left the cabin.

"Lola, are you okay?" I asked.

"Shit! Georgia forgot the damn spoon," Lola snapped.

"Oh, here." I rushed to the minibar in the corner, where the miniwine bottles and mimosa mixes were. I grabbed a spoon in plastic wrap and walked back to hand it to her.

Lola accepted it, then sighed. "Thank you, Ivy."

I sat on the bottom of her bed as she took the lid off her ice cream, as well as the seal. She stuck her spoon right into it and scooped some into her mouth. She made a gagging noise and spat the ice cream right back out.

"Ugh. Oh my God. Okay. That is disgusting. If they didn't pay me so well, I wouldn't be endorsing that shit." She capped the ice cream and shoved it back into the bag, then she tossed the comforter off her legs and made her way to the minibar.

She filled a plastic cup with wine and downed it, then she poured another but took it down slowly. She finished it, though. After one more pour, she was pacing back and forth in the cabin with her cup, staring down at the ground.

"Is Keke okay?" I finally asked, and she slowed her pace, side-eyeing me.

"Far from it. She has a severe concussion, as they said, and not only that, the doctor doesn't know when she'll come to. He said it could be days. Weeks. Hell, maybe even months because it's so bad." She sat on the bottom of Keke's bed, nursing her wine.

"Lola, I'm so sorry."

She went on as if she hadn't heard me. "They stitched her up, put casts on the broken bones. Broken arm and broken shin. I'm sure she'll be covered in bruises tomorrow."

I remained silent.

"The only thing I can't understand is how she fell. I mean—we've been going to this camp for *years*. Keke has walked that trail, jogged it, sprinted on it, and not once has she fallen." Lola's brown eyes shifted up to lock on mine. "You were out this morning. You didn't happen to see any-thing, did you? Maybe someone else was out there too?"

"No, I didn't see anyone," I responded with a shake of my head. "Why? Do you think someone caused this?"

Lola swallowed hard and stared me in the eye before dropping hers to the cup of wine in her hand. She took a big swig. "I don't want to jump to conclusions. For all I know, maybe Keke tried something new and got too close to the edge. But . . . well, never mind."

"No." I stood up and moved closer, sitting on the rug on the floor right in front of her and giving her all my attention. I was the friend she needed right now. The one who wouldn't judge and would only listen. "You can tell me anything."

"Can I?" she probed, and for a moment there was some-thing hostile and defensive about her. I wasn't sure if she was directing that hostility toward me or if she was just upset about the situation.

I hesitated.

She let out a wet gasp, shuddered a breath, and then said, "Ignore me. I'm just a mess." That, she was. "It's just that there are a lot of volunteers here who don't like Keke. They all think I favor her, that I put her first, but it's not that at all. I mean, do I have a weak spot for her? Of course I do. She and Bailey mean a lot to me. But when it comes to the charity, I try to separate that, you know? But Keke, as I'm sure you've noticed, likes to hover. She doesn't believe in keeping the distance, and I don't want her to think I'm purposely trying to avoid her, so I just let it happen."

"I understand."

"The police came to the hospital. Talked to me." She swallowed. "They asked me things about Keke, if she may have had any enemies at the camp, or gotten into an argument with anyone. I lied. I told them everything was fine, and that I was sure it was an accident, but . . . I don't know. Something in my gut is telling me this was no accident—that someone had it out for her. But . . . why would they do something like this? Try to kill her? I mean . . . I just don't get that. Keke can be obnoxious and self-absorbed at times, but she's a good person. She has a good heart. And oh God, Bailey," she cried, throwing her head back and squeezing her eyes shut. "Keke's mother came with Bailey to the hospital and the poor girl didn't even know what was going on. I mean, can you imagine a sweet four-year-old girl not having her mother? Bailey is the one who relies on Keke the most. Without her, she'd be motherless."

I lowered my gaze to focus on the rug. If I hadn't known any better, Marriott, I would think Lola was trying to guilt-trip me, but Lola knew nothing. She thought I was good. Nice. And to be fair, I only wanted to hurt Keke and send her off, not kill her. Her being in my way wasn't *that* serious.

"Lying to the cops was a stupid move, but it had to be done. To protect my charity. This event. Everything I've worked for. It's better if it looks like an accident."

"But if your gut is telling you that someone did this, how will you be able to sleep knowing that they're probably here under our noses?" I questioned with a voice full of concern.

Lola took a long drink, and I admit I was laying it on pretty thick. I mean, why would the person who pushed Keke ask such a question? Oh right, because they would never. This was the way I could lower Lola's suspicions of me the most. By allowing her to think I was terrified, afraid for my life.

"So, what are you saying? That I should go to the police? Tell the *truth*? That would ruin the charity, Ivy. It would ruin the event. You're the only person I have told this to, okay? I can't have this kind of news leaking out, so if it does, I'll know who they've heard it from, but I'm trusting you. I trust that you'll keep this between us. Won't you?"

"I don't know, Lola. I mean, yes, you can trust me, and I won't say a thing, but after telling me this, I'm a little worried about staying at this camp."

"Ivy, sweetie . . . please don't worry." Lola briefly closed her eyes and then opened them again. I noticed a small tic at her jaw. "I'll take care of this. For our sake, let's agree that Keke fell—that this was an accident. No one here knows Keke as well as I do, but for her safety and ours, we'll just let this blow over. I'll have security keep an extra eye out and, unfortunately, turn the cameras back on. The rangers will be doing double patrols. Everything will be fine." She drank the last gulp of her wine and then pushed off the bed, going to the cart again.

As she filled her cup, I couldn't help thinking that this was exactly what she did while under pressure. She drowned her stress with wine and pretended everything was okay, even though things were definitely *not* okay. Where did she learn that? Who taught her how to ignore her issues and blanket them with alcohol?

Lola wasn't confrontational, and I knew that, but seeing as she was so quick to put the whole Keke conspiracy to bed just for her own peace of mind proved to me only one thing.

She was a very selfish woman, and I had every right to continue ruining her fucking life.

CHAPTER SEVENTEEN

Lola visited Keke every day after the accident. I mean of course she did. Keke was hurt and she felt sorry for her and Bailey. Not only that, but she felt a threat was at the camp . . . only she couldn't say anything because she wanted to keep the situation under wraps and her reputation intact. Selfish, selfish woman she was, Marriott. You can't tell me I was wrong about her.

Lola returned every night of camp, a little after nine each time. She drank her wine. Put on a brave face for her friends. I mean surely her pity party couldn't last for long.

Did she still feel bad about what she did to me? To my life? No, she didn't. She could spare me with this Keke bullshit. At least Keke was still alive and Bailey could still see her.

I'd had enough of it. I needed to get her back on track, change the course. It was the last night of Ladies with Passion Camp. It was pedicure and movie night. The women were going to be getting their toes painted by the staff of a local salon and then watch a movie afterward with whatever snacks they were craving. I saw no need for Lola to be there for the movie, so I came up with my own escape for us.

As the pedicure stations were being set up in the welcome

hall, I went to the nail polish cart and picked out a few colors, placing them in my tote bag. I made sure to steer clear of Vonyetta, Noah, and Olivia. They had a bad habit of spotting me and asking me to do little favors for them, and I always did them because I had a reputation to keep clean with all Lola's peers.

After collecting some cotton balls and nail polish remover, I took the back exit out of the welcome hall and made my way to Lola's cabin.

As I approached, I saw her standing in front of our cabin, her honey-blond tresses piled on top of her head and wrapped in a white scarf, talking to one of the pregnant women.

She was putting on a façade, pretending she was okay, that nothing had ever happened. I guess it had to be that way, right? Mrs. Perfect couldn't ever be Mrs. *Imperfect.* Honestly, as the week carried on, it was as if the whole fall with Keke hadn't even happened, and it was strange to me.

How many times had she done that, Marriott? How often did she pretend things were okay, even though she'd wrecked lives? After all, none of what happened to Keke would have happened if she hadn't ruined my life in the first place.

I passed by, making sure she noticed me. As the pregnant woman spoke, Lola glanced my way and smiled. I returned a half smile, making sure my expression was clear enough for her to notice something was bothering me. After entering the cabin and setting down my bag on the bottom of my bed, it didn't take long for Lola to walk in after me, just as I'd expected.

"Hey, you," Lola said from the door, giving me an apprehensive stare. "Everything okay?"

"Oh yeah. I'm fine." I forced a smile at her, but kept an even, enthusiastic tone.

She noticed my forced smile and closed the door behind her. Her arms folded across her chest as she took two casual steps toward me. "You know, I've always been pretty good at reading someone. You aren't fine. You seem bothered. Tell me what's wrong."

Who was she kidding? She couldn't read people worth a damn. If she could, she'd realize all her friends were garbage and didn't have her best interests at heart. She also wouldn't have been standing in front of the woman who was slowly tearing her life apart.

"I'm just . . . well, I guess I didn't expect to feel so overwhelmed by all the events for Passion Camp. I also keep thinking about what happened to Keke. I don't know. It's like every time I go out there, I think the person who pushed her is probably looking for someone else to push. How do we know anyone here is safe?"

"Oh Ivy." Lola sighed, unfolding her arms to place her palms on my shoulders. "I told you, you don't have to worry about any of that, okay? I have close eyes on the camp. No one is coming after you, or me, or anyone else here."

I nodded, but I still pretended to be anxious. "Do you think we could stay in tonight? I, um . . ." I turned and picked up my tote bag. "I grabbed some nail polish and supplies from the welcome hall. Maybe we can do our own manicures and watch a movie on your portable projector thing?" I'd watched a reality show on her projector with Arabel, who had said Lola was okay with us using it during our free time.

"Oh." Lola pressed her glossed lips and then rubbed them together. "Well, because it is the last night, I do have to give a little farewell speech to the attendees and volunteers tonight."

"Oh—right. I'm sorry, I completely forgot about that." I placed my tote bag back down on the bed.

Lola was quiet for a moment. "But you know what? I'll tell Vonyetta I'll give the speech in the morning. No big deal. Better they receive it with rejuvenated minds anyway."

"Really?" I asked, elated.

"Yes, of course. I could use a night in." She gave me her warmest smile . . . and there it was, my dear therapist. I felt it.

Our connection had grown. Our bond was strengthening. I had her. My vulnerability was a treasure for her, and she couldn't just let it go. She could never leave someone so vulnerable on their own—someone in need of her attention and care.

Lola stayed, drank her wine, and I laughed at her jokes, gasped at her stories. I even painted her toes for her. She wanted blue on her toes. I wanted to laugh at how predictable she was.

This was the night when I knew. I knew that Lola Maxwell was considering me a very close friend and a gift to her. I was slowly becoming the little sister she'd wished she had while growing up—the friend who indulged in her picture-perfect life and absorbed every detail of it.

The friend who oohed and aahed about her trips to Belize, Greece, and Thailand. I was the friend who accepted her, and allowed her to be herself, and she would love it. Crave it. *Need it.*

I had her confidence, witnessed her vulnerability, and accepted her flaws. She could be slightly imperfect around me, trust me with secrets, confide in me about Corey, whom I loved hearing about, even if it came from her.

She wouldn't let me go. No, in fact she'd want me everywhere she went from that moment forward.

She'd need me . . . and that was my plan all along.

Gain her trust, then ruin her.

CHAPTER EIGHTEEN

The perks of having a rich best friend were so much more than I'd imagined. I didn't think it would all happen so quickly, yet there I was, living it up and getting text messages from my new bestie every day.

I spent many evenings at Lola's mansion, or just with her in general. Sometimes we'd cook together while talking about Lola's day, or we'd sit on her patio and sip chilled white wine while reading a new book she thought would be good for us to read together.

I would post on my Instagram about the new book my bestie and I were reading, or take a picture of me holding a glass of her expensive wine in the air with the pool lightly blurred in the background. I'd tag Lola and she'd like my Instagram posts and even comment sometimes and, surprisingly, being her new bestie brought a lot of followers my way.

I understood it now, Marriott—the craze over social media. It's addicting as hell to watch the number of followers you have grow with every new post.

I realized that Lola liked to be in control of those who were close, though. She also loved being complimented. She liked to feel as if she *owned* a person—that she could control what they wore, what they drank, what they read.

When we'd go to restaurants and order, it was always she who picked the wine we'd drink as well as the appetizer. The choice of entrée was all mine, but she'd always mention how much she recommended a certain course.

I went into her office once while she was on a call by the pool and saw she had two calendars, one with dates of her events and one with dates of Corey's. A bit much, if you asked me. I was sure Corey could keep up with his own events, but I had a feeling they weren't there as reminders for herself. They were there so she could know everywhere he'd be in the future. So she could notice patterns, perhaps? She was a smart woman. She knew what she was doing.

Corey was never around, and that was strange to me, considering how often I was at Lola's place. *In due time*, I told myself.

To my luck, my budding friendship progressed without interruptions. Three weeks had passed and Keke was still comatose. Lola's visits to the hospital happened less frequently, but she did send flowers every day, straight from Keke's flower shop. She'd mentioned to me that it would be her way of letting Keke know she had the shop being tended to for her while she was out, and a way to support her company. Pathetic, really.

I visited the hospital every day, sporting my black cap, making sure Keke was still out cold. I never went into the room, just passed by. The door would always be wide open during the day, with a clear display of colorful flowers in vases placed on the counter in front of the window. Sometimes her mother would be there. Sometimes no one would be there at all.

Keke's head was once wrapped in bandages. Eventually, the bandages were gone, which meant she was healing. I wasn't looking forward to the day she'd wake up. I hoped the damage was so bad that she'd forgotten everything.

Faith and Arabel I didn't have to worry about much. They visited Lola once a week and talked about their husbands and how all men were alike. For a bunch of women I was certain were dying to get married at one point in their lives, they sure did complain a lot about their marriages.

And speaking of Faith and Arabel, Lola sent me a text informing me that she was having dinner and drinks the second Saturday of July and that I was invited. She'd also invited Arabel and Faith.

I wasn't looking forward to the dinner. I preferred spending time *alone* with Lola and getting as much information out of her as I could, but in order to keep Lola's trust and remain close, I *had* to go.

After cleaning my kitchen and making my bed, making sure the corners were tucked in the way I liked, I got dressed. I wore the lacy green dress Lola had picked out and bought for me when we went shopping, along with black heels she let me pick. I made sure my makeup was subtle but noticeable, to let her know I put in some kind of effort for this dinner. Apparently, it was going to be formal and Lola wanted her girls to look great. Like I said, she was controlling. Why couldn't we just wear what felt right?

I drove straight to Biscayne Bay, pulling right up to Lola's mansion and parking in the roundabout driveway. There were two other vehicles parked in the driveway, as well as a polished black Chrysler.

Ahh. Dr. Corey Maxwell was around. Was he going to be joining us ladies for dinner? I sure hoped so. I'd missed him and needed to see him. It'd been way too long.

As I walked to the front door, it turned out that I rather appreciated that Lola had made this night formal after all. I needed to look my best for Corey, and this dress hugged me tight in all the right places and revealed all my curves. It definitely made my new breasts look good.

Ideas began to sprout in my mind, taking root.

I rang the doorbell. As always, Georgia answered. "Good evening, Miss Elliot. Glad you could make it to dinner." I never got over the way Georgia greeted me—as if I were a nuisance. As if she could read me like a book and didn't like me, only entertained me for Lola's pleasure. She was protective of Lola. That was fine. She could protect her all she wanted as long as she didn't get in my way.

"Glad I could make it too." I walked in as she took a step back.

Georgia shut the door behind me. "Right this way."

I followed her down the corridor, and as we got closer to the kitchen, I could hear voices. Several of them. Faith and Arabel were already laughing, and then I heard a deep, familiar voice. It was a voice I'd been fantasizing about ever since hearing it. *It was him.*

I followed Georgia into the kitchen and there he was. Corey fucking Maxwell. Immaculate and devilishly handsome. Dressed in a tailored, navy-blue blazer and jeans, his dark hair brushed in deep waves, and dimples revealed as he uncorked a bottle of champagne. The popping noise rang in my ears, the women gasped and guffawed, and he chuckled.

There weren't many men who could get me to lust after them, but there was definitely something about Corey Maxwell that made me want him so damn much.

Perhaps it was due to the fact that he belonged to Lola and I wanted everything she had to belong to me to make up for what she'd done. But he was married, and happily in love from the looks of it. The way he topped off his wife's glass with the bubbly liquid couldn't be missed. His eyes flickered up to hers as he poured, and then he smiled. She blushed, holding his gaze. He was infatuated with Lola.

She was his prize. His dainty little gem.

But not for long.

"Miss Elliot is here, Mrs. Maxwell," Georgia said over the commotion.

"Oh! Ivy! Finally! I'm so glad you're here, girl!" Lola's voice was shrill. "You came right on time! Corey just opened up an amazing bottle of champagne he bought while he was in France!"

France. So that's where he was. He'd never posted about being there, and I knew because I checked his Instagram every day for updates.

Lola sashayed my way in ruby-red heels, and of course she looked like a goddess. Her hair was braided in a halo, and the silky, knee-length gown she wore was nothing short of breathtaking. Her breasts, which Corey had lifted and filled himself—I found out that little tidbit about two weeks ago—were the main display of her ensemble. The front of the dress was cut in a plunging V, revealing a lot of cleavage, and also making it perfectly clear to everyone that she wasn't wearing a bra.

"You know Faith and Arabel, and of course you've met Corey," Lola said. I could tell she was tipsy already. And yes, I had met Corey already. Three times now, and she knew that too.

I wished that number was higher. I thought I'd see him around the mansion more often since Lola and I were hanging out more, but normally when it was time for Corey to come home—he left off work around seven thirty every night—Lola was making some excuse, pretty much telling me I had to go before he arrived.

If I hadn't known any better, Marriott, I would have thought she was threatened by me when Corey was around. Or maybe they truly did have plans. They were rich, after all, with lots of money to burn.

"Nice to see you again, Ivy." Corey came closer to me, extending his arm and offering me a hand.

I took it. Shook it. Smiled. As our hands connected, I remembered his fingers kneading my breasts after I recovered from surgery. He had soft hands. He took care of them. "Nice to see you too, Dr. Maxwell."

"No, no. None of that." He chuckled. "Just call me Corey."

I kept myself together. Couldn't flirt in front of my new bestie, right? Especially not with her husband. "Okay, Corey it is, then."

"So, dinner should be ready in about ten minutes," Lola said when I faced her again. "Georgia and the crew are taking care of some final touches. Come join us for a drink while we wait." Lola led me to the island counter and poured some champagne into a flute for me.

Accepting the drink, I took a sip and felt eyes on me as I swallowed. I had hoped it was Corey, but it wasn't. It was Faith. I gave her a smile as I lowered my flute. She exchanged a smile, but it was definitely not genuine.

For a while the women chatted back and forth, and Corey stood on the sidelines, eyes bouncing back and forth between each woman who spoke, casually sipping his champagne. I did the same, mostly because I had no clue what these women were even talking about.

"You can't tell me you two don't want to at least try again," Arabel said, looking between Corey and Lola. I perked up. Wait . . . when did we get on the topic of trying again?

"Well, we've considered it before, but honestly, we're too high up there in age now, Arabel. It would cause complications, and I'm just not sure if I want that risk again."

"Aw, I understand," Arabel cooed.

"Not only that," Corey chimed in, "but Lola's career is

doing great. A baby would interrupt all that. She's thriving and she's told me herself that it's best if we adopt instead if it comes down to it. Trying again may result in more heartbreak, and we want to avoid that if we can." Corey sighed. "Sacrifices."

"Yes, exactly, honey." Lola lifted her glass to her husband and tilted it toward him. He did the same and they both sipped.

I didn't understand this whole charade they were putting on. Lola wanted to try again. Corey didn't. She'd never flat out told me that, but I could read between the lines. She always went on about, *We have our careers to think about now,* and *It's better this way. Last thing I want is another scare.* And by scare, she meant a miscarriage. I could understand that, but I knew the maternal part of her wanted to try again, just to see if things would work out, but Corey must have told her it wasn't wise. It was okay if Corey didn't want kids. I could live with that.

"So, Ivy, Lola tells me that you plan on quitting your job to work for the Ladies with Passion charity full-time soon?" Faith said, snapping me out of my thoughts.

"I am, yeah. I've already put in my two-week notice. I'm finishing there, and then I'll be on my way to becoming a Lady with Passion." Oh right. I forgot to tell you about that, Marriott. During one of our lunch dates, Lola told me that she was opening a new position at the office for the charity. The job would be similar to Noah and Olivia's. It was for a creative consultant. She'd practically handed me the job, so I took it. The pay was higher, and the schedule was way more flexible. I was moving on up.

"That's nice. I think it's so great that Lola created jobs within the charity. And you'll be working at the office with Noah and Olivia, who have been there for about five years now?"

"Yes." Her tone seemed accusatory. I wasn't sure what she was getting at.

"Stop it, Faith," Arabel chortled.

What the fuck was so funny?

"Stop what? I'm only asking questions," Faith said with a smug smile.

So, this was some sort of inside joke? Something they'd spoken about? And to think I'd actually liked these bitches at first. Well, "like" was a strong word. I just figured they were so wrapped up in their own rich lives that they didn't give a damn about the mediocre girl who worked at Banana Republic.

I glanced at Lola, who was now frowning at Faith. "Faith, what are you trying to imply?" Lola demanded.

"Nothing! Nothing!" Faith chuckled, then sipped her wine. "I just can't help thinking that . . . well, you've just met Ivy, Lola, and she already has her hands in so much of your stuff. You two sunbathe together, shop together, and now she's working with you?"

"And your point is?" Lola's frown deepened.

"I just think you need to slow down with the poor girl. To me, it seems like you're trying to replace Keke with Ivy. One friend's absence has opened up a chair, and Ivy has the seat now."

Okay. Faith was a bitch, plain and simple. And maybe she was jealous too. She wished she was in my position, tanning and reading and sipping crisp white wine with Lola Maxwell. The room went still, an awkward crackle of tension in the air.

Footsteps sounded on the marble floors, and Lola turned as Georgia appeared at the mouth of the kitchen. "Dinner is ready when you are, Mrs. Maxwell."

"Good." Lola put her attention to Faith again while saying, "Arabel, Ivy, why don't you two go ahead and get seated. I need a word with Faith."

I nodded and trailed behind Arabel, following Georgia to the dining room. Over my shoulder, I watched Lola murmur something to Corey, and then she gave him a pat on the chest. He nodded and sighed, following right after us.

When I sat, I couldn't see Lola or Faith in the kitchen anymore, but I hoped Lola was sticking up for me.

"You know how Faith gets when she starts drinking," Arabel said as Corey took his seat. "She loses that filter of hers."

"I see," Corey said, but he wasn't amused.

Arabel looked my way. "To be honest, I like you much more than Keke. I think you're good for Lola."

"That I can agree with—you being good for Lola, that is," Corey said. "I haven't seen her so relaxed in so long. You're a good listener, from what she's told me."

I nodded. "Well, I try to be. It seems like she needs an ear here and there."

"She has me and Faith to talk to too," Arabel countered.

Yeah, once a week, and only so they could come over, eat all Lola's food, drink all her wine, and complain about their older husbands while Lola fidgeted and listened.

"She does. She talks about you and Faith a lot with me. She loves you two."

Arabel put on a cocky grin after my statement. That's all these women wanted, Marriott. They wanted their egos stroked and their pride in good standing. Never demean them. Never make them feel replaceable or irrelevant. How did I know? Because I'd studied Lola for over a year to figure it out.

Speaking of, Lola sauntered into the dining room with Faith trailing behind her. "Sorry about that," she said as she pulled back the chair beside Corey and sat down. Faith took the seat next to Arabel, not once looking my way.

"Before we dig into our delicious meal, I'd like us to pray," Lola announced. "And Faith will do us the honors." She gave Faith a stern look in the eye.

Faith pursed her lips a moment and then said, "Let's bow our heads." Her prayer was straight to the point. Nothing fancy.

"Amen," everyone said in unison when she was done.

"Thank you for that, Faith," said dear Lola, and I caught the sarcasm in her voice. She wasn't happy with Faith at the moment.

Georgia entered the room with two men in white button-downs and black vests following her. Each man had white plates occupying both hands that they placed on the table in front of us.

"This is our appetizer," Georgia murmured, setting a plate in front of Lola. "It's a crab-stuffed portobello mushroom and of course for you, Lola, a *crabless* stuffed portobello mushroom to cater to your vegan needs. Enjoy."

"Thanks, G." Lola looked around the table. "Let's dig in, shall we?"

Everyone dug right in as the men with Georgia filled our wineglasses. The mushroom was good, but the entrée they brought out minutes later was divine. A duck roasted in butter and garlic and served with a cranberry-orange sauce. Along with it, asparagus and a baked potato. Lola only had the as-paragus and potato.

Rich people ate so well, Marriott. I could really get used to that.

"So, there's a reason I invited you ladies over tonight," Lola said as everyone was close to finishing their entrées. "I mentioned a while back during one of the volunteer meetings that we were trying really, really hard to get the Green Garden Hall for the Passion Gala this September. It took a lot of work and *a lot* of swaying, but I am so happy to let you girls know that we got it! It'll be our first time hosting the gala in New York!"

"Oh my goodness, Lola! That is incredible!" Arabel sang.

"What? That is amazing!" Faith added.

Corey gave a proud smile, as if he'd known this news for a while now.

"I'm so happy for you, Lola!" I exclaimed. No, really, I was. Lola was mentioning the gala to me more and more every time I saw her, and I knew about her getting the Green Garden Hall. I saw an email pop up on her phone from the events coordinator there when we were baking vegan raisin and walnut cookies last week.

"Thank you, ladies. Of course the event will still be in September. If you know about the Green Garden Hall, you'll know it's a beautiful venue, which will make for a lovely night. I've been talking to the event planner about the vision I have as far as decorations. Expect lots of fairy lights and drapery and candles. With the greenery the venue has on the walls, it will all come together. So, right now I am officially inviting you three to the event."

I almost choked on my water.

"Oh wow!" Faith said a little too loudly.

"Wait, Lola, are you serious?" I gasped.

Lola gave me a sure nod. "Of course I am, Ivy. I *want* you there. You've been so good to me, and I know you'd have a great time. Plus, you'll be working for me soon, so you're pretty much obligated to go now."

Pretending to be surprised was easy, but I knew Lola would eventually invite me to the gala. I didn't think the official invite would happen until *after* I started working for her, but knowing now was just as good. I was in. Really in. No more doubts about it.

"You should be so honored, Ivy," Arabel said to me as dessert was brought out. "I mean, getting an invite to this gala requires a lot of leg-pulling and money, and yet you get invited by the queen herself. That's a huge honor. Lola sees something in you."

I gave her a sweet smile. "Thanks, Arabel."

One of the men gave me another refill of wine. This was my fourth drink, including the champagne. Everyone else was downing theirs drinks like water, cheery and jubilant. I couldn't keep up . . . but I knew I could use not keeping up to my advantage tonight.

Things carried on with lots of excitement as we transitioned from the dining room to one of the sitting rooms with dim lighting. Lola discussed her big ideas and plans for the gala, and even started talking about the dress she was going to have custom-made for herself. As she did, the drinks continued, glasses filled to the rim, and Arabel and Faith became giggly, while Lola became downright sloppy.

She hugged Corey around the neck too tightly, clung to him like a baby monkey. She kissed him too much on the face and neck, and through it all, he seemed to be made uncomfortable by her actions. He was a man who loved his affection in private. Even I could see that.

"Well, tonight was amazing, but if I don't get my ass home and to my bed soon, I might just pass out on this chair," Arabel broadcasted.

Arabel's remark wasn't the least bit funny, but I broke out in a laugh, and everyone looked my way. Faith and Arabel decided to ignore my outburst, but Lola and Corey seemed surprised by it. I was pretending to be drunk. I had to let it be known.

The couple bid their friends farewell and Arabel gave me a hug and told me goodbye. Faith didn't even come near me. I noticed she hadn't said another word to me after what happened in the kitchen. Lola must have set her straight, but I knew Faith would never apologize to me. Not to someone she thought was beneath her.

When the chatty duo was gone, Lola and Corey turned to me in the corridor.

"You okay to drive, Ivy?" Corey asked, concern etched on his forehead.

"Oh—yes, I'm great. Well, actually, I'm a little fuzzy, but I'm fine. I can catch an Uber and come back for my car in the morning."

"What? Hell no! Are you kidding?" Lola's voice was too loud, and it made my head throb. "You can stay the night here or stick around until you sober up. I'm not letting you go out alone with drinks in you. Not in Miami. No ma'am."

I bit back a grin, pretending I didn't know what to say, or how to react.

"If you aren't comfortable staying, I can have Felix drop you off," Corey offered quickly. "He drives for us on call when we need him."

"No, absolutely not." Lola took me by the hand. "Ivy, please stay here until you're okay. I would hate for something to happen to you. We drank a lot tonight. Best thing you can do is sleep it off. Besides, we have plenty of space. You wouldn't be in anybody's way."

"Are you sure, Lola? I don't want to interrupt your night or invade—"

"Nonsense," she blurted out, then snickered. "Matter of fact, if you're staying, join me for another glass by the pool."

"Oh-kay," Corey intercepted, moving between me and Lola. "I think you've had enough to drink tonight, Lola. Let me get you upstairs and to bed." Lola pouted as Corey grabbed her hand. "Ivy, I'll have Georgia show you to the guest room."

"That's okay," I said as Corey started down the corridor with his wife. "Lola showed me where one is. If it's okay with her, I'll just go to that one, sleep for a few hours."

"That's my favorite guest room!" Lola exclaimed. "Just don't vomit on anything and you're good. I'm teasing! Seriously! There are pajamas and nightgowns in there, but you aren't sleepy, are you, Ivy? Corey, come on! Just one more glass by the pool," Lola pleaded, tugging on Corey's hand to stop him as he started leading the way to the staircase.

"Lola, enough." Corey's voice was firm but low. He was facing her now, brows drawn together. I supposed he'd had enough. I guess Dr. Maxwell could see his wife's flaws just as well as I could.

Lola narrowed her eyes at him for a brief moment. Tension sparked between them as they stared each other down. It was so quiet that we could hear the dining room being cleared, the dishes clinking and being stacked.

Lola looked away and put her focus on me, giving me a grin that must have required all her willpower. "Good night, Ivy. Stick around until morning. I'll have a nice breakfast ready."

"Thanks, Lo." Lo? I'd never called her that one. Maybe I did have one too many drinks. By the way she winked, I assumed she liked the new nickname.

Lola took off, leaving Corey behind. He huffed and trailed after her, and I watched them disappear around a corner, heading for the marble staircase.

I waited a moment before going in the same direction, taking each step slowly to make it up to the second level. I knew exactly where the guest room was. Lola's favorite.

I stepped right into it, closing the door behind me and kicking out of my heels. I stripped out of my dress and was left standing in only my nude bra and panties. It was a matching set. I always made sure to match sets now that I was visiting Lola's mansion so much. I never knew when I'd bump into Corey, or get the chance to be alone with him, so I was always prepared.

I moseyed to the closet and spotted the silky pearl robe I'd had my eye on many times before. Whenever I visited Lola, I'd make at least one trip to this room, pretending it was mine, dreaming of this exact moment—the moment when I'd be able to lie in the bed, soak in the tub, shower beneath the rain-forest showerhead. Tonight was going to be the first night of many, and I'd worked hard for it.

I took out the robe and slid my arms into it. Then I stood in front of the floor-to-ceiling mirror I'd grown to love, with the gold-and-pearl frame, and studied my body in the robe. I tied it at the waist, and it accentuated my curves—my new breasts, my hips.

I heard something rattle outside and walked to one of the windows in the room to look out. From the window I could make out the Miami skyline and Lola's pools and, right below, there were the pool chairs and umbrellas.

The lights were out by the pool, so only a blue light illuminated the area. The water shimmered like turquoise crystals, and standing in front of the larger pool, holding a glass of liquor, was none other than Corey Maxwell himself.

My heart beat a little faster.

I supposed the shower could wait.

Now was the time to make my first move.

I left the bedroom as quietly as I could and clicked the door shut behind me. I didn't need anyone noticing I wasn't inside.

The lights in the dining room were out now, as well as the lights in the kitchen. Everyone was in bed. Lola didn't have cameras inside her home, only on the outside. The camera recorded the perimeter of the bay and the pools. Not much past the umbrellas.

She valued her privacy and was very adamant about the way hackers could get into the camera systems inside houses and share the content.

As I entered the kitchen, the rippling blue light from the pool poured on me. Corey was standing right there, casually sipping a drink he'd most likely made himself. Thinking, it appeared.

Thinking about what, Corey? Your drunk wife? Me?

To my luck, the sliding doors were already open. I walked out, and as if he heard me, Corey turned his head and spotted me.

"Oh shit. Ivy!" He turned halfway, releasing a breath of relief. "You scared the hell out of me. What are you doing out here?"

"I couldn't sleep, figured I'd come down for some air."

"Ah." He lowered his gaze, and that's when he caught it. My breasts—*his* breasts—were on full display for him. He swallowed thickly and turned back around to face the pool.

"Yeah. When I drink, it's hard for me to go right to sleep for some reason. That's why I don't drink much. Kind of throws off my sleep schedule." I took a step forward and was standing right beside him.

"Yeah, tonight got a little awkward at times. Sorry about the whole thing in the hall with Lola. She can get carried away." He paused. "Sometimes she drinks like she's trying to suppress certain thoughts and feelings." He shrugged and sipped the last of his drink. "I don't know what's up with her sometimes."

"It's okay. You don't have to apologize for that. Does she always do it?" I asked. "I noticed she drinks every day and I didn't know whether to be worried about that or not."

"You noticed that too, huh?" He chuckled, low and deep, and it made me want him even more. He set down his empty glass on a nearby table. "She wasn't always a big drinker. It started becoming heavier after her last . . . well, you know. But that was over ten years ago. I assume it still haunts her, though. She always tells me she doesn't feel like a real woman. I think she's just too hard on herself."

"That she is."

Corey sat on the edge of one of the chairs, dropping his face in his palms. "Apparently I've had too much to drink myself. I don't even know why I'm telling you all this. I hardly know you. You probably think I'm crazy."

I looked up, at the windows that were soft with gold light inside. No one was around. The cameras couldn't see us from where we stood by the umbrellas.

"Well," I murmured, taking a step closer to him, "maybe you can get to know me. You know, the same way Lola has." He picked up his head and slowly dropped his hands, confusion seizing every single one of his features. I closed the gap between us, pressing him back by the shoulders so he was resting against the lounge chair. "But perhaps with more benefits."

"Whoa—hold on, Ivy." He pushed me back lightly, and I paused. "What the hell are you doing? Lola is upstairs—you're her *friend*."

"When is the last time she's fucked you, Corey?" I demanded. He was pissing me off now, acting like he owed Lola the world.

"You're drunk. You should sleep this off and—"

"Just answer my question."

Corey swallowed visibly and shook his head. "What does that have to do with what you're doing right now?"

"Lola hardly does a thing with you anymore. And you know how I know? Because she tells me. She doesn't even remember the last time you two had sex. The way you act around other people when you're together is just for show."

"I love Lola."

"Does she love you?" I countered. He dropped his head, but I lifted his chin back up, placing my knee down on the outside of his hips. I was closer now. "She thinks she owns you. That's not love, Corey."

"Ivy, this isn't right. You should really go back upstairs—"

I'd had enough of his talking. I needed to kiss him.

Cupping the back of his head, I pressed my lips to his and then moaned, sinking down on top of his lap. I pushed him back again so that his back was on the chair, and then rocked my hips. He'd gotten rid of his blazer but was still wearing jeans, no belt. I felt his dick harden and twitch between my thighs as I kept grinding my hips.

He held his hands away, though, refusing to touch me, so I grabbed one of them and made him caress my ass until, eventually, I didn't need to assist him. He was doing it all on his own.

"I can make you feel like a *real* man," I breathed on his lips after breaking the kiss. I dropped a kiss on the crook of his neck, and he groaned. His dick throbbed. "I would let you fuck me *whenever* you want. Take me *however* you want. I would put you first. But . . ." I sighed, and gently sank my teeth into the lobe of his ear, "only if that's what you *really* want."

I faced him again, kissing him deeper this time, slower, so he could savor it, swirling my tongue around the inside of his mouth. His next groan was guttural, conjured from the base of his throat. Primal and hungry. He was straining in his pants now. That was all I would give, though. I couldn't feed him too much at once.

I pulled away, climbing off his lap and then walking around his chair. His arms remained halfway in the air. He was dazed. Confused. Horny as hell.

He'd think about this for weeks, but he wouldn't act. No,

of course he wouldn't. Why would he? He was a good man. A good husband. Devoted. Passionate. So extremely in love. Corey would never cheat on his wife . . . unless it was with the right woman. A woman he knew would keep all his dirty little secrets.

"Good night, Dr. Maxwell," I murmured over my shoulder, and I smiled on my way back to my room, licking my bottom lip, savoring the taste of him.

CHAPTER NINETEEN

Of course I didn't see Corey the next morning. And truth be told, I didn't want to see him. At least not so soon.

Lola was nursing a hangover, so she had Georgia send me off with croissants and fresh jam. Georgia apologized for her as I walked out of the mansion.

As I made my way to my car, I noticed one of Corey's was gone. It didn't take a genius to know he'd avoid me for as long as he could, all the while letting thoughts of what happened by the pool consume him.

I would have to keep a distance from Lola for a few days too, so that he wouldn't assume I was clinging to this fantasy. He'd wonder about me. Probably ask Lola about my whereabouts in a casual way once he noticed I wasn't around as much. He would think I regretted it more than he did, which in turn would make him wonder why.

But he'd had a taste, Marriott, and he hadn't put much effort into stopping it either. He would want more. It was just a matter of time.

I suppose at this point you're wondering why I'm taking this revenge thing so far. Perhaps you were right when you said I wasn't completely sane. Truly, after everything I'd done so far to get to where I was, I realized that I'm not sane, Marriott, and you know what? I'm cool with that.

At first, this was about ruining Lola's life—and don't get me wrong, it's still about that— but, like I said, Corey Maxwell had some kind of pull on me. When I first laid eyes on that fine-as-hell man, I was instantly attracted to him. I pined for him. I had dreams about him in between hatching plans of taking down his wife. I wanted him so badly it made me burn inside.

So, I'd worked on a plan that would eventually lead him to me and make him want me just as badly as I wanted him.

I dated Xavier and thought I was in love with him back then, but Xavier was no good for me. He verbally and physically abused me. He promised me good times and joy but only delivered pain and anarchy. All we ever did was argue, and if we weren't arguing, we were fighting. Still, I'd loved him somehow . . . until I didn't, and I left him, getting thrust back into the system and fitting in with the bullshit stereotypes for young black girls like me.

And then there was a man like Corey, with eyes as brown as chocolate and a voice as smooth as silk. One look at him and I wanted him. Who *wouldn't* want him? I knew for a fact Lola didn't deserve him. He needed someone better—someone who would give him whatever he wanted, and in exchange, he would give me whatever *I* wanted.

He had the money; I had the body. It would always be an even exchange. If he took care of me, I'd take care of him. It was that simple. It was what every good man wanted, but women loved to make it harder. Women like Lola especially, because she knew her worth and knew she'd be fine without him, and that she didn't have to fulfill his every need.

This motive of mine went much deeper than the troubles of my past at this point. I wanted more than to ruin Lola Maxwell's life. I wanted her husband, and I wanted him to want me just as much, to the point he'd be willing to end his marriage for me. To the point he'd break her heart and leave her miserable and alone, just as I'd been.

I knew it was going to require a lot of work—I mean, that was sixteen years of marriage I had to break up—but things like this happened all the time, Marriott. Men would leave their wives as they got older and staler and would give all their money to the younger, prettier girls with the tighter pussies and fuller asses.

Corey was a man of need and hunger. If Lola wasn't going to fulfill his appetite, it had to be me. I wanted to be his woman, and only his.

That would be what I took away from Lola. All that bliss? Her supposedly happy, perfect marriage? It would be mine, and she wouldn't be able to do shit about it because once he and I were together, there would be no turning back.

CHAPTER TWENTY

Just because I didn't like Lola didn't mean I didn't like her money. Being her go-to girl and new best friend had many great perks, one of which was the shopping.

Lola was going to be flying in a private jet to New York City, where she would be meeting a designer who would be fitting her for a dress he custom-designed for her.

She insisted I come with her—well, me and my new coworker, Olivia. Olivia was only invited for work purposes. It was officially gala season, and Lola needed to be kept up-to-date on everything. She'd need to give immediate responses to questions certain donors had, and to stay in touch with Green Garden and the event planner about specifics. Olivia was the middleman.

Riding in a private jet was something I'd never thought I'd be able to do. It was a two-and-a-half hour flight, but I relished it, accepting the complimentary drinks and snacks and sitting next to a window, staring out of it, pretending I was in Lola's shoes while she spoke to Olivia and Olivia typed away on her laptop.

We landed in no time, and a black car awaited us at the private airway, taking us straight to the bustling city. I'd never been to New York City before, but I'd heard many things about it. It was the city of dreams and wonder. The city where you could catch a cup of coffee on every corner. The city that never slept.

It was a dream for some to be surrounded by yellow taxis, fast cars, and steaming potholes, but a place this busy wasn't meant for someone like me. I thought Miami was bad, but New York City was completely over the top.

The chauffeur parked in front of a boutique painted black and white and named Bobbi Sleek's. I was out of the SUV first, and as I waited for Lola to give the driver instructions, I absorbed my surroundings and the city life around me.

Men and women were in a rush, as if late for the most important meetings in the world. Their eyes were laser-focused. They didn't give a fuck that people were around them, in front of them, behind then. Some shouted for taxis, waving their hands in the air like maniacs, while others strolled with coffees in hand or shouted into cell phones.

It was the first week of August and there was a coolness in the morning air that we didn't get in Florida around this time of year. I was glad Lola had suggested I bring one of her jackets from her closet, just in case it got cooler later on that night. I'd never been in her closet by myself, so to go in it alone was exhilarating.

She had a whole rackful of designer shoes, and don't even get me started on the amount of clothes she had hanging neatly on hangers. Some of them still had price tags on them.

I'd grabbed a tan leather jacket from the coat and jacket rack, and as I slid my arms into it, it smelled like her perfume. I would keep it too. I was sure she wouldn't miss it.

"All right. Come on, ladies." Lola led the way to the boutique. "Bobbi is waiting for us."

Air from the A/C poured out of the vents as we walked inside the boutique. The shop was full of thin mannequins in stunning dresses, each dress completely different from the next, with only small details that proved they were from the same designer, like the way the buttons were stitched on or how the sequins were patterned.

A light scent of jasmine and sandalwood was in the air, giving the boutique a sense of calm in comparison to the chaos outside its doors. Bubblelike chandeliers hung from the ceiling, the walls were painted a smooth ivory, and a song by Alicia Keys played softly from hidden speakers.

"Good morning, ladies!" A very tall, lanky man came into view, strolling between black mannequins and past the fitting rooms to our left. He had dark brown skin and a double nose piercing, a stud in one nostril and a hoop in the other.

"Bobbi!" Lola sang, meeting the man in the middle of the boutique.

I glanced at Olivia, who pressed her lips together and fought a smile. I did the same. Really, it was hard not to laugh at the encounter, but only because of Bobbi's unusual look. He had a bold, neon-yellow afro. His jeans had many holes in them, and he had to have had on the oldest pair of white Chuck Taylors I'd ever seen, but that wasn't the kicker. He wore a suit jacket as red as Lola's lipstick.

He was eccentric and definitely fit the bill as a unique personal designer. One look at him and I knew he had some sort of fashion sense, despite the old Chucks.

"Oh honey, it's so good to see you again another year," Bobbi crooned over Lola's shoulder as he hugged her. "You can't keep letting me spoil you like this, girl, or I'm gonna let it go to my head one day."

Lola tittered, as he did. "You know this is my favorite place to be when I need a dress for the gala, Bobbi. I wouldn't be anywhere else." She turned sideways and gestured to me and Olivia. "This is Olivia and Ivy. They work at the Ladies with Passion charity with me, though Ivy is off today but decided to tag along with me to play dress-up." She gave me an appreciative smile. "Ladies, this is the wonderful Bobbi Sleek. I get all my dresses for the galas from him. He is phenomenal."

Bobbi moved toward us, extending both his arms so we could shake at the same time. "Nice to meet you, ladies."

"Nice to meet you too," Olivia and I said in unison.

"Lovely. So, what's happening today? Am I going to need to find dresses for all three of you or just get you fitted, Lola?"

"Actually, Olivia already has her dress. She's had it for a couple of weeks now, right, Liv?" Lola asked.

"Yep, sure do. I still need to get it tailored, but it'll be ready by gala night."

"But on the other hand, Ivy just started working for me, and seeing as this is her first time attending a Ladies with Passion Gala, I think I need to treat her." She gave me a wink.

"What? Oh—no, Lola, that is *way* too generous. I seriously can't let you do that." Oh but I could. It was the least she could do, right?

"Don't even try to be modest with me, Ivy!" Lola walked my way in her nude, red-bottomed Louboutins. "Let me do this for you. I want this night to be magical for all of us. You never went to prom, right?" she asked. "I remember you telling me you didn't."

"No, I didn't," I confirmed. "I couldn't afford it." And that was true. Prom was expensive as hell, and I'd much rather have been fed than attend a dance in a tulle dress.

"Well, let's consider this your prom night. We'll get you into a nice dress, and when it's go time, we're going to doll you up. It'll be great."

"That's so much to ask, Lola. Really, I can just find a dress the next time I go shopping."

"I'm not taking no for an answer. This will be my treat. After helping at the camp and being there for me after *everything*, this is the least I can do. Let me treat you, babe." By "everything," she meant that little secret about Keke's fall.

I sighed, pretending I was at war with this decision of hers. But Lola knew I'd do whatever it took to make her happy, and she knew I didn't like to say no to her, so I smiled and said, "Okay, okay. Fine."

"Wonderful." She clasped her hands together and spun in her heels to face Bobbi again. "All right, Bobbi. I've been waiting for this day forever. Show me what you've got."

Bobbi Sleek's Boutique had everything we needed, from complimentary coffee and fresh-baked pound cake to large fitting rooms for the biggest, puffiest dresses.

I now understood why Lola was so excited to get to New York City to this place, and why she couldn't stop talking about it. Bobbi was attentive and kind and swift. Apparently, he had an assistant, but from the looks of it, he didn't need him or her because he handled everything with a cool head. He was made for this.

As Lola tried on several blue dresses Bobbi had designed, Olivia fed her details and asked her questions the event planner was asking. I was glad I wasn't working that day. To know I was going to be wearing a ten-thousand-dollar dress had done me in and I couldn't think about anything else.

I couldn't hate Lola right now. Not for this.

Truthfully, no matter how much I pretended I didn't care about not going to prom, I was the girl who had always wanted to go. Call me old-fashioned. It was every girl's dream to get dolled up and look great after enduring so many years of teachers droning on and nagging you.

None of the guys in school would ever ask me to go with them. No one even wanted to date me in school. I was the girl without parents, who got shuffled around in the system too much. I was the girl who cried in the bathroom stalls because my days had become too much, and who got picked on for taking meds to control those emotions. I wanted to be normal, trust me, Marriott, I did, but my life refused to give something so simple to someone like me.

Attending this gala would be my prom. I may not have been going with a hot date, but there was hope that I could be hooking up with one by the end of the night.

"Ivy, I have the perfect dress for you," Bobbi said as I ran my fingers over a silver satin gown. "Follow me." I followed him to the fitting area, where he instructed me to stand where the mirrors were. "Give me just a second."

He went around a corner and then returned with a champagne gown. He hung it on one of the racks close to me, and I moved next to him to get a better look. I was completely awestruck.

"Now, I know this doesn't come close to being the hottest gown ever, but this is a dress I've been working on for a few months now. I could never find the person with the right look who could rock this dress, so I've kept it in the back as a little treasure, but when you walked in with Lola, I saw it. You were made for this dress, love. You're the one I've been looking for."

Isn't it funny how destiny works, Marriott? Bobbi had been waiting for a girl like me—a girl who was meant to disrupt Lola Maxwell's life, all so I could try on a dress he was passionate about. See, it couldn't be all bad that I was here. Someone was getting something out of my presence in Lola's life.

"Wow, Bobbi, it's—it's stunning." I ran my hands over the silky fabric. It was a spaghetti-strap mermaid dress with a plunging neckline and white lace trimmings. The dress made just for me spilled down to a puddle of silky champagne fabric on the floor and was embroidered with more white lace at the hem. It was simple, and the complete opposite of Lola's dress as far as the style.

It screamed Ivy Hill, the real me, as you know, and I loved everything about it.

"Do you want to try it on?" he asked.

I thought he'd never ask. "Yes please."

Bobbi carried the dress by the hanger to one of the fitting rooms. As he hung it up, Lola came wandering out of her fitting room in one of the custom-made gowns, and of course it was stunning.

Mine was so simple in comparison to Lola's, but for once I didn't care about hers being better. Lola had to be the star of the evening—the best dressed. It was her charity. Her event. If it weren't for her, there wouldn't have been a Ladies with Passion Gala to begin with. She needed to stand out the most.

She waltzed out in a one-shouldered, sky-blue satin dress that was pinched at the waist to flaunt her curves. It appeared to be made entirely of sequins at the top, but slowly transitioned to sky-blue and white feathers at the bottom. A front side split revealed one of her long, slender legs and even her upper thigh.

That dress *screamed* Lola. It was custom-made to appeal to her tastes. She'd mentioned wanting feathers on her dress, and Bobbi really came through with them. A train followed her, the feathers swaying beneath the golden lights as she walked.

"You look amazing, Lola." I fed her the compliment as she stood in front of the mirror.

"You think so? I might have to get back with Dre, work on losing about ten to twelve pounds to fit better in this thing." She picked up the dress at her thigh, ruffling the feathers.

"Oh, stop it," Bobbi said, fixing her train. "You look incredible. Just imagine you with some banging jewelry, your hair all done up, and your makeup on point, and everyone will be drooling all over you at the gala, Lady Maxwell."

I clenched my fist at that name. *Lady Maxwell.* Though this was nice, what Lola was doing for me, I couldn't forget my plan. She still had Corey. She was definitely gorgeous in that dress. Corey wasn't going to be able to keep his hands or eyes off her. I hated her all over again.

Why couldn't I just have him, Marriott? Why did she have to find him first?

"Is this the one?" Bobbi asked her, his hands clasped in front of his face.

"Yes," she breathed. "This is the one, Bobbi."

"Yes!" Bobbi shouted, doing a little bounce on his toes. "Okay, so Ivy, go ahead and try on your gown," Bobbi said over his shoulder to me. "I'm going to take Lola's measurements and then I'll come check on you. Be gentle with the zippers."

I entered the fitting room, and as soon as I got the door to close, I wanted to scream. I couldn't let Lola win on gala night. My only hope was that I could get to Corey sooner—way before the night of the gala.

She'd look great, have him on her arm for the photos, and as she introduced herself to the donors, but as long as he had my panties in his pocket, I didn't care. I'd be winning.

CHAPTER TWENTY-ONE

I'd gotten the perfect dress from Bobbi's little boutique in New York City and was even more excited for the day of the gala to arrive.

After returning to Miami, I kept my distance from Lola and only appeared when she needed me. She was busy with organizing the event, and I didn't want to come off as clingy. Not only that, but I had to work too.

Ladies with Passion needed me, and as easily as I could have sabotaged the entire gala by working for Lola, I needed this one night to work in my favor.

I deserved to attend the Passion Gala. I deserved to dress up, look pretty, and mingle like a normal person . . . or perhaps I was getting spoiled with this new life of mine, becoming obsessed with material things instead of my original motive. Didn't matter. I could take a little break from that. I wanted this night, and you know how I get when I don't get the things I want. I work harder at getting it.

But there was one little problem—well, a really big problem, actually—that I'd completely forgotten about until I saw Lola the next morning.

Lola and I were supposed to be getting coffee and discussing the final itinerary for the gala. She wanted to know my thoughts on the schedule and wanted to ask my opinion on a pair of shoes Bobbi had suggested she wear with her dress.

Instead of doing that, though, Lola bustled into the coffee shop, met me as I waited in line for a coffee, and said, "Guess what?"

Confused by her excitement, I asked, "What's up?"

"You'll never believe it, but I got a call from Keke's mother this morning."

As soon as she said Keke's name, my heart plummeted to my stomach. Fucking Keke. I'd forgotten all about her, Marriott!

"Keke is finally awake!" Lola squealed.

Shit. Those were not the words I wanted to hear that day, especially not a month before the Passion Gala. All those weeks spent building up to the gala and getting so much one-on-one time with Lola, and I'd let my duty of checking on Keke fail me. I knew it was only a matter of time before she'd wake up, but thought surely I'd get at least another week without issues.

It was just like her to interrupt while things were finally running smoothly. I'd become the number one lady in Lola's life, and now she was back. Just like that, ready to shove me out of the way and be in Lola's face all over again.

"That's great, Lola!" It fucking was not. This was bad. Really bad. "Is she doing okay?" I started to ask, "Does she remember anything?" but decided against it.

"Her mother said she's doing fine but that she wants to see me. Let's take our coffees to go and pay her a little visit. I'm sure she'd love to see you too."

"Keke hates me," I said with a nervous laugh as Lola waved at the barista who was waiting to take our order.

"That's absurd. She'll be happy to see you."

Shit . . . would she? Would she remember everything that happened? All the way down to the very last detail? She'd suffered a lot of head trauma from what Lola was told, but she was conscious, and there was no guarantee that she wouldn't remember who pushed her.

We took our coffees to go and I sat in the passenger seat of Lola's Tesla, my heart banging hard against my rib cage and my palms sweaty.

Lola was thrilled. All she kept talking about was how much Bailey had missed Keke and couldn't wait to talk to her mommy again.

When she pulled up to the hospital, my tongue felt swollen in my mouth. Lola parked and unclipped her seat belt in a flash. I unclipped mine slowly, pushing open the car door and stepping out.

It was unbelievably humid and my tank top stuck to me like glue, my jeans feeling twice as heavy on my legs. My knees almost gave out on me, but I kept it together, following the ever-so-eager Lola to the entrance of the hospital.

She checked in, and as soon as she had the green light, off she went, going straight down the hallway to Keke's room.

I lingered behind as everyone in the hospital moved in quick paces. Maybe if I'd made an excuse and told her I wasn't feeling well, I could have avoided seeing Keke. I could have pretended to pass out. That could have worked, right?

My heart was beating harder.

I didn't want to do this, but what could I say to get out of it? It would have been wrong not to show my face, pay a little respect to Lola's dear friend who suffered a horrible fall.

I drew in a deep breath as Lola knocked on the door, and as she went inside, I exhaled.

This was it. I knew it.

This was going to be the moment my entire plan fell apart.

CHAPTER TWENTY-TWO

Fresh flowers were on top of the counter. Dozens of them. They were the first thing I noticed as I walked into the sterile room. Apparently, many people knew Keke was awake and back in good health; there were cards attached to each bouquet, even boxes of chocolate stacked near them.

"Keke!" Lola squealed, and I watched her run to the hospital bed to meet her old friend.

"Lola! Goodness, girl, I missed you so much!" Keke cried out. Lola bent down to hug Keke tight around the shoulders, and Keke returned a hug just as tight.

Her eyes were closed as she did, but in a matter of seconds her eyes were open again, and they landed right on mine. She frowned then, pulling away from Lola rapidly.

I waved at Keke. "Hi, Keke. How are you feeling?"

"What is she doing here?" Keke demanded, focusing on Lola. "I thought it would be just you today."

"Ivy rode with me to come see you. I told her you were awake now, and that you'd love to see her. She was really worried about you."

I nodded and smiled. Did she know? Could she see through my smile?

Lola looked between Keke and me, then she cleared her throat and pulled up a chair next to the hospital bed. "How *are* you feeling? How's your memory and everything after the fall?"

Keke sighed and rested her head against the bed. "I can't remember shit."

Relief. Sweet, instant relief. She couldn't remember, Marriott. This was good.

I moved to a chair in the corner, allowing my heart to settle and my shoulders to relax.

"Everyone tells me I fell, that I probably tripped. One of my shoelaces was untied and all that when they found me."

Lola rubbed her arm. "I was surprised to hear you'd fallen."

"I don't think I fell," Keke said, her voice serious and her eyes locked on Lola's. "I don't know why, but when the doctor was asking my questions, I kept getting this weird sensation that hands were on my back, like someone pushed me. But who would do that? A lot of those pregnant women have been through some traumatic shit, but a pregnant woman wouldn't have been able to keep up with me on the trail." Keke turned her head to look at me. "So, what's going on? You two best buddies now? I checked out your Instagram, Lola. Y'all have been hanging out a lot."

Lola scoffed at Keke's remark. "Ivy is a good friend, yes. Why do you sound so defensive about us hanging out?"

"You just met her," she answered without hesitation.

"I've known Ivy for three months now. She's a good friend to me, and she came here to check on you with me, Keke." Lola gave her a sympathetic rub on the arm. "Are you okay?"

"Oh, I'm fine. I just don't trust *her*."

"Keke." I stood up and moved closer to the bed. "I'm sorry if you feel like I've gotten in your way, or if my being here isn't what you wanted. I didn't mean to intrude. I just know how much you mean to Lola, and I know you had a bad fall, so I didn't mind tagging along to say hello."

"Where did you even come from, Ivy? Huh?" Keke snapped. "Lola may have fallen for your sad-girl story, but I don't fucking buy any of it."

We stared at each other.

She was a miserable bitch.

"Funny enough," Keke went on, "I don't remember much from camp, but I do remember telling you there was something about you I didn't like, and I still stand by that. A little fall isn't going to change my mind about you."

Oh, that bitch. If Lola weren't in the room, I would have strangled her with my bare hands. But I was the victim here. She was attacking me, and by the looks of it, Lola was seeing it the same way.

"Okay . . . you know what? I'm just going to give you some space. I can see I clearly overstepped," I murmured, going for the door.

"No, Ivy. Stop right there." Lola's voice was stern. She stood up from her chair.

"It's okay, Lo. She clearly needs some space."

"Lo?" Keke scoffed, looking up at Lola. "Now she's got nicknames for you? I can't with this girl."

"Keke, that's enough!" Lola snapped. She glared at Keke, her eyes wide and partially confused. "We came here to see you, and to show you some respect, and you're acting like a selfish bitch! I don't know what's gotten into you, but this is not the Keke I was expecting. Perhaps you need more rest, so I'll visit you tomorrow."

"No, wait—Lola, I'm sorry. I just—"

"No, Kee. Just . . . just get some more rest. I have to get Ivy back anyway. We have to discuss a few things for the gala next month."

"The gala? Next month already? Is she going?" Keke

asked, her eyes misty now. She could feel the bond severing. Lola was letting go.

Ha.

Lola peered over her shoulder and exhaled. "She works for the charity now, so yes, she's going."

"You mean she's taking my spot?" Keke asked blandly.

Lola paused. "Kee, you were in a coma. Even if you wanted to come, you couldn't. You'd still be recovering, getting things in order with Bailey. Right?"

Keke folded her arms over her chest. "Wow." She was looking out the window now. "Replaced. Just like that. You know what, Lola, just take your new best friend and get the fuck out. Don't even bother visiting me tomorrow. We're done."

Lola was stuck for a moment, taken completely off guard. She looked between Keke and me, then she shook her head disappointedly and walked in my direction.

"Let's go, Ivy." Lola's heels clicked as she left the room and carried herself down the hallway. I gripped the door handle and looked back at Keke, but she was already glowering at me.

"I know it was you," she said, dropping her arms. "I know you pushed me, you *dumb bitch*."

I stood there a moment, staring right back at her.

My heart was beating a mile a minute, my mouth dry, tacky.

Then I said something I probably shouldn't have said. Something I knew would bite me right back in the ass one day: "Prove it, *bitch*."

CHAPTER TWENTY-THREE

"I am so sorry about Keke's behavior back there, Ivy."

Watching Lola drive away from the hospital in a mood the complete opposite of the way she'd arrived was somewhat comical. It was the end of a friendship . . . at least for now. She'd chosen me over Keke, and perhaps I should have been thankful for that, but I knew it wasn't about one person over the other for Lola. It was about who was more emotionally available for her, and Keke wasn't that person anymore. Not only that, but she needed me to make sure the boat sailed smoothly for the gala as I worked with Olivia and Noah.

"It's okay, Lola. Don't apologize for someone else's behavior." I sipped my semicold coffee. "But I told you she hated me."

"Keke still needs to grow. She thinks everyone is after her because of the situation with Bailey's father. She hates feeling replaced."

"What situation?"

"Bailey's father left Keke for another woman. Got married to her six months later."

"Really?" I gasped. This I did not know. I just assumed

the father was a deadbeat, the way Keke talked about how in-dependent she was.

"Yes, but he's good with Bailey, and so is his wife, and Keke can't stand it. They share custody, so he gets Bailey every other week. Sometimes Bailey calls his wife Mom. Keke doesn't appreciate it and teaches Bailey these awful habits. I can't sit here and judge her for it. I know it must be hard raising a child alone, but the problem with Keke is she makes every-thing about her. If she's not first, no one else can be happy. Her behavior today proved that. She should have appreciated that we came out of our way to see her at all, but instead she tried to berate you. I won't stand for it."

Aww, how nice of Lola. *Not.*

"Listen, I feel awful. I shouldn't have made you go if you really weren't comfortable about it. Let me set up dinner tonight. We'll eat, have some wine, go over the itinerary, and hang out a while. Maybe take a swim today. It's a nice day, right?"

"Okay." I nodded. "Sure. I'll need to stop by my place for a bathing suit."

"Okay. I'll take you back to the coffee shop, let you grab your car. Maybe I should follow you to your place and you can ride back with me. I'd love to check it out."

"Oh—no, you really don't want to come out there. There is nothing spectacular about it."

"What? Do you think I'm going to judge you?" she asked, side-eyeing me with a smirk as she turned into the parking lot of the coffee shop.

"Not at all, I just don't think you should be driving a Tesla through Liberty City is all. You can't tell me you've never heard of *Grand Theft Auto?*"

"*Grand Theft Auto?*" She frowned, confused.

"It's a video game where the characters steal random cars

or, most times, rich people's cars. One of the locations for the game was Liberty City."

Lola chuckled. "Ah, I see." She parked the car. "Fair point. Well, meet me tonight around five thirty. I'll have the wine and food ready."

Whew. That was a little too close. She could *never* come to my apartment. It was the only place I felt safe, the only place that didn't have a touch of Lola. I always thought of it as my secret lair. The place where Ivy Elliot unmasked herself so Ivy Hill could come out and play.

"Okay. I'll see you tonight." I smiled as I left, but that smile slowly disappeared as I made my way to my car. I was tired of smiling for her. Tired of playing nice and pretending I was hurt because her friend didn't like me.

My only hope was that Corey would be there tonight. He was in town. I knew because I'd driven by Maxwell Aesthetics before going to the coffee shop and seen his car parked in his assigned spot.

It'd been three weeks since he last saw me. It was time to make another move.

CHAPTER TWENTY-FOUR

Let me share a little memory with you, Marriott. A memory that I'll never forget.

Every summer in July since I was a little girl, my parents would take me to the water park. They'd pack a cooler full of cold cut sandwiches, juices, and freeze pops. I'd bounce out to the car from the apartment we lived in with my towel and my favorite doll, ready to enjoy a full day of fun.

We'd get there early just to get the best seat in the house, which was only a few feet away from the biggest slide in the water park. From that special spot, there'd always be a cool mist to shoot on us from all the people who'd go down the big slide while screaming their hearts out. Plus, it was a shady spot, not too much sun, just enough to soak some of it in. My mother would squirt and smear cold sunscreen on my back as the sun beat down on us. She always wore this white sun hat with an orange ribbon, and my father always had one of those old fishing hats on to block the heat. As Mama rubbed sunscreen on my back, Daddy rubbed it on hers.

I looked forward to those summers. Our water-park escapes happened every single summer since I was five until one day it just stopped. I had turned fourteen, and long gone were the days when I was an only child with loving parents.

My parents could no longer take me to the water park. I could no longer suck on fruity freeze pops or feel the coolness of the sunscreen on my back colliding with my mama's soft hands.

Daddy couldn't watch me do cannonballs at the deep end of the pool, or teach me how to hold my breath under the water anymore. Those precious memories had ended—stolen away from me as quick as night and day, and it was all because of Lola.

Now, Lola was rubbing sunscreen on my back, talking about her rich people problems, and I was trying my hardest not to say anything I didn't mean. Memories like that don't just fade away, Marriott, especially not when you had a good life before.

By no means were my parents rich. For the most part they lived paycheck to paycheck, but they always provided for me, always took care of me. They saved up every summer just to create those memories at the water park, and even though some of the slides would be out of commission and the concession stands always ran out of snacks, it didn't matter. We had one another, and it was fun.

Sometimes I looked at Lola and wondered how she could live with herself after what she'd done to them. How could she continue smiling? Living a grand ol' life when she'd destroyed another?

Did she not feel guilt? Shame? Hurt? Did she not realize how much she impacted my life, created all this mental blurriness inside me?

I am the way I am because of what happened to my family, and how my childhood flipped upside down overnight. I had no family in Florida. My parents had no siblings and my grandparents were dead. Whatever kin could be found had no idea I even existed, so they didn't take me in.

I was left alone.

Lost.

Confused.

Crushed.

I watched Lola dive into the pool and resurface. Her hair became curlier, water dripping from it and running down her chest. I wanted to jump in on top of her and shove her head under the water . . . but I knew better. She had house staff on duty, and not only that, but it would have been too quick and way too easy for her. I spent *years* suffering because of her. It was her turn to suffer now.

I walked into the pool in my white bikini, allowing the cold water to wrap around me. Lola smiled from the other end of the pool and I forced one back at her. Then she sank under the water and swam my way. As she resurfaced, she laughed in my face, droplets trickling over her lips.

"I needed this," she breathed out.

"It's the perfect day for a swim," I said in agreement.

"Right? So, I told Georgia to make chicken for you tonight, and I'm going with a strawberry walnut salad. Is that okay? If you want a salad, I can tell her."

"No, chicken is okay. I'll take it." I didn't need to starve myself like she did to feel good about my body. Unlike her, I didn't mind eating.

After our swim, we took showers in her mansion—me in my new, favorite guest room and her in her bedroom—and then met for dinner on the deck on the second floor.

The sun was setting behind the horizon, the water in the bay sparkling like wet gems. A warm breeze blew by every once in a while, carrying the salty scent of the ocean with it. I cut into my baked chicken with grilled pineapple as I looked over the itinerary for the gala, all the while curious as to where Corey was.

Was he not coming home tonight? Did he have plans? I needed to see him.

As Lola went downstairs to answer a call from Olivia by the pool, I pulled out my phone and checked Instagram. I went to Corey's profile and saw he had a new story up. A video played of him recording one of his buddies throwing a dart at a dartboard. From the looks of it, he was at a bar. That explained why he wasn't around.

I picked up the bottle of wine and poured myself another glass. I refused to go home tonight without seeing him, and if I needed to pretend to be too drunk to drive again, I would.

Lola returned to the deck as I finished my last bite of chicken. "Someone was hungry," she noted, smiling.

"I was. Swimming always leaves me starving."

"So, the itinerary looks good? Not too overwhelming?" she asked, picking up her raspberry cocktail.

"No, I think it's fine. There will be food, and unlimited drink cards, and gambling. No one should complain."

"I agree." Lola took a sip of her drink, quiet for a moment. "So, I should probably tell you now that some of the donors attending the gala can get very handsy. Especially the men."

"Really?" I asked, amused.

"Yes. Last year Gary DeAngelo had one too many drinks and kept trying to kiss Olivia on the cheek during dinner. It wasn't a fun night for her, but it did result in a two-hundred-thousand-dollar donation from him."

"Really?" I choked on a laugh as Lola smiled. "Well, I'm sure I can handle it. I've dealt with my fair share of assholes."

She was quiet again. "If any of them do seem a little infatuated with you, just try to get them to spend as much money as they can, if you know what I mean." She winked.

"You mean act like a hooker for the night?" I asked, cocking a brow, smiling only a little.

"No, no." She giggled, and I forced a laugh. "I just mean while you have them like putty in your hands, you may as well use that to the charity's advantage."

I tried to keep an even face, but she had no idea how ignorant and selfish she sounded. She was probably kidding, but I couldn't ignore the swirl of urgency in her eyes.

Let these rich men take advantage of the simple, pretty girls so she could raise as much money as she could for her stupid charity? That's what she was saying, and even if she wanted me to believe it was a joke, I knew she meant it.

I glanced at my wine. "I think I'm starting to get a little headache," I murmured, rubbing my forehead with the tips of my fingers.

"You are? Did the swim wear you out?"

"Just a little."

"Do you want to go inside? Lie down in one of the guest rooms?"

"Only if you don't mind. I would drive home, but I'm worried this might shift into migraine territory. My mom used to get them really bad." And she did. My mother had a condition where her migraines would sometimes morph into seizures if they ever got too bad.

"Your parents are no longer with you, right?" Lola inquired. "I never have gotten around to asking about your parents, have I? Do you remember them?"

I froze in my seat as Georgia appeared and began taking away some of the empty dishes. Damn it. I shouldn't have mentioned my mom. My eyes swung up to Lola's, whose were sympathetic but burning with curiosity. I couldn't back myself out of this one. I'd brought it up, after all.

"They passed away when I was twelve," I said. "So, yes, I remember them pretty well." Twelve was what I'd told her purposely, Marriott. I didn't need her putting my age together with her past.

"They passed away at the same time?" she asked, her head tilting.

"Yes. It was during a . . . really bad fire. I was at a friend's house when it happened."

"I'm so sorry to hear that, Ivy." Lola reached across the

table and rubbed my hand. I had the urge to snatch it away, but I remained perfectly still. "My parents weren't the greatest," she declared with a dry laugh. "My father was a drunk and my mother was . . . well, let's just say she always had a new partner when I was growing up. Never a dull moment with that woman."

"What happened to them?"

"My father died from a heart attack and my mother . . . she's still alive. I just pretend she isn't because she's a very entitled woman. She sees or thinks of me and only wants money."

I nodded. I didn't know how to respond positively to that, as she was one to talk about entitlement. Lola pulled away and grabbed her wineglass again, sipping slowly, and for a moment I could feel for her. I'm not completely emotionless, you know.

With our parents, we could relate. Though the situations were different, and it was her fault mine were taken away from me, we grew up as teens in a cold world without parents, and that was never easy for anyone.

So, I decided to ask her a question—one that I'd hoped would change my mind about her. It wouldn't change my motive, but maybe it would change the way I felt about her in the long run.

"I have a question," I said as a warm gust of wind bristled by. The sun was sinking now, replacing the daylight with inklings of night.

"Yeah?" Lola's eyes latched on mine.

"Do you have any . . . regrets?"

"Regrets?" she repeated, confused.

I nodded.

"Like . . . with life in general or with my parents?"

"For anything," I said firmly. I needed to calm down. I couldn't get too defensive or she'd likely catch on. I relaxed my shoulders a bit.

She seemed surprised by that question and sat back in her seat, swirling her wineglass so the liquid moved. "Well, I do regret not being there when my father died. He'd called me the day he passed. I was sixteen, but I didn't want to see him, so I stayed at my cousin's house often so I could avoid his drunken mishaps."

Okay, and?

"But I chalk that up to something that was meant to happen. He was unhealthy. Ate lots of red meat." *Well, that explained her vegan diet.* "Other than that, though . . . no. I don't have any regrets. Everything I've done and have gone through was either supposed to happen or was a lesson in my life. I don't regret those things."

Wow.

Wait. Was this a joke?

She had to be kidding, right, Marriott?

All I could do was stare at her. I mean, she couldn't have been serious. So, she didn't regret killing two people? She didn't regret covering it up and lying about it? Paying off the police so her name wouldn't be put in the system so no one would ever know and confront her lying ass about it? I knew that was what she'd done. She paid them. Why else would Detective Shaw have been so unyielding about her name? He was bought.

I pushed back in my chair a little too abruptly, and Lola's forehead creased with confusion as she looked up at me. "Are you okay?" she asked, her face etched with concern.

"Yeah—I'm okay. I think I just really need to lie down. My head is throbbing."

"Of course, Ivy. Don't let me hold you up. Go ahead."

I turned and walked away quickly, through the kitchen and up the stairs to the guest room. I shut the door behind me and pressed my back to it. My breath came out heavy and hard, and for a moment it felt like the room was spinning around me.

I needed to get my breathing under control. Get myself under control. What was that thing you used to make me do, Marriott? Count to ten and then think of my favorite song?

I closed my eyes and counted to ten. I felt silly doing it, but I had to admit it worked. Then I hummed "Glory" by Dermot Kennedy and slowly opened my eyes.

The song stopped. I took a look around the guest room. I wanted to break every single item in it, from the shiny, dust-free lamps to the floor-to-ceiling mirror on the wall.

That bitch had no regrets about what she'd done. None. But I knew she did it. I could see it in her eyes. There was no way she felt nothing . . . and I was going to prove it. Maybe not today or tomorrow, but I would make her confess. That lying, stuck-up *bitch*.

I shut off all the lights in the room and walked to the window, watching Lola pick up her wineglass and the half-full bottle of wine as she stood on the deck. She carried them away from the table with a small smile on her lips.

Did she not realize just how similar she was to her father? He was a drunk, and all she did was drink. No matter how much she tried to escape it, she would always have parts of her parents in her. Things like that were engraved in your DNA. No matter how hard you tried to run from it, a person would always develop the habits of their parents.

Lola's entitlement came from her slutty mother, her drinking came from her alcoholic father, and yet she thought she was better than them just because she could wear flashy clothes and shoes and drive a Tesla? She was a fucking joke.

I heard her heels click as they came up the stairs, and I cracked the door open, watching as Lola walked down the opposite end of the hallway to get to her bedroom, still with her wine and her glass.

The door snapped shut behind her, and as soon as it did, I hurried out of the room and went across the hall to her office. One of the double doors let off a gentle creak as it opened, and I closed it quietly, going to her desk. This was something I'd wanted to do for a long time.

I sat in the leather chair and opened the first drawer. I had no idea what I was looking for, but there had to be something here that proved she was responsible. A journal, maybe, or some kind of letter.

I know what you're thinking. Something along the lines of *But the incident happened thirteen years ago. Did Lola even live in that mansion then?* I don't know, Marriot. And for all I knew, all evidence was long gone. Buried deep or burned in a fire. But I had to at least try to find something.

I got to the bottom drawer and shuffled around, and then I came across a little blue book. It was a hardback journal, but the edges were peeling, and it was bent at the spine, as if it'd been used many times. Lola's name was monogrammed on the front of it. I held my breath as I pulled it from the drawer and placed it on top of the desk.

I couldn't read it in there. There was no telling whether Lola would make a visit to her office to work, or if Georgia or someone else would pass by, so I picked up the journal, tucked it under my arm, and pushed the chair back under the desk.

I left the office, tiptoeing back to the guest room and locking the door behind me. I climbed on the bed and turned on the bedside lamp, opening the journal and flipping through it.

It was her journal all right. Her cursive script couldn't be mistaken. The first few pages were dated all the way back to February 2005. My parents died in April 2007. She'd had this journal way before they died.

I flipped like a madwoman when I found the dates, skipping over the parts about Lola's worries, her new marriage, her wonderful sex life.

Then I reached April 12, 2007, a page where Lola mentioned it was a good day and that she couldn't wait to see a Dr. Gilbert.

And then I flipped to April 13, 2007, the day my parents died . . . only there was no April 13. There were no more journal entries at all after April 12, 2007.

They'd all been ripped out.

CHAPTER TWENTY-FIVE

I ran my fingers over the ripped edges in the book. What had she done with the entries? My guess was that she'd torn them out in a drunken rage, hoping to rid herself of her imperfections. Of proof.

A door slammed in the distance and I looked up. I tucked the journal under my pillow and hurried to get up from the bed. I cracked the door open, but the hallway lights were off now and the hall was empty.

I walked quietly out of the room and went to the railing near the stairs, leaning over it as I heard footsteps below. I saw someone pass by, catching only their feet, and from the polished shoes, I knew exactly who it was.

My heart galloped as I slowly took the stairs down and checked the kitchen, but no one was there. I looked out the window to see if he'd be near the pool, but he wasn't there either.

Leaving the kitchen, I ventured down the hall and went past the staircase, peering up to make sure Lola wasn't around.

A door creaked on its hinges on the other side of the hall and I followed the noise. But as soon as I stepped around the corner to find the creaking door, a hand cupped my mouth, while another snaked around me from behind and reeled me back.

I started to scream, but then I smelled his cologne, Bleu de Chanel, and instantly relaxed. I knew it was his. I saw it on the sink of their master bathroom. I felt his solid body against my back, his breath running down the curve of my neck.

My back hit a wall and the hand around me was gone, but the front side of his body pressed against me, pinning me there.

It was dark inside the room, minus one floor-to-ceiling window that allowed the moon to shine inside, creating a cool, white glow. I focused on the dark silhouette in front of me, locking what I could make out of his eyes.

"Why the hell are you following me?" Corey asked gruffly.

"I'm not," I said.

"You were waiting for me to get home," he said, and he wasn't wrong. I'd been waiting for him all day.

"So what?"

"I'm married, Ivy." He sounded exasperated. But I wasn't the one who'd brought someone into a dark room on the opposite side of the house.

"And yet you're sneaking around with me right now."

"This isn't sneaking around. I need to talk to you. I haven't seen you in weeks. It's like you're trying to avoid me now after what happened by the pool that night."

I lifted my chin defiantly. "Nothing happened."

"I wasn't that drunk and neither were you. You remember what happened."

"Yeah, well, I regret it. Lola is my friend. I shouldn't have done it. I was stupid and drunk and she's not worth losing for that mistake."

Corey pushed in, and I felt something hard dig into my lower belly. "Mistake?" he mumbled on my mouth. "What happened to doing whatever I want? Giving me whatever I want?"

"That's off the table. Like I said, I was drunk and stupid."

His eye twitched.

He continued staring at me, and then he gripped my face between his fingers and dropped his head to kiss me. The kiss was rough and damp and possessive, and I wanted to smile behind it because I did it. My plan to avoid him and fake my regret worked. I won. As our lips parted and he panted raggedly, he said, "You may have been drunk, but I know you meant every word you said."

"Lola is upstairs," I told him.

"This house is too big." He kissed me again, then sucked on my bottom lip, coaxing a moan from me. I could taste the scotch on his breath. He was drunk. "She won't hear a thing."

He unbuckled his belt and then unbuttoned and unzipped his pants, lowering them to his ankles. As he pressed a hand to my shoulder, forcing me lower, to my knees, he said, "This stays between us." His voice was raspy. "If Lola gets suspicious, we take a break."

Which led me to ask, "Have you ever had an affair before?"

"No. Never."

I lowered my chin, facing his erection. "Good. Then I'll be your first," I said, and then I took him into my mouth.

We didn't have sex, but I did give him the best head of his life. He'd said it to me as I let him release down my throat, so no, I wasn't exaggerating, Marriott.

I couldn't take the affair too far with him yet. We still had plenty of time to be together later on. Lola was around, and I wasn't in the mood to risk so much just yet. I still had the gala to think about, an event I was actually looking forward to.

I left Corey in the room I figured out was his man cave as

he flipped on a light switch. There were signed jerseys hanging on the wall in expensive-looking frames and a basketball
in a glass case, signed by Dwyane Wade.

As the door clicked shut behind me, I walked through the
house, smiling like a dazed idiot. But just before I reached the
staircase, my fingers wrapping around the cool wrought-iron
rail, a voice rose behind me.

"Can't sleep, Miss Elliot?"

I gasped and twisted around, noticing Georgia standing at
the opening of one of the sitting rooms. She had a cup of tea
on a saucer in hand and was wearing a silver nightgown.

I narrowed my eyes at her. Was she watching me? Did she
see me leave Corey's man cave?

"I was going for some water but couldn't figure out where
the bottles were." The lie slipped right off my tongue.

Georgia sipped her tea and then took a step forward. "I
can show you where they are."

I swallowed thickly. "Sure."

She walked off, toward the kitchen, and I followed her.
The kitchen remained dark as she placed her teacup and
saucer on the counter to open the fridge.

I stood by the entrance, watching as she opened one of the
drawers inside the fridge and took out a water bottle. It was
easy to find. A toddler could have found it. She knew I was
lying.

She walked my way and placed the bottle in my hand. I
tried taking it, but she held on to the end of it a little tighter.

"What are you—"

"Careful in this house, Miss Elliot," she said in a hushed
tone. "The last thing you want is to get caught between the
Maxwells."

"Is that supposed to be a threat?" I asked, looking her in
the eye.

Georgia said nothing. Her face remained expressionless. I
couldn't read it.

Who did this bitch think she was? So what if she saw me leaving Corey's man cave? What could she do? What could she say?

"Look," I said, keeping my voice solid. "You and I both know that if this home so much as crumbles, you'll be out of a job. Lola won't stay if she's pissed at Corey. She'll leave, because this home is under Corey's name. Corey is hardly here as it is, so I'm sure he wouldn't need you, and I'm sure the last thing *you* want is to lose a job that pays you well, so how about you mind your own business and stay out of mine?"

It was harsh. Cruel.

I didn't care. I didn't need this woman fucking up my plans. My future.

Her expression didn't change. Honestly, it was strange that she didn't at least react or seem surprised by my statement.

Instead, she released the water bottle and lifted her chin, still holding my eyes. "Have a wonderful night, Miss Elliot," Georgia murmured, walking past me.

I looked over my shoulder and watched her leave the kitchen without turning back, and as she rounded the corner and disappeared, my heartbeat settled.

It was fine. No, really. It would be.

I was going to tell Corey that Georgia saw me leaving his man cave, and that he'd need to tell Georgia to keep quiet if she wanted to keep her job. She would.

Georgia lived here. She'd be out of money, a home, and a purpose if she mentioned this to Lola. She wasn't going to jeopardize everything she had over a measly affair that had nothing to do with her.

It would have been foolish, and I didn't take her as a foolish woman.

PART TWO

START OF THE RUIN

CHAPTER TWENTY-SIX

GEORGIA

Well, hello there, Ivy. Ivy Elliot, is it?

Interesting. I always thought your name was Ivy Hill.

I've been looking forward to writing these words to you. Not that you'll ever get to read them—I can't take a risk like that—but pretending to write to you as I deal with what I've done does seem like it will work. I read something about it online once—how to cope with high levels of remorse and guilt—and it said to write letters to the person you feel guilty about, even if the person never receives the letters.

Well, here we are. Here I am.

I mean, don't get me wrong, I know that after everything, you probably hate me, and you most likely assume that I hate you too. In all honesty, I don't hate you. I don't even come close to hating you.

I know what hate is. Hate is an emotion you carry in your heart. It's a burning, gnawing sensation that burns in your veins, one that you can't escape or get rid of. Hate is an emotion you wish you could release because it has so much control and power over you, but that's not how hate works, is it? Hate is loyal. It's there to stay.

Speaking of loyalty, I'm sure you know I've been loyal to

Lola Maxwell for quite some time now. I started working for the Maxwells when I was twenty-six years old. I'm forty-one now as I write this, but I'd dedicated about a decade and a half of my life to the Maxwells. Fourteen years. That's a lot of time to really get to know someone, don't you agree?

I remember the day I applied for the job like it was yesterday. My second cousin on my father's side of the family forwarded me an email about the position. She worked with an employment agency and always had access to the elite jobs that would fill fast.

In her email she'd mentioned that the pay was great and that I'd get to live in the home if given the job, but that I had to fill out the application quickly because many people were applying and submissions would close in two days.

The job was for Lola Maxwell. *The* Lola Maxwell. Everyone was running to apply.

There was a lot of responsibility with the job, but I could handle it. I'd grown up being responsible for people. My grandmother was one of them. She'd become sick in her fifties, diagnosed with ALS, and I lived with her until I was twenty, so I felt it was my responsibility to look after her. I took care of her, changed her wet diapers, and fed her when she lost control of her hands.

And don't even get me started on my mother, who always came home smelling like weed, her hair a mess and her attitude on ten. She wasn't a very kind woman, but I loved her, and when she was down, sick, or had had a little too much to drink, I took care of her . . . that is until I no longer had to. She died when I was twenty-three.

I was good at being responsible. Apparently, the Maxwells were looking for someone young and sharp—someone who could remember small details and handle all their orders for their new home. Household manager. That was the position.

Do you know what a household manager does, Ivy? A household manager is one level down from an estate manager, but the Maxwells didn't feel the need to have an estate man-ager when they had a household one who could cover the tasks. A household manager manages the rest of the staff, han-dles employer needs, is able to think the way the employer thinks, plans the events in the home, minds the security, or-ders and replaces luxury items that might break, and so much more.

There is always something hands-on to do for the home, or the employer. It was a job one had to be dedicated to, you see, so it was understandable that the Maxwells didn't want someone with thin skin or with too many family members and friends. They needed a champion, someone accessible at all times, someone willing to dedicate years of their life to make them comfortable and satisfied at home. I knew I could be that woman for them.

Other than my cousin, who I'd asked to forward me job listings she thought would fit me, I had no one.

So, I filled out the application, and to my surprise, I was sent an email a week later with a number, an address, and a confirmation that I had an interview at the new Maxwell es-tate.

I was *ecstatic*! I mean, this was Lola Maxwell we were talk-ing about. I'd heard so many great things about that marvelous woman. She was the richest woman of color to live in Florida—other than Oprah of course—and admired by many.

Lola Maxwell had opened up several clothing stores all over Florida called Lolita's and sold clothes only people in her high-profile class could afford. Basically, her stores sold clothes for millionaire women or the wives of millionaires.

She'd gotten a loan from her husband, Corey Maxwell, the year they got married, and invested it in her first store. From there on, things took off for her, getting to the point where she began to make more money than he did, which said a lot, because Corey was very wealthy.

The couple had just gotten married and her stores were

thriving, so they bought a multimillion-dollar home off Biscayne Bay to live happily ever after in.

I remember driving to the home for the interview, in awe of the place. They had it all, and I felt a slight twinge of envy as I parked in front of the house. It was amazing, and I wished I could have my own home just like it.

Seeing as I was sharing an apartment with a friend at the moment, I needed this job. Oh how wonderful it would be to live in a mansion, even if I did work there every day. It was a great perk to have.

Someone would ask me, *So, what do you do for a living?*
Oh I live in Lola Maxwell's mansion. No big deal!

I collected my résumé and purse from the passenger seat and climbed out of the car, smoothing down my black pencil skirt and adjusting the blouse I'd borrowed from my roommate's closet. She was going to curse me out when she realized I'd taken it without her permission, but right now I didn't care. If I got this job, I wouldn't have to worry about my roommate's tantrums.

I knocked on the door, nervous as hell but giddy, and a woman answered. I knew exactly who she was. Lola Michelle Maxwell. Prior to getting married, she was Lola Reyes. A half Black, half Puerto Rican woman who was even more stunning in person.

The many photos of her online hadn't done her justice. Her beauty was almost intimidating, and suddenly I felt like my blouse was too tight, my skirt too snug. I instantly regretted the greasy, fast-food burger I'd eaten the night before as I studied her in her slim, plum maxidress. Her body was everything mine wasn't. While I was frumpy and had stress acne, she was thin and had glowing, clear skin. Granted, she probably paid for her skin and body to be so great, but it didn't matter. She looked ten times better than I did on any given day.

"You must be Georgia," Lola said, showing off her perfect

white teeth. "Come on in. I've been looking forward to meeting you."

Obviously I nailed the interview. How else would I have gotten the job? I had to get personal to secure it, but it worked in my favor. The thing about Lola was, she loved a good sob story. It was almost like she fed off the sad parts of other people's lives.

"I'm sold," Lola said to me with a smile as we sat in her lavish sunroom. "I've interviewed quite a few people and though some of them were qualified, I didn't like how arrogant they were. Some of them have worked for lots of famous people, but there was nothing personable about them. But you . . . I like you," she said. "There's something vulnerable about you, and I could use that around here. The job is yours."

Never had I been so excited to be hired. This wasn't going to be an ordinary job. This would take me to the next level. Lola insisted that to keep the household running strong, I needed to live with her, and I was pleased to hear that. She gave me a tour of her immaculate mansion, even showed me a room on the second floor that would be mine. The room was in its own wing, had lots of privacy, and I shouldn't forget to mention it was enormous. The bathroom was luxurious, all marble and clean porcelain and sparkling glass. It was more than enough. It was perfect and would definitely beat sleeping in the cramped-up room I was currently in any day.

Lola wanted me to start the following week. I signed a ten-year contract to become her household manager, which meant I'd take care of everything in the mansion.

If Lola needed a particular dinner, I'd inform the chefs. If the grass needed to be cut, I'd call the mowers. If the pool needed cleaning, I'd contact the pool cleaning company.

It seemed simple enough . . . but even I should have known that every good thing came with a price.

CHAPTER TWENTY-SEVEN

For the first four months living with Lola was wonderful. Her husband was a nice man and didn't ask for much other than a scotch on the rocks after a rough day.

Lola was the one who was a bit of a handful, but I had gotten used to her ways. I took pride in being the household manager for Lola, and nothing could stop that pride.

I loved cleaning, so picking up after them wasn't a problem. There was no need for her to have a maid or butler around every day when I was there. The maids only came twice a week to man the bedrooms and bathrooms, dust in the higher places, and so on.

I made sure to always be at the top of my game because I knew I could easily be replaced by some other woman, so if Lola told me to jump, I asked her how high. If she needed me to fetch a certain treat for her raging sweet tooth, I ran off to do it in the car she provided.

Lola despised my car. It was a green 1999 Volkswagen Beetle with brakes that squealed like a baby pig. She'd told me to get rid of it the first week I was hired and said that if I was to work for her, I needed to *look* like it. She allowed me to drive her SUV to run errands for her and the home, and I sold my car.

My life revolved around Lola Maxwell, and you know what? I enjoyed it. I loved being needed. Being called upon when Lola wanted to talk or rant about a long day.

We'd spend many nights chatting about her goals and dreams. She'd have a glass of wine here and there, but never too much at first.

Lola also surprised me with early nights off, or even nights out quite often.

I'll never forget the night she took me to a lounge in downtown Miami. It was an open mic night, so we listened to people sing or read poetry over drums or jazz music and sipped fruity cocktails in a VIP section.

That was a night that changed my life forever.

"So tell me, Georgia. Why don't you have a man?" Lola had asked me over the music that night. She'd had two drinks at this point, and I was still babysitting my first. I'm not much of a drinker.

Her question caught me off guard and I blushed and bowed my head.

She let out an excited laugh. "Oh, come on! Don't be shy! You can tell me anything!"

"Well," I said, placing my drink on the table in front of me. "I work for you, so I'm busy with that. I also live at the mansion, so I can't exactly bring anyone there to hang out or anything."

"Well, maybe you could hook up with a guy and go to his place or something," Lola suggested with a playful shrug. She looked great that night, clad in a gold dress that stopped just above her knees and heels to match. Gold eye shadow on her eyelids and plum lipstick. I couldn't help feeling like she was trying to escape something that night, though. Or someone.

I shrugged and laughed. "I could . . . but I'm not really looking for love right now."

"Well, just so you know, there's a guy at the bar who keeps staring at you." Lola smirked and looked past me to the bar. I looked with her and, sure enough, there was a guy standing there with a beer in hand, looking right at me. He sipped from his beer bottle and then smirked, and my heart pounded faster as I snatched my eyes away.

"Oh my gosh," I gasped. "Wait . . . how do you know he's not looking at *you*?"

"Trust me, he's not looking at me. He's ogling the hell out of you, Georgia. Don't underestimate yourself. You're gorgeous and he sees that."

Her words made me light up like a million watts. I'd never had anyone tell me I was gorgeous. I mean, I knew I wasn't hideous, but I was a plain Jane, you know? I didn't get recognized often for my looks, though I had to admit, as Lola and I got ready at the mansion and she did my makeup in her master bathroom, I felt prettier. My grandmother always used to tell me my brains would be my moneymaker.

It'd been a while since I'd worn makeup. Lola had a small policy about it at the mansion. I couldn't go crazy with my makeup while working for her and needed to appear professional while on duty. Luckily for me, I didn't care for makeup all that much. I wore mascara here and there, but nothing over the top.

"I'm going to tell him to come over," Lola said, shooting to a stand.

I gasped. "Oh no! Lola, I can't talk to that guy."

"Why not?" she asked, smiling her perfect smile.

"Because it's . . . it's been so long since I've talked to a guy. I can't even remember how to flirt if we're being honest."

Lola gave me a once-over, and when she realized I was serious, she huffed a breath and sat next to me. "Okay. Here's the thing about guys at clubs. Flirting isn't that hard with them. They're here looking for someone to go home with, so they can't be choosy. He's already been drinking and he's eyeing you. Just have a little conversation and see where it leads."

"I'll mess it up. I know I will."

"Just try," she encouraged. "If not for you, then for me. I don't get to be all flirty anymore. I have Corey now." She pursed her lips, and I didn't miss the slight eye roll she passed after saying that. "Just because you work for me doesn't mean you shouldn't get to have a little fun every once in a while."

She was right . . . but I was serious about not knowing how to flirt anymore. I was broken in that way. I'd taken care of people my whole life, so that when it came to men, I was just . . . *awkward*.

"Okay," I said. "But let me go to him."

"That's my girl," Lola chanted.

I stood up and smoothed out the wrinkles in my banana-cream dress. I had no idea what the hell I was going to say to the guy at the bar, so I thought about how I'd start the conversation as I crossed the room. A man with dreadlocks was on stage, rapping to the melody of a saxophone about his struggles with an ex-girlfriend.

I couldn't think, and the words of the man on stage weren't setting the tone for flirting, so when I met up with the guy at the bar, I just stared at him. His thick brows shot up to his forehead as he waited for me to speak. I fumbled with words.

"I, um . . . my boss . . . told me I should come . . . speak to you." Damn it. I was butchering this. Were you ever this bad with guys, Ivy?

The man appeared amused by my remark. Up close he was handsome as hell. His hair was cut clean, lined up, and faded at the edges, and his skin was a shade or two darker than mine. He was tall, with a goatee, and he smelled like sandalwood and some other scent I couldn't quite place. Leather, maybe? His clothes were simple. Navy-blue, V-neck t-shirt, jeans, and Jordan's.

"You're out tonight with your boss?" he asked, stifling a laugh.

"Well, yeah. I work at her house for her. But it's not like that, you know? We're also good friends."

The man chuckled. "Well, your boss must be pretty chill if she's out with you tonight." He looked across the club at Lola. I looked with him, and Lola was giving me a thumbs-up. I was so embarrassed by that thumb. I felt like a child who was nervous to play her first soccer game, Lola being the mom in the stands with the thumbs-up to encourage me.

"Be honest." I sighed. "You were looking at her, weren't you?"

"What would make you think that?" He put on a slight frown.

"Well, she's the prettiest woman in the room. Everyone stares at her when we go places."

"Well, if you believe that, you're wrong."

"If I believe what? That everyone stares at her when we go out?"

"That's she's the prettiest woman in the room."

I was confused.

He went on. "She can't possibly be the prettiest woman in the room if I'm looking right at the prettiest woman in the room."

Wait. He meant me. He was looking at me. My heart did cartwheels. I pressed my lips to fight a smile, but it was pretty much impossible. He'd gotten me with that line. He was flirting with me. Why couldn't I be that smooth?

The man stretched out his arm and offered me a hand. "I'm Dion," he said.

"Georgia," I said back, taking his hand and shaking it.

I had no idea that all my life I'd been looking for this man named Dion. Dion McNeil. We met at this club, and even after exchanging numbers and parting ways, I couldn't get him off of my mind.

He sent me text messages every single day. Every morning he'd send me a **"Good morning, Beautiful"** text, and I'd respond with **"Good morning, Handsome."**

Dion eventually became the love of my life. I did all my duties at the mansion in a timely fashion, just so I could go to meet him for dinners or for a drink at a bar. I became a much better flirt, but I think I was just becoming comfortable with him altogether.

As time progressed, he would invite me to his apartment, where he'd cook dinner for me and let me watch him prepare it. He was a great cook, had even gone to culinary school for two years but never finished.

I suppose it didn't matter, though, because he was currently a sous chef in a really popular Miami restaurant called Louie's. I'd learned that about him when we first hooked up, along with other facts. His favorite color was red. He'd lost his parents when he was two and grew up with an uncle named Brandon. He also used to be a hand model. He did have nice hands for a chef, I would admit.

For a while, life was great with Dion and at the mansion with Lola. And then, around Christmas of 2006, nearly a year after I'd started working for Lola, Dion asked me to marry him.

We didn't do anything big. We went to the courthouse and sealed the deal with a kiss and two gold wedding bands. I was Mrs. McNeil, and I was so damn proud to have his last name.

But it was after we got married when things started to change.

CHAPTER TWENTY-EIGHT

Dion wanted me to move in with him. But he knew about my job. He knew I had to be at the mansion every day and night so the Maxwells' ship could continue running smoothly.

"Just quit. I make enough money to take care of both of us," he'd said to me as we lay in his bed one night. We'd been married for a little over a month then. I was naked beneath his sheets and he was shirtless, his back pressed to the headboard. He was running the pads of his fingers up and down my bare arm.

I ran my hand over his chest and sighed. "I know you can, but Lola needs me at the mansion. I'm also under a contract, Dion. Even if I wanted to quit, I can't for another eight or so years."

"Eight?" he repeated, and I sensed irritation in his voice.

"It's a ten-year contract, babe. I told you that before."

I looked up and his mouth twitched. Then he moved my arm from his torso and climbed out of the bed. I pushed up on my elbow, watching as he tugged on his boxers. "Dion?" I groaned.

"Don't call my name like that, Georgia. So, you're telling me I'm going to have to wait ten years to live with my *wife*?"

"Why are you acting surprised by this, Dion? You knew when we first met that I had obligations to Lola and the mansion."

"You're choosing her over me," he muttered.

"No, I'm not! Don't say that!" I sat up fully. "This job pays me well. Look, maybe I can't quit, but if I talk to Lola, maybe she'll be okay with me leaving the mansion a little earlier from now on to spend time with you, and coming in a little later."

Dion turned around then, and his eyes softened. "And if she isn't?"

"She'll have to let me, Dion. We're married now. She'll understand. She knows what married life is like."

He sighed and came back to the bed, and relief unfurled in my belly. He grabbed one of my hands and wrapped his around mine. "I just don't want to live without you, G. I want to come home to my wife. I love you too much for you to be away from me all night."

I leaned forward and kissed him. "I know, I know. I'll talk to her."

And I would . . . I just wasn't sure when. When I'd applied for the job, it was never my intention to fall in love or get married, so I was fine signing a ten-year contract with Lola. I didn't think I'd find a man who loved me as much as I loved him, but life is funny like that. It throws things at you that you don't quite see coming. I'm sure you know all about that.

I arrived at the Maxwell mansion at six the next morning and got straight to work. I handled everything that needed to be handled, and around nine that morning Lola came downstairs.

She was dressed up, which meant she probably had to meet someone for work or had a breakfast date with a friend. I was standing at the counter, sipping some caramel tea as her silver heels clicked on the marble floors and she entered the kitchen with a bold smile.

"Good morning, Lola," I greeted her in a soft voice.

"Morning, Georgia." Her voice was harmonious.

"Breakfast is ready for you by the pool."

"Oh, I meant to tell you to cancel that. I have to run." She put on a mischievous smile. "I have something to tell you, but I didn't want to say anything until it was confirmed with a test."

"A test?" I asked, confused.

"Yes!" She walked closer to me. "I'm pregnant, G! I took a test last week!"

"Oh my goodness! That's amazing, Lola! I'm so happy for you!" And really, I was. I knew how hard she had been trying to get pregnant. She'd mentioned to me only weeks before that she and Corey were going to be trying to start a family.

"Thank you! Dr. Gilbert squeezed me in today. I told her I couldn't wait to be seen. Only problem is, her clinic is in St. Petersburg, so I have a little drive ahead of me, but it's for the best gynecologist in Florida, so it's fine. I haven't told Corey yet, though. I want to make sure everything is okay first before I give him the news, so don't mention it to him if you see him."

"Of course not. My lips are sealed." I pretended to zip my lips.

Lola smiled and turned, and when she left the kitchen, I huffed. I couldn't ask her about not being in the mansion right now. She was pregnant, and the last thing I wanted to do was pull away in her time of need.

Dion wasn't too happy about it. I mean, of course he wasn't. He didn't give a damn that Lola was pregnant or starting a family. He just wanted me with him so we could discuss starting our own. For the time being we compromised. I'd leave the mansion at eight every night to be with him, and that was okay for a while.

It became a little trickier now that Lola had fallen pregnant, though. She was moody and tired, always complaining about something I had no control over. But this was my job. I had to make it right.

I worked tirelessly to make the house comfortable for her. Prior to being pregnant, Lola loved seeing fresh flowers in the kitchen, particularly lilies. Now, she swore she hated the smell of them. The chefs couldn't cook certain foods because they made her want to vomit. She was also very sick every morning, and I could sense tension between her and Corey that wasn't there before.

Something told me Corey didn't want Lola to be pregnant, that he wasn't ready to start a family. The way he looked at her sometimes made it obvious, like he was horrified by the idea of it. He also started asking for his favorite scotch more than usual.

I kept out of their business, though. The Maxwells argued often. Most times they argued after attending certain events or parties together. Lola would come home in a rage, slamming doors and accusing Corey of flirting with someone at a party, and he would turn right around and point out that she was flirting too.

I was glad Dion and I didn't have to worry about petty things like that. I realized being rich could bring too many problems to a marriage while living with the Maxwells. You weren't ever really 100 percent happy, even with all that money.

I always found it shocking the way people could buy into Lola and Corey's happiness. I'd witnessed firsthand how much they yelled at each other, slammed doors, broke glasses, and even slapped each other around, but, as I said, it was none of my business.

I was under a certain confidentiality too. Being her household manager meant keeping my mouth shut. But even if I hadn't been, Lola was my boss and my *friend* and I wouldn't have had any right telling anyone. I didn't even tell Dion about Lola and Corey's marital problems. I felt she trusted me to keep quiet and keep it private; that was my obligation.

Crazy thing is, though, that Lola began to change with the pregnancy. She wasn't as nice anymore, or caring of anyone else's feelings but her own. I tried to chalk that up to her hormones, and how fatigued and sick she'd become, but after the night of April 13, 2007 . . . it was no longer about the pregnancy.

No. It had become much, much deeper than that.

CHAPTER TWENTY-NINE

I remember arriving at the mansion on April 13, and Lola wasn't there. Neither was Dr. Maxwell. The house was oddly quiet, but I did my duties, made my calls, and cleaned whatever needed cleaning.

Something was off about that day. Rain isn't unusual in Florida, especially during spring, but it was really pouring down outside, the windows getting slapped with water and wind.

Lola normally didn't leave until nine in the morning or after if she had somewhere to be. She'd have a list on the fridge of what she wanted for lunch or dinner, along with instructions if she had guests coming over, but not that day.

I was worried, but I didn't want to be annoying by calling or checking in if she was busy. For all I knew, she'd traveled somewhere and forgotten to tell me . . . but she never forgot to tell me things like that. She loved to brag about her trips to different cities or countries.

Day transitioned to night, and finally Lola came home. The rain had settled and become a light drizzle. I didn't notice her arrival at first. I'd just finished eating a quick dinner when she trudged past the kitchen and I caught her thin silhouette. It was nearing ten at night. I was late to get to Dion and had sent him a text to let him know, but I didn't want to leave until I knew what was going on, or if she'd have any requests.

"Mrs. Maxwell?" I called, shooting off my stool and going after her. She was halfway up the stairs at that point. "Mrs. Maxwell?" I called again. "Is everything okay? I didn't know what you wanted for dinner, so I told Tonia to make roasted veggies and a soup."

Lola stopped walking up the stairs but didn't turn to look at me. Something was wrong. She seemed agitated. Was she about to fire me? Maybe she didn't like that I was leaving early most nights anymore.

Lola finally looked over her shoulder, but not right at me. Something was definitely wrong, though. Her face was pale, her lips dry, and her hair a bit disheveled. I noticed stains of blood on her blouse and gasped.

"Oh my God, Lola. What happened?" I took a step up.

"No, Georgia. Don't." She dropped her head, her hair curtaining around her face. I stopped moving. "Take the rest of the night off," she ordered.

"But, what about your dinner—"

"For fuck's sake, Georgia! Just take the fucking night off! Go to your stupid husband and stop bothering me!"

Her tone had caught me completely off guard, but what caught me off guard the most was the way she stormed up the stairs and slammed a door behind her. I stepped down, utterly confused, but I wasn't going to ignore her orders. It was clear she wanted to be alone, so I grabbed my things and left . . . but for the record, my husband wasn't stupid. I didn't know what her problem was, but that was just rude.

As I was leaving, Corey was climbing out of his car. "Hey, Georgia," he greeted me as I reached the SUV. "Taking off?"

"Yes. Mrs. Maxwell told me I could go. I'm sorry if you wanted dinner," I murmured.

"Don't apologize. It's okay. I'm sure I'll find something."

He seemed too chipper. Compared to Lola's attitude, I could only assume he had no idea what was going on with her.

"Have you talked to Mrs. Maxwell at all today?" I asked, glancing at the front door of the mansion and then focusing on him.

"No, I haven't. I called her after a surgery, but figured she was busy when she didn't answer."

"Oh." He was going to be in for a rude awakening. "Well, good night, Dr. Maxwell."

"Drive safe, Georgia."

I climbed behind the wheel of the SUV, watching Dr. Maxwell enter the house. When the door closed behind him, I couldn't help feeling something was very, very wrong.

I tossed and turned the whole night and got out of bed around four the following morning to get ready for work. I couldn't get that bloodstain on Lola's shirt out of my mind. Did someone hurt her? What the hell happened?

Dion wasn't pleased with me leaving so early, and he didn't understand my stance. I hadn't told him about the blood I saw on Lola's shirt, or how she'd yelled at me. I didn't want him to have any more reason to feel like I needed to break my contract and quit.

I drove to Biscayne Bay and parked in the roundabout driveway around six that morning. Both Corey and Lola's cars were there. It was strange for Corey to still be around. He normally was leaving or long gone by the time I arrived. He went to work early and came home late most nights. Cosmetic surgery wasn't an easy job.

I used my key to get inside the house. It was too quiet. I flipped on a few light switches in the kitchen and placed my keys on the hook by the fridge.

I waited several hours for one of the Maxwells to show their faces, but it wasn't until a little after one in the afternoon that Dr. Maxwell left the mansion without stopping in the kitchen and then, an hour later, Lola came downstairs.

I was on the phone with the landscaper, scheduling a time for him to come, when I noticed her enter the kitchen and grab a bottle of water from the fridge.

"Let me call you back," I said hurriedly before hanging up. I rushed into the kitchen, where Lola was now pacing in front of the counter, chewing on her thumbnail.

"Morning, Mrs. Maxwell. Are you feeling better today?"

Lola whipped up her head, as if she'd just noticed me. Her face was clear of makeup, still pale, her eyes puffy. "Georgia— what are you doing here? I thought I told you to take the day off."

"You told me to take the rest of the night off last night. I didn't realize you wanted me to take today off too." Just as I said that the doorbell rang.

She panicked then, looking from me to the way out of the kitchen. "Oh, fuck. I can't do this!" she cried.

"Do what?" I asked as the bottle of water slipped from her hands and dropped to the floor. She clutched the edge of the counter.

"That's a cop at the door, Georgia. He called me twenty minutes ago and said he needed to speak to me right away. Something horrible happened last night and now he's here to talk to me."

"What do you mean? What happened, Lola?" I walked closer to her and picked up her hands in mine, giving them a squeeze.

She sniffled, and her nose was red now. "I . . . I don't know. It was all so sudden. So scary." She took a moment to collect herself, and then she used her fingers to wipe the tears from under her eyes. "Okay . . . um, do me a favor. Tell Tonia to get a quick snack ready—maybe some fresh-cut fruit and yogurt for parfaits. I'll get the door."

This wasn't like her. She never answered the door, but a cop was knocking, and she looked sick with worry.

I followed her orders and went to the chef's kitchen,

where Tonia was just walking in with groceries. I told her to get some parfaits going and that it was urgent, and then I left the kitchen, following the sound of Lola's voice.

I stopped in the hallway near the front den as I heard Lola say, "It truly was an accident and I can't have this on my hands."

"What are you saying?" the cop asked.

"My reputation is important to me. This would tarnish all I've built. If people find out about this, it will ruin me, you get that, right? They'll blame me and look at me in a different way. I was—I was visiting my doctor for an emergency appointment. The weather wasn't on my side, and then . . . well, things happened, you know? I felt some pain and I lost control."

It was quiet. My heart pounded. What the hell was going on?

Lola said in a quieter voice, "I would like my name to be off the record for this. I don't want any journalists getting hold of the information from this accident and using this to spark a scandal. My lawyer already came to you to discuss this incident. He said you told him my name would remain anonymous when the story was reported—that this wouldn't jeopardize my reputation just yet because you're still investigating."

"Whether it was an accident or not, Mrs. Maxwell, two people are *dead*. You got off last night with your lawyer and the whole *distress* thing, but this is you and me. One-on-one."

"I called my lawyer right after you called and he's on his way right now. He knows you're here. Until he gets here, I'm not discussing anything one-on-one with you."

"If it weren't for the health risk you were under yesterday, I would be having you arrested for manslaughter right now, Mrs. Maxwell. And not for just one count but two. We don't need him here. Like I said, this is between you and me."

"What is it that you want?" she demanded. "What will it

take for you to let this go? You're obviously here to get something out of this because you didn't instantly arrest me yesterday, there were no witnesses, and you drove over three and a half hours to get here, so don't hang that manslaughter bullshit over my head. What is it that you want, Detective Shaw?"

I took a step forward with bated breath.

The detective remained quiet for some time. I almost thought he'd left, until he spoke up again. "You know, I looked into you after you and your lawyer skipped off to your doctor's appointment. From the look of things, you make a pretty penny."

Lola sniffled. "Okay?"

Silence again.

Shaw cleared his throat. He sounded like a smoker. "Now, I don't ask for much, but for my family, I'll do anything, the same as you would for your sparkly clean reputation. My daughter needs to go to college," Shaw said in a low, serious voice. "There's nothing I can do about the two people who died at this point. They're gone, and as you stated, you were under distress during the accident, so I suppose I can rule this as just that—an accident—so long as I get what I need for my little girl."

"Okay," Lola breathed.

"We both know college is expensive . . . and we also know that if you live in a place like *this*, and drive cars like the one you were driving last night, you have the money to cover tuition. So, you're going to write me a check for five-hundred-thousand dollars and I'll make sure your name doesn't appear in the file. You'll remain anonymous and no one will know you were ever part of this."

Lola was silent. "Fine. I can do that."

"You don't sound so sure," Shaw countered.

"I'm sure I can manage that much. But before I do, I will need you to sign a nondisclosure about this with my lawyer. Guarantee confidentiality."

The detective chuckled and then said, "Fair is fair, I suppose."

"Okay, then. Let me just go get my checkbook and I'll get the money to you right away."

I gasped as I heard instant footsteps, but there was no time for me to run off. Lola was already rounding the corner and coming my way. She noticed me first thing, and her damp, red eyes stretched two times wider.

"Georgia!" she hissed, hurrying toward me. "What the *fuck* are you doing here? Go to my office!" She shoved me on the back and I sucked in a sharp breath. "Go!"

I hurried up the stairs and made a right, Lola hot on my trail. Opening one of the double doors of her office, I stepped inside, and Lola came in after me, slamming the door behind her.

"Were you eavesdropping on my conversation?" she demanded, grimacing.

"I'm so sorry, Lola. I—I told Tonia about the parfaits and then I came to look for you to see—"

"Bullshit!" she snapped, then walked around me to get to her desk. "What did you hear?"

"Nothing," I lied as I watched her shuffle through the top drawer of her desk. She took out her checkbook and grabbed a pen.

"Well, whatever you heard, I'm doing this for your safety too. You still want this job, right? The only way you'll keep it is if I write this check for that dirty-ass cop downstairs."

"What did you do?" I asked, my voice breaking.

"That's none of your business."

"You killed two people," I said, my eyes stinging now. "I heard him say two people are dead."

She whirled around, pointing a finger in my face. "I didn't fucking kill anybody!" she snarled. "And if you repeat those words to anyone—*anyone*, Georgia—I will fucking *end* you!"

She glared daggers at me, and I worked hard to swallow

the bile that was slowly creeping up my throat. "Does Corey know?" I whispered.

"No. All he knows is that I lost the baby yesterday." She sniffled then, wiping hard at her nose. I didn't know what to say. All I could do was look at her. I had no idea she'd lost the baby. That explained the blood on her shirt.

"Lola, I'm so sorry."

"Don't." She held up a hand. "Don't call me by my first name. It's Mrs. Maxwell to you from now on."

Her words were like knife wounds. I blinked quickly to bat away the tears. The hurt. Why was she treating me like this over an accident? I wasn't judging her. I just had questions and was concerned about her.

"Okay," I whispered.

She turned away and marched to the door. "I want steak tonight. Tender and fresh. After the horrible night I had, I need meat, and for dessert I want fudge brownies and ice cream."

I bobbed my head as she snatched open the door. "And I meant what I said, Georgia. You tell *anyone* what you heard and I'll fucking fire you and make your life a living hell. That goes for your husband too. As of this moment, what went on downstairs never fucking happened."

CHAPTER THIRTY

IVY

I couldn't believe it was the weekend of the gala, Marriott! I'd been humming all day, imagining all the songs the DJ would be playing and the drinks that would be on the menu. There were going to be three signature drinks. I helped Noah pick the flavors. One had strawberries, another mint and lime, and the last peach. I was leaning toward choosing the peach.

I'd been waiting *months* for the Passion Gala and now it was happening, and I had all the ins. For starters, I was flying to New York in a private jet with Lola, Corey, Olivia, and Noah.

Don't worry, I was keeping a safe distance from the sexy Dr. Maxwell. I kept busy with Noah and Olivia on final touches for the event, but every once in a while, I'd give Corey the eye. His poker face sucked, so of course he tried to avoid looking at me altogether.

When we landed, we went straight to the Mandarin Oriental, where Lola checked us all in with pride. Everyone had their own room. Lola and Corey would be sharing a presidential suite overlooking Central Park and with views of the city, while Noah, Olivia, and I had suites with views of the Park and the New York skyline.

Walking into my room was like walking into a dream. The first thing I noticed were the picture windows and the way they revealed the skyline. The view was stunning.

We'd arrived the night before the gala to settle in and get ready for the big event; now the sun was just setting. I stood in front of the window, taking in the steady blur of red and white lights from the cars driving by, even noticing people strolling through Central Park.

For the first time I had a real taste of luxury. I'd looked up this hotel when Lola had mentioned where we would be staying during one of the meetings at work. The rooms she'd booked for us started at $2200 a night, while hers started at $14,000. That was a lot of money. I couldn't even fathom having that much money to spare for hotel rooms. Her room alone was probably a third of my yearly salary.

There was a bottle of champagne on ice on the table next to the window, along with a flute. I opened the bottle, and when the cork was out and the room sounded with a loud *POP*, I squealed and then giggled, pouring myself a glass.

"A toast to you, Miss Hill. You did it. You're here." I sipped. Stared out of the window. Chuckled.

There was a knock at my door, and I put down my glass, going for it. I checked the peephole and saw it was Noah. I stepped away from the door, rolling my eyes.

Ugh. Couldn't work wait? He'd mentioned finding me to discuss a few things tonight, but all I wanted to do now was revel in my suite, roll around on the Egyptian cotton, and put on the fluffy, expensive bathrobe that was hanging in the bathroom after taking a long, hot bath in the oversize tub.

I cleared my throat and put on my best smile, swinging the door open. "Hey, Noah. What's up?"

"So, I was talking to Lola, and she told me she wants to take us out to dinner to one of her favorite restaurants tonight. You down?"

"Sure. What time are we going?"

"She said within the hour. We're meeting in the lobby. Should be enough time to refresh, right?"

"Yeah, more than enough. I'll see you down there."

I closed the door and picked up my suitcase, laying it on the bed. I'd done some shopping before the trip. I'd decided to spend more of my paycheck over the weekend and shopped for tighter-fitting dresses and new shoes. This was New York City and I wanted to go all-out. Plus, Corey would be around more often than not, and I needed to quietly seduce him.

After I was dressed and had done my makeup, I checked myself in the mirror. I had to admit I looked good. Black stockings, a leather skirt, a simple white blouse that hugged my body, and fuck-me heels.

I was out the door in no time, pressing the button for the elevator. To my surprise, as the doors opened for me, Lola and Corey were already inside.

"Hey, Ivy," Lola greeted me as I walked in. "Don't you look great!"

I laughed. "You're one to talk! Look at you!" As always, she looked dolled-up. A little black dress and petal-pink heels, with jewelry to match. "I figured because I was in a new city, I needed to look the part." I don't know why I was feeding her an explanation. I really didn't care what she thought.

"Well, you look amazing." She winked at me.

"I'm so glad we're doing dinner. I'm starving," I said as the elevator began going down.

"Of course. I could use a bite too. I had my hands full this morning. Didn't even get to eat."

"You probably already do this, but you should have your food prepped more. I like prepping when I'm too busy and it's a lifesaver." I couldn't believe I was getting so good at making small talk, Marriott. You'd have been proud of me in that moment. Acting like a normal human being.

"Yeah? Maybe I'll tell Georgia to start prepping meals for me."

Three more floors until the lobby. I glanced at Corey. He was avoiding me completely.

"Oh, babe, you'll have to try the halibut tonight. It was my favorite thing on the menu when I came here last year with Arabel."

Corey nodded when Lola spoke, nothing more. Wasn't Lola a vegan? Halibut was fish . . . gah, she was so full of shit. Only a vegan when she wanted to be.

The elevator finally stopped and the doors spread apart. Corey was out first, with Lola trailing behind him. He was uncomfortable, that much was clear. The least he could do was try to play it cool.

Dinner was at an Italian restaurant with a view of the Hudson River. This particular restaurant was located on the rooftop of a building. Candlelight and jazz music made the restaurant feel warm and welcoming and slightly romantic. If it had been only Corey and me, it would have been romantic. But it wasn't just us. It was us, his wife, and two other people who talked too damn much.

Lola was chatting with Noah about the gala, and while she did, I brushed the tip of my foot across Corey's upper thigh under the table. His eyes stretched, and then he cleared his throat, picking up his water, and chugging it down as a distraction.

"Don't worry, Corey," Lola said to him as he adjusted in his seat. "The boring stuff will be over soon." She laid a kiss on his cheek. I wanted to cut off her lips. That was my cheek. My man.

After what had happened in the man cave, I was becoming more territorial with Corey. Anytime Lola talked about him, it angered me, but I smiled to push through it. Anytime she complained, I wanted to slap her across her face for being so ungrateful. She didn't appreciate him at all, Marriott. Not one bit.

Corey picked up his fork and cut into his halibut. I couldn't believe he'd ordered it just to please Lola. He didn't even seem to be enjoying it.

Once dinner was over, we all walked back to the hotel, absorbing the city life. Cars and taxis zipped by, couples walked hand in hand, and people rushed into nearby bars or restaurants, dressed like superstars.

I walked next to Olivia and listened to her go on about some novel she was reading, pretending to be interested. Noah was in front of us, checking things off his list for the gala—he was very organized that way—and Corey and Lola were ahead, arm in arm. *Ugh.*

We'd have an early start in the morning, getting things organized, so as soon as we were inside the hotel, we parted ways to go to our rooms.

Just after I'd kicked off my shoes, peeled out of my stockings, and poured myself another glass of champagne, someone knocked on my door.

Hesitant, I took slow steps toward it. If it was Noah again, I was going to flip. I mean, how organized did he have to be? I checked the peephole, and my heart did a little flip.

It wasn't Noah at all.

With haste, I snatched the door open. On the other side was Corey.

The red tie he wore for dinner was gone, his white, button-down shirt unbuttoned at the collar. One of his forearms was pressed on the frame of the door, the other at his hip, as if he'd been standing there for a while.

His eyes shot right up to mine. Then he dropped his arm and charged right in, cupping a hand around the back of my neck. I held back a gasp as his solid, warm body pressed mine and the door clicked shut behind him. His lips were instantly glued to mine and I ended up spilling my champagne on the floor.

Then the glass hit the floor. Thank goodness it was covered in carpet.

My back landed on the king-size bed and Corey climbed between my legs, still kissing me. Groaning as he palmed one of my breasts.

When he finally broke the kiss, he looked me in the eye with his warm, brown irises and said, "All I could think about was your ass in that skirt." His eyes ventured down to the black leather riding up my thighs.

"Where is your wife?" I asked. I loved pretending I didn't want him. The truth was, I wanted him more than anything.

"She went to meet one of her donors for a drink."

"And you didn't go with her?"

"No. I was tired."

"And now you're here." I couldn't fight my smile as I dragged my palm over his erection. My teeth sank into my bottom lip for a brief moment before I said, "You don't feel so tired, Dr. Maxwell."

"Quiet," he ordered, and then he somehow managed to shove the tight skirt up to my waist. I busied myself with unbuttoning and unzipping his pants, then shoving them down, and he wasted no time when his dick was free.

He thrust his way inside me and let out a loud groan, like being inside me was the best feeling in the world.

When was the last time he did anything with Lola? I was curious. The way he recklessly rocked into me, it seemed he hadn't had any in weeks, and it had been about two weeks now since that night in his man cave.

I was surprised Georgia hadn't said anything, but I assumed he had spoken with her, making it clear to her that she had to be quiet when I filled him in.

Corey took a moment to withdraw and lay on his back. I

took the initiative and climbed on top of him, my palms flat on his chest, giving him the best ride of his life. His groans were like gold. His hands on my body were like winning an award.

It didn't take him very long to come. Corey was so sexy when he did, especially as his neck tensed and his muscles tightened beneath my hands, and I relished the fact that I'd caused him to. I didn't care that I didn't get pleased myself. Watching him let go because of what I had between my legs was enough for me. I felt powerful. In control. He was at my service, and my job was to please him.

I rolled over after the final upward thrust of his hips and sighed as I lay on my back beside him. We both stared up at the ceiling, breathing through the moment. It was our first time having sex, and it was just as great as I'd imagined it would be.

Quick. Passionate. Intense. Thoughtless.

"I'm pretty sure Lola is cheating on me," Corey finally said after a while.

That caught me by complete surprise, and what a fucking buzzkill. I sat up to look him in the eye. "How do you know?"

"I just know. She has before. She has her moments, I guess." He sat up and put his back to me. "I know she didn't just go meet a donor. She went to meet her current fuck boy."

"But why would he be in New York?"

"Oh, come on, Ivy. Don't act like you know nothing about her affair," he grumbled, looking over his shoulder at me.

"I don't," I confessed, and he looked away. "I didn't even know she was having an affair until now. I didn't know she'd cheated on you before either."

"She doesn't talk to you about him?"

"No," I retorted. Why were we even talking about Lola? So what she was having an affair? So was he. Shouldn't he have been focused on me instead?

"I guess that's a good thing. Means she doesn't take him

seriously. He'll probably be at the gala tomorrow. Some guy named Eddie. I looked him up when I saw his name in her phone one night. Fucking asshole."

I climbed on my knees behind him, draping my arms over his shoulders. "How can I help?" I asked, laying kisses on the crook of his neck. I was tired of talking about Lola. For once I didn't want our time together to have anything to do with her.

I took his groan as a sign to continue. All he needed was to be distracted. With my hand, I turned his head so that he was looking over his shoulder. I kissed his supple lips, and then I climbed onto his upper thighs, nestling my sex on top of his.

"Why don't you just leave her?" I asked, rocking my hips forward and backward, grinding on top of his hardening cock.

"Why would I? We've been married for sixteen years."

"Because you could have someone who would never cheat on you. Someone who would be ready to please and take care of only you. Does Lola do that?" Damn it. I was just like him. Could never keep her damn name out of my mouth.

"No."

"Has she ever?"

"She used to . . . before she opened her stores and started the charity."

"So, what, you only got one or two years of Lola pleasing and taking care of you?"

"Our sex became empty very quickly. She'd only want me if she wanted to try for a baby. Eventually, I got fed up."

I leaned up and sank down his hard length, and he shuddered a wet breath. "You poor thing," I crooned. "Well, you should consider making some changes," I breathed on his mouth and he cupped my ass in his hands. "Do something that will make you happy."

"Like what?" he groaned, squeezing.

"Like be with me."

"I just met you."

"So what?"

"So . . . I know nothing about you."

"But you love how I feel around you."

He didn't respond to that, but he didn't have to for me to know it was true. Corey held me close to his body, splaying one of his large hands on my upper back and using the other to guide my hips.

"What are you after, Ivy?" he rasped on my lips, and then he thrust his way up, burying himself inside me, making me moan.

I could only smile as that question left his lips. "Only you, Dr. Maxwell. Only you."

CHAPTER THIRTY-ONE

Let me ask you this, my dear therapist. Is it wrong to be infatuated with a woman's husband? Does it matter that it's the husband of a woman you despise? No, really, what do you think?

Most people involved in affairs feel some kind of guilt or shame, but I felt none of that while sleeping around with Corey. In my eyes, Lola deserved what was happening behind her back, and hell, me fucking her husband was the least I could do.

Maybe Corey felt some shame, but that was only because being with me was his first affair. He'd soon come to realize that he had nothing to feel sorry about because I was perfect for him.

His wife cheated, so he cheated. He felt good with me and not with her.

Fair was fair.

None of that mattered at this particular moment, though. No, no. It was Passion Gala night! Showtime, baby! I had to show the world just how stunning I could be.

I was currently sitting next to Lola in her presidential suite with bright lights in my face and a makeup artist studying my features, trying to figure out what look would match the dress I had hanging up in the back of Lola's closet.

My hair was done, courtesy of a woman named Pamela who Lola had hired for us. She'd wrapped my hair in rollers that resulted in big, bouncy curls and then pinned my hair in a half-up, half-down hairdo.

Lola mentioned that Corey had decided he would get ready after our makeup was done, so he was nowhere in sight. Not that I needed him to be. The night before he hadn't left my room until shortly after midnight, and amusingly enough, I'd taken a shower and gone down to the bar after he left and guess who I saw? Lola! Hanging off the arm of some delicious silver fox. He was handsome and definitely looked like more than a typical *fuck boy*, as Corey had called him.

I was close to having my makeup finished when Lola looked at me through the mirror in front of us. "So, are you excited about tonight?" she asked, her eyes wide and hopeful.

"I am. And you were right. This does feel like I'm getting ready for prom. I can't believe I missed out on this feeling."

"It's like a high, right?"

"Yes, a high."

"Told you." The witch grinned.

The artist started on my makeup, leaving me no room to continue a conversation with Lola. Good. I needed to focus on myself.

As expected, my makeup was everything and more. The artist did an amazing job and snapped a picture for his portfolio so he could remember this look forever.

Then it was time. I needed to squeeze into my dress. I stepped out of my regular clothes as I stood in one of the corners in Lola's room, then picked up the designer dress by the hanger, sliding off the spaghetti straps.

I dressed carefully, making sure not to stretch the dress too much at the bosom or tear anything. Everything had to be perfect. I needed to be perfect. "Lola, can you zip me?" I asked as she stepped around the corner in SPANX.

"Of course." She stepped behind me and lightly tugged on the zipper, bringing it up to the center of my back. Then she stepped around me and beamed. "You're a doll, Ivy. So beautiful."

I could only smile at her. I picked up the scarf Bobbi had made to go with the dress and ran it through my fingers. It would cover my shoulders and block some of the cold from the A/C as we entered the Green Garden Hall.

In no time, Lola was dressed, and then there was a knock at the door. Corey was back. He needed to get dressed too. "I'll leave you two alone and find Noah," I said as I made my way to the door.

Lola slid a foot into a silver heel. "Okay. We should be down in a few moments."

I glanced at Corey. He gave me a faint smile as he began unbuttoning his shirt. I bet he was still thinking about the night before. Our own dirty little secret.

I left, and I felt good, Marriott. I was glowing. At first I'd hardly even recognized myself in the mirror when my makeup was completed. It was the most I'd ever worn, but now I understood why so many women wore lots of it. It makes you feel good—sexy even. Your lashes are longer, your lips look fuller, and your flaws are concealed.

I sent Noah a text and he responded quickly, telling me he was already in the lobby, and that the limo was waiting.

"Look at you!" Noah squealed when he saw me coming toward him. "You look like a million bucks, girl!"

I blushed. It felt good to be noticed.

Olivia was in the lobby too, standing near the door. Her dress was an A-line, pale yellow tulle dress. It was a simple dress. Nothing too extravagant. I liked that about Olivia. She didn't care for attention. Noah had on a simple black-and-white tux.

Olivia's phone was pressed to her ear for a moment, and then she lowered it and rushed to us. "Okay, first off you look great, Ivy! Second I think we really need to get going. Genevieve said she needs us to look over a few things before they open the doors."

"I just texted Lola because I got the same text from Genevieve," Noah said. She said she'd catch another black car and will meet us there. She's okay with us handling whatever needs to be done."

Ugh. It was just like Lola to be fashionably late. Most times she was on time, but for this? No. She'd glide in wearing her feathery gown and everyone would notice and gasp and stare, awestruck.

"Okay," I said. "Well, let's get this show on the road, then."

So, Passion Gala wasn't exactly like prom, Marriott. For starters, I didn't think I would be *needed* so much. The ceiling light above one of the bars was flickering, so we had to tend to getting the bulb changed. One string of fairy lights wasn't lighting up in the hall, so Genevieve and Noah had to quickly get a new pack from the storage room and replace it. It was too cold in the ballroom, so we had to wait for the room to heat up before letting anyone in.

It was annoying . . . well, at first. After the doors opened and guests rolled in, it got better. Drinks were passed from the bars and hors d'oeuvres began to shuffle through the crowds, and it wasn't so bad. I'd had a drink myself to loosen up.

The gambling was first, and the laughter was boisterous, and people were jolly, which was Lola's endgame. To her, the drunker a person was, the more they'd gamble, and the more a person gambled, the more money the charity made.

All would have been well for me if I hadn't caught a man's

eye. His name was John Hampton. He was co-CEO of a popular yacht club and owned several golf clubs all over the States. He was also married, which I didn't care so much about, but he constantly told me how much I reminded him of his wife, and that was not cool. What woman wanted to be hit on constantly just to be reminded that they looked like the man's wife? Lola had arrived around twenty minutes after the doors opened and noticed him talking to me. She gave me a keep-it-up-buttercup wink. Ugh. She sucked, Marriott.

According to Olivia, John Hampton was a huge donor. He gave heftily to Lola's cause. He also loved to refer to Lola as a sister and close friend, but he spoke of her like an old fling.

"You know Lola and I went to college together?" John said to me during dinner. Lola was on the opposite side of the table, next to Corey, flat out ignoring him. "She was the one girl every guy wanted. I remember telling her that she'd go places; now look at her." John sipped his whiskey. "So, what about you? Where'd you come from and how long will you be in New York?" He gave me a sleazy smile.

I was repulsed. To put it simply, John wasn't all that attractive. He was balding badly but trying to hang on to what hair he could, and his breath smelled like sardines. Not only that, but he wasn't where my sights were. My eyes were only on one target, and that was the doctor sitting on the opposite side of the table, right next to Lola.

A woman named Samira was seated on the other side of me with her fiancé, a retired professional golfer named Roland Graham. Samira and Roland were an interesting couple. He hovered around her like a shadow. When she spoke, he was very attentive, and if any man dared look her way or tried to mingle with her, he was in that man's face, giving him a silent threat to back off. But for the most part they seemed like a nice couple. Strange, but nice. I wished I had a guy who was possessive with me, but in a healthy way, you know?

As the night carried on, I noticed that Lola was drifting further and further away from Corey. Corey hung out in a corner with a few men, sipping his drink and pretending not to notice, but I took note of the subtle slide of his eyes as he looked for his wife.

Lola had been drinking, it was clear. She was loose. And it didn't help that the silver fox from last night was there. He came in an hour late, dressed impeccably in a tuxedo and black tie. He walked in as if he owned the place, catching the eye of several women.

"Who is that man?" I asked Olivia as we stood by the bar with our drinks.

She looked where I was looking, watching the silver fox carry himself across the room. He was tall and broad-shouldered, with a chiseled jaw and a thin nose. "Oh! That's Eddie Witherspoon. He used to be a professional basketball player, but he retired and started up his own real estate agency. He only invests his time in selling mansions and high-dollar condos, and because he used to be a big-shot athlete and is known as this delicious bachelor and all that, he gets the best clientele. Closes easily on most of the mansions and condos he sells. Lola says he's really good at what he does."

Yeah, I bet he was.

I couldn't help watching Eddie make his way to the bar. He ordered a drink, and when it was handed to him, he turned and gave the room a scan. I knew who he was looking for.

He went straight for Lola and pressed a hand to the small of her back. She turned to him and smiled, laced one of her arms around the back of his neck to hug him—because the other was occupied with a drink—and then placed a not-so-friendly kiss on his cheek. I glanced at Corey. He'd watched the whole encounter.

His jaw ticked, and as Lola continued speaking to Eddie—

or should I say flirting with him—Corey carried his drink with him out of the ballroom.

This was my chance.

"Text me if you need anything," I told Olivia, and I walked away, steering my way through the crowd to get to the exit. I entered the hallway, where fairy lights were strewn between white drapes and vine garlands, giving the gala elegant vibes. I moved past the candles in lanterns, my heels clicking on the marble floors, and rounded a corner.

Corey was standing in the hallway to the restrooms, his head bowed and his back against the wall. "Corey?" I called, and he picked up his head instantly. "Are you okay?"

He blinked. Once. Twice. "I'm fine."

"I saw what happened. Eddie talking to Lola. I saw her with him last night too, by the bar in the hotel. It was after you left my room."

Corey sighed. Shook his head. "That explains why she wasn't back in the room when I got there."

I stepped closer to him and grabbed one of his hands. "I'm sorry you're going through this." I felt bad for him, Marriott. I loved him, cared about his feelings, and he was hurting. I needed to make him feel better.

I lifted a hand and cupped his cheek, turning his head so he could look at me. His eyes flickered down to my lips. My breasts. Then my lips again.

I leaned in and kissed him on the lips, and I was pleased when he lowered his guard and deepened the kiss.

I pulled back and looked down the hall. No one was around. Everyone was in the ballroom, drunk and oblivious. I took his hand and went past the restrooms to get to one of the closets. It was one of the bigger closets, with folded tables inside, and table covers and leftover decorations.

Corey closed the door behind us and had me wrapped up in his arms in a matter of seconds. I moaned when he bundled my dress up to my waist just to pick me up in his strong arms and attack my throat with kisses. My back slammed into the edge of a shelf. It hurt a little, but I didn't care. I had Corey in my arms, right in front of me, and it was what I'd wanted since he had to leave the night before.

He placed me back on my feet and turned me around. I let out a wet gasp as he pushed up my dress again, breathing raggedly and entering me from behind. My fingers gripped the edge of the wooden shelf, a loud moan escaping me.

"Yes, Corey," I breathed. "Fuck me. Forget about her and take me."

And he did. He fucked me, slammed into me, and my moans grew louder while his grunts and groans mixed with my sounds of pleasure. The wood of the shelf felt raw against my palm as I held on to it to keep my balance, but he was raw inside me, cupping one of my breasts in his hand.

For a split second I wondered if I would end up pregnant with Corey's baby. He didn't use protection and I wasn't on birth control of any kind. He wasn't being careful, and I wondered if maybe he didn't care if I ended up with his child. That would certainly be good enough reason to leave Lola and be with me. She couldn't carry a child in her womb for him, but I could. He'd have an obligation to leave.

I guessed I would get to that when it happened. Until then, I took joy in letting Corey release some of his aggression with me. Lola wasn't thinking about him and he knew it. She was more concerned about the contributions and Eddie Witherspoon's dick than her husband.

Corey let out a raspy groan and pressed his forehead to the back of my head as he performed one last thrust. "Fuck. You're so good, Ivy."

So good? He thought I was *so good*.

I sighed as he pulled out, and as he adjusted his pants, I fixed my dress.

It was quiet for a moment.

"We should leave early," I said.

"Why?" he asked without making eye contact.

"She won't notice."

"Then she'll leave with him." Corey fixed his tie. "I need to get back."

He turned and walked out of the closet, leaving me standing in the dark. What the hell was up with him? Why couldn't he just get over her already?

Oh yeah. Right. Because he'd been married to her for sixteen years. I swear, Marriott. He was making this harder than it needed to be. He had the perfect woman right in front of him—me—and he was wasting the night worrying about Lola and Eddie.

Inhaling and exhaling, I opened the closet door and walked out. I went back to the ballroom. The atmosphere had changed since I walked out to find Corey. The lights were dim, and only the strings of fairy lights on the white drapes across the ceilings gave visibility. It was louder now, and the bars were overcrowded.

Everyone was drinking. Laughing. Chatting.

And then a song came on and I froze. "Keep Ya Head Up" bumped out of the speakers and Tupac's voice brought back memories.

Back rubs and forehead kisses. A warm bed and a night-light. Glowing star stickers on the ceiling. Quick spaghetti dinners with dollar corn bread. Daddy teasing Mama over dinner about her new hairdo, when really he loved it. Me laughing when Mama scrunched her nose and teased him back about his naked chin.

Daddy always looked weird without his beard.

Why was I thinking about my parents? Why was I here? My heart beat faster as the lights above spun around me. I wanted to cry . . . but I was over that phase of my life. I was done crying, Marriott. I was here now. I'd gotten into Lola's life, slept with Corey . . . but was it enough? Was it really worth it?

A woman laughed, and I looked over, watching as she

threw back her head and pressed a hand to her chest. Pearl earrings in her ears and a pearl necklace on her neck.

They had no worries. No problems.

Everyone was so self-absorbed. Bragging about their million-dollar homes, Ferraris, and Porsches.

Trips to Cambodia, Egypt, and Croatia.

Money, money, money.

It was too much, Marriott. So many unappreciative people in one room—trust-fund kids or people who'd embezzled all they had and somehow never got caught.

I needed to get out. I needed to get these thoughts out of my head.

I turned to go back out, but before I could, Lola was walking up to me. Faith and Arabel were with her, and Corey was trailing behind her.

"Tonight has been so amazing!" Lola sang. Then she took my hands and dragged me to the dance floor. "Dance with me, Ivy! We deserve this!"

But I didn't want to dance with her. She made me, though, and I couldn't reject her in front of everyone, so I twirled with her and let the bass of the music run up the soles of my heels, but I didn't put much effort into it.

Corey came to the floor to cut in and dance with Lola, but she turned her back on him, preferring to dance alone. I frowned at Corey, and he frowned as Eddie met up with Lola, doing some goofy dance move that made her giggle along the way.

She started dancing with him. Not touching, but their eyes were connected.

Corey was pissed now. He stepped between them, and I saw him mouth the words, *I've had enough of this shit!*

"What are you talking about?" Lola said, shocked by his outburst.

"You don't have to do this shit in my face, Lola!"

Eddie looked uncomfortable, but he didn't move.

Lola lightly moved Corey aside, but only after placing a kiss on his cheek and telling him to calm down, that they were only having a good time and it was all business. Then she looked up at Eddie and said, "Sorry about that." And she walked off with him, arm in arm, not once looking back.

I was stunned. Fucking stunned. Just like that, she'd chosen Eddie over Corey. In his face. In *everyone's* face. Samira was there. She was just as stunned as I was. She saw it all, but pretended not to, instead turning to her fiancé when he came up to her with a fresh drink and a tense smile.

Livid, Corey stormed off the dance floor and out of the room. His elbow bumped into Noah's arm, and Noah spilled some of his drink on the floor.

I needed this distraction. I left the dance floor.

"What the hell is wrong with him?" Noah asked as I walked by. He was clearly upset by the spilled drink.

"No idea. We should probably go check," I said, and hoped Noah would decline.

"No, girl. That's okay. I think I'm going to cling to my positive attitude and stay right in here." He walked away to talk to Faith and Arabel and their husbands by one of the poker tables.

I left the ballroom. Corey wasn't in the hall or the lobby, so I checked outside.

He was standing on the sidewalk, talking on his phone. "See you in a minute." Corey lowered the phone.

"You're leaving?"

"Yes." His voice was cold and standoffish.

"I'll come with you."

"For fucking what, Ivy? I don't need you to come with me. Stop being so goddamn desperate."

I blinked quickly. "What did you just say to me?"

"I said you're being desperate. Stop following me around." He took a step away from me.

"Stop trying to shut me out, Corey. You're upset and I get that, but I'm here for you."

He narrowed his eyes. He was about to say something, but a car pulled up to the curb. The driver climbed out and went around to open the back door.

Corey gave me his back and climbed into the black car. The driver looked at me, confused about whether I was included in the ride or not. I put my focus on Corey again.

"Just come on, Ivy," Corey finally muttered, and my heart raced. I got in the car. The black leather was warm and it smelled like roses.

We rode in silence back to the Mandarin, and once we were out of the car, Corey tipped the driver and we went inside, where the heat was blowing and classical music serenaded from hidden speakers.

Corey didn't say a word to me as we rode up the elevator. He stopped on my floor and walked out first. I opened my clutch, taking out my room key card and swiping it through the lock on the door.

I walked in and put down my phone and clutch.

Corey went to the minibar and poured himself a drink. Scotch. I should have known.

Is it bad that I was really starting to reconsider this affair with him? I didn't realize Corey was so . . . *emotional*. It was obvious Lola didn't love him all that much—that she had fallen out of love with him years ago—so why was he clinging to her like some lost puppy? Why hadn't he fallen out of love too and tried to move on?

He could be with me, right, Marriott? Leave her, take me, and be happy? I knew I could make him happy. I had it in me. I was good at putting smiles on people's faces, even if I had to fake it a little bit. I hated working retail, but I was good at faking that.

Corey sipped his drink and looked at me through the corner of his eye. "Come here," he commanded.

And I did. I walked to him.

He put down his glass behind him before lifting one of his hands to grip a handful of my hair. It ripped at the root and I hissed at the sting of it.

"What are you doing?" I asked, and my heart beat harder because this felt familiar to me . . . and not in a good way.

Corey pushed me forward with his body until the backs of my knees hit the edge of the bed and I fell down. Then he climbed on top of me and locked a hand around my throat.

"I want you to pretend to be Lola tonight."

"What?" I croaked. He was out of his damn mind. The last thing I wanted to be was Lola.

"Shut up," he snarled, and he gripped my throat tighter. "I'm so sick of your shit. Flirting with that motherfucker, Eddie. Doing it in my face. Dancing with him. How is his dick, huh?"

I tried to swallow. He squeezed. "Okay—Corey, no, I don't like this. I don't want to be Lola." I tried to sit up, but he forced me back down with a heavy hand.

I panicked, then, and his eyes widened. He lowered his face. "How is his dick, huh? I know it's not bigger than mine. And you want to know how I know?" He was pushing up my dress as he asked, and one of his hands forced my legs apart. He moved my panties aside with rough fingers.

"Corey." My voice broke.

"Just shut up." He was working on unfastening the button of his pants. Unzipping them. His dick was hard and free. I tried to sit up again. Another hand came down on my chest, forcing me back on the bed.

"Stop this," I demanded, but my voice came out weaker than intended. "I'm done with this game."

"Who said it was a game, Ivy? Give me whatever I want. Please me whenever I want. You said you would do it." He bent over me and propelled his hips forward to thrust himself inside me. A sharp breath broke out of me. "So, do it, Ivy. Be Lola. Give me what I want."

Fuck him. I wasn't Lola. He was out of his fucking mind, and I was about to shove him off me and tell him to get the fuck out until he said something I didn't quite expect.

"I know what you're after," he growled in my ear, and my blood ran cold. "You want my money. You want *her* life. Well, you want it so bad," he rumbled on my neck, "this is how you get it. No one said having me would be easy, babe."

CHAPTER THIRTY-TWO

The gala was over.

That high I'd had as I was getting ready for the night and as I'd fucked Corey in the supply closet? It was gone. Dust.

I hated him . . . well, I felt like I did the day after. My emotions were all over the place. I felt betrayed.

Corey reminded me of bad things that night. Reminded me of Xavier. Too handsy. Too aggressive. Too mean. He'd taken advantage of me, just like Xavier always had. He was drunk, yes, but he knew what he'd said to me. He remembered because after he finished, he left my room and didn't show his face the next morning for breakfast.

I hated that I had to see him on the jet back to Florida, but it was much easier for me to keep a distance and look away. There was also tension between him and Lola. Noah and Olivia sensed it and pretended to sleep in their seats. I sat in my seat, staring out the window, tormented by his reckless behavior.

You don't get it, Marriott. Corey was supposed to be a gentleman. He was supposed to be different, but he'd made me look at him a different way the night of the gala. My perfect night in my perfect dress was ruined because of his reckless, selfish actions. God, I was so sick of everyone being so damn selfish.

I purposely stayed away from Corey and Lola when we got back to Miami. I was grateful Lola was giving us the week off with pay to recover from the success of the gala.

I mean, who was I kidding? I'd said once before that all men were pigs, and I was right. I didn't take Corey as the kind of man who choked women and then forced them to have sex with him.

Now I could see why Lola didn't fuck him as often as he wanted—why she'd walked off with Eddie that night. Corey must have done this to her too.

Corey was an asshole who thought the world revolved around his dick. He needed to get himself under control . . . but I needed to work on forgiving him eventually because he was right about one thing. I *did* want his money and I *did* want a life like Lola's.

I knew that without him, I wasn't going to get any of it, and I'd worked so damn hard. I needed this. I deserved it. I'm not saying money was going to take care of all my problems, but it would be a start.

Forgiveness is such bullshit, though, Marriott.

The one who forgives first never really wins.

I was used to Lola sending me messages and asking me to meet her, but the text I received from her four days into my week-long break didn't settle well with me.

WE NEED TO TALK. COME TO MY PLACE AT 6.

I wasn't sure what to expect, but something in my gut told me she knew about me and Corey. Had he told her about us? Did someone see us in the hallway? See me get in the car with him?

There were so many ways this could go, but for all I knew,

she could just want to talk to me about the gala or Eddie since I saw the whole thing happen.

It wasn't like Lola to demand me to come to her, though. She always asked if I had plans, to which I'd respond that I didn't, and then she'd rope me in and tell me to meet her somewhere, along with a little incentive, like sharing a bottle of wine or going shopping for new shoes.

It was best to get it over with.

I drove to her house in a somber mood and parked in front of the mansion. The door wasn't answered by Georgia this time, though. It was Corey.

I took a step back when I saw him. I wasn't ready to forgive him yet.

"Ivy," he murmured, and his chocolate-brown eyes twinkled like he had actually been longing to see me. He started to form a smile, but when he realized I wasn't pleased to see him, he sighed, then looked over his shoulder.

Realizing the coast was clear, he took a step close to me and said, "Look, Ivy. I'm sorry about what happened the night of the gala. I'd had too much to drink and I was really, really upset with Lola. I'm sorry."

"You choked me," I spat at him. "Do you do that to Lola too when you can't have your way?"

"No—I just let my emotions get the better of me." He lifted a hand to stroke the apple of my cheek. "Don't let this change what we have. I've been thinking, you know. About you and me. You were right about how I need to make changes. Lola isn't going to leave Eddie alone—I know that now after the gala—so I'm working on being separated from her."

"Why not just get a divorce?"

"It's . . . complicated. I have to go about it the right way. We've been married a long time and it would cost a lot of money. I'd have to negotiate so I don't lose too much in the process."

"Sure, okay. I don't have time for your excuses." I rolled my eyes and pushed past him to get inside the house.

Corey caught my hand. "Wait—Ivy, I—"

"Ivy, you're here!" Lola said from down the hall, and Corey quickly released my hand from his and stuffed it in his front pocket.

I focused on her as she stood there, waving and giving me a small smile, but it didn't reach her eyes. Something was off with her today. She was made up as always, wearing a teal blouse, jeans, and sandals.

Corey closed the door with his foot, side-eyeing me as he walked past. I watched him go past Lola, who peered over her shoulder to watch him saunter off. There was still tension between them, I could see.

"You wanted to see me today?" I asked, stepping closer to Lola.

"I did. Let's go out by the pool."

She clearly didn't see Corey grab my hand; otherwise she'd have spoken up about it, right?

I followed her through the kitchen and met her by the lounge chairs under the pool umbrellas. It was fall in Florida—still warm outside, but not deathly hot like it is over the summer.

Lola sat down, and on the table was a bottle of red wine and two glasses. I took the seat across from her, forcing a smile at her as she poured the wine into the glasses. She didn't smile back.

She handed one of the glasses to me and I took it, nodding appreciatively. She sipped hers and I did the same.

"So, you're probably wondering why I asked you to come over." She gulped down more wine. "Well, there is no easy way to have this conversation, but I, um . . . I spoke to Georgia a few days ago."

Georgia? Oh fuck. So she did tell Lola about me and Corey? That bitch! "Okay. What's going on?"

"Well, she seems to think that . . . well, that you're relevant to something that occurred in my past."

I put down my glass on the table. This wasn't what I thought I'd be hearing.

"Your name isn't Ivy Elliot, is it?" Lola questioned, and my heart slammed to a standstill.

I tried to move my mouth, but it remained glued shut.

"You don't have to answer that. I know you aren't." Lola sighed. She crossed her legs and looked toward the bay.

"Lola, I don't know what Georgia told you, but—"

"She didn't have to tell me much. She thought that perhaps she was overthinking things, so she let it go. But when she told me that she'd seen you snooping around in my office, I hired a private investigator to get answers for me, had him look into you."

I swallowed hard, unable to pull my eyes away from hers. She knew. She fucking knew. It was happening now.

"Your name is Ivy *Hill*. Your parents were Dante and Carol Hill. They died on April 13, 2007, in a car wreck. They died because of me." Lola's eyes were full of tears at this point and fuck, Marriott, I didn't know what to do. All I could manage was a blink to battle my own tears.

This wasn't the way I thought the conversation would go. Why did it feel like she had the upper hand? Like she was going to make me feel guilty when, really, she should have been the one lost, scared, and nervous as hell? I was supposed to be the one to shove this news in her face. I was supposed to be the one who won, got Corey, took half her money through him, and then told her that she was a selfish bitch afterward.

"Lola, I—"

"Why didn't you tell me, Ivy?" she asked, and her voice broke, as if she were really hurt. And maybe she was. She trusted me. Liked me. Told me things. "All this time you knew so much about me, pretended to be my friend, and you were their *daughter*."

I bit into my bottom lip until I tasted blood. "You have no right to be upset with me for lying," I said in an even tone. "Yes, my name is Ivy Hill. Yes, I found you and pretended to be your friend, but that's only because you ruined my fucking life! I loved my parents. They were all I had, and you took them away from me. It wasn't proven, but I know you made the detective on that case keep your name out of the files just so you could protect your own name! You made it virtually impossible for me to find you, let alone get answers about that night! You would have let me live my entire life lost and confused!"

Lola was flabbergasted. Her eyes stretched wide and she stood up and I couldn't believe it, but she dumped her wine in my face. I let out a sharp gasp, standing with her in complete shock.

"You don't know the whole story, you little bitch!" she hissed at me. "You don't know what the fuck happened that day, so don't you stand there and accuse me of ruining your life! I didn't even know the fucking Hills had a daughter until now!"

"No?" I shouted as wine ran over my lips. "Well, what happened that night, then, Lola? Please enlighten me, you fucking *liar*!"

Lola's bottom lip trembled as she stared me in the eye. She slammed down her wineglass on the table and I was surprised it didn't shatter.

"Fine," she muttered. "I'll tell you. I was in St. Petersburg visiting my gynecologist," she said, looking me hard in the eye. She sat back down and I hesitated before doing the same, but I did anyway, only because I needed to hear everything she had to say. "I was nine weeks pregnant at the time. Happy as could be. But on that day I felt like something was wrong. I was getting cramps, feeling ill. I needed to be checked. My doctor couldn't squeeze me in until the afternoon, and it took me about three hours to drive there, so I drove alone. Three hours is far, yes, but this was the best doctor in the state. I was willing to make the drives. I didn't tell Corey about the pain I was having, I just went, but I knew what was happening because it had happened to me before." She drew in a sharp breath. "By the time I got to St. Petersburg it had started to storm, but I needed to get to the clinic as soon as possible. The pain had become even more intense by this point and I was crying. I was—I was driving so fast. Racing through the rain. My GPS told me to take a back road to get to the clinic faster, so I did, but it was a shadowy road, and with the sky so dark from the storm and all those trees, I could hardly see. My phone started ringing and I tried to reach for it, but it fell through the crack on the side of the passenger seat. I was reaching for it while also trying to hold back tears *and* drive. God, I was in so much pain that I couldn't even see straight. Then, before I knew it, I saw a car in front of me pull out of nowhere. I ran into the back edge of the car, and because the roads were slick, the car did a tailspin and slammed into a tree. I was lucky enough to slam on my brakes and stop with minimal damage to myself, but the crash was so loud. I knew someone was going to be hurt. I got out and saw the front of my car was completely wrecked, but it was nothing in comparison to the car that had hit the tree."

Blinking my tears away was impossible at that point. I thought of my parents and the fear they probably felt as they realized their lives were in danger and, soon, coming to an end. I'd heard about the car hitting a tree. It was the same tree I used to climb when I was a little girl.

My parents were cleaning out my grandma's house that day. I remember, because they'd dropped me off at my friend Retta's house to spend the day there while they went to clean it up and toss out old furniture.

My grandma had passed away about eight months before that day and they were thinking about moving into the house, but also considering the responsibility of it. It was an old house—a small, ranch-style, vintage home with a big wooden porch, painted a pale yellow that Mama said would be the first thing to be changed on the outside of the house. The shutters were dark green, and I remember them needing a fresh coat of paint too.

It was close to a lake where gators sometimes roamed, and I had to always be careful there. I could never go past the fence in the backyard. Grandma would scold me.

My grandma didn't have many neighbors close by. The closest was Mrs. Stevens, who was a little over half a mile away, and she was hard of hearing and much older.

They went to that house often to make it a home for us. For *me*. There was a long street in front of the house that led to the freeway, but not many cars took that road because of the cavernous potholes. Across the street was this really big Southern live oak tree. The same tree my parents hit.

The front of their car slammed right into the tree. They both went headfirst through the windshield, their bodies hanging out. I could picture all the blood, their mutilated faces. I always wondered why they didn't pick up the phone—why Retta's mom was so concerned about me that night.

I lowered my head, my throat thick with unshed emotion.

"Ivy, it was never my intention to hurt anyone. I was just trying to get to my doctor so I could get checked. I didn't want to lose the baby because I had lost one already. It was with a guy I met before Corey, and it was the worst pain of my life. This was much, much worse, though," she said, her voice thick. "Because of my recklessness, I killed *two people*, and because of the wreck, I lost the baby. There was no saving it. I suppose that was my punishment."

I stared at the wineglasses.

"If—if you want, I can give you money. Just name your price and I'll give it to you, but you have to promise to *never* say anything about this to anyone, and you have to agree to sign a confidentiality agreement."

I stood up and knocked over the wineglasses and the bottle of wine. The burgundy liquid leaked on the cement ground, pooling around Lola's feet, and she frowned down at it before focusing on me.

"Fuck you and your fucking money!" I snapped. "This is what you did with the detective too, right? Shoved your millions in his face? You're such a fucking coward!"

I stormed through the house and through the corridor to get to the front door. Fuck her, Marriott. She can rot in hell.

As I stormed out, Georgia was coming from the driveway with brown paper bags of groceries in her arms. She seemed surprised to see me. I glared at her as I passed by, then snatched my car door open.

"Wait—Ivy!" Lola called, but I refused to let her catch up to me. I started the car and left, tires screeching along the cobblestones of the driveway.

So, this was the truth, Marriott. I knew it now. Lola had a miscarriage and it caused my parents' death. Now I knew why the detective always used words like "accident" and "confidential." I was right. She'd paid him to keep her name off the books.

Could I completely blame her for her pain? No, but she still covered it up. If it hadn't been for some unknown person telling you Lola's name, I never would have known it was her at all.

But . . . there were only two people who could have fed me Lola's name. There was Corey, but if he'd known who I was from the start, he never would have slept with me, and considering how hooked on Lola he was, he wasn't going to sabotage their marriage with this. It would have ruined him too.

That only left one other person.

The same person who'd informed Lola that I was relevant to her past, that I'd been snooping around in her office. Why else would Lola have dug for information about me? Georgia had facts about me. She had proof of some kind.

But why in the hell would Georgia, Lola's *household manager*, do something like that?

PART THREE

THE *PERFECT* RUIN

CHAPTER THIRTY-THREE

GEORGIA

By now you know the truth, Ivy. You know I'm the one who got in touch with your therapist and told her to give you Lola's name. You're a smart girl. I was sure you'd figure it out.

Trust me, it wasn't an easy choice. For starters, I didn't trust you with that kind of information. I knew it could make or break me if you had the name. You were just a little girl. An angry, lonely, little girl. You'd made so many mistakes that it was almost sad to know you only made them because you grew up without parents.

What was with that boyfriend of yours anyway? Xavier. A drug-dealing hothead who had been arrested three times for possession. What did you see in him anyway? I've always wanted to know. He was six years older than you and lived in a shitty apartment, and you called his place home. You became obsessed with the idea of him, until you realized he was a no-good man. Just as you did Dr. Maxwell.

See, that was your problem. You obsessed and obsessed until you became bored with the ideas, the fantasies, and I didn't know if I could use that to my advantage or for what needed to be done, but I decided to take that risk. Why? Because I saw something in you, Ivy. I saw potential. I saw fury, and I knew that fury would lead you to do things you never thought possible.

All those years you spent wondering who killed your parents, and why the person was never named in news outlets, why Detective Shaw refused to tell you. Well, you found out, and you can thank me for that.

Before I take this any further with you, let me go back to Lola.

I kept her secret in the depths of my heart, and you know what she did? She resented me for knowing the truth. I realized after a while that Lola wasn't ever going to fire me. Firing me would have meant losing my confidentiality, and she didn't want that.

I knew too much, and with what I had on Lola, I could have tarnished her entire career. But I didn't. I still cared about her—cared for her like a sister—but it wasn't until later that I realized she didn't see me the same way I saw her.

Lola's miscarriage and the fact that she killed your parents set something off inside her. I don't know how to explain it, but she became bitter in a sense. I mean, don't get me wrong, she was always the perfect friend for all her rich besties, and even that talkative bitch Keke, but when she was home alone, she was the complete opposite of perfect.

No, in fact she was a fucking *bitch*. She requested her favorite drink every day, a raspberry gin cocktail with lime. It was always that, or wine. Either way, she'd have three or four glasses of whatever drink was available. She drank heavily, hoping it would mask her guilt and shame.

Lola felt like she had some kind of power over me. My marriage was rocky, so I finally built up the courage to ask Lola if I could move out of the mansion and live with Dion. She flat out told me I couldn't.

"I need you in this house more than ever now, Georgia.

I'm sure your husband will understand," she said while reading an article in a popular magazine about herself.

But Dion didn't understand. He was fed up, and things
became much worse at home when he lost his job weeks later.
Fired and replaced. No longer the hot sous chef of Louie's.
He was struggling to find another job because he had no culinary degree. The head chef at Louie's had given him the job
as a spur-of-the-moment thing, as an opportunity, but apparently Dion was becoming stale and making too many mistakes
in the kitchen. He blamed his mistakes on me not being there
for him, his problems at home.

That meant I *had* to work. I really, really had to work, and
I couldn't fight Lola about moving out. I couldn't quit my job
when we needed the money more than ever. I had to make
my marriage right again.

Dion hated knowing that I couldn't quit. He hated my job
because it was the reason I was never home. He hated that the
only time I could come to him was after ten at night, when
Lola and Corey no longer needed me or had evening plans.

And don't get me started on the sex. We hardly had sex
anymore because I was so tired after working. Lola's demands
were catching up to me, and I swear, they were going to drive
me crazy.

Georgia, I thought I told you I wanted a vegan dish tonight?

*Georgia, you're really starting to be the worst household manager
I know! Don't you realize that?*

Georgia, what the fuck is wrong with you?

Lola asked me those questions often, but the very last was
the one she asked when I dropped a dish in front of her. The
dish shattered on the floor and I was really set off. It was my
last straw for the day.

What Lola didn't know was that Dion wanted a divorce.
It turned out he was cheating on me, and had been for going
on five months. He'd found someone else—someone more

available to him. Someone who could soothe him, and she made pretty great money too, so he could mooch off her.

"What is going on with you?" Lola asked when she hung up the phone. She stared down at me with her judgmental hazel eyes.

"I just . . . I think I need a small break today," I whispered.

"Well, take a break, and then get your shit together, G. I can't deal with this right now. You're supposed to be taking care of my house and causing me less stress, not feeding into it."

"I know. I'm sorry," I apologized. "I'll clean this up."

Lola gave me a repulsed once-over and then shook her head and left the kitchen. I picked up the pieces of the broken dish and threw them away, then went upstairs to my room to take a shower. After that, I stared at the divorce papers, which were on my desk, trying to figure out how I'd gotten there.

Only a year before, I was happy with Dion. We would lie in bed or on the sofa watching movies and munching popcorn and M&M's. He'd cook special meals for me. He'd make me forget about my long days and nights at the mansion with foot rubs and stories from his childhood. I thought we'd be stronger than this—that we could be spending a few hours apart a day for our marriage. But that's the thing about love, Ivy. Love is no good for you, and it can blind you.

For the most part I did what needed to be done for Lola. But I wasn't feeling any better doing it. I felt sicker, and the smell of the cleaner I used to wipe the counters suddenly made me want to vomit. The food I had to set on the table for Lola and her guests always smelled spoiled or rotten.

Something was wrong with me, you see . . . and then it hit me what it could possibly be, and I drove to the nearest pharmacy, bought a pregnancy test, and took it home.

And just like that, after peeing on a measly stick, I found out I was *pregnant*. It was Dion's baby of course. I didn't see this as a bad thing, though. I figured this would be my way back to him. I was pregnant with his child. He'd forget about his new girl toy, cancel the divorce, and be with me again to start our family. He'd forgive me for not being as present for him as I should have been.

I thought that would work, Ivy, I really did. But it didn't. The first question Dion asked when I called and told him the news was, "Are you quitting your job at the mansion?"

To which I replied, "Why would I quit? You haven't found a job yet and with a baby, we'll need the money."

"You can find another job," Dion snapped. "I'm sick of you working at that damn place."

"But, Dion, she pays me good. We need the money."

Dion sighed, clearly fed up. "You know what, G, talk to me when you can put me before that fucking job. If you're so good at it, you can get another one with flexible hours. You know how many people would be glad to have a woman who worked for *Lola Maxwell* working for them? I'm sure many of them will let you negotiate your hours." He groaned, sounding irritated. "That woman abuses your freedom, and you just let her. What the hell are you gonna do when you get bigger with the baby and can't do shit around her house? You think she's going to keep you? No. She's going to toss your ass aside and find someone who is more committed. Someone who doesn't want a damn baby."

And you know what? Dion was probably right. I hadn't thought that far ahead. What would Lola have done if I told her I wanted to start a family? It was never stated in my contract that I couldn't start a family while working for her. There was even a clause for maternity leave and everything, but would Lola live up to that? Would she be fair about it? There was no way she would just shove me aside like trash, not after all I knew and how hard I worked for her.

Dion didn't want a baby—at least not with me. That

much was clear from the way he hung up on me. But I wanted it, so I decided to keep it, despite what he had to say. Lola wouldn't release me or shove me aside. She had been pregnant herself, and even though it hadn't lasted long, she'd understand.

She had to . . . right?

CHAPTER THIRTY-FOUR

Wrong.

For someone who'd started up her own charity for pregnant women and single mothers, Lola didn't understand my side of this one bit.

I told Lola I was pregnant the same week I found out and mentioned that if I was slower around the house, that was why. I saw she didn't want to flat-out get rid of me, so she hired some girl named Viola to step in and perform household manager duties whenever I felt too sick to.

That didn't last long, though. Viola sucked at her job, and seeing as I didn't want to be replaced, I sucked up my pregnancy woes and was back on my A game.

Lola had her charity up and running by this point. She left me notes telling me to prepare for an official dinner she'd be having. Some of the wealthiest people in Florida were coming to the dinner to celebrate the charity.

Lola was no fool. Her charity wasn't a real nonprofit organization. She pocketed most of the money that was donated, leaving just enough to pay her staff and to run events.

She was full of shit, but I kept my opinions to myself. After all, I didn't care so long as I was getting paid on time.

Anyway, the day of her dinner party, something was wrong with me. I wasn't feeling well and was a little queasy. I'd assumed I was having some first trimester sickness. There were many aromas floating through the house from Tonia and her cooking staff. Too many for my pregnant nose to keep up with.

I was getting the house ready with the caterers and making sure the servers were ready for the night with their white gloves and serving trays.

Lola wanted everything to be perfect. Many of the donors had never been to Lola's home, so she had some new furniture and décor delivered. She wanted to show off her mansion, let everyone know she had it made.

It was June of 2010. The party was going to be an indoor-outdoor mingle, with special cocktails on the menu. A bar would be set up by the pool, with a bartender to serve guests and get them drunk and happy, and dinner would be in the dining room inside.

As I said, I wasn't feeling well, and as day became night and stars cloaked the dark, lavender sky, I began to feel worse.

Lola traveled through the house, acting as if she were a queen. Her sequined red dress hugged her body tight, accentuating her hips and breasts.

She flirted with several of the male donors, ready for them to sign checks with her name on it. One thing I could say about Lola was that she was very committed. She had grace and charm when need be, and she knew how to talk a man into donating five hundred thousand dollars to support women in need as if she were a car salesman selling Ferraris to retired sixty-year-old men. It was that easy for her.

I think a lot of the men assumed they'd get a peek under that flashy dress of hers, and Lola ran with that. She led a lot of them on, making them believe they could have a piece of her if they donated to her charity.

As I checked in with the chef to make sure dinner was close to being served, a wave of nausea hit me, and I ran out of the kitchen and up the stairs. I couldn't make it to my room, so I headed for the guest bathroom—the one Lola had decorated herself. Lola had decorated several rooms: her bedroom, her office, her thinking room with the big chandelier that I'd watched be installed, and this particular bathroom.

I puked my guts out in the toilet, hoping it would make me feel better. It didn't. I sat on the commode for a while, holding my head, sweat building on my upper lip, trying to get myself together. I had to be perfect for this party—Lola needed me to be—and I tried, I really did, but then a pain came over me, one I'd never had before.

My stomach began to cramp, ten times worse than menstrual cramps. I stood up, and that was when I heard something pitter-patter on the floor. When I looked down, I saw blood.

"No," I whispered. Not on Lola's premium marble floors— the floors she'd spent sixteen thousand dollars on. I picked up the roll of toilet paper and pulled off a big wad, wiping up the blood, but all it did was smear, and more blood trickled down until eventually it became a small puddle around my feet.

I knew exactly what was happening. I'd been pushing myself too hard lately, trying to make sure the Maxwell home was stable so that I wouldn't get fired. But it was too much for my body, apparently. My baby.

"Georgia!" I heard someone call. It was Lola. "Georgia! Where are you?"

I waddled to the door with tears in my eyes. She'd help me. I didn't know what to do. "Lola," I whisper-hissed as I cracked open the door.

She spotted me and I waved for her to come. She frowned, rushing my way. "What in the hell are you doing in there? I need you downstairs," Lola said. "Dinner is supposed to be starting soon."

I opened the door and she looked down at the floor and gasped. "Oh my God! What happened to you?"

"I think something is wrong with the baby, Lola. I need to go to the hospital."

"What?" she snapped. She charged in and stared down at the floor. "How could you bleed all over the floor, Georgia! You do realize guests have to come up here too, right?"

"Lola, didn't you hear me?" I pleaded. "I'm in a lot of pain. I need to go to the hospital right now!"

"Georgia, I told you I would need you tonight! Why would you let this happen tonight of all nights? I have really important people downstairs who are about to donate lots of money to my cause. I can't take you to the fucking hospital right now! I have to be here!"

"I can drive myself," I groaned. "It's no problem. I'll go myself."

"No—you can't go back downstairs right now. The party is shifting inside. People will notice you and I can't have this night ruined." Could she hear herself? I mean, really, could she? I was literally losing my baby and all she cared about was her fucking party.

"I'll tell Corey to call Clyde. He's a good doctor. He can tend to you in your room."

"But, Lola, he'll take a while to get here and I—"

"*GEORGIA!*" Lola screamed in my face. She'd turned red, veins appearing on her neck. "Get the fuck out of here! Go to your room! You'll be fine! I'm fine, aren't I?" She tugged on my arm, pulling me out of the bathroom and shoving me toward my wing of the house. "Go!" she screeched. "While I find someone to clean up this shit."

"Oh my God, why are you acting like you don't care?" I shouted, turning back to face her.

"Because I *don't* care, Georgia! I really don't give a shit about you or a baby you shouldn't even be having! You always need some kind of attention, but I can't give it to you tonight!"

"But I *wanted* this baby!" I cried.

"And I wanted mine, but you don't see me wallowing about it, do you?"

"That's because you killed *two people!*"

A hand struck my face and I released a sharp gasp. She'd slapped me. The slap was loud and it stung. I cupped the left side of my face and stared at her, horrified.

"You wouldn't make a good mother anyway, Georgia. Look at you. You're pathetic. Why do you think I hired you? Someone who has no independence? You work here under contract and I'm damn sure not letting you go. Not after everything you know about me. I let you slide when you married Dion. I figured a lonely girl like you needed a man to get through life, but don't get carried away with your tongue. Now go to your room and wait for Clyde to get here."

This was comical, wasn't it? Well, in a dark way. I thought Lola's miscarriage would make her take this matter more seriously. But all she cared about was her party and the money. My baby meant nothing to her. Hell, *I* meant nothing to her, and I realized it that night.

Corey's friend Clyde did show up and checked me over. He wrapped me in a few blankets and, per Lola's instructions, took me through the kitchen when the guests were outside again, to his car and then to the hospital, but by then it was too late.

The baby was gone. I'd bled everywhere, tried to stop the blood with a pad. The pad was soaked by the time Clyde showed up.

He had no words.

Neither did I.

I stayed the night at the hospital, sobbing. I was alone, with no one to check in on me or talk to me. I called Dion so

I could tell him what had happened, but he didn't answer. Didn't even respond to my text messages. Clyde didn't know me, so of course he didn't stick around. I thought Lola would come to see me the next morning, but she didn't. And you know why? Because she didn't give a fuck about me. She'd said it.

Instead, I checked out when it was time and caught a bus back to Biscayne Bay. I was still hurting, my uterus raw and achy. As I spotted that mansion on the hill with the terra-cotta roof perched beneath the sun, with the big sapphire ocean behind it, something inside me just . . . *snapped*.

It takes a hell of a lot for a loyal woman to snap, you know? I was patient and kind and forgiving before, but I couldn't forgive this. I'd lost something important to me—the only thing that was keeping me going, pushing me through the long hours at the mansion. Getting me through the constant yelling and scolding and coldness. Through my divorce. That one thing that was keeping me going was gone and I was left with nothing at all.

Long gone were the days when I cared about Lola's well-being. Long gone were those memories I'd had of her, when I'd considered her a long-lost sister. I thought I'd take Lola's secret to the grave, but she didn't deserve that from me. She didn't deserve *anything* from me.

Though I could have walked away in that very moment and never looked back, that wouldn't have worked in my favor. I couldn't just leave, not when I knew I had just as much leverage over her as she had over me.

I walked into the mansion, and Lola was sitting by the pool in an orange bathing suit. She just sat there beneath the sun like nothing had ever happened—like she hadn't just told me the night before that she didn't care about me or my baby, who was now gone.

She heard me walk out and sat up on the chair. "Oh, Georgia! I'm so glad you're back home safe, girl!"

"Yeah," I murmured. "Me too."

She stood and came in my direction. "Listen, I'm sorry about last night. I was stressed and had too many drinks and I let my words and actions get the better of me."

I didn't say anything to that. That was more than her actions getting the better of her.

"I know miscarrying is hard. Trust me, it's a horrible pain. Losing something you love instantly and unconditionally." She sighed. "But . . . take this with a grain of salt. Do what I did and let it *empower* you."

Empower me? Wow. She called herself empowered? She was anything but. She was a straight-up piece of shit.

"So, this is what I want you to do. I want you to go upstairs and take a long, hot bath, and when you're done, come back down and I'll have a nice meal ready for you." She turned me around, and I trudged ahead, but before I could disappear, I looked over my shoulder at her. "Go on," she murmured. "I have to go meet Faith in a bit, but I'll be back in time for dinner."

I did take the bath, and I did sit there for a long time. A very, very long time. The water was cold and cloudy by the time I got out. I didn't sit there and wallow, though. No, if anything, Lola was right about not doing that. I couldn't accomplish anything by wallowing about a baby I'd lost, no matter how much I'd loved the idea of becoming a mother. But what I could do was change the course of my future so that I wouldn't suffer again.

So you want to know what I did? When Lola left to meet Faith, I went out to the shed by the pool. I grabbed one of Dr. Maxwell's golf clubs and took it back to the house, then I stomped up the marble staircase and walked right into Lola's thinking room.

There was her chandelier—the most prized possession in the house. She'd been in awe of that stupid chandelier since she'd bought it. She'd told me a million times that it was an embodiment of her. It was a representation of her hard work, a treasure. She'd bought it shortly after opening her charity, with her first check from a donor. She was proud of this chandelier that was worth twenty thousand dollars.

And you know what I did?

I lifted the golf club above my head and slammed the end of the club right into the crystals of the chandelier. I swung at it over and over again, like a kid bashing a piñata, and I have to say, it was fun. Hella fun.

The chandelier fell eventually, crashing down on the waxed floor. I felt just like a lucky kid, then—as if I'd broken the piñata open and revealed all the delicious candy inside.

I was sick of Lola telling me what to do—sick of her for ruining my life. If she'd let me go to the hospital as soon as possible, I wouldn't have lost the baby to begin with. Clyde had even said I should have gone to the hospital as soon as I felt pain, but I was so consumed with helping Lola for the party and doing my damn job that I decided against it.

I suppose I should blame myself for that, but Lola wouldn't have let me leave anyway.

She came back home just in time for dinner, as she said she would, and I told her I'd heard something crash in her thinking room and discovered that the chandelier somehow had fallen and crashed.

She was mortified. Hysterical. She started blaming the staff—the maid who had been on duty earlier that day. She fired that maid and for that I truly was sorry. Coco was a good maid . . . but she'd find another job, I was sure.

I told her I'd clean up the mess, get rid of it, and I swear I saw tears in her eyes as she stared down at her broken crystal treasure. She was obsessed with that chandelier, honestly. She really saw it as a piece of her ice-cold heart.

"I can't even look at this," Lola muttered. "Clean it up immediately, then contact Alonzo to order a new one. Custom-made, just like the first. It won't be the same, but at least I'll have another."

"Yes, ma'am," I muttered, and she stormed off. Lola literally didn't enter that room again until her new chandelier had arrived and she watched the men install it, repeatedly telling them to be careful with it.

It took three months for the new chandelier to come in, but that was my doing. Alonzo would have replaced her precious chandelier right away, rushed the order, but I refused to contact him until a month after her demand for a new one. I rather enjoyed seeing the broken chandelier on the floor. I took my time cleaning it too. I was in no rush to replace it. In fact, I spent the entire next week getting rid of the crystal pieces. I'd walk by the room with a cup of tea and smile at my destruction. Lola's hard work, shattered. All thanks to me.

That chandelier was just the start. I realized I had sacrificed so much for Lola Maxwell and what did I get in return? A divorce. A lost baby. A broken soul.

She'd done that. Lola had broken me.

Now it was my turn to break her.

CHAPTER THIRTY-FIVE

"I want you to rewrite my contract." Three days after losing my baby, this was my demand.

As I'd mentioned before, I had a contract with Lola as household manager that I had printed out and read thoroughly the same night I broke the chandelier.

Per the contract, I was to perform ten years of service for her in her mansion. I could receive up to three vacations a year and take them whenever I wanted, so long as they didn't coincide with any important events or dinners the employer of the home (Lola) had planned, and I also had health care benefits, which came in handy for my tragic and brief stay at the hospital.

I was also under confidentiality, and if I broke it, my employer could terminate me, but we were past that point now. She wasn't going to fire me, so that promise was out the window.

What wasn't included, however, was some kind of bonus or premium after my tenth year, and that didn't sit well with me for some reason. You'd think after working for someone for ten years you'd get something bigger out of it in the end, right, Ivy? Maybe some sort of early retirement fund as a thank-you for dedicating ten years of your life to two of some of the richest people in Florida, or a brand-new car? *Something.*

Lola looked up from cutting her grapefruit to focus on me. She was seated on the deck beneath the pool umbrella, a fresh breakfast laid out for her, and a magazine open next to her dish. "Excuse me?"

"My contract," I repeated. "You're going to rewrite it."

"And why would I do that?"

"Because if you don't, I'll tell the journalist who was sniffing around during the time of the accident you caused that *you* are the reason those people are dead. The journalist had a theory about it being someone famous. Perhaps I'll tell him what I know."

Lola's face turned stoic. She put down her knife, the silver tip glittering as it caught a ray of sunlight, and looked me in the eye. "That accident was almost two years ago. No one would believe you."

"Detective Jack Shaw. He's the one you paid off, right? What if I report him to whoever his boss is? Tell him he wrote you out of the files so he could have five hundred thousand of your dollars? Then he'll have no choice but to confess and hope it will save him his job. You forget, there is a paper trail."

She narrowed her hazel eyes. "Why are you doing this?"

"Because I should be promised something at the end of my contract, especially after everything I've lost because of you."

She scoffed. "Georgia, you're the one who applied for this job—you're the one who wanted to work here. I didn't force you."

"Yes, I did, but I didn't realize what I was signing up for, or that you would be so horrible to me."

Lola ran her tongue over her teeth before saying, "So, you're going to blackmail me into rewriting your contract? And what exactly do you want to change about it?"

"Everything can remain the same. I'll finish my ten years with you and then I'll leave, but I want to be promised ten million dollars by the end of the contract. A million for every year I had to deal with your shit."

Lola lifted her chin. Her eyes shimmered. "You're serious, aren't you?"

"Do I look like I'm kidding?"

"Wow. Okay, Georgia." Lola huffed. "You want me to rewrite the contract, I will. But you will have to sign a non-disclosure agreement immediately, in which you will agree not to use what happened over me anymore. You won't get to hang what you know over my head again, and if you try to blackmail me again, you won't get the ten million dollars you're asking for."

"Fine," I murmured. "But I won't sign it until I see you have the contract written up to guarantee the money."

"Very well." She rolled her eyes. "Now, Corey said he has some news to tell me tonight. Have a steak made for him and something special and vegan for me."

I nodded, but I didn't miss the icy look in her eyes. It was clear she hated me now, but I didn't care. Lola's reputation was precious to her, and ten million dollars would leave a small dent in her finances, but nothing too major, considering she had the charity and her stores to keep her afloat.

It was a small price to pay to keep her perfect reputation, and for what she'd put me through.

I was surprised to see Lola had the contracts ready the following day.

She called me into her office and was seated on one of the chairs, the contracts on the coffee table, pens carefully placed on top of them.

I carefully read the part about the ten million first, but there was one clause I didn't quite like. "What the hell is this?" I demanded. "I have to work for you for *two* terms to get the ten million?" I reread that part of the contract incredulously.

Lola had a smug look on her face when I looked up. "It's that or nothing."

"I'll contact the cops, Lola! I'll tell them everything I heard and what you did!"

"No, Georgia, you won't," Lola snapped, rising from her chair. "And you know why?" she asked. "Because telling the cops or a journalist is too easy, and you'd get nothing out of it. You'd lose money, and you won't find another job like this one because I damn sure won't write you a recommendation letter and no one will want to hire a *snitch*. You want the ten million, you'll have to work for it, G."

Wow. I couldn't believe this.

"What?" She almost laughed. She was cruel that way. "You thought I was just going to hand that much money over to you because you felt you could wave something from my past over my head? You aren't the one at the top, Georgia. You aren't in charge! Didn't you realize that without me you would have nothing? All those stories about how you were desperate for this job, how no one ever appreciated you. Well, I gave you a purpose, and you fucked it up, just the same as you fucked up your marriage. You went into that knowing it wouldn't work out!"

That bitch! I wanted to slap her, pull her hair, even strangle her. But I held it together because she was right about one thing: The ten million was important to me. I needed it so I could start fresh somewhere else, forget about Lola and live my damn life for once.

I'd never get another job as good as this one if I left, and I would have needed Lola's recommendation if I looked for a job with anyone else, especially if I wanted any credibility. I was getting older, you see, and these days rich people were looking for younger people with fresh minds and healthy bodies to keep up with their homes and their lives.

"Just do yourself a favor and sign the NDA," Lola grumbled. "Once that's done, we'll both sign your new contract, you'll finish your first term, and then your second will begin in a few years. It's that simple."

I was vibrating with rage. I flipped through the contract several times, assaulted with emotions I couldn't quite explain. But then I stopped at a clause that I'd misread at first, and I read it three times to be sure I understood it.

Suddenly, I was no longer shaking with anger.

I was fighting a smile.

That clause, and that clause alone, was the *only* reason I signed the new contract. It would have to do, and it was my only way out. It would make me perform the lowest of all lows, but I would have to use it. At that point I was willing to do *anything* to rid myself of Lola. *Anything*.

I willingly signed the NDA because I knew I'd no longer need it. She could have the wreck. Several ideas had hatched in my mind, and now they were sprouting wings, and they were much, much worse than blackmail.

Lola thought she'd won by getting me to sign both contracts. She'd put on a superior grin as she looped the *l*s of her last name. She thought she'd conquered her troubles and put me back in my place.

But the truth was, Ivy, she had no fucking idea what was coming to her.

CHAPTER THIRTY-SIX

IVY

I hated Lola Maxwell with a passion.

My hatred for her was one of the main reasons I'd agreed to meet Corey in Destin for a getaway. Just us two, one-on-one. He'd found my number in Lola's phone and sent me a text after I stormed out, asking me what had happened. I didn't know what to tell him. I didn't need him looking at me differently, and Lola had been vague with him.

According to him, Lola had no idea about our getaway. He had told her he was going golfing with some buddies. Lola also hadn't told Corey who I really was, but she had mentioned that she was heartbroken over finding out some horrible things about me.

She was trying to make me seem like the bad guy while she played the victim. Fortunately, Corey hadn't fallen for it, nor did he care what I'd done to Lola that broke her heart. He was glad that we were no longer friends. It meant he could have an affair without more guilt than necessary, and that it would stay out of the house.

My time spent with Corey was great, though. What, Marriott? Don't think of me like that, okay? I'm not weak. This wasn't just for his benefit.

Anyway, he'd had his boat taken down to Destin, and we spent many special moments on it, having sex in every place we could, sipping mimosas in the morning and guzzling hard liquor at night. His favorite was scotch on the rocks with a lemon peel. I made it for him every night, and he thanked me and gave me a deep kiss.

I could overlook the way he had choked me the night of the gala and the pretending-to-be-Lola shit. After all, no one is perfect. Corey was still ten times the man Xavier was. Plus, I could tell he really wanted more with me, that he wanted to take our relationship to the next level.

"I think I'm going to take my chances and divorce Lola," Corey said one night. We were at our hotel, seated on the oceanfront balcony. It was our third night there.

The moon was the only thing in the midnight sky, with just a smattering of stars. No clouds were in sight. He was sitting in one of the cushioned chair and I was on his lap, stroking the stubble on his chin. I loved when he let his beard grow. Lola loved his face bare. The moon shone down on us like a beacon, as if revealing to the whole world that we were together and having an illicit affair.

"Really?" I asked him.

"Yes. I think we've run our course. She'd be better off single."

"But if you leave her, what does that mean for us?"

"What do you mean? We'll still be together. I want you."

I beamed. "I want you too."

"So, it's settled then. I've looked into a divorce lawyer already. I'll do what needs to be done, and then it'll just be you and me."

I giggled like a schoolgirl and then we made love on the balcony. I wish I could say things were great after that, Marriot, but they weren't.

Our trip was over two days later, and we went our separate ways—me back to my run-down studio apartment in Liberty City and Corey back to Lola. I hated the idea of him being around her, kissing her, pretending to love her. He loved me now, and I'd worked hard for that love. Lola didn't deserve his affection or his attention. He was a good man and she didn't appreciate it.

To my utter surprise, though, Lola sent me a text the Sunday after our trip. Apparently, she wanted to have dinner at seven and make up for what she'd said to me.

I found that bizarre, but then again, it was just like Lola to try to mend things with me so she wouldn't feel guilty for covering up what she'd done. She was lucky I hadn't run off with the information I had to *The Breakfast Club* on the radio, or to *Good Morning America*. But that wouldn't have done me any good.

Corey wouldn't have forgiven me for it, even if he didn't know the truth about his wife or me. He would have hated finding out about me that way anyway. There was no point in telling him about it. Lola did what she did, and she'd confessed to it. Now I had Corey and he was going to divorce her to be with me. That was all I needed.

I figured why not go and meet her? She'd offered money before, and though Corey would have enough for both of us, I knew once he was done with the divorce, it would suck him dry, emotionally and financially.

I would ask her for money now—as much as I wanted. She'd pretty much given me a blank check after dumping her wine in my face. It was time to put that to use, but if that wasn't what she was offering, I'd need a new plan. I needed some way to shut Lola down to soften the blow for Corey after the divorce. My man wasn't about to suffer because of her too.

I dressed well but kept it subtle—a short, floral sundress and sandals. I brushed half of my hair up into a ponytail and then grabbed my keys, heading to Biscayne Bay.

I parked in the driveaway, spotting Corey's car there too. My heart did somersaults at the sight of it. My future husband was around, and that made me one happy girl.

I picked up my purse from the passenger seat, the five-thousand-dollar Prada bag Lola had handed down to me because *she never used it*, slinging the strap over my shoulder and marching to the front door.

Georgia answered, and I scowled at her. It was her fault that things blew up with Lola in the first place. All her suspiciousness and nosiness and watching me at night. If she hadn't opened her big mouth, Lola and I would still be fine and I still would be living the best of both worlds, sleeping with Corey and spoiled with riches by Lola.

I started to walk in, but before I went too far, I turned back to Georgia just as she closed the door. "You're the one who told my therapist Lola's name, aren't you?"

Georgia placed her hands behind her back. "I did, but only because it seemed like it was what Lola wanted at the time. Now, I'm not so sure."

"Why?" I demanded. "What are you not sure about?"

"You're trying to ruin Mrs. Maxwell's life. I suppose feeding that information to Dr. Harold wasn't wise."

"How do you even know about me? About Dr. Harold?"

"I knew about the accident the day after it happened."

"The *accident*?" I snapped. "What makes you think it was an *accident*?" I said through clenched teeth.

"Because Mrs. Maxwell didn't intentionally try to kill your parents, Miss Hill. She was under distress. It was a mistake."

Miss Hill. I hated that she was now using that name, like she couldn't wait to use it—like she'd known it since the day she met me. "A mistake that cost my parents their lives," I grumbled.

Georgia sighed. "Perhaps you should take this up with

her. Mrs. Maxwell is waiting for you by the pool. Would you like me to take your purse? Get you something to drink?"

I looked her over in her uniform and then shook my head. "Whatever." I tossed my purse at her and she caught it with a small grunt. Then I went through the house and into the kitchen to get to the pool. Georgia knew nothing about my past. She had no idea what I'd been through, so she could shut the fuck up. Why she defended Lola so much, I had no clue. Lola treated her like shit.

As mentioned, Lola was standing in front of the pool. Her arms were crossed, her feet wide apart, and her hip cocked. She was wearing a white gown with a gold belt at the waist. There was a cocktail glass in her hand with pink liquid, half empty.

I took a step out and, to my surprise, Corey was also standing out by the pool. I hadn't noticed him from where I was standing by the door. A pillar was in the way, blocking my view of him.

I remained still as Lola turned and faced him. It seemed they were in the middle of a heated conversation.

"I just don't understand why now," said Lola. "Of all the times, and all the years, you want a divorce *now*? There is someone else, isn't there? Someone you've fallen for?"

Corey turned to face Lola, preparing his lips to speak, but when he did, he caught me standing behind her and clamped his mouth shut.

Lola spun around and caught me behind her, and her frown deepened. "What the hell are you doing here?" Lola snapped, clutching her glass tighter.

"What do you mean? You sent me a text asking me to meet you for dinner at seven."

Lola's expression morphed to one of confusion. "I never sent you any sort of text," she spat back. "Why would I want to meet you for dinner? Why are you still lying?"

"You said you wanted to mend things, Lola. I have the message on my phone."

What a cunt. Because Corey was here, she wanted to act like she didn't want me around? I could see I was getting nowhere with her.

Lola wobbled a bit on her heels and then she sighed, walking to an empty chair under the umbrella. "I don't have time for this shit." She groaned, lowering her head and rubbing her forehead with the pads of her fingers.

"How much have you had to drink?" Corey demanded, moving toward her. He had his signature drink in hand, but polished it off. Nothing remained but ice and lemon peel.

"Why do you care?" Lola barked at him, picking up her head. "You don't want to be my husband anymore, right? I'll drink however much I fucking want!"

I remained perfectly still.

"You're angry and you're drunk, just like your father. You knew this divorce was coming one day, Lola. We haven't been happy since that damn wreck."

"What? Why are we even continuing this discussion, Corey?" she shrieked. "Why are we talking about this in front of—"

And just like that, Lola knew. She knew exactly why Corey was continuing this discussion with her in front of me.

She shot off the chair. *"Are you fucking kidding me?"* she screeched. "With *her*, Corey? The fucking *foster* girl? Wow, and I thought finding out about the stripper you fucked in Vegas was bad, but this? This is an all-time low for you, honey! I mean, really!"

Lola stumbled sideways. What? What did she mean, the stripper in Vegas? I was Corey's first affair. And what did he know about the wreck? Did Lola tell him about it? Had he always known she'd done that?

"Lola—" Corey reached for her hand, but she jerked away from him and shook her head.

"Fuck both of you," she seethed, and then she stomped to me. "Especially you, Ivy. You low-down, dirty *slut*. Keke was right about you. You're a psychotic, thirsty bitch."

Lola stormed away, rushing into the house and through the kitchen. "Georgia, get me another drink!" Lola shouted. "Now!"

When she was gone, I turned my attention on Corey. "What did she mean about the stripper in Vegas?" I asked. "And the—the wreck? What did you mean, the wreck?"

"Not now, Ivy," Corey muttered, putting down his glass on a nearby table and rubbing his forehead.

"Yes, now, Corey! How many people have you slept with? You told me I was your first affair!"

"Well, I fucking lied, Ivy! You aren't my first fucking affair!" he bellowed. "I mean, did you really think I would risk my entire marriage over a girl like *you*? You have nothing to offer me but your body! I was fine with that before, but seeing how naïve you are now is making me reconsider a lot of shit!"

I felt like I'd been shot in the heart. He'd lied to me. I'd forgiven him for what he'd done before. He'd snaked his hands around my throat and choked me, tried to get me to be a woman I hated, and I forgave him, but this lie was much worse.

He made me feel special. He made me think I was important to him, but what was this? I was just a pawn in his game—his way out of a bad marriage. He . . . used me, just like everyone else in my life.

"The wreck," I said. "You knew Lola did that? That she killed the Hills?"

"What? What the hell do you know about that?" he asked, glaring.

"Those people were my fucking *parents*!" I screamed. "And she killed them! She ruined my life and you went along with it! You're just as bad as she is!"

Corey seemed confused. I didn't care. I was pissed. I saw red, Marriot. Red. I couldn't think straight. Could hardly breathe. The sun felt too bright and my belly was in knots. I wanted to vomit. Then I wanted to kill him.

I charged toward him with a foreign scream leaving my lungs, slapping him right on the face and then shoving him into the pool. When he was in the water, I jumped in too and pounced on top of him, forcing his head down in the water.

I refused to let up, blinded by rage. I wanted to kill Corey for breaking my goddamn heart. For staying with Lola even after knowing she'd covered up a bloody trail.

And then I heard a scream—a scream so loud it pierced my eardrums.

CHAPTER THIRTY-SEVEN

I looked to my left, noticing Georgia standing in the kitchen. One of her hands was cupping her mouth, the other trembling as she reached for something on the floor. She was petrified.

I released Corey and stared down at him. He was still face-down in the water.

"Corey! Get up!" I snapped.

But he didn't get up. I tugged on his arm, but he didn't budge. "Corey!" I screamed, panicking now. Why wasn't he getting up?

I panicked.

I flipped him over and his lips were blue, his eyes closed. Blood was trickling from his nose. "Oh!" I screamed. "Oh fuck!" My heart was practically beating out of my chest. I splashed away from him and ran to the steps to get out of the pool. Water dripped from me as I ran for the house, my throat thick and my vision blurry.

What the hell was going on? What had I done?

I ran hard and fast in my sandals, but I didn't make it far into the kitchen. I slipped on something wet—the water from the pool on my feet, I assumed—but when I hit the floor with a heavy smack, I realized it wasn't water I'd fallen into at all.

Crimson liquid stained my palms, my clothes.

It was blood.

And not just any blood. *Lola's* blood.

She was belly down on the floor, her head turned sideways. Blood was oozing out of her nose, her mouth parted, blood trickling over her pale blue lips. Her skin was blue too, just like Corey's. Her dress was stained in dark, dark red.

Her blood.

Her body.

Her white dress.

Broken glass close to her thin fingers. A single raspberry on top of one of the shards, blending in with the blood. *Her blood.*

Georgia screamed again, backing away into a corner to get away from me, her eyes wide and her hand pressed to her mouth. Never had I seen Georgia so afraid.

"Ivy!" she screamed hysterically. "What did you do? Oh my God! Please! *Please don't kill me!*"

CHAPTER THIRTY-EIGHT
GEORGIA

I have to admit it, Ivy. You were hard to track down on my own.

It took me a lot of digging to find the name of the Hills—surprisingly, not many people wrote about the wreck and two people dying; it was almost like no one cared that your parents had died except for that one conspiracy theory journalist—but fortunately, I discovered their names, and your mother had a Facebook page she didn't keep very private.

I had done a quick search about the crash around the time I thought to make Lola rewrite my contract and discovered the couples' name. I had no luck finding your father—I assume he was a pretty private man—but I found your mother with ease.

I discovered then that she had a fourteen-year-old daughter at the time of the crash—a daughter she was very proud of and loved with her whole heart.

She'd named you in one of her public posts, and from the moment I found your name, I knew I needed to find the *real* you. I knew you could help me in ways I couldn't help myself, so long as you had the right information and so long as you were smart.

So, with the check I received from Lola every month and the money I had been saving for the baby prior to my miscarriage, I hired a private investigator. He found you in a matter of three days and filled me in on all the details about you. You were seventeen at that point.

According to him, you were a rebel. You'd gotten into many fights at school and you were bounced around from foster home to foster home. When I found you, you were living with a woman named Miss Cathy. Remember her? Boy, she wasn't good to you, was she?

I can recall the times I drove by Miss Cathy's house and saw you sitting on her rickety wooden stoop. She'd always be yelling at you about something. I guess I can understand why you ran away from her to live with that older guy. Miss Cathy's house was no home for you. You were lost. Sad. Broken. That was a good thing for me.

My investigator informed me that you were seeing a therapist named Marriott Harold. Marriot seemed like a lovely woman, like she had your best interests in mind. As much as you pretended to hate her, I think you rather enjoyed your visits with Marriott. Though she was a strange bird, she was protective of you, and she showed that she cared and you secretly loved that.

You loved when anyone cared about you. That's why you moved in with your now ex-boyfriend, right? Because he showed you a little attention, told you that you were pretty? He was no fool. He took advantage of a young girl, and you were desperate enough to stick around for two years and endure his sick ways.

When I found out you were seeing a therapist, I needed to know why. The government had covered your trips to see Marriot which meant your mental condition had to be serious.

And what did I find out? That you have a serious disorder.

An obsessive-compulsive disorder with *people*, which I didn't even know was a thing until the investigator told me what your therapist had on file for you. You also suffered a while with abandonment issues and from a post-traumatic stress disorder, which was understandable. You lost your parents in a horrible tragedy because of someone else. It was a thing you couldn't control, and perhaps that tragedy is why you'd developed your other disorders.

Please don't hate me for realizing you were the perfect candidate to carry out some of my plans. Granted, I knew nothing about you when the wreck first happened, but when I found out the Hills had a daughter, well, it was game on.

I didn't exactly get the chance to start grooming you to hate Lola until you were eighteen. Do you remember attending a group discussion for lost teens? It was rather easy to put together, held in the gym of a middle school. I paid the coordinator of that little group discussion and told her to pretend to care about the teens, to act as a mediator. I knew you'd go once and never go again.

I left a flyer on your boyfriend's doorstep while you were on your way to school and you picked it up. You read it, then stuffed it into your back pocket. The next thing I knew, I was in the parking lot, watching you enter the school for the discussion. You didn't say much. You just sat there, listening to other people's stories, desperately trying to relate to someone else. To make a friend. I'd spent a lot of my vacation time looking out for you, Ivy.

I had one girl named Alexa come to talk to you. I paid her to be your friend. You liked her for a while. She made up a story about how she lost her parents during a store shooting, remember? She blamed the gunman, said she hated him. Then she asked you if your life would be different if the person who'd caused the crash hadn't done it.

It was the start of something. I knew it. That question sparked something inside you and got you to *really* think about what had been done and why you never got any real answers.

From that moment on Marriott was writing in her notes often about you. I know because my investigator would break into her office after hours to read them and send me pictures of them. He went above and beyond and was well worth every penny.

Marriott said you were asking about the person responsible for your parents' death. She mentioned that you'd asked about the person before, but that you brushed it off because the detective in charge of the case wouldn't tell you. You were becoming obsessed with knowing who had caused the wreck, and that was a good thing. I always believed you deserved to know.

You'd suspected foul play and my dear, you were correct. There *was* foul play. Lola Maxwell played the system, paid to have her name cleared . . . only you didn't know it yet. But you would.

My plan? It took time. I endured years of Lola's shit, even after having my contract rewritten. For the most part she pretended what I'd asked for hadn't even happened, but her demands increased and she treated me like nothing more than her maid or a woman who was forever indebted to her, and I suppose I was that woman for a while. I'd set myself up for it by trying to blackmail her, after all. I had to be there for everything she wanted and needed.

I didn't bother you much as you went through college. Boy, those were four long years that I hated. I did have my investigator keeping tabs on you, though. He filled me in about you once a week. I often had to sneak out at night to meet him outside Biscayne Bay. You were doing well for yourself. Becoming more stable, more confident.

That was good. I was proud of you. It was as if I'd watched you blossom from a child to a woman . . . but I didn't want you to forget your roots, or how much your life had changed because of Lola.

The time never felt quite right while you were in college, so I agreed I'd let you finish—let you enjoy your scholarship—while I endured Lola's bullshit. You should thank me for that. It gave you a little more freedom.

When you graduated, I knew it was the perfect time. I had been patient, even endured five extra years of working for the Maxwells just to carry out this plan of mine, but I was growing sick of Lola's bullshit, dealing with all of her demands.

I needed my freedom too . . . and that all came down to you, my poison Ivy.

CHAPTER THIRTY-NINE

I was glad Marriott made you continue your therapy through college. She really adored you, and eventually I had to pay her a hefty amount of money, but things worked in my favor. Still, the things I had to do to get ahold of you were almost too much, Ivy. But the biggest step was getting through to Marriott.

I went to her myself to discuss Lola. I knew she'd never listen to a man, otherwise I'd have sent my investigator. She needed someone who knew Lola personally—who could prove things about her that no one else could.

My goal was simple: convince Marriott to tell you Lola's name and let you run with it. That was it, but she made it so much harder than it needed to be.

She wasn't having it at first.

"Why would I do that after all these years?" Marriott demanded, staring at me with confusion and anger. "Ivy is finally doing well for herself! She's thriving and has graduated college, and now you want me to tell her the name of the woman who pretty much tore her life apart? You are outrageous. Get out of my office."

I needed to think of a lie, and quick. If I didn't get Mar-

riott on board, all would be lost. It wasn't like I could just go
to you and tell you Lola's name. You would have known I
was up to something when you showed up at Lola's . . . because you *would* show up. I knew you. You wouldn't have
been able to resist.

"Lola, the woman who caused the wreck, asked me to
do this," I stated. "She was too afraid to come here herself,
so she told me to find Ivy. Trust me, I could have gone to
Ivy myself, but I wanted this to be right for her. I know Ivy
trusts you and she'll believe you over some random woman
she's never met."

Marriott looked at me sideways as she sat behind her desk.
That was the thing about Marriott. She liked being depended
on. Talked to. Trusted. Why do you think she became a psy-
chologist?

I sat in the chair in front of her desk, giving her an earnest
look. "I've worked for Mrs. Maxwell going on thirteen years
now. She has regretted the accident since it happened and
now she's ready to make amends with Ivy, and I'm her mes-
senger. All Mrs. Maxwell wants is for Ivy to know her name.
With that, she can do as she wishes. She can come to her or
drop it. And if she comes, Mrs. Maxwell will most likely apologize and help her out. End her struggles."

"But Ivy has certain quirks, Mellie." Mellie. That wasn't
my name. My real name was Georgia, as you know. I wasn't
foolish enough to give Marriott my *real* name. All of this could
have backfired if she'd decided not to do what I suggested.
Just as easily as I'd shown up at her office, she could have
shown up at Lola's to speak to her. "She isn't mentally stable
enough to have this kind of information," Marriott went on.
"Something as simple as knowing the name may throw her
completely off track, push her right back out of reality."

"She's a big girl, Dr. Harold. I'm sure she can handle it,

and if not, I'm sure Mrs. Maxwell will be happy to cover the care she needs."

"That's where you're wrong about Ivy. I know for a fact she won't take the news well. Ivy has a—a problem of becoming *obsessed*. She spent nearly two years pleading with me and the police for answers. I always promised her I'd find out the truth for her one day, but I only said that so she would hold on to hope. What I really wanted was for her to eventually forget about it and move on, and now that she's starting to, you want me to feed her this name? How do I even know it was this woman? Lola Maxwell, is it?"

"Because I was there the night it happened. She had blood on her clothes. She was distraught. I also overheard her speaking to a police detective the next day, the same detective who was supposed to investigate the wreck. His name was Jack Shaw, right?"

Marriott's throat bobbed. "You could have gotten that information from the Internet."

"She paid off the detective, Dr. Harold. That's why he never gave Ivy a name or any details. Mrs. Maxwell gave him five hundred thousand dollars so he'd keep her name out of the investigation, and that was the end of that."

"She did *what*?" Marriott gasped. "Why would she do such a thing? Why didn't she just own up to what she'd done?"

I shrugged. "I suppose Mrs. Maxwell was trying to protect her reputation."

"Well, that's mighty selfish, isn't it? Who is this Lola Maxwell? Why is her reputation so important?

"Look her up. A quick Internet search and you'll see why."

Marriott sighed and shook her head. "I don't know," she said, still hesitant. "I know Ivy. She'll want to face this woman.

That could bring harm to both their lives, lead to unnecessary drama at the least."

"Well, and this is just my opinion . . . Mrs. Maxwell deserves to at least be confronted about this, don't you think?"

"Ivy will obsess," Marriott went on, her eyes on her notes. "She's a lonely girl. Information like this may be lethal. I understand what you and Mrs. Maxwell are trying to do, but Ivy would be better off without this knowledge in her possession."

See what I meant? Dealing with her was like dealing with a piece of food stuck between your teeth. "What if Mrs. Maxwell offers you thirty thousand dollars?"

Marriott whipped up her head and looked deep into my eyes. That caught her attention. I suppose I'd learned a thing or two from Lola. Money was powerful, could shut any man or woman up if it was the right price. "Just for me to tell Ivy her name?"

I nodded.

Marriott drummed her nimble fingers on the edge of the desktop. "Well, I guess I could do it for that. I would just have to keep a close eye on her."

"Let's not play modest, Dr. Harold. You work on a government-need basis. You live in a one-bedroom apartment that's too small for you and your three cats and you're in debt up to your neck. You want better for yourself. You've always wanted better for yourself. Thirty grand will come in handy for someone like you."

Marriott's jaw dropped. "H-how do you know that?"

"I know a lot of things."

Her hands were shaking now. She knew the deal. I wasn't here on Lola's behalf. I'd tried to use that and she wasn't taking the bait, so I had to get assertive. "What are you? Some kind of investigator?"

"No. I just have really good resources."

She worked hard to swallow. The room was quiet. "How do I know the money is guaranteed?"

"It is . . . but it won't all show up right away. I'll wire it to you in increments, just to make sure you hold up your end of the bargain. I'll start with ten thousand and increase from there." I adjusted my purse on my lap.

Marriot was quiet for a beat. She looked all around her. "This will go against all my codes—all my work ethics."

"You'll be fine, and so will Ivy."

She drew in a deep breath and then exhaled. "Fine," she said, lifting her chin. Her bottom lip was trembling. "Make it forty thousand and it's a deal."

And a deal it was.

Marriott would get every check I received from Lola. I wasn't joking about how well Lola paid me: eight thousand dollars a month. Kind of low when you consider everything I'd done for her and how filthy rich she was, but it was all right. I could afford to pay Marriott and I didn't need much anyway while living in the mansion. Food was provided. Clothes were a uniform. Gas was covered by one of Lola's business credit cards. It wasn't like I went shopping or had a personal life anymore, so I'd saved several thousand dollars over the years—ever since Lola showed me her true colors. Not only that, but my ten million was well on the way. It was only a matter of time before I would receive it, so this small sacrifice would be worth it.

I asked Marriott for a pen and then scribbled Lola's name on a sheet of paper, sliding it across the desk. "Just in case you forget."

Marriott took it and placed it in her top drawer, giving me a wary glance.

As I climbed into Lola's SUV and started the ignition, I

could feel Marriott watching me go. I didn't care. I knew she would keep quiet and do what she was told if she wanted the money and a better life.

She would feel remorse for telling you, Ivy, but she'd get over it and realize your decisions afterward were your own.

This was a plan being set in motion and nothing was going to stop it. Nothing at all.

CHAPTER FORTY

You did everything much better than I could ever plan, Ivy. You were a wise girl, something I adored about you.

You didn't jump the gun and run with Lola's name. You took your time. You came up with your own plan. You had to have known that Lola hadn't sent that name herself, but that was what Marriott told you, right? I know it is because that's what I told her to tell you.

You had to have hoped and prayed Lola knew nothing about you, but you took the risk anyway and showed her your face, which proved to me you had several tricks up your sleeve for her. I liked that.

What were you thinking when you realized Lola didn't know who you were? I bet you were relieved, thought you were ahead of the game and extremely smart, but you didn't think to ask yourself who had really given you that name, did you? You just assumed what was happening was meant to be, and that you were smarter than the originator—than me.

I admit, it was a nice touch signing up for Lola's charity. I always thought you'd slink your way in some other way. She was obsessed with that little charity of hers. Good job.

But I have to tell you, even if you'd used your real name on the application, Lola wouldn't have known who you were. Matter of fact, Lola had no clue the Hills had a daughter.

She didn't give a fuck about the deceased couple, she just wanted the situation buried, and she didn't care how. You should hate her for that. You really, really should. She never would have owned up to her wrongdoing if it weren't for me leading you to her.

I'm confused, though, by why your motive changed. You wanted to destroy Lola, take her down at first. I saw that anger in your eyes as you left Marriott's clinic. You wanted to ruin this Lola woman. Destroy everything she touched. But let me guess . . . you saw Dr. Maxwell and became mesmerized. I had a feeling that would happen.

You went to him several months later, he fondled your breasts, and suddenly you felt connected to him. I suppose I should have seen that one coming. Your obsessive disorder was going to kick in one way or another; I just expected you to continue obsessing over Lola, not become crazed with the idea of being with him.

I could have told you from the jump that he wasn't all that great. All he ever did was cheat on Lola, and she did the same in return, but he loved playing the victim. He loved having the women he fucked around with think they were his first affair and that his wife was no good. That's how he got the ladies. That's how he got *you*.

You thought he was sweet and perfect and innocent. But he wasn't. No one is fucking perfect, Ivy, and you should have known better. Hell, Dr. Maxwell was just as bad as Lola, that's why they were perfect for each other. All that damn arguing and fighting they did. It was no wonder they were miserable with each other. And trust me, he knew about your parents and how that situation was covered up. Lola had foolishly taken the five hundred thousand dollars she'd given the detective from their joint account and Corey noticed, and she most likely explained. But like Lola, he decided it wasn't relevant, that it was smart of Lola to bury it the way she did.

If I were you, I'd fucking hate him too.

You did everything and more, Ivy. You destroyed a friendship of hers at your own will. Shit, I can't believe you pushed Keke off a cliff. I know you did it, and I won't lie, I was proud of you. You were willing to go to great lengths to get close to Lola and eventually work to steal her husband, and I admired that. It was more than I would have done, but still!

Lola had gone on and on, swearing Keke was pushed, and as she did, I had to stifle my laughter because I knew. I just knew it was you. Good thing those cameras weren't on during camp, huh?

You knew what you wanted and you went after it, and from that moment forward, I figured maybe I'd done the right thing—that maybe you could still be useful to me, despite the affair you were ready to spur.

Who do you think suggested that you stay in Lola's cabin during camp? Who do you think suggested she invite you over more often because it seemed like you had her best interests in mind and would make a good friend?

I *raved* about how wonderful a girl I thought you were, and Lola liked to think everything I said was her idea, so she fed into it. Yes, Lola may have despised me, but she still listened whenever I spoke, mainly because after I'd signed those contracts, I made it my mission to not speak to her on a personal level again. At least not until you showed up.

Lola loved taking in broken girls, and she could see the brokenness in you. She wanted to rub her money in your face, the same way she wanted to rub it in everyone else's.

She wanted you to *need* her, brag about her and her wealth, because no one else really needed or bragged about her much.

Why do you think she kept Keke around for so long? Keke was a needy little bitch, with an even needier daughter. Keke loved to post on social media when she hung out with Lola to make her other friends jealous. That worked for Lola. It made her feel important—like some goddess.

You were envious of Lola's life, and rightly so. She'd built herself up and acted like this empowered, perfect woman after her miscarriage, while you struggled for everything you had. She lived the good life while for years you cried yourself to sleep every night after your parents' death.

It wasn't fair, was it? How she continued being a selfish, entitled bitch while you wept? How she went to exotic countries and soaked in new cultures while you were abused?

It *wasn't* fair. She always got what she wanted, while everyone she touched with her greediness suffered.

You deserved more.

I deserved more.

Unfortunately, only one of us could come out on top, and for what I did to you, I do apologize. But, I mean, you *silly girl*! You fell for that idiotic husband of hers. You fell for his stupid charm like a fool, thought you'd run off into the sunset with him, take his money with you, and live a new, wonderful life. I couldn't have that happen. It would have thwarted my plan.

I liked you because you weren't that materialistic at first, but then you got hooked on the finer things, had a little taste of luxury and a stroke of rich dick, and thought you were invincible. I thought you were smarter than that.

What I did needed to be done, though, so this demise would have happened regardless. It had taken me years. I couldn't let it all just go down the drain.

I had to pin the blame on someone, and who looked more like the perfect suspect than the girl whose parents tragically *died* because of Lola Maxwell? They would investigate, you know? After such a tragedy. Two rich people dead. A huge scandal that would be talked about for weeks—months.

There were witnesses who could testify against you too. Faith and Arabel. Keke. *Me.*

We were all suspicious of you, and we loved Lola like a sister, right? You were weird and came out of nowhere, and we didn't like you. That was your own fault. You needed to enhance your people skills. I should have worked on that with you, but it's fine. The weirder you seemed to the others, the better it was going to work out for me in the end.

No one was going to suspect me, a woman who had dedicated her life to the Maxwells.

Wouldn't it look strange to the police that you'd only come around four and a half months ago, yet you became Lola's best friend practically overnight? You moved from St. Petersburg to Miami just to get closer to her. You visited her house every day, most times when Lola wasn't even around— and yes, that's all on tape. Security records everything at the gates.

You slept with her husband, which I could attest to after watching you hump him by the pool on one occasion, and leave his man cave on another, and you got jealous that he still loved her, so you poisoned her with the crushed antidepressants found in your purse.

You didn't put the pills there. Of course not, but the cops would never know that. They'd just put two and two together. A girl with mental issues shows up on the day the Maxwells die. Pills in your bag with your name on the prescription bottle—the five-hundred-dollar bag Lola gave you, but they'd think you stole. Security cameras perfectly angled with views of the pool and sitting area, watching your every move.

The text message from Lola? She'd been arguing with Dr. Maxwell all day long while also trying to drink her stress away. She'd left her phone on the kitchen counter, and somehow a text was sent in the midst of the chaos.

Lola was getting hostile. Corey was being pathetic and demanding drinks too. Things were getting out of hand, and all the while I had your own pills in my hand. They were already crushed. I'd chopped them up weeks before, waiting for the perfect opportunity to use them.

You'd stopped taking the pills. My investigator confiscated them from your apartment while you were in New York and you never even noticed. It would work. I'd done my research. I knew what I wanted to do, I just needed the supplies to do it—something with your name written all over it.

I mean, it was the perfect plan, don't you think? It took some time and *a lot* of patience, but in the end, I'd say it all worked out in my favor.

It was *the perfect ruin.*

And I bet all this time you thought you were the one doing the ruining, didn't you? The heartbreaking? The sabotaging?

This was never your plan, Ivy. All of the events that led up to this very moment happened because of *me.*

You were never the one in control, no matter how sure you were of yourself. I only made you think you were. It was better for you to think you were taking Lola down yourself, ruining her friendships and her marriage and her life. Let you feel powerful, invincible.

You carried out a plan, and though I was worried at first and did feel a little bad, you handled it so much better than I ever could have imagined. I knew you were smart, desperate, and a little bit crazy. All the things one would need you to be in a situation like this. But if you were just a tad bit smarter, you would have left it alone and moved on, like your therapist begged you to do.

Lola and Corey are dead. Everyone thinks you did it.

Meanwhile, because she is gone now, I have ten million dollars in my bank account, and it's all thanks to you, sweet Ivy.

I am sorry about the situation you're in now, but you should know that I truly, truly couldn't have done any of this without you.

CHAPTER FORTY-ONE

IVY

Breathe . . . breathe . . . *breathe*.

Count to ten. Breathe. Hum your favorite song. Think of a happy moment.

The water park. Fruity freeze pops. Sticky fingers wrapped around a warm, soft hand . . .

No.

Blood on my hands. A white dress soiled in the same blood. Broken glass on the floor beside the body, a single raspberry next to glass shards.

Not my blood. Not my fault.

Breathing wasn't going to save me. In fact, I would rather have been doing anything other than breathing.

Apparently, I had killed Lola and Corey Maxwell. The evidence was so stacked against me that not even my court-appointed lawyer believed my story. He gave me a look and told me to accept a plea bargain. Confess to the crimes, do the time, and hope for parole. But I didn't kill them. I wasn't going to confess to something I didn't do!

"For the last time, I didn't kill them!" I said as Detective Hughes glared at me from across the table. He was a lanky man, with long, skinny fingers and a bald head. His suit hung from his bony shoulders like he'd lost a lot of weight recently and hadn't gotten around to getting new clothes. "You have to believe me. I didn't do it!" I was on the verge of tears. I didn't want to go to prison. That wasn't me. I never would have done something like this.

"The security camera footage at the Maxwells' home says otherwise, Miss Hill. We also ran toxicology on the Maxwells. Turns out they overdosed on antidepressants and traces of rat poison were found in their blood. A witness said they saw you dumping something into the Maxwells' drinks while they were arguing."

"A witness? Who?" I snapped. "The only person who was there other than me and Lola and Corey was the household manager, Georgia. Why aren't you questioning her?" I demanded. "She's the one who did this! S–she had to have sent me the text to come to Lola's house! She set me up!"

I'd been questioned for hours, going back and forth with Detective Hughes with a lawyer at my side. Though the lawyer told me I didn't have to answer some of the questions if I didn't want to, some of them I couldn't help but speak up on, especially when they mentioned Georgia.

"Georgia McNeil gave a full confession. She told us everything. She told us that you'd been coming by the Maxwells' home, even when Mrs. Maxwell wasn't there, and that you were having an affair with Dr. Maxwell. Lola was your friend, was she not? Why would you sleep with your friend's *husband*? What were you going to get out of it?"

"She was never my fucking friend," I seethed.

"So, you admit to killing her because she didn't want to be your friend?"

"No—I didn't kill her!" I shouted.

"But you wanted to."

"No!"

Detective Hughes let off an irritated sighed and sat forward, opening a maroon folder. "We received the Maxwells' home security footage an hour ago. Can you tell me what you see in this picture?"

I blinked away my tears and looked down as he slid a photo across the silver table. It was an image of me in the pool, my curly hair wet and sticking to my face, my hand gripped around the back of Corey's neck. Corey was facedown in the pool, his arms stretched out wide, as if he'd drowned long ago. It looked as if I'd drowned him. But I hadn't. I couldn't have. There was no way he could have drowned that fast.

The pills—the antidepressants. They were in his drink too. Georgia had to have made those drinks. She always made the drinks, always served them, always asked if we wanted more. She'd even asked me if I wanted a drink. He was probably dead as soon as his body hit the water.

"Tell me what you see, Miss Hill," Detective Hughes said, his voice harsher than it was a moment ago.

"It's a . . . it's a picture of me with my hand around Corey's neck." A tear slipped down my cheek.

"And what were you doing to him in this photo?"

"I was—I was angry with him. I was mad because he'd used me, but he wasn't even in the water that long," I pleaded, looking into the detective's gray eyes. "I swear I didn't kill them! I was framed for this! You have to believe me! G-go ask Detective Jack Shaw in St. Petersburg! Lola bribed him, and then there's Georgia, who went to Marriott to tell her to give me Lola's name!"

"Ivy," my lawyer whispered, laying a hand on my arm.

"I didn't do this!" I sobbed, turning my head and looking him the eye. "I didn't."

Detective Hughes was clearly fed up. "We contacted Detective Shaw, as you suggested last night, and he said there is no file of any kind with Lola Maxwell's name in it."

I wanted to die right then and there. Take Detective Hughes's gun out of the holster and blow out my own damned brains.

"Back to this image." Detective Hughes stabbed a finger on the black-and-white picture. "You're telling me that you had an affair with Dr. Maxwell, found out he'd used you, and suddenly he was facedown in the pool the same day? Please tell me how this adds up, Miss Hill? Lola was found facedown on her kitchen floor. A witness stated that you seemed unbothered by Lola's blood on your hands, that you were sitting in it until she screamed that she was calling the police."

I groaned. A witness. *Georgia.*

I know what this looked like, Marriott. It looked like I killed them. But I didn't. You believe me, don't you? I guess this was what I deserved. You told me not to obsess over Lola and I did anyway. Now look at me. Set up. Framed for two murders I didn't commit.

There was no way they were going to believe me at this point. I couldn't quite explain why I drove by Lola's house so many times before really getting to know her. I couldn't explain the testimony against me, and why Lola's friends thought it was strange that she had suddenly just taken me under her wing. I couldn't explain why I'd moved nearly four hours away from my hometown to live in Lola's and then become her friend two months later. I couldn't explain getting the boob job from Corey. No, if anything, I looked obsessed to the detective.

I couldn't explain the footage of me running from the pool in a panic, running away from Corey's dead body, only to run into another, although they didn't see that part. I couldn't explain any of it. All I could do was say I wasn't guilty, that it wasn't me, even as things progressed to trial. But do you think the jury would believe me? The judge?

A man named Henry Thatcher, a prosecutor representing the state, laid it all out for the jury. Apparently, because Lola had gotten into a wreck while suffering a miscarriage, per Dr. Gilbert's testimony—and Detective Jack Shaw confessed that Lola paid him off, but that wasn't enough to help me—she'd caused a domino effect. She killed my parents and I grew up into an angry girl.

Thatcher reported the fights I'd gotten into, and how I'd run away from home. That I'd stabbed my ex-boyfriend, but that was only because he attacked me first. He didn't die anyway, and I got off with self-defense.

According to Thatcher, I blamed Lola for my horrible upbringing and thought to take advantage of Lola and her elitist life. He made his case about jealousy, hatred, rage, and greed. He made Lola look like the victim, despite everyone knowing about the wreck she'd caused—which only made people sympathize with her more and donate even more money to her charity—and I was the bloodthirsty, obsessed murderer who wanted to steal Lola's life. Corey had rejected me and I was angry, so I drugged and killed him too. Lola trusted me, Thatcher stated, and I broke her trust by having an affair with her husband and then murdered them.

But they had it all wrong—well, some of it. Yes, I hated Lola, but it was never my plan to *kill* her. I didn't want to kill anyone.

But you want to know what sold the jury?

Fucking *Keke*.

Keke went to the stand with a limp and told them how she had a feeling I would be dangerous to Lola—that she was sure I had pushed her off the cliff at camp, and that I'd admitted to doing it when I went to the hospital with Lola after they'd had their little fight.

The prosecutor showed them photos of Keke's broken shin, arm, and the stitches on her head while she was in a coma. She couldn't prove it, but she always had this hunch that I wanted her out of my way so I could be closer to Lola. According to Keke, I envied her friendship with Lola and even ruined it in the end. Faith and Arabel reported that I wasn't in the cabin when they woke up the morning Keke fell.

Keke had no proof, but the media ate up her testimony like a decadent chocolate cake. I was a threat to society . . . and I was sentenced to life in prison with no chance of parole.

I was set up, Marriott. It was Georgia who did all of this—who created this destruction and ruin in my life.

I swear, I'm not capable of killing anyone. How stupid would I be to do all of that, just so it could all come back to me being the primary suspect? You know I'm much smarter than that, and you know my mind better than anyone else. I didn't murder Lola and Corey.

But, alas, I've been in prison for two months now and I haven't heard a peep from you. I guess I need to send this to you, just to show you my side of the story, even if it is a little ugly.

I'll be honest with you. Now that I've had time to think, I wish you'd never given me Lola's name. After all this shit, I'd much rather be the clueless, hopeless girl I was before than a woman rotting in prison for the rest of her life.

Lola would still be alive and nameless to me and I'd still have my freedom.

I've made up my mind. I'm sending this to you, and I'm *begging* you, please come visit me, Marriott. I know you're ashamed of me, and I never thought I'd say this, but I need you.

Please don't leave me like everyone else has.

Please help me.

CHAPTER FORTY-TWO

Three months, six days, and fourteen hours.

That's how long it's been since I was sentenced and shoved into prison, convicted of a crime I didn't commit.

Time is slow in prison. So goddamn slow, and no one trusts me here. I'm always hungry. My cell partner attacked me the first week I was here to assert her dominance, and I promised her my meals for a month in exchange for my life.

I don't deserve any of this shit. I should be on a boat, drinking fruity drinks and dancing under the stars at night.

Out of all the close encounters in my life and all the trouble I've caused, I didn't ever think I'd end up here. I'm not perfect, but I know where I stand, and I'm not a killer.

I've thought about appealing, but where would that get me? Lola was the beloved beauty of Florida. People adored her, many came out to her funeral to show respect, and I'd killed her. Not many were going to risk dipping their toe in this case again to save a lowlife girl like me, even if they had plenty of evidence.

Something hard clanged on my cell door and I looked up at the guard behind it. "Get your ass up, Hill. You've got a visitor."

A visitor? I haven't had a visitor before. Maybe it's Marriott. Yes! I knew she'd come to see me one day. She was most likely waiting for all of this to blow over. I wrote to her all those times. She always said she'd be there for me no matter what.

I hurry to stand, shoving my hands through the small space between the cells so she can cuff me. She opens the door, tugging on the chain so I can step out and then slamming the door shut behind her and locking it.

"Don't know who the hell is visiting *your* crazy ass," she grumbles, walking ahead of me. That's the thing around here. I'm the *dumb psycho bitch* to everyone, from the inmates to the guards. There's shouting and screaming. My fellow inmates aren't pleased that the *dumb psycho bitch* has a visitor and they don't.

I ignore them all, keeping my eyes ahead, trudging along in my brown prison uniform. It feels strange entering the visitors' block—I've never been here before, but I've always envied the girls who can go here every week to speak to someone they care about.

There are two sections. One where you speak over the two-way phones, one where you can sit at a table, right in front of your visitor if you want. It's the visitor's choice of course. All about safety.

I'm sent to the two-way phones, and that's how I know it's not Marriott who's visiting me today. Marriott would want to be in my face, pleading with me, telling me everything is going to be okay. I get the feeling she's never coming to see me.

"Number three," the guard says as I look at the phones separated by thin, scratchy glass and black blocks between each booth. "Warden doesn't want you out for long." Yeah. Because the Warden admired Lola and hates me for what everyone thinks I've done. "You've got twenty minutes."

I glance over my shoulder at her before moving ahead. As I do, I can see someone sitting on the other side of number three. They're wearing black. Their skin is brown.

I stop in front of three . . . and I can't believe my eyes. *You have to be fucking kidding me!*

I look back at the guard, who isn't paying me any attention. Instead she's chomping on her gum, glancing at the clock. I sit, and feel my weight sink onto the stool as I stare through the glass, right at Georgia.

She smiles from the other side of the glass, that same weird-as-fuck smile she gave me when she tended to Lola's home and when she answered the door and greeted me.

There's something different about her now, though. Her hair has been straightened and is now glossy and cut in a bob. There are diamond earrings in her ears and she has on make-up, which I've never seen her wear before. Her brows have been plucked, and expensive rings are on her fingers.

There's a familiar Cartier rose-gold watch on her wrist and I instantly recognize it. It was Lola's. She wore it the first day of Passion Camp.

Georgia picks up the phone, still holding my eyes. I snatch the phone off the hook and press the receiver to my ear.

"Oh, Miss Hill. I have to say, you've had better days."

"Fuck you," I hiss at her from my side of the glass. "What the hell are you doing here? I can't believe you have the fucking nerve."

"I'm here for a brief visit. I figured *someone* should see you after everything you've been through."

I narrow my eyes at her. "How could you do this to me? I know it was you!"

"How could I do what?"

"You know what you did! You set me up!" I hiss into the black phone.

Georgia says nothing for a while, and then she finally sighs and smiles. "I think you and I can both agree the world is a better place now."

I stare her in the eye. "Rat poison? I never bought rat poison. You dumped it in their drinks with those antidepressants, not me. You're fucking insane."

Still, Georgia says nothing, and now I'm getting pissed. "Why did you do it? I—I get Lola, I guess, but why Corey?"

"Most would say loose ends are . . . deadly."

Great choice of words. *Cunt.* I grit my teeth. "Why haven't I seen Marriott? Have you done something to her too?"

"Other than give her forty grand so she could tell you Lola's name during one of your therapy sessions? No. And you really shouldn't have stopped seeing her. She was good for you."

My eyes stretch and my heart sinks. So that's why Marriott hasn't responded or shown up. She was bought . . . just like everyone else. Marriott didn't show up to my trial to speak up for me when I requested it—didn't even so much as check in on me. Now I knew why. I knew she was too good to be true. And all this time I thought Georgia had killed her too. I was worried.

"Let's not pretend you had a conscience when it came to ruining Lola's life, Ivy. You wanted her dead. She took your parents from you."

"Why would you do something like this? I barely even knew you and now I'm in here for life! And for what?" I look her over in her fancy attire. "So you could get some of Lola's money? Wasn't she paying you enough?"

"Lola ruined my goddamn life, the same way she did yours. But unlike you, I took some initiative."

"By *framing* me?"

She makes a tsk-tsk noise through her teeth. "The people in this world can make it a selfish place, Ivy. I thought you'd have figured that out by now. Believe me, you would have ended up in here one way or another. I just did you a favor and got it over with."

"Why?" I ask, my voice breaking. "Why did you do it? Why me? Don't you think I've lost enough?" I want to cry.

Georgia studies the ring on her middle finger, a red ruby on a thin gold band. "Because, just like me, you were angry. You wanted revenge, but you got stupid and lazy with it. You fell for a man who wasn't going to love you back. I had to make my move before you got carried away with your own plan to run off with him and the money owed to me. I know girls like you. You don't share. You think the world owes you. You would have gotten all that money through Corey if he and Lola had divorced and run off with it. You would have left me in a pit—with nothing. I couldn't have that. Not after all I'd been through."

It feels as if something has been lodged in my throat. "What are you even talking about?"

"Oh, what the hell? It isn't like anyone is listening on these crappy two-way phones anyway. I dealt with the Maxwells for fourteen years," Georgia whispers into the receiver. "I was the one who cleaned up their shit, planned their dinners, and made sure their house was an actual home, but they never appreciated that. Rich people never appreciate anything." She studies her manicured cuticles. "To put it simply, I asked Lola to rewrite my contract as her household manager and told her I wanted ten million dollars at the end of my ten-year term. I knew her dirty little secret about your parents that she so sloppily covered up and tried to blackmail her with it for the ten million, but it backfired on me. She rewrote the contract and gave me a nondisclosure to sign, but she wasn't fair with it. In order for me to receive the ten million she knew I deserved, I had to work for her for *another* ten years. That would have been twenty years too long working for Lola and I just couldn't do it. After everything she'd put me through, I simply refused, and hell, going four years into the second term was brutal.

"But one thing Lola always did was underestimate me, and we all know with every contract, there has to be some kind of way out, even if it's nearly impossible to make happen." Her throat bobs. "There was a clause in my new contract. It stated that if, in the unlikely event something was to happen to both Lola *and* Corey, my contract would be null and I'd receive my ten million dollars immediately. An executor handled their will and all of their assets. I ran my contract by him and the money was deposited into my account. But you have to realize that in order for that to happen, both of them had to be *gone* so I could get the money right away or I had to wait the ten more years and continue dealing with her shit. I wasn't about to wait."

I draw in a breath. This couldn't be real. What I was hearing couldn't be true.

"So . . . anyway, I did some digging. Sought you out. Spoke with Marriott about two years ago to get the ball rolling . . . and from there, everything just sort of pieced itself together. Lola had ruined my life, so I ruined hers." She pauses, inhales, and then exhales and looks me in the eye. She really has the nerve to pretend to be sympathetic. "I feel bad for you, I really do, but I couldn't have any of this circling back to me. Lola and Corey needed to go, and you had the perfect motive I could use. Kill the woman who'd taken everything from you. Then kill the man who'd broken your heart. Technically, he was never supposed to break your heart because you were never supposed to fall for him. An affair? Yes, but not fall in love. But it worked out. In all reality, you brought this upon yourself, Ivy."

"But I didn't do this! I loved Corey!"

"I see you're still a fool."

I slam down the phone on the short table in front of me, pushing myself off the stool. "You're fucking demented!" I shout at her. I know there's soundproof glass between us, but I'm sure she can read my lips. I know she can hear every word. I lean forward and slam two fists on the glass. She doesn't flinch, as if expecting me to react this way. She came here to torment me—to let me suffer from these truths. "You set me up, you selfish bitch!" I scream, and I can't believe it, but she smiles.

"All right, Hill! That's it!" the guard shouts from behind me. "You had one chance and you just fucked it up!"

"This is her fault!" I scream as the guard grips my arm and tows me back. "She set me up! She just confessed to it! She framed me!"

Georgia casually hangs up the phone and stands, watching as the guard wraps an arm around my middle and drags me back. "You must be off your fucking meds!" the guard grunts.

"You're a fucking bitch, Georgia!" I scream, pointing a finger at her, blinded by tears. By rage. "You'll get what's coming to you! I promise you, you will!"

It doesn't matter what I say, though. My words hold no weight, and they don't faze her. She steps away from the glass with a subtle smirk, and when she turns away, I realize it.

She wins . . . and I am going to live the rest of my life in this shithole. And she doesn't care. Of course she doesn't. The ten million in her pocket is all she needs to start a new life.

She's gotten away with everything without so much as a double check and I got pinned.

Who was going to believe a young black woman who's been convicted of murder? A girl who lost her parents at fourteen? A girl who was known to be mentally unstable? A woman who grew up to stalk another woman, fuck her husband, and supposedly drown him because her heart was broken? No one, that's who. And that bitch Georgia knew it.

That was why she was smirking.

That was why she was here, because she knew no matter how much I say she framed me, no matter how hard I try to convince anyone of the truth, no one will ever believe me.

I said it before, and I'll say it again.

I *never* should have told Marriott to give me that fucking name.

CHAPTER FORTY-THREE

GEORGIA

Seeing Ivy locked up with my own two eyes gave me satisfaction. I needed to see for myself, up close and personal, that she couldn't get out. The poor girl is miserable, but I'm sure she's used to misery by now. She'll be okay.

I've never felt like I belonged in Miami. I grew up in this city, which is notorious for its night life and beach parties . . . and the high crime rate.

I'd spent many years in Wynwood, witnessing many of my friends and family turn to drugs. It was a bad place. I knew I deserved better, so I sought better for myself.

I must part ways with this city—this city that has not always been so kind to me. I've had lots of time to think about where to run off to. There are many places I'd like to see and things I'd like to do, like get full on pasta and wine in Italy, or ride on a camel in the Red Dunes and then make my way to Dubai.

But for now, I just need to get away. I waited until things blew over with the murder trial. I've paid my visit to Ivy like I told myself I would, just to confirm. Now, it's time to start anew.

I'll begin again in London first, a city I've wanted to visit since I was a little girl. My grandmother used to tell me stories about how she'd dated a man from London for two years. It didn't work out because she was too hotheaded and he was too sensitive, but she said he was romantic. Sweet. Loved to feed her.

Perhaps I'll find a man who will love to feed me. Be romantic with me. A man who will never, *ever* know my background or where I've come from. A man who won't abandon me like Dion.

I will start over. I will start now.

I packed my suitcases last night and am now printing off my schedule. My flight leaves in three hours. After picking up the paper, I head for the kitchen of the condo I'd bought, which faces the ocean, preparing my final cup of caramel tea in Miami.

I do it with diligence, starting up my kettle, letting the water boil, and then dumping two tea bags into a bone-china teacup on a saucer. I pour the water carefully, allow the tea to steep, and then remove the tea bags, giving them a light squeeze with my fingertips before discarding them in the waste bin.

Then I take my tea on the saucer to the living room and sip as I watch the ocean. It is peaceful doing this. I can't remember the last time I've been so relaxed.

But my peace doesn't last for long. There's a knock at my door. I have no idea who it can be. Probably my neighbor, Pete. He's been interested in me, and though he is quite handsome, I can't afford to get mixed up with him. I'm leaving Miami and all it entails behind, and I refuse to fall for another Florida man.

Placing my saucer and teacup down on the white porcelain counter, I make my way to the door in brand-new red stilettos and open it.

I'm ready to greet Pete, tell him that it was nice knowing him . . . but this isn't Pete.

In fact, it's no man at all.

"Hi, Georgia," Faith says. A wide smile is on her lips, but

it doesn't reach her eyes. Her eyes are intense, her lashes clumpy from too much mascara. She's dressed well, but then, so am I.

When you are well off, it's better to play the part. You receive more double takes and get seated faster at restaurants when you look rich. I can see now why Lola was always so eager to dress up to go out on one of her lunch or dinner dates.

"Faith," I say, and there is curiosity burning in my voice. "Hi—what are you doing here? How do you know where I live?"

"Lola's lawyer told me." Her smile slowly fades, but her eyes remain the same. Intense. Dark.

"Lola's lawyer?"

"Yes. May I come in?"

"I was actually just about to leave. I have a flight to catch and have to be gone within the hour if I want to beat traffic."

"This won't take but a minute." I grit my teeth as she saunters past me and into the condo. "Beautiful place. How much does it cost you?" I can't help sensing an underlying accusation in her tone.

I close the door, realizing this is not a sweet meet and greet.

"I know everything, Georgia. You might want to cancel that flight."

Oh. I see.

The script has flipped.

You, Faith. You are here for deeper reasons.

CHAPTER FORTY-FOUR

"Excuse me?" I ask.

"I wanted to wait until Ivy's case blew over before I came to see you."

I remain standing by the door as you look around my apartment. It's fully decorated. I told my landlord he could keep it all and charge more for the next tenant if he wants to. I wasn't going to need any of it where I was going.

"Okay . . ."

"Do you remember when you asked Lola to rewrite your contract, and how she guaranteed you ten million after you fulfilled a twenty-year term with her?"

My heart beats faster. "How the hell do you know about that?"

"She told me, Georgia. She met me for brunch the day after you asked and told me everything, and I recall her specifically mentioning that you blackmailed her and that she was making some arrangements. Then, the week before she passed away, she told me something felt off with you, and with Ivy, and mentioned that if anything happened to her, I should look to you for answers. She didn't go into details about anything, but she made it very clear that she didn't trust you."

I clench one of my fists. I want to punch you. Strangle you.

"So . . . I went to Lola's lawyer, asked him for a favor, and he showed me the new contract Lola had come up with for you." You slide your purse down to your forearm and open it, pulling out a folded packet of paper. Unfolding it carefully, you clear your throat and say, "I have it highlighted here. 'In the unlikely event that something should happen to the employer (i.e.: loss of memory, diagnosis of incurable disease, or *death*), the household manager will receive the agreed amount of ten million dollars at once and the contract and all responsibilities of the employee shall be null and void.'" You lower the paper and give me a smug smile. "So, tell me, *household manager* . . . were you involved in the killing of Lola and Corey too? I mean, I know Ivy was in on it . . . but you helped her, right?"

No. Nah-uh. There is no way I am letting another ignorant rich bitch ruin my damn life. I have had enough of Lola and her demons. Her lies. She won't haunt me like this and you will not take advantage of me. I deserved this money and she knew it.

"She told you about my contract?" I breathed. "And who else?"

"Just me. Lola trusted me more than any of her friends." You seem so sure about that, but from what I remember, Lola liked Arabel the most.

I rub my nose, forcing myself to summon tears. You need to see that I am distraught by this news—this accusation. "Did she tell you what she did? Why I blackmailed her?"

"Not exactly. I asked, but she said she didn't want to talk about it, just that I needed to believe her about you. Now that I've had time to think, I'm sure it was about that wreck."

"Right—exactly so. Then you have to know the whole story, Faith. Don't accuse me of things I didn't do until you listen, okay? I loved Lola, but she wasn't perfect, and she hated me because I could see all her flaws."

"Why do you think I came here? I could have gone to the

police and told them what Lola told me, especially after getting hold of this contract, but I came here. I'm giving you a chance because I know Lola wasn't perfect, and I know she liked to lie and play the victim. But that doesn't mean I can't use this contract to my own advantage."

You maneuver through the furniture and pass my three-thousand-dollar, bamboo coffee table to get to the sofa.

"So, I'm all ears. Convince me that you had nothing to do with what happened, get me to believe you, and then we can discuss how to split the ten million dollars so I can keep my mouth shut about it." You grin.

I fight a grimace.

This is interesting. See, I'd heard from Lola while eavesdropping on one of her phone calls with Arabel that you, Faith, were on the brink of a divorce and were lashing out at your friends because of it.

What is it now? Is your husband getting tired of you? Did you catch him in an affair? Are you bored now, and looking for ways to keep money in your pocket when he leaves you?

It explains your behavior during the dinner Lola set up, when she announced the location of the gala and invited you and the others to join her for the event. You lashed out at Ivy, accused Lola of moving too fast with her, and you were drinking too much. Yes, I saw and heard it all.

I assumed the divorce thing was a rumor because Lola never spoke of it again, but now I see. It wasn't a rumor. Your husband is about to leave you, and now you want to lash out on someone else.

Well, not today. Not with me, bitch.

I am going to London and no one is going to stop me, especially not you.

I make my way to the kitchen and pull down a box of tea, my back to you, and then I open my purse, which is right below the tea cabinet. I have several prescription bottles inside. Antidepressants. Opioids. Take too many at once and they'll likely kill you, you know?

The antidepressants were prescribed for me by a therapist I forced myself to see, just to cover my tracks. People needed to know I was deeply affected by Lola's death. They had to know that despite inheriting ten million dollars, my heart was broken. You can understand that, I'm sure.

Sadness is an easy emotion to pull off. My therapist helped me to cope by prescribing antidepressants so I could get back on my feet. As for the opioids, well, I suppose growing up in Wynwood had its perks. I still know people who can get these kinds of drugs for me for a fair price.

I turn to look at you, Faith, after taking out the pill bottles and tucking them into the pocket of my jumper. You stare at me with a glint in your eyes and a cocked brow, as if you have the advantage—as if you have me all figured out.

But Faith . . .

Faith, Faith, Faith.

There is this thing called minding your own fucking business. All you had to do was forget about me and suffer through your damn divorce, but instead, here you are in my face, threatening to take the money I worked my ass off for.

That doesn't sit well with me, Faith.

"Before I begin," I murmur, wiping away a tear, "would you like to share some tea with me? I think it will calm me down a little."

You hesitate at first, but then you give me an oh-what-the-hell kind of shrug. "I don't mind a drink, but I'd prefer something stronger than tea. Got any wine?"

And I nod. "Of course." Then I turn and I smile, bending down to open my wine fridge. Wine and antidepressants. The same cocktail Lola was so quick to scarf down while she was arguing with Corey over their pending divorce, right before requesting her favorite cocktail.

I lower to a squat and pretend to clang around in the wine fridge below the counter. I name some of the wines for you, to see if any are familiar to you that you might want. Your last drink should be a good one, no?

But you don't know any of them, so you tell me to bring the best one.

So, I do. But oh—the wine bottle opener is in my bedroom. I tell you I had a glass in my room last night as I was packing. I go and get it, and as I round the corner and step into my bedroom, the pills come out.

And with one of the heaviest lamps on my nightstand, I quietly smash, smash, smash the pills, then scoop the dust back into the bottle. I do it as quickly as I can. Use all my strength. Can't have you getting suspicious.

I return to the kitchen. You're scrolling through your phone. Who are you texting, Faith? Are you telling people where you are just in case something happens to you while you're with me?

Ah. That's okay. I'll take your phone, pretend to be you for a while. Make everyone think you ran off and got tired of your life—afraid of the divorce. Afraid of losing everything.

I pour your wine at the counter with my back to you, making chitchat about how heartbroken I am that you'd think I'd do such a thing to Lola. You are still smug. You don't believe me. I really, really don't like you, so I dump more of the pill dust into your drink than necessary, swirl it a bit, then pour another glass and turn around to leave the kitchen.

Why didn't you watch me? You know how Lola died. She was poisoned. You are an idiot.

As I hand you your cocktail, I immediately sip from my glass so you won't suggest that we swap, just in case maybe you were on to me.

You sigh, and for a moment I think that surely you must know deep down that I would never commit such a heinous crime—that I would never have killed Lola Maxwell—because you take a long sip.

Perhaps you think I just got something out of it but want to see if I'll slip up, but if you knew for a fact that it was me—all me—you wouldn't have come here. You wouldn't be seated on my sofa, sipping my wine. You'd know I was dangerous . . . but you are just like Lola, I see. You underestimate me.

As you sip your wine and type in the passcode for your phone, I make a mental note of the six digits you plug in all while taking a moment to breathe. And then I tell you the truth—the whole truth—to waste time. To get you to stick around longer as the pills and alcohol settle in your veins.

And your eyes get bigger. You're frightened, moving away toward the edge of the sofa. Your pupils have dilated. Your breathing seems much, much faster.

Goodness, Faith, you're sweating now. Are you okay? You look sick. Pale. You're up now, rushing across my living room to get to your purse on the counter. But before you can make it, you fall, and your body slams right down on my marble floor.

Your eyes are wide open, your mouth ajar. Just like Lola, your face seems a little blue now. Blood drips from your nose. Your lips. I get up and flip you onto your back. Can't have too much blood that I have to clean up. Shit. I think I may have put a little too much dust in your drink. But that's what happens when you piss me off.

I'll miss my flight because of you, but that's okay. I'll just schedule another, and all will be well. No one will know about this because you will have disappeared—considered a grown woman who ran away from her life—and I will still be free.

Free, free, free.

Oh, finally.

CHAPTER FORTY-FIVE

*F*orgive me.

    I have not wronged you or forgotten you. I've just needed time to think. Things like this require a plan, as you know all too well.

    I feel awful, guilty, ashamed. The situation you're in is all my fault. I have read every word you've written and taken it all in with tears in my eyes because I know you. I know you like a daughter. I know that deep down, you are good.

    I'm going to fix this. My first step? Catch a flight to London. Get on the same plane she does.

    The woman who framed you, she's booked a flight. I'll follow her. I'll feed Detective Hughes as much intel as I can until we build a good case. You'll get that damn appeal even if it kills me, and I know this woman is dangerous, so maybe it will.

    Believe it or not, I think some of what you said to Detective Hughes about Georgia got to him, especially when he found out about the contract she had with Lola Maxwell. He dug and dug, and all of it led to dead ends, but something about that contract didn't sit well with him, only he had no proof. No way around it.

    Then I showed up. I'd made notes about the woman's visit after she left my office and had written a very in-depth description of her. I showed him the deposits she sent from her account to mine. I told him that the woman who framed you said her name was Mellie. That she'd lied to me. That she said she had Lola's best interests at heart, but that she'd also hired a private investigator.

I never should have told you the name, you're right. I don't know what I was thinking. It was a lapse in judgment. I became greedy, heard about the money and lost myself for a while. But I knew the woman was watching, and you were pulling away. I prayed you wouldn't do anything bad, and then I found out you left St. Petersburg. I knew it was happening. You'd fallen into whatever trap she had set for you.

I saw the images of you with Lola Maxwell on your Instagram. I sobbed. I hurt for you. I'd hoped you'd let it go. I tried calling so many times. You'd changed your number.

But it's okay. You'll be okay.

Georgia . . . she's a bad woman, Ivy, and she must be stopped. I'm going to do that with the forty thousand dollars she so willingly handed over to me.

You'll be angry with me right now for keeping my distance—letting this breathe—but in the end, you'll thank me.

I'll save you. I promise.

ACKNOWLEDGMENTS

I would first love to thank my husband for supporting me through the writing of this novel. This was one of the hardest books I've ever written. It took me months to get through it and to figure it out, but he stayed close and encouraged me to work on it night and day while taking care of our boys, and I love him dearly for that. So thank you, Juanito. You're the best husband ever.

I also have to thank my agent, Shawanda Williams. If it had not been for you and your confidence in me, I would not have gotten this deal. You are a powerhouse and you keep me so motivated, even when things get rocky. I will never be able to thank you enough for seeing in me what I could not see in myself.

Selena James, you got my foot in the door at Kensington. You're incredible and you believed in my words enough to make this dream of mine a reality, so thank you! I will never, ever forget it.

Dani and MJ Fryer, y'all are the best alpha readers and friends an author could have! Your critique and confidence in this project really pushed me and made this feel all the more real. Thank you for cheering me along.

To Norma and Esi of Dafina, you make the best team, so diligent and wonderful and passionate. While we worked on this book, I know so much was going on and life tried to get in the way, but you persevered and still delivered greatness. Thank you for believing in this story and in me . . . and for putting up with my many, *many* annoying emails!

To my readers—my queens in Shanora's Queendom. I would not be where I am today without all of you. Many of you have supported me since 2012, pushed me through each book I have written (even the ones that now make me cringe), and now I am here writing acknowledgments for the first book of mine that will ever sit on a shelf IN STORES. I am so humbled and so grateful for all of your love and support. You have made my dreams come true and it means so much to me to know you all have my back. I hope to keep you forever.

And lastly, to the person reading this very sentence right now. Thank you for giving this messy, dramatic, intense debut thriller of mine a chance. I am so grateful for you.

Discussion Questions for *The Perfect Ruin*

1. *The Perfect Ruin* contains chapters in first, third, and even second person point of view. Why do you think the novel was written this way?
2. Do you wish Lola had been able to share her point of view during the story too? Why or why not?
3. If Ivy had never been given Lola's name, do you think that she'd have turned out to be a different woman?
4. Considering Lola's reputation and all she'd done to become Miami's sweetheart, do you understand why she tried to bury the tragedy? Should she have faced the consequences and backlash from her actions?
5. In your opinion, was what Georgia did to Lola understandable after all she'd gone through while working for her?
6. Why was Lola's chandelier such an irritation to Ivy and Georgia?
7. Ivy can be an unreliable and untrustworthy narrator. Though many chapters were told from her point of view, we don't know if she's being truthful or lying about certain events. Was Ivy telling the truth about never wanting to wish harm on Lola and Corey in the end?
8. What were Ivy's relationships to other female characters in the novel? Do you think that deep down Ivy wanted a best friend or someone she could call a sister?
9. Considering the life-threatening act Ivy made toward Keke, and how determined she was to get what she wanted, do you think she got what was coming to her in the end?
10. What do you think the final chapter means for Georgia and Ivy's future?

A Q&A with Shanora Williams, author of
THE PERFECT RUIN

- **Can you talk a little bit about the relationship between your two main characters in *The Perfect Ruin* and why it's important to you to depict it?**

The relationship between Ivy and Lola was bred through secrets, lies, and hate. It felt important to me to reveal in *The Perfect Ruin* how Ivy's hatred was born and how it festered and took control of her life, and to show that there can be personal consequences if a person does not work to heal their traumas.

There's also the factor of jealousy that Ivy has of Lola, which is especially a large issue for women and has been for centuries. Women are always expected to be held up to really high standards in society and that can be overwhelming in itself, whether it comes down to being a mother, daughter, sister, wife, co-worker, friend—whatever the role may be. Any little imperfection or mistake and there's automatic judgement and this is made even worse during a digital age where social media is practically the core of many people's existence. With that as a factor as well, the health of our minds can eventually take its toll because there is the issue of comparisons, which is a thief of joy. In the case of my characters, Ivy compared her life to Lola's quite often which eventually led to her hating everything about her own life and wanting to claim Lola's, even though Lola's wasn't perfect either. Sadly, the people who are usually holding women up to such high standards are other women.

- **Can you talk a bit about the role mental health plays in your book, and how it factors into the relationship (and relationships between women more broadly)?**

Ivy has the tendency to become obsessed with certain ideas and with people too. If someone enters her life and they feel important to her (whether it is from love, lust, or hate), she obsesses over that person to the brink of madness. Seeing as she'd found out who Lola was and knew what Lola had done, her obsession consumed her and nothing else mattered but getting involved in Lola's life somehow and seeking revenge. I believe if Ivy hadn't had the tendency to become obsessed and would have continued her therapy, then perhaps she wouldn't have stalked Lola, pretended to be her best friend, or aim to ruin her life. With the help she needed, she may have been able to find a healthier option in regard to Lola.

- **Why is this issue important to you?**

I have dealt with it. I have lived through it. I have had moments of depression, but I have overcome it and I pour it all into my writing. As I mentioned, for the longest time I refused to get help. I refused to reveal what I was feeling because I always thought I had to be this guarded woman who always had to be strong, when in reality it only made me feel weak and angry. I'd had enough, so I did things to push myself out of it and bring myself to a new light, I talked about my issues with people I trusted, and I felt so much better. Sometimes all it takes is a simple talk or even a pen to paper to write down every single thing you are feeling and allowing all of that negative energy to pour out of you.

- **How does *The Perfect Ruin* stand out among other domestic thrillers?**

I've noticed there is a bit of a formula to popular domestic thrillers. They include a wife; a husband; a mistress or female outsider; one party is usually very wealthy; there is a twist and a big reveal. And the characters are mostly all Caucasian.

The Perfect Ruin embraces many of these elements. There's Lola Maxwell, with her perfect marriage and perfect life within Miami's elite upper class. There's Ivy and her plot to infiltrate Lola's life. And there are certainly more than a few big twists. However, this novel changes the narrative around race because the characters are primarily people of color.

That said, I write for all types of reader, from brown to white. I don't believe in limiting myself and my writing to just one race, by only allowing one race to connect with the story. I believe *everyone* should be able to read it and connect and feel for the characters. You will know the characters are of color by certain descriptions, and you will know that they take pride in the skin they are in, but while reading, you will only see these characters as people.

- **What is one thing you hope readers will take away from your novel?**

I hope readers will simply enjoy the novel for what it is. Yes, mental health is a very important topic to me, but this is also a work of fiction that I had a lot of fun breathing life into. I especially loved bringing representation to Black women in the thriller and suspense genre and shining light on our flaws and moments of weakness, as well as our moments of power and strength. I hope to see more of this kind of content as publishing continues.